Sun, sea and champagne,
...the perfect ingredients for

JET-SET
SUMMER
Affairs

Three luxurious romances
Three super-sexy heroes
One steamy summer book!

JET-SET
SUMMER
Affairs

PENNY JORDAN
SARAH MORGAN
SANDRA FIELD

JET-SET SUMMER AFFAIRS
© by Harlequin Books S.A. 2009

Master of Pleasure © Penny Jordan 2006
Million-Dollar Love-Child © Sarah Morgan 2006
The Jet-Set Seduction © Sandra Field 2006

ISBN: 978 0 263 87537 9

025-0609

Harlequin Mills & Boon policy is to use papers that are
natural, renewable and recyclable products and made from
wood grown in sustainable forests. The logging and
manufacturing processes conform to the legal environmental
regulations of the country of origin.

Printed and bound in Spain
by Litografia Rosés S.A., Barcelona

Penny Jordan has been writing for more than twenty years and has an outstanding record: over one hundred and sixty-five novels published, including the phenomenally successful *A Perfect Family, To Love, Honour & Betray, The Perfect Sinner* and *Power Play,* which hit *The Sunday Times* and *New York Times* bestseller lists. Penny Jordan was born in Preston, Lancashire and now lives in rural Cheshire.

Don't miss Penny Jordan's new book,
The Sicilian's Baby Bargain, available in
August 2009 from Mills & Boon® Modern™

Sarah Morgan trained as a nurse and has since worked in a variety of health-related jobs. Married to a gorgeous businessman, who still makes her knees knock, she spends most of her time trying to keep up with their two little boys, but manages to sneak off occasionally to indulge her passion for writing romance. Sarah loves outdoor life, and is an enthusiastic skier and walker. Whatever she is doing, her head is full of new characters, and she is addicted to happy endings.

Don't miss Sarah Morgan's new book, *Powerful
Greek, Unworldly Wife*, available in September
2009 from Mills & Boon® Modern™

Althought born in England, **Sandra Field** has lived most of her life in Canada; she says the silence and emptiness of the north speaks to her particularly. While she enjoys travelling and passing on her sense of a new place, she often chooses to write about the city which is now her home. Sandra says, 'I write out of my experience; I have learned that love with its joys and its pains is all important. I hope this knowledge enriches my writing and touches a chord in you, the reader.'

Master of Pleasure

PENNY JORDAN

PENNY JORDAN'S GUIDE TO
ROMANCE IN SARDINIA

I was so pleased when I learned that my book
Master of Pleasure was being reissued. Its heroine,
a single mother in difficult circumstances, has to
make some difficult choices for the benefit of her
children, like so many women today.

I'd always wanted to set a book in Sardinia; the
combination of its history, the alpha men who
made that history, the complexity of the countryside, savagely harsh in some areas and yet with the
most beautiful coves and beaches and a clear
turquoise blue sea along the coast that includes the
famous luxury holiday resort of the Costa
Smeralda, seemed to me to be created to be
together – rather like my hero and my heroine.

The resort of Costa Smeralda was originally created
by Prince Karim Aga Khan for the enjoyment of
his rich, titled and glamorous friends. The coastline
with its small bays and incredibly clear sea is very
beautiful. My favourite place to stay would be the
Romazzino, long and whitewashed and set against
the hills.

A room there, opening directly out to face the
sea, is perfect for lovers, along with the privacy of
its garden. The scent of myrtle and juniper drifting on the sun-soaked air is almost aphrodisiacal.
For those who enjoy people-watching, the hotel's
private deckchairs on the beach are one of the area's
'places to be'.

Porto Cervo is the village area of Costa Smeralda
– ideal for strolling hand in hand, locked in that
special private world that belongs to lovers, perhaps stopping for a glass of wine and, of course, a
cappuccino, whilst nearby is the Porto Vecchio,

with the Piazzetta Hotel Cervo, the Passeggiata and the Sottopiazza shopping boutiques and luxury restaurants. A local favourite to look out for on the menu is *pasta alla bottarga*, a Sardinian speciality made with salted mullet roe.

It would be impossible to visit Costa Smeralda and not find somewhere secluded and romantic to eat, perhaps sitting outside and watching the lights twinkle on the water.

Sardinia is everything that is Italian, and romantic and sexy but, like a cool drink with that all-important extra zest from a slice of lemon, Sardinia has something that is all its own, an extra machismo, a deeper, hotter sensuality, a stronger awareness of what it means to be a woman and very much in love with one special man.

The capital city of the island is Cagliari. Cagliari was originally built by the Phoenicians. If you visit the island at the beginning of May, be sure to visit the city for the Festa di S. Efisio, when you will see the softer side of the island and its people, who are deeply committed to their traditions and their history.

CHAPTER ONE

SASHA turned her head to look at her nine-year-old twin sons. They were playing on the beach like a pair of seal pups, wriggling and wrestling together, and jumping in and out of the waves that were washing gently onto the secluded Sardinian shoreline.

'Be careful, you two,' she warned, adding to the older twin, 'Sam, not so rough.'

'We're playing bandits.' He defended his boisterous tackling of his twin. Bandits had become their favourite game this summer, since Guiseppe, the brother of Maria who worked in the kitchen of the small boutique hotel that was part of the hotel chain owned by Sasha's late husband, had told them stories about the history of the island and its legendary bandits.

The boys had their father's night-dark hair, thick and silky, and olive-tinted skin. Only their eye colour was hers, she reflected ruefully, giving away their dual nationality—sea-coloured eyes that could change from blue to green depending on the light.

'Told you I'd get free.' Nico laughed as he wriggled dexterously out of Sam's grip.

'Careful. Mind those rocks and that pool,' Sasha protested, as Sam brought Nico down onto the sand in a flying tackle that had them both laughing and rolling over together.

'Sam, look—a starfish,' Nico called out, and within a heartbeat they were both crouching side by side, staring into a small rock pool.

'Mum, come and look,' Nico called out. Obligingly she picked her way across to them, crouching down in between them, one arm around Sam, the other round Nico.

'Come on. And I'm the Bandit King, remember.' Sam urged Nico to get up, already bored with the rock pool and its inhabitant.

Boys, Sasha thought ruefully. But her heart was filled with love and pride as she watched them dart away to play on a safer area of smooth sand. She turned to look back towards the hotel on its rocky outcrop, while still keeping her maternal antennae firmly on alert. This hotel was, in her opinion, the most beautiful of all the hotels her late husband had owned. As a wedding gift to her he had allowed her a free hand with its renovation and refurbishment. The money she had expended had been repaid over and over again by the praise of their returning guests for her innovative ideas and her determination to keep the hotel small and exclusive.

But with Carlo's death had come the shock of discovering that the other hotels in the group had not matched the financial success of this one. Unknown to her, Carlo had borrowed heavily to keep the business going, and he had used his hotels as collateral to secure his loans. Bad business decisions had been made, perhaps because of Carlo's failing health. He had been a kind man, a generous and caring man, but not the kind of man who had taken her into his confidence when it came to his business and financial affairs. To him she had always been someone to be protected and cherished, rather than an equal.

They had met in the Caribbean, with its laid-back lifestyle and sunny blue skies, where Carlo had been investigating the possibility of buying a new hotel to add to those he already owned. Now, in addition to having to cope with the pain of losing him, she had had to come to terms with the fact that she had gone overnight from being the pampered wife of a rich man to a virtually destitute widow. Less than a week after Carlo's death his accountant had had to tell her that Carlo owed frighteningly large sums of money, running into millions, to an unnamed private investor he had turned to for help. As security for this debt he had put up the deeds to the hotels. And, although she had begged her business advisers to find a way for her to be able to keep this one hotel, they had told her that the private investor had informed them that under no circumstances was he prepared to agree to her request.

She looked back at her sons. They would miss Sardinia, and the wonderful summers they had all enjoyed here, but they would miss Carlo even more. Although he had been an elderly father, unable to join in the games of two energetic young boys, he had adored them and they him. Now Carlo was gone, his last words to her a demand that she promise him she would always recognise the importance of the twins' Sardinian heritage.

'Remember,' he had told her wearily, 'whatever I have done I have done with love—for you and for them.'

She owed Carlo so much; he had given her so much. He had taken the damaged needy girl she had been and through his love and support had healed that damage. The gifts he had given her were beyond price: self-respect, emotional self-sufficiency; the ability to give and receive love in a way that was healthy and free of the taint of destructive neediness. He had been so much more to her than merely her husband.

Determination burned steadfastly in her eyes, turning them as dark as the heart of an emerald. She had been poor before—and survived. But then she had not had two dependent sons to worry about. Only this morning she had received a discreet e-mail from the boys' school, reminding her that fees for the new term were now due. The last thing she wanted to do was cause more upheaval in their young lives by taking them away from the school they loved.

She looked down at her diamond rings. Expensive jewellery had never been something she'd craved. It had been Carlo who had insisted on buying it for her. She had already made up her mind that her jewellery must be sold. At least they had a roof over their heads for the space of the boys' summer holidays. It had hurt her pride to ask Carlo's lawyers to plead for them to be allowed to stay on here until their new school term began in September, and she had been grateful when they had told her that she'd been granted that wish. Her own childhood had been so lacking in love and security that from the very heartbeat of time when she had known she was pregnant she had made a mental vow that her child would never have to suffer as she had suffered. Which was why...

She turned her head to watch her sons. Yes, Carlo had healed so much within her, yet there had been one thing he couldn't heal. One stubborn, emotional wound for which she still had not found closure.

The worry of the last few months had stolen what little spare flesh she had had from her body, leaving her, in her own eyes, too thin. Her watch was loose on her wrist as she pushed the heavy weight of her sun-streaked tawny hair back off her face and kept it there with one slender hand.

She had been eighteen when she'd married Carlo, and nineteen when the boys had been born, an uneducated but street-smart girl who had been only too glad to accept Carlo's proposal of marriage despite the fact that he was so much older than her. Marriage to him had provided her with so much that she had never had, and not just in terms of financial security. Carlo had brought stability into her life, and she had flourished in the safe environment he had provided for her.

She had been determined to do everything she could to repay Carlo's kindness to her, and the look on his face the first time he had seen the twins, lying beside her in their cots in the exclusive private hospital in which she had given birth, had told her that she had given him a gift that was beyond price.

'Watch, Mum.' Obediently she obeyed Sam's demand that she watch as he and Nico turned cartwheels. One day soon they would be telling her not to watch them so closely. As yet they hadn't realised just how carefully she did watch over them. Sometimes, with two such energetic and intelligent boys, it was hard not to be over-protective—the kind of mother who saw danger where they saw only adventure. Her own thoughts silenced the ever ready 'be careful', hovering on her lips. 'Very good,' she praised them instead.

'Look, we can do handstands too,' Sam boasted.

They were agile, as well as tall for their age, and strongly built.

'You have made good strong sons for me, Sasha,' Carlo had often praised her. She smiled, remembering those words. Their marriage had bought her time and space in which to grow from the girl she had once been into the woman she was now. The sun glinted on the thin gold band of her wedding ring as she turned again to look at the hotel on the rocks above them.

She had travelled all over the world with her late husband, visiting his chain of small exclusive hotels, but this one here in Sardinia had always drawn her back. Originally a private home, owned by Carlo's cousin, Carlo had inherited the property on the cousin's death, and had vowed never to part with it.

Gabriel stood in the shadow cast by the rocks and looked down onto the beach. His mouth twisted with angry contempt and something else.

How did she feel now? he wondered, knowing that fate had reneged on the bargain she had struck with it, and that the security she had bought with her body was not, after all, going to be for life. How had she felt when she had learned that her widowhood was not going to be one of wealth and comfort?

Had she cursed the man she married, or herself? And what of her sons? Something dark and dangerous ripped his guts with razor-sharp claws. Just watching them

had brought to the surface memories of his own childhood here on Sardinia. How could he ever forget the
cruel, harsh upbringing he had endured? When he had
been the age of these two boys he had been made to
work for every crust he was thrown. Kicks and curses
had taught him how to move swiftly and sure-footedly
out of their range. But then he had been an unwanted
child, a child disposed of by his rich maternal relatives,
abandoned by his father, to be brought up by foster
carers. As a boy he had, Gabriel acknowledged bitterly,
spent more nights sleeping outside with the farm animals than he had inside with the foster family, who had
learned their contempt of him from his mother's relatives.

Gabriel believed that such an upbringing either made
or broke the human spirit, and when it made it, as it had
his, it hardened it to pure steel. He had never and would
never let anyone deflect him from his chosen path, or
come between him and his single-minded determination
to stand above those who had chosen to look down on him.

His maternal grandfather had been the head of one
of the richest and most powerful of Sardinia's leading
families. The Calbrini past was tightly interwoven with
that of Sardinia. It was a family riven in blood feuds,
treachery and revenge, and steeped in pride.

His mother had been his grandfather's only child.
She had been eighteen when she'd run away from the
marriage he had arranged for her, to marry instead a
poor but handsome young farmer she had believed herself in love with.

Strong-willed and spoiled, it had taken her less than
a year to realise that she had made a mistake, and that

she loathed her husband almost as much as she did the poverty that had come with her marriage. But by then she had given birth to Gabriel. She had appealed to her father, begging him to forgive her and let her come home. He had agreed, but on condition that she divorced her husband and left the child with his father.

According to the stories Gabriel had been told as a child, his mother hadn't thought twice. Her father had paid over a goodly sum of money to Gabriel's father on the understanding that this was a once and for all payment and that it absolved the Calbrini family from any responsibility towards the child of the now defunct marriage.

With more money that he had ever had in the whole of his life in his pocket, Gabriel's father had left his three-month-old son and set off for Rome, promising the cousin he had left Gabriel with that he would send money for his son's upkeep. But once in Rome he'd met the woman who was to become his second wife. She had seen no reason why she should be burdened with a child who was not hers, nor why her husband's money should be wasted on it.

Gabriel's foster parents had appealed to his grandfather. They were poor and could not afford to feed a hungry child. Giorgio Calbrini had refused to help. The child was nothing to him. His daughter had also remarried—this time to the man of his choice—and he was hoping that within a very short space of time she would give him a grandson with the lineage his pride demanded.

Only she hadn't, and when Gabriel was ten years old his mother and her second husband had both been killed when the helicopter they were in crashed. Giorgio

Calbrini had then had no alternative but to make the best of the only heir he had—Gabriel.

It had been an austere, loveless life for a young boy, Gabriel remembered, with a grandfather who'd had no love for him and had despised the blood he had inherited from his father. But at least under his grandfather's roof he had been properly fed. His grandfather had sent him to the best schools—and had made sure that he was taught everything he would need to know when the time came to take over from him and become the head of the house of Calbrini. Not that his grandfather had had high hopes of him being able to do so, as he had made plain to Gabriel more than once. 'I have to do this because I have no choice, because you are the only grandson I have,' he had told Gabriel, ceaselessly and bitterly.

Gabriel, though, had been determined to prove him wrong. Not to win his grandfather's love. Gabriel did not believe in love. No, he had wanted to prove that he was the better man, the stronger man. And that was exactly what he had done. At first his grandfather had refused to believe Gabriel's tutors when they praised his grasp of financial politics and all the complexities that went with them. But by the time he was twenty Gabriel had quadrupled the small amount of capital his grandfather had given him on his eighteenth birthday.

Then, three weeks after Gabriel had celebrated his twenty-first birthday, his grandfather had died unexpectedly and Gabriel had inherited his vast wealth and position. Those who had predicted that he would never be able to step into his grandfather's shoes had been forced to eat their words. Gabriel was a true Calbrini, and he possessed an even sharper instinct for making money than his grandfather. But there was more to his life than making money. There was also the need to make himself emotionally invulnerable.

And that was exactly what he was, Gabriel reflected now. No woman would ever be allowed to repeat his mother's rejection of him and go unpunished.

Especially not this woman.

He could hear Sasha speaking to her sons, the sound of her voice, but not her words, carried to him by the breeze.

Sasha! By the time Gabriel was twenty-five he had become a billionaire. A billionaire who trusted no one and who kept the women he chose to warm his bed as exactly that—bedmates and nothing else. The rules he laid down for his relationships with them were simple and non-negotiable. No talk of love, or a future, or commitment; absolute fidelity to him while they were partners; absolute and total adherence to his safe sex and no babies policy. And, just to make sure that this latter rule wasn't broken 'accidentally on purpose', Gabriel always took care of that side of things himself.

Over the years he had endured his share of angry, bitter scenes, with weeping women who had thought they could change those rules and then learned their mistake. Magically those tears had quickly dried once they were offered a generous goodbye gift. His mouth twisted cynically. Was it any wonder that he had become a man who trusted no one, and most of all a man who despised women? So far as Gabriel was concerned there wasn't a woman in existence who could not be bought. His mother had shown him what women were, and all the other women he had come into contact with since had confirmed what she had taught him when she had abandoned him for money.

Not that he didn't enjoy the company of women, or rather the pleasure of their bodies. He did. He had inherited his father's good looks, and finding a willing female partner to satisfy his sexual needs had never been a problem.

'Sam, don't go too far. Stay here, where I can see you.' Sasha's words reached him this time, as she raised her voice so that her son could hear it. A caring mother? *Sasha?*

Like his bitterness, the past wouldn't let go of him. It was here around him now, gripping him so tightly that he could feel its pain.

After his grandfather's death he had had closed up his grandfather's remote and uncomfortable house in Sardinia and bought himself a yacht. With financial interests in property, it had made sense for him to travel, looking for fresh acquisitions both material and sexual. And if a woman invited him to use her for his sexual pleasure then why should he not do so? Just so long as she understood that once his appetite was sated there would not be a place in his life for her.

By the time he was twenty-five he had also already made the decision that when the time came he would pay a woman to provide him with an heir—a child to which he would make sure *he* had exclusive rights.

Gabriel watched Sasha with cold-eyed contempt. Six weeks ago, just after his thirty-fifth birthday, he had stood beside the hospital bed of his dying second cousin—the Calbrini family was extensive, and had many different branches—listening to Carlo pleading for *his* help for the two sons Carlo loved more than anything else in the world.

The same warm breeze that was playing sensually with Sasha's long hair was flattening the thick darkness of his own to reveal the harsh purity of a bone structure that bore the open stamp of Sardinia's human history—the straight line of his Roman nose a classic delineation of masculine features that echoed the works of Leonardo and Michelangelo, coupled with the musculature of a man in his prime. Centuries ago the Saracens had invaded Sardinia, leaving their mark on its history and its inhabitants through the women they had taken and impregnated. It had been Carlo who had told him that legend had it that boy children born to such women were said to possess the physical stamina and legendary merciless cruelty of the men who had fathered them. Gabriel knew that there was Saracen blood in his own family's past, and he knew too that it showed in his attitude to life. He had no mercy for those who double-crossed him.

Eyes as golden and as deathly watchful as those of an eagle studied the two boys. Privileged, and loved by a doting elderly father. Their childhood was so very different from his own. The sunlight gilded his skin, warmly gold rather than deeply olive. He looked on the promise Carlo had begged from him as an almost sacred trust, an admission from his cousin without words being spoken that he was entrusting his sons to Gabriel's care because he did not trust their mother—because on his deathbed he had finally been prepared to admit that she could not be trusted.

But still Carlo's last words to him had been of her.

'Sasha,' he had told Gabriel. 'You must understand…'

He had been too weak to say any more, but there had been no need. Gabriel knew all there was to know about Sasha. Just like his mother, she had walked out on him. The memory of that was like a constant piece of grit rubbing against his pride, exacerbating the darkness within him. She was unfinished business, the cause of a blow to his pride against which it had banked a debt of compounded interest—which he was now here to claim in full.

A roar of protest from one of the twins caused Sasha to turn to look in maternal anxiety, and then to call out, 'Stop fighting, you two.'

Something—no, *someone* had moved between her and the sun. Immediately she shielded her gaze to see who it was.

There were moments in life that happened both so quickly and yet so slowly that they could never be ignored or forgotten. Sasha felt the abrupt cessation of her heartbeat, then a suffocating sense of shocked disbelief, streaked with fear and panic—and something else so painful that she refused to give it either life or a name. She listened to the slow heavy thud of her heart as though it belonged to another woman, distantly aware of it propelling the blood into her veins, keeping her physically functioning while, emotionally, every nerve felt as though it had been tortured and then severed. Just one word was torn from her throat.

'Gabriel!'

CHAPTER TWO

JUST one word, but it was so filled with anger, shock and fear that it seemed to reverberate between them.

Sasha had to tilt her head back to look up at Gabriel, and she could feel the panicky beat of the pulse at the base of her throat. She resisted an urge to place a covering hand over it.

'What are you doing here? What do you want?' It was a mistake to ask him that. He would be able to hear the panic in her voice and see how she was having to fight to control her fear. The way his mouth was twisting into that cruelly unkind and satisfied smile she remembered so well told her that.

'What do you think I want?'

His voice was so soft and gentle that it could almost have been the tender stroke of a lover's touch against her skin, or the brush of an angel's wings. Just for a second her body reacted to the memories it evoked. She was seventeen again, a desperate bundle of aching, emotional need she had kept hidden beneath a shield of bravado. Her body was bereft of its sexually challenging armour of short skirt and minuscule vest top, and her long hair, with its amateur blonde streaks, was still damp from the shower Gabriel had insisted she have. She was watching him watching her, overwhelmed by the feeling, the longing suddenly shooting through her; knowing for the first time in her life what it felt like to experience physical sexual desire. And she wanted him, *desired* him so very badly.

A door had swung open on her past. She didn't want to see what lay behind it, but it was already too late. She remembered how she had been too impatient to wait for him to come to her, running to him instead. He had caught hold of her, holding her at arm's length whilst he studied her naked body. Even her flesh had signalled its eager readiness to him, her breasts firming and lifting as she imagined him touching her there. But when he did she had realised that her imagination had not had the power to tell her just how his touch would feel, or what it would do to her. The flesh of his fingertips had been hard and slightly rough, the flesh of a man who worked and lived physically, not just cerebrally. She had shivered, and then shuddered with uncontained delight when he had slowly explored the shape of her breasts. The erotic roughness of his touch had increased her arousal so much that she had suddenly become aware of not just how much she wanted him, and how excited she was, but how ready her body was for him, how hot and wet and achingly sensitive that most intimate part of her had felt. As though he had sensed that, too, Gabriel had trailed his hand down over her body, smoothly and determinedly. When he had allowed it to rest on her hip, cupping the gently protruding bone, she had been seized with impatient urgency and the need to feel him caressing her more intimately.

Had she then moved closer to him, openly parting her legs, or had he been the one to propel her closer to him, moving his hand to her thigh? She couldn't remember. But she could remember how it had felt, how she had felt, when he had bent his head to kiss the smooth column of her throat at the same time as he had stroked apart the swollen lips of her sex to dip his fingers in the slick moist heat that was waiting for him. She had almost reached orgasm there and then.

A shudder punched through her. What was she doing, thinking about that now? She could feel the strain of her own emotions. Fear? Guilt? *Longing?* No, never again. The girl she had been was gone, and with her everything that that girl had felt.

Sasha looked down towards the beach, where her sons were still playing, oblivious to what was happening, and then looked quickly away, instinctively not wanting to contaminate them with what was happening to her. Her sharpest and most urgent need was not to protect herself but to protect them. As she looked away she stepped to one side, as though to draw Gabriel's attention to her rather than her vulnerable young. There was nothing she would not do to protect her sons. Nothing.

Gabriel tracked the involuntary movement she made away from the two boys. Carlo had claimed that she was a very protective mother, but of course she would have been while she believed that Carlo was a wealthy man and her role as their mother gave her unlimited access to that wealth. Carlo, like many men who come to fatherhood so late in life, had worshipped the flesh of his flesh, evidence of his potency. His heirs… Now the heirs to precisely nothing. Gabriel's tiger-eyed gaze

pounced on the visual evidence of their privileged cos-
mopolitan lifestyle—expensive Italian clothes, healthy
American teeth, upper-class English accents, their flesh
and bones that of children who had from birth been well
fed and nurtured. At their age he had been wearing rags,
his body thin and bony.

He switched his gaze from the beach to the woman
in front of him. She too had good teeth, expensive
teeth—paid for, of course, by her doting husband. Her
doting and now dead husband. Her hair was cut in the
kind of style that looked artless but, as Gabriel knew,
cost a fortune to maintain. The 'simple' linen dress she
was wearing, with its elegant lines, no doubt possessed
a designer label, just as her hands and feet with their un-
coloured but carefully manicured nails spoke of a
woman who had the kind of confidence that came from
enjoying position and wealth. But not any longer. What
had she felt when she had learned of Carlo's death?
Relief at the thought that she would no longer have to
give herself to an old man? Avaricious pleasure at the
belief that she would now be wealthy?

Well, she would have one of those two feelings to
keep, he acknowledged brutally, although probably not
for very long. She must be close to thirty now, and if
she wanted to find another rich old man to support her
she would discover she was competing with much
younger, unencumbered women. The kind of women
who fawned around *him* wherever he went.

One of Gabriel's mistresses had once told him that
it was his Saracen ancestry that gave him the dark and
dangerous side to his nature that his enemies feared
and his women loved. For himself, he believed that any

child growing up as he had done—unwanted, harshly treated, both physically and emotionally—quickly learned to give back as good as it got. A child who had to literally fight off the farm dogs for a scrap of bread was bound to develop a hard carapace to protect both his flesh and his spirit.

An unexpected smile dimpled his chin as he watched Sasha swallow and saw the telltale darkening of her eyes, but there was no warmth to that smile. 'Yes, it must have been hard for you, lying there in bed, letting an old man take his pleasure with your body and being unable to give you any pleasure back. But then, of course, you had all that money to pleasure you, didn't you?'

'I didn't marry Carlo for his money.'

'No? Then why did you marry him?'

Ah, now he had her. He could hear the uneven ratcheting of her breath escaping from her lungs. How well he knew that fierce need to protect oneself from a death blow. Unfortunately for her it was too late. There was no protection for her here.

'It certainly wasn't for love,' he taunted her unkindly. 'I saw him just before he died. He was in the hospital in Milan. You, I believe, were in New York—shopping. Very conveniently you had also boarded your sons at their school, in order to give yourself the freedom to do so.'

All the colour bled out of her face. Infuriatingly Gabriel recognised that even now, almost bleached of blood and life, she still managed to look impossibly beautiful.

Sasha was terrified she might actually faint, so great

was the pressure of her anger. She had gone to New York in secret, to meet with yet another specialist to see if there was some way that Carlo might be saved. She might not have loved her husband as a woman, but she had been grateful to him for all that he had done for her and for the twins. The decision to ask the school if the boys could board was not one she had made without a great deal of soul searching. For her, the boys' emotional security was always paramount, but she and they had owed Carlo a huge debt. What kind of person would she be if she had not done absolutely everything she could to find a way to give her husband more time with them? It wouldn't have been possible to travel to New York to seek a second opinion with the boys. And then there had been the added worry of how it would affect them to watch Carlo slowly dying. She had needed to be on hand to visit the hospital and then the hospice sometimes twice or three times a day. Carlo had wanted to die in Italy, not London, where the boys were at school. She had made what she had believed was the best decision she could at the time, but now Gabriel was pin-pointing the guilt that still nagged at her for having had to leave the boys at school for a term.

'You know, of course, that the business is ruined and that all he has left you is debt?'

'Yes, I know,' she agreed bleakly. There was no point in even attempting to conceal the reality of her financial situation from him, or trying to explain to him how she felt about Carlo. He would not understand because he was incapable of understanding. Their shared experience of damaged childhood years, instead of forging shared bonds of mutual compassion, had turned them into the bitterest of enemies. He would never understand why she had left him for Carlo, and she would never tell him—because there was simply no point.

'I suppose I should be honoured that you've actually come to gloat in person. After all, you weren't at the funeral.'

'To watch you cry crocodile tears? Even *my* stomach isn't strong enough for that.'

'But it is, of course, strong enough for you to come here and verbally stone me. It's been over ten years, Gabriel. Isn't it time—'

'Isn't it time *what*? That I claimed the debt you owe me, along with its accrued interest? I'm a man who likes payment in full, Sasha. Carlo knew that.'

Something—either old knowledge or female instinct—iced down her spine in a cold trickle of awareness she didn't want but couldn't ignore.

'What do you mean? What did Carlo know?'

'He knew that when he asked me to lend him money that money would have to be repaid.'

'*You* loaned Carlo money?'

Gabriel inclined his head. 'Against the security of the deeds to his hotels. He had overtraded, and badly. I told him that, but he believed he could borrow his way out of trouble, and since we were family I could not refuse him the help he wanted. Unfortunately for him he did not manage to turn the business around. Fortunately for me his debt was covered by his assets. My assets now. Including this place, of course.'

Sasha stared at him.

'Yours?' She couldn't comprehend what he was saying. 'You mean that *you* own this hotel?'

'This hotel,' he agreed, 'and the others. And your

home, the money in your bank, the clothes on your back. It all belongs to me now, Sasha. Everything. Carlo's debt is repaid,' he told her softly, 'but yours to me is still outstanding. Did you think it had been forgotten? That I wouldn't bother to seek retribution?'

She wanted desperately to look at her sons, to reassure herself that they were there, whole and safe, and that none of this could touch or harm them. But she was afraid that somehow just looking at them would draw Gabriel's attention to their vulnerability.

Instead she drew in a deep, unsteady breath and said, 'You seek retribution from me? I was the one who was the victim in our relationship, Gabriel. You were the one who—'

'You were the one who sold herself to the highest bidder.' Somehow she made herself look at him. 'You left me with no other option,' she told him quietly.

It was, after all, the truth. She had gone to him looking for all those things she'd never had, still able to believe that miracles could happen, even for girls like her, and that all the wrongs in her life could be made right. She had still trusted in her dreams then. She felt pity for the girl she had been, was glad that she was gone, and even more glad to be the woman who had taken her place.

Before Gabriel could say anything else she demanded, 'What is it exactly that you want, Gabriel? I assume you haven't wasted your precious time coming here just to gloat? Or did you think it would be amusing to throw us out personally? Well, I'll save you the bother. It won't take us long to pack.' Of all the luxuries she would have to give up this was the one she would miss the most. The luxury of pride. Because she knew so well just what a luxury it was.

'I haven't finished yet,' he told her.

There was more? What? Surely it wasn't possible for things to be any worse?

'Before he died, Carlo appointed me as his sons' legal guardian.'

It was a joke. A cruel deliberate attempt to frighten her. Payback time with a vengeance. But of course it couldn't be true.

'What's wrong?' she heard Gabriel demanding softly when he caught her swift indrawn breath and the shocked disbelief she was trying to hide. 'Surely Carlo told you that he intended to appoint me as their legal family guardian in accordance with traditional Sardinian law?'

He knew, of course, that Carlo had done no such thing because his cousin had told him so himself.

'It is for the best,' Carlo had whispered painfully to Gabriel. 'Even though I know Sasha won't see it that way at first.'

She certainly didn't, Gabriel recognised. Her eyes were wild with disbelief as she shook her head in denial.

This couldn't be happening, Sasha thought frantically. This was the nightmare to end all nightmares. The ultimate betrayal. A knife-sharp edge of fear sliced into her heart and paralysed her defences.

'No!' she told him, shock bleeding the colour from her face, clenching her hands into small, anguished fists. 'No. I don't believe you.'

'My lawyers have all the necessary papers.'

This wasn't some kind of malicious joke, Sasha recognised numbly. This was real. Her head was aching, bursting with unanswerable questions. She was too distraught to maintain the protective distance of remote disinterest.

'I don't understand… Why would Carlo do something like that? Why?'

Gabriel shrugged, a small movement of powerfully strong shoulders. Sickeningly for a second the scene in front of her swung crazily out of focus and she was seeing another, younger Gabriel, sea water sluicing from the bare tanned strength of those same shoulders as he hauled himself up out of the ocean onto the deck of his yacht, his body naked and unashamedly ready for her, just as hers had been equally ready for him.

And she had always been ready for him. Ready, eager, wanting. Hungry for the intimacy of any sexual act that would bring him closer to her and keep him there. She had had no inhibitions, and she suspected he would not have allowed her to have any. With their privacy guaranteed she had thought nothing of shrugging on one of his shirts and wearing nothing else, as turned on by the knowledge that beneath it she was openly available to his touch as she knew he had been. As a lover he had opened her eyes to a whole new world of pleasure, and he had imprinted that pleasure on her body in such a way that she knew she would never be able to forget it. There had been long hours when he had held her on their bed and caressed and kissed his way over every inch of her—the curve of her throat, the tender flesh inside her arm, her fingers. If she closed her eyes she knew she would almost be able to feel the slow wet curl of his tongue as he drew slow patterns of almost unendurable erotic stimulation along the whole length of her.

Aroused to a fever pitch, she would invariably forget his command to remain still and reach for him, arching her back, spreading her legs, moaning with raw delight when he carefully held apart the outer lips of her sex and stroked his tongue-tip the full length of it. Her orgasm would begin before he entered her, her body welcoming his fierce thrusts even while deep down inside herself a part of her ached to feel him there without the barrier of the condoms he'd always insisted on using.

Abruptly Sasha realised the danger of what she was doing. *No!* Her silent tortured denial reverberated inside her skull. What was happening to her? How could he be making her remember that now?

'Isn't it obvious?' she could hear Gabriel saying coolly. 'Carlo knew the state his financial and business affairs were in. He told me himself that he wanted to do everything he could to protect his sons and their future. Obviously by making me their guardian he believed he would be morally compelling me to provide for them financially.'

'No, he wouldn't do that,' Sasha protested. But even as she said the words she knew that she was deceiving herself. It was exactly the sort of thing Carlo would have done—albeit for the best of motives. Carlo had had such a deep-rooted sense of family. He had been proud of being a Calbrini, proud too that the twins would bear that name. He had cared about her, and he had protected her from the pain of loving Gabriel and being rejected by him, but the boys had Calbrini blood in their veins, and in the end that had mattered more to him than her.

Sasha was trying hard to remain strong, to focus on what Gabriel was saying instead of slipping back into the past, but the memories Gabriel was evoking had a dangerously strong hold on her and were making her feel frighteningly weak. How could it be that just standing here with him could awaken the kind of erotic thoughts she had truly believed she had left behind in her past?

'To provide for them financially,' Gabriel repeated, adding as smoothly as though he were sliding a knife up through her ribs and straight into her heart, 'and to protect them from their mother.'

It took several seconds for her brain to absorb what he was saying, and then several more for her to react to the cruel injustice of his words. 'They don't need to be protected from me, and neither do they need you.'

'Carlo obviously didn't agree with you, and neither will the law. I am their guardian. They are my wards. That was their father's dying wish.'

'But I am their mother.'

'The kind of mother who some might say they would be better off not having.'

'You have no right to say that. You know nothing about my relationship with my sons.'

'I know you. You went to Carlo because he was prepared to give you what I would not. Now he is dead, and sooner rather than later you will be looking for another man to take his place. Obviously Carlo feared that should you remarry your new husband might not have Carlo's sons' best interests at heart, and he wanted to protect them.'

'I would never marry a man unless I thought he would love them as though they were his own.'

'Wouldn't you?'

Sasha suspected she knew what he was thinking. 'You still haven't forgiven your mother, have you? Well, I am not her, Gabriel. I love my sons—'

'Enough! This has nothing to do with my mother.'

Sasha wasn't going to argue with him. What was the point? It would be like trying to break down granite with her bare hands. But she knew that she was right. Gabriel measured women by the yardstick of his mother's failure to be a mother to him, and he condemned them all along with her. He wanted to believe that all women were capable of abandoning their children for money because he needed to believe it; because not to do so meant accepting that his own mother had left him because of some failure within himself to merit her maternal love. He spoke his beliefs as though they were a truth written in stone, and Sasha knew that inside his head, in what passed for his heart, they were. In his eyes she was already condemned and would remain condemned. What he believed could not be changed, because he did not want it to be changed.

She had learned so much on her own sometimes difficult and painful journey to maturity and acceptance of her own past. And most of all she had learned that it was impossible to make another person's journey of self-knowledge and healing for them.

Gabriel had decided a long time ago to sacrifice the ability to love and be loved in exchange for the protection of a bitter pride that would not allow him to see her sex as motivated by anything other than the most callous form of self-interest.

Carlo might have believed he was doing what was right, but Sasha wished he had not brought Gabriel back into her life—and more importantly into the lives of her sons. They meant everything to her. There was nothing she would not do to protect them, no sacrifice she would not make.

'You didn't have to agree to Carlo's request,' she forced herself to point out. 'Why did you? My sons mean nothing to you.'

Gabriel could hear the hostility in her voice. He looked towards the two boys. Sasha was right, of course; they meant nothing to him beyond the Calbrini blood in their veins. His initial reaction when Carlo had told him his intention had been to refuse. Why should he burden himself with the responsibility of his cousin's sons, especially when he knew what their mother was? It was obvious what Carlo was trying to do. He was bankrupt and in debt, his sons were too young to fend for themselves, and their mother could not be relied on to protect them; she would sell herself to the first man who could afford her. All this must have gone through Carlo's mind as it would have done his own. So Carlo had turned to him, on his sons' behalf, knowing that morally Gabriel could not and would not reject the claim of their shared Calbrini blood.

Since then, however, Gabriel had had more time to reflect on the situation. He had reasoned to himself that in accepting the role of guardian to Carlo's sons he could spare himself the necessity of producing heirs of his own with all the potential legal pitfalls that could entail. Carlo's sons were Calbrinis. He had decided that he would spend some time with Carlo's sons to evaluate for himself whether or not they were worthy of raising as his own heirs. If they were, then as their guardian he would raise them exactly as he would have done his own sons, to become the heirs his vast empire and wealth required. As for Sasha...

He could feel the burn inside his body like that of an old unhealed wound. Their shared history was a page of his life he had never been able to remove. The women who had gone before her, like those who had come after, had never managed to leave the imprint on his senses that she had. She was a payment owed to him in the balance sheet of his life. Fate was now giving him the opportunity to salve his wounded pride.

Once he had collected the capital and interest on her debt to him, once he had reversed the past and forced her into a position where *he* would be the one to walk away from her—for nothing else would salve his pride—then he would make it plain that there was no place for her in the new lives of her sons, and certainly not in his. Gabriel did not envisage any real problems. He knew Sasha. She was a hedonist and a sensualist, driven by sexual and financial greed. He was not foolish enough to think that he could simply trick her into doing what he wanted. The minute she guessed what he was planning she would cling to the boys, determined not to let go of her passport to his wealth. He would have to be subtle and thorough.

And ultimately, if she refused to relinquish her claim to her sons...?

If she was foolish enough to do that then she would soon realise her mistake.

'No, but they meant a great deal to Carlo.' Gabriel answered Sasha's question coolly. 'And my word means a great deal to me. Since I have given him my word that

I will act in all ways towards them as though they were my own, that is exactly what I intend to do.'

'What?' His own? The shock of what Gabriel had said rocked Sasha back on her heels. Why hadn't she anticipated this? She knew how much Carlo had loved the boys, but she knew too how deep his Sardinian roots went, and how important his family and its honour were to him. If only Carlo had told her what he was planning she could have done something, anything—whatever it would have taken. Pleaded, begged, demanded that he didn't do this to her. He had known how Gabriel felt about her, how much he despised her. And he had known too...

She took a deep breath. She hadn't thought about any of this in years. She hadn't allowed herself to—not once since she had slipped from Gabriel's bed in the pale light of a false dawn while Gabriel slept, unaware of her intentions. She had taken nothing with her when she left the yacht—not the expensive clothes he had bought her, nor the jewellery—only her passport. And enough money to get the hotel where Carlo was staying, to give herself and her future into his keeping. She had been eighteen then, and Carlo had been in his mid-sixties. Small wonder that a month later, when he had married her, the officials had thought he was her elderly father. She had not cared, though. All she had cared about was that now she was safe.

She could see Gabriel looking at the boys, and she reacted immediately to what her maternal instincts translated as a threat, reaching for his arm, wanting to stop him from going to them. But before she could touch him Gabriel swung around, his own grip on her wrist making her wince. His body was tensed like that of a hunter, a *predator*, waiting for her to try to escape so that he could punish her. A shudder of recognition ripped through her belly as she was subjected to the once-familiar signs of her own body's arousal. How could this be happening? It was over ten years since Gabriel had last touched her. The twins' birth had flooded her senses and emotions with an intensity of a different kind of love that had obliterated all she had once felt for Gabriel. Or so she had told herself.

How could one touch do this to her? How could *he* make her feel like this—her lower belly hollow with anticipation, her legs trembling, sweat springing up along her hair line and adrenalin forcing its way along her veins? It was a trick of her own imagination, that was all, she tried to reassure herself. She did not want or desire him. How could she? But the ache of longing inside her was intensifying and drowning out rational thought. Arousal and anger, desire and dislike, all the sweet, savage sexual alchemy of their shared past swept back over her.

She had, she remembered, felt like this the first time she had seen him. Only then the liquid heat erupting inside her body had not been shadowed by either pain or knowledge. The physical ache of her longing for him had seduced her before he had even touched her, and when he had touched her… She closed her eyes, not wanting to remember but it was too late. Inside her head she could hear her own voice as she cried out to him, caught up in the grip of her own unbearable pleasure, her eyes wide open with the awed shock of it while he leaned over her in the shadowy coolness of the yacht's main cabin, watching her as the expert touch of his fingers brought her to orgasm. Her first orgasm. He had waited until its shuddering hold on her body had eased before giving her the look of hooded triumph that would become so familiar to her and saying laconically, 'Perhaps now would be a good time to tell me your name?'

She opened her eyes abruptly. Her face burned now at the memory of her own behaviour then. She had only been seventeen, she reminded herself shakily. A child whose head had been stuffed with daydreams. Still, she had felt she knew all there was to know. She was now twenty-eight, a woman who knew enough to realize how dangerous her past had been, and how lucky she was to have escaped from it, and from Gabriel. She was free of that now. Of that and of him, and of all that he had made her feel and want.

She could feel Gabriel looking at her, focusing on her, the intensity of his concentrated gaze making her tremble. He couldn't guess what she had been thinking, what she had been reliving. She was far too mature now to betray herself to him. Nevertheless, the dull ache inside her was refusing to subside and, as though she had no control over it whatsoever, she could feel her gaze being drawn to his body, to his throat, and the vee of sun-warmed flesh exposed by the neck of his polo shirt. Beneath it his torso would be ridged with muscle, the darkness of his body hair arrowing downwards over the tautness of his belly. Her gaze followed the downward arrowing of her thoughts, coming to rest where her hand and her lips had once rested so intimately and so pleasurably. She could still remember the hard sleekness of male flesh over rigid muscle, its smooth supple movement beneath her eager touch...

What was she *doing*? Frantically she pushed back the memories. She wanted badly to swallow, to wet the nervous dryness of her lips, but she was afraid of doing so in case…in case what? In case Gabriel guessed what she had been remembering and subjected her to the kind of savagely sexual possession she had once found so exciting? Here, with her sons less than ten yards away?

'Let go of me,' she breathed, trying to pull her wrist free.

'Are you sure that is what you really want? Once you begged me for my touch. Remember?'

She couldn't help it. She shuddered violently.

'Ah, yes. I see that you do,' he taunted her as he released her. Her flesh felt cold without his next to it. Cold and bereft. She mustn't let herself think like that.

'Let me warn you, Sasha, just in case you have forgotten. I know exactly what you are.' He studied her body with a contemptuous and knowing sexual inspection that made her want to hit him.

'I am the twins' mother, and that is the only way you will ever know me from now on, Gabriel,' she fired back at him. Were those words for his benefit, or for her own? He released her arm so quickly she almost lost her balance. She looked at him. His back was turned towards her. She shuddered. How could she ever have been so foolish as to have loved him? But she had. Desperately, wholly and completely, hungering for him to return her feelings, believing that she could trade sex for love. What a fool she had been. But she wasn't that fool any longer.

CHAPTER THREE

STILL gripped by shock, Sasha watched Gabriel turn towards the boys. She couldn't get her head around the enormity of what Carlo had done. But they were different from other men, these Sardinian men. They lived by a different code; theirs was a paternalistic society, and the belief in their right to order the lives of their families absolute.

When Carlo had told her about Gabriel's mother she had seen that he did not share her shock that Gabriel's father should seek to force his daughter into a marriage of his choosing.

'No wonder she ran away,' she had commented.

Carlo had frowned at her and shaken his head. 'She was fortunate that her father forgave her and that he was powerful enough to persuade Luigi to marry her despite the humiliation she had forced on him.'

'But to make her marry a man she did not love—'

'It was his right as her father.'

'And forcing her to abandon Gabriel, her baby? You can't believe that was right, Carlo.'

'Not right, no, but Giorgio was a proud man and the head of our family. The purity of the Calbrini bloodline was a matter of honour to him, and to accept as his grandson a child whose blood—'

'But in the end he had to accept Gabriel, didn't he?'

Carlo had inclined his head, as though in acceptance of her argument, but Sasha had known that in his heart he was as old-fashioned and traditional as Gabriel's grandfather. She suspected that he had only told her the story of Gabriel's birth because, despite what Gabriel had done to her, Carlo had still felt he had a duty to stand by his second cousin. He might have offered her the protection of his money and his name, but he had still been a Calbrini. And so were her sons. Carlo had never forgotten that, and neither must she—although for very different reasons.

Gabriel was still watching her sons.

'There isn't any point in me introducing you to them. After all, you are hardly likely to be playing a hands-on role in their lives, are you?' she challenged him.

'On the contrary. I intend to make my duties as their guardian a priority—which is why I am here. Who knows how badly they may have been damaged by the circumstances of their life?'

He had answered without even looking at her.

'They miss Carlo, but his death has not damaged them…'

Gabriel swung round to face her.

'The damage to which I refer is not that caused by the death of their father but rather by the life of their mother.'

A terrible cold stillness had her in its grip.

'You have no right to say that.'

'I have every right. They are my wards. It is my moral and legal duty to protect them.'

'From me? I am their *mother*!' Her hands were curled so tightly her nails bit into her flesh.

He turned slowly to face her, the golden eagle eyes as flat as polished stones.

'You may be their mother, but you are also a woman who craves the lifestyle only a very rich man can provide. When such a man pays you for the use of your body he will not want his enjoyment of that body to be interrupted by the needs of a pair of nine-year-old boys. In the eyes of most courts such a mother would be considered derelict in her maternal duty and not worthy of the name.'

She could almost feel the acid burn of his bitterness.

'Just because your own mother abandoned you—'

'You will not speak of her.'

Sasha had never felt more angry, nor more afraid.

'I have decided that it is in the best interests of my wards that they remain here, on the island that was their father's home, while I consider what is best for their future.'

'That is not your right.'

Sasha was afraid, and fighting hard not to show it, Gabriel recognised. The pulse in her throat was fluttering like a trapped bird struggling to be free. He could almost feel the waves of panic and fear beating up through her body. He could certainly see the shocked outrage in her eyes.

'They are my sons,' Sasha insisted fiercely. '*My* sons.'

'And my legal wards now, under traditional Sardinian law. This is a patriarchal society, as you well know.'

Sasha was shaking her head. 'You can't do this. I won't let you.'

'You can't stop me.' He gave her a cold smile. 'You cannot afford to go to court. You have no money. Carlo is dead, and you need to find another man to support you. A man who, like Carlo, is blind to the reality of what you are. Don't bother denying it,' he told her harshly before she could protest. 'After all, we both know, don't we, that you are accustomed to selling yourself to whichever man will pay the most? After all, that is why you came to me…and why you left me. Isn't it?'

He had tossed the question at her almost casually, but Sasha wasn't deceived. Nothing Gabriel ever did was done casually or without purpose. Even knowing that, she couldn't stop herself from betraying her own agitation as she told him quickly, 'That was all a mistake.'

'Yes—your mistake,' he agreed.

'No, that wasn't…' she began, and then stopped. 'It was a long time ago.' What was she *doing*? She had no need to explain herself to him, and every need to protect herself from the contempt he had always felt for her. Gabriel was dangerous, he always had been and he always would be, and she now had the two best reasons in the world not to re-enact her own past like a moth drawn to the flame that would ultimately destroy it.

'Not that long ago. It's only just over ten years ago since I picked you up off the street where your previous lover had left you. Remember? You told me that you'd been offered the starring role in a porno movie mogul's latest skinflick, but you'd star in a private one for me instead. Your words, not mine!' He was walking away from her now and heading for her sons. 'The she-leopard does not change her spots.'

'Where are you going?' she demanded frantically, even though she already knew the answer. The smile he gave her made her bite down hard into her bottom lip to stop herself from shuddering in open dread.

'I am going to introduce myself to my wards,' Gabriel answered her softly.

For several precious seconds Sasha was too caught up in her own emotions and the past Gabriel had evoked to move, but somehow she managed to break free of them to run after him, calling out fiercely, 'Leave them alone! Don't you dare touch my children.'

Entering a new decade had added to her beauty rather than taken from it, Gabriel admitted reluctantly as he watched her speed towards him. Her breasts were rising and falling with emotion and exertion beneath the thin covering of her dress when she finally reached him. It caught him off guard to look at her and feel the familiar hunger grip his body. She had always had good breasts—firm-fleshed and erotically real, warm and pliable to the touch, the skin tasting of woman and sunshine and sex, her dark brown nipples always greedily eager for the attention of his fingers and his lips. In his mind's eye he could still see her, virtually naked on the private deck of his yacht, her head thrown back so that the sea breeze could tousle her hair, her lips curved into a smile of wanton, intensely sensual pleasure as she offered herself up to him.

Now, as then—although for different reasons—she was standing immediately in front of him, between him and her children in fact, so that it was impossible for him not to look directly at her. Motherhood had given her breasts a softer fullness that suited her, but it didn't seem to have taken away the narrowness of her waist, nor the sensuality of a body that was made for sexual pleasure. A body he had once known as intimately as he knew his own—perhaps more so. As a lover Sasha had had an incomparable blend of fierce sexual passion and a feminine ability to lose herself and give herself so completely in the act of sex that it had felt as if she was handing every bit of herself over to him for their mutual pleasure. But of course he had been far from the only man to enjoy Sasha's sexuality, and he certainly hadn't been the first to pay for it—if not in money, then certainly in kind, with the lifestyle of a rich man's mistress. She had as good as admitted that to him the night he had picked her up, if not actually out of the gutter, then certainly heading towards it.

He frowned darkly, angered by the power she still had to occupy his thoughts, even though he assured himself it was no longer with the white-hot overwhelming desire for her that had once burned inside his brain as well as his body. She had got under his skin and left an ache he could still feel ten years later, even if the savage heat of the need that had once threatened to consume him had ultimately burned out. Burned itself out, or been ruthlessly stamped out by him? What did it matter which? He had known from the first time he had taken her to bed that the intensity of his hunger for her was not something he wanted in his life. If he had aided in its destruction then he had acted wisely, out of self preservation. What he was feeling now was simply an echo of a long-dead feeling.

But not so dead that the embers didn't smoulder with the heat of his desire for compensation. It had been bad enough that she had walked out on him for Carlo. But the fact that Carlo had fathered two sons on her and taken pride in them had struck painfully at the carefully guarded wound left by the misery of Gabriel's own childhood.

For him—a man who had received neither love, compassion nor kindness—to be given the responsibility of protecting the childhood of these children was either an act of great foolhardiness or great trust. It had certainly been an act of moral desperation. Not that Gabriel would ever punish two innocent young lives for the sins of their mother—not after the way he himself had suffered.

He had received word that Carlo had died a matter of hours after he had seen him. Alone, without Sasha at his side, because she had been shopping.

Sasha. He didn't want to think about the past they had shared, but it refused to be thrust away. Inside his head he could see her clearly as she had been the night he had first seen her. Her hair longer than it was now, inexpertly streaked and slightly tangled in the warm evening breeze. She had been wearing a cheap short skirt and a top that had revealed more of her breasts than it concealed, making her look every inch exactly what she was as she stood on the roadside in St Tropez. He wouldn't even have contemplated stopping if she hadn't virtually thrown herself in front of his car. Pretty, available, hungry girls like Sasha were ten a penny in St Tropez in the season, going from lover to lover, climbing upwards while they could towards their ultimate trophy of a man foolish enough and rich enough to offer them more than a night's sex in return for a thick wad of euros. Sasha, he remembered, had been carrying a large straw basket which, she had told him with a small shrug, contained all her belongings.

'I had to leave quickly, so I just brought what I could,' she had told him disarmingly, when she had by some sleight of hand managed to get herself into the passenger seat of his Ferrari without him actually having invited her to do so.

That had been in May. From the little she had told him about herself he'd gathered that the man she had left had been part of the detritus swirling around in the wake of Cannes Film Festival—a 'producer' looking for young flesh to satisfy his own jaded appetite and those of the debased human beings he made his skinflicks for. But Gabriel hadn't wanted to waste time listening to her talk when there were so many far more pleasurable uses for those soft full lips of hers. There was a practical streak to Sasha, as there was to all successful courtesans. She had quickly worked out that having to satisfy only one man would be a far more cost-effective way of using her body than risking being passed hand to hand by the producer and his friends.

Oh, yes, she was very practical. Within a year she had made plans to move onward and upwards—not just into another man's bed, but more profitably into his whole life. As his wife. And that man had been his own second cousin Carlo—a man old enough to be *his* father, never mind hers. It had been unthinkable that she would leave Gabriel; he was the one who controlled their relationship, not her. He paid the bills and called the tune; she was his for however long he desired her to be. But she had walked out on him, leaving behind an unpaid debt to his pride.

A debt for which fate was now giving him the opportunity to claim payment in full.

Sasha saw the familiar cruel smile curl down the edges of Gabriel's mouth. How many times had he taunted her with that smile before giving in to her pleas and satisfying the aching wanting that he himself had aroused within her flesh?

She had thought when she had met Gabriel that she knew all there was to know about sex and her own body. The truth was she had known nothing whatsoever about pleasure, and too much about need.

When Carlo had offered her an escape route from Gabriel and from the life she had lived before him, she had told herself that the only way to save herself was to seize it with both hands and never look back. And that was exactly what she had done.

But, while she might never have consciously looked back, in her dreams she had gone back so many times, and in such dreadful pain. She shuddered, blinking fiercely. In the years since her sons' conception she had taught herself to walk tall and to be proud for them, and for herself. She would never deny her past, but she believed she had learned from it, *grown* from it, and when the time came and her sons asked she would not lie to them about it.

For now, though, they were too young to be exposed to and tainted by her mistakes, and she would fight with everything she had to protect them from that and to keep them safe. The only way Gabriel would ever take them from her would be by taking her life first and then stepping over her lifeless body to get them, she told herself fiercely.

'I'm not going anywhere without my sons.'

'And they will be staying here. With me.'

'With you? In Sardinia? Where? You don't live here yourself,' she reminded him.

'I didn't, it's true, but now that I own the hotel I intend to turn it back into a private home. The boys will live here when they are not at school, so that they can grow up in their father's culture, his old home.'

On the surface it was both a sensible and a compassionate plan, but compassion was an emotion that simply didn't get under Gabriel's defensive radar. There was something he wasn't telling her. Some hidden agenda motivating him that he was keeping to himself. She looked quickly at her sons, her heart thudding with apprehension. It was easy to see their Calbrini heritage in their looks, even if they were too young to have developed the predatory Sardinian profile shared by both Carlo and Gabriel. Carlo had always said proudly that they were true Calbrinis, and he had promised her…

Her fingers curled tightly into her palms. Carlo had been a man of honour, she reassured herself. He would not have broken the promise he had made her before their birth.

'The boys are due back at school in London in September,' she told Gabriel warningly.

'It is only July. They have the whole summer to enjoy being here, and to get used to my role in their lives.'

'You're planning to spend the summer here?'

'Why not? Sardinia is my home, after all. It makes sense for me to be here to supervise the turning back of the hotel into a private home, and to spend time getting to know my wards.'

She lifted her chin.

'You do realise that I shall be here with them?'

'Hoping to make time to slip away to Port Cervo and find someone to take Carlo's place? Another rich old man to sell yourself to? Or perhaps this time you're hoping for a rich young one? Don't get your hopes up too high, will you, Sasha? You're getting older, and you've got a lot of competition. Plus, not every man wants to be burdened with another man's sons. But then, of course, I was forgetting—that problem is easily solved, isn't it? You'll just put them in boarding school and go off and live your own life without them, like you did when Carlo was dying.'

'You have no right—' Sasha began, but it was too late.

Gabriel was ignoring her, stepping past her to walk determinedly towards the boys. She started to run over the slippery rocks, instinctively wanting to put herself between him and her sons, wincing as she slipped and the corner of one of the sharp rocks scraped against her bare leg, piercing the flesh. As though they sensed her anxiety, the boys had stopped playing to watch the two adults approaching them. Both of them now immediately hurried over to Sasha and stood one on other either side of her in a way that would normally have made her smile almost ruefully because of its instinctive maleness. The boys were totally identical, so much so that even she was sometimes almost deceived when they played tricks on people and pretended to change places. There were subtle differences between them, though, that only a mother could see,

She looked magnificent, Gabriel admitted. A tigress

guarding her young, ignoring the blood trickling down her leg and the broken strap of her flimsy footwear.

Out of nowhere, raw, primitive and unwanted emotions savaged him.

Sardinia's family hierarchies and patriarchs had long memories, and the history of the island was filled with tales of revenge and bitterness waged between warring families. He came from those people who truly believed in the rule of an eye for an eye, even though in these modern times they paid lip service to modern laws, and that ancestral history rose up inside him now. He had believed that Sasha was *his*, and that she would remain his until he no longer had any use for her. That he had been the one who controlled their relationship, and through it *her*. It had been the primary unwritten law that governed their relationship. But she had broken that law, and in doing so she had offended his pride.

He could never forget what his mother had done to him, and how she had chosen to reject his claim on her. As he had grown to manhood he had told himself that he would not have his power or his emotional security challenged or threatened by any woman. In those relationships with women he chose to have *he* would always be the one who ended them. He *had* planned to end his relationship with Sasha. But she had walked out on him before he could. And, worse, she had walked out into the arms of another man. His cousin! Oh, yes, Sasha owed him—and he intended to drink his fill of his chosen cup of revenge.

CHAPTER FOUR

SASHA wasn't going to be parted from her sons, not for a minute—even if that meant she had to stay here with Gabriel, Sasha told herself fiercely. But thankfully it wouldn't be for long. Not even Gabriel could hold back the start of the new school year. Which reminded her... She looked down at the rings on her fingers. Thanks to her diligence and determination she now had the satisfying credentials of a degree and an MBA. And thanks to Carlo's generosity the sale of her jewellery should give her enough to buy a small house in London close to the boys' school, pay their school fees and put some money in the bank for a rainy day.

'Come,' Gabriel demanded autocratically, holding his hand out towards the nearest boy.

Sasha could feel Sam looking up at her questioningly.

It would be so easy to turn them against Gabriel, and to fill their pliable minds with thoughts of bitterness and resentment, to drip poison into them so that they became filled with hatred and fear for the man their father had appointed as their guardian. But, no matter what she felt personally, she could not do that to them. She would not damage them in that kind of way. They came before everything and everyone else, in her life and in her heart.

Forcing herself to smile, she gave Sam and then Nico a small gentle push towards Gabriel.

'Your father has appointed Gabriel to be your guardian, and that means that we can stay here in Sardinia for the rest of the summer,' she told them as lightly as she could.

It was better to keep things simple and easy for them to accept and understand. They both loved Sardinia, and why shouldn't they? This country was, after all, a big part of them and their family history. They had spent every summer here since their birth.

It felt odd to receive the formal handshakes of these two miniature representations of his own family genes mingled with those of their mother instead of embracing them in true Sardinian fashion, Gabriel acknowledged. But then their father had been an elderly father, very much of the old school, and part educated in England himself, so naturally their manners reflected that.

'What are we to call you?' Sam asked shyly.

'Gabriel is the second cousin of your father,' Sasha explained quickly, not willing to give Gabriel the opportunity to take control even in this small matter. 'So perhaps you should call him Cousin Gabriel?'

'Cousin Gabriel.' Sam rolled the words around his tongue. He was both the more serious and at times the more reckless of the two boys, whereas Nico tended to follow his twin's lead. 'I like it,' he announced judiciously.

'Good. I am glad that you do,' Gabriel told him cordially, neatly taking charge of the conversation. 'I used to call your father Cousin Carlo when I first knew him.'

Oh, very clever, Sasha acknowledged, as she saw the way her sons were starting to relax and move closer to him, like to like, male to male, the boys drawn instinctively towards this new figure in their lives.

Carlo had loved them deeply, but when he had become ill two energetic youngsters had been too much for him to cope with other than for a few minutes at a time. So she had set herself up as buffer between her sons and her husband, wanting to protect both from pain—emotional pain on the part of her sons, and physical pain on the part of her frail husband.

'Can we do some fishing this afternoon?' Nico asked her eagerly.

Fishing was a new passion, and most days the three of them spent time sitting on the rocks, waiting for fish to bite on the lines Sasha had taught the boys how to bait.

But it was Gabriel who answered, before she could, saying calmly, 'There are some matters I need to discuss with your mother, so we must return to the hotel. But perhaps this afternoon you can show me the best place to fish.'

He was seducing her sons every bit as easily as he had once seduced her, Sasha recognized, as the twins danced up and down with delight, eagerly falling into step beside Gabriel and abandoning her as they all made their way back to the hotel.

'Can you play football?' she could hear Nico asking Gabriel with eager shyness.

Immediately Gabriel stopped walking and turned to

look down at the small earnest-looking face turned up towards his own. 'Do fish swim?' he teased Nico, adding with a small shrug, 'I'm Italian, aren't I?'

'Sam supports Chelsea, but AC Milan is my team.' Nico beamed.

'I support Chelsea because half of us is English,' Sam informed Gabriel seriously. 'So it's only fair, isn't it?'

Her sons were so engrossed in talking about football with Gabriel that she might as well not be here, Sasha decided with a sharp pang.

'You need to get that leg cleaned up.' They had reached the hotel, and Gabriel's terse instruction brought Sasha's lips together in an usually tight line.

'Oh, please.' Her voice dripped sarcasm. 'Don't try to pretend you're concerned. The compassionate act doesn't suit you, Gabriel, and besides, we both know that you have no compassion for the female sex in general, and me in particular.'

She turned to look at her sons, who had been lagging behind but who had now caught up with them. 'Boys, go and get cleaned up, please, and then down to the kitchen for lunch.'

Sasha believed in nurturing her sons with loving but firm boundaries. She upheld the importance of good manners, but this, in her opinion, was a double-lane highway. If she expected her sons to behave politely, and to understand the importance of good manners, they deserved to be on the receiving end of them them-selves. So far—backed up, thankfully, by the same kind of attitude in their school—they were developing a happy mixture of automatic pleases and thank-yous accompanied by natural boyish high spirits and occasional forgetfulness.

'You're a fine one to talk about concern,' Gabriel said as soon as the boys had raced upstairs, out of their hearing. 'You may be clever enough not to employ full-time care for those two—Carlo would never have agreed to that, as we both know—but you obviously make sure you aren't left with *too* much responsibility for their day-to-day care.'

'Just because they asked you a few questions about football, that hardly makes me an uncaring or uninvolved mother,' Sasha told him scornfully.

'That wasn't what I meant. I was referring to the fact that you are sending them down to the kitchen to eat while you, no doubt, will enjoy your lunch somewhere a little more elegant and without their presence. If you were left to your own devices you would probably also import a lover—possibly the same one you were seen dining with in New York.'

Sasha stared at him in outraged fury. She was too angry to even think about responding to him. She owed him nothing. Less than nothing. And she wasn't going to give any kind of legitimacy to his accusations by bothering to defend herself from them. Why should she?

'It's a pity there isn't something you could take for that perverted and warped sense of reality of yours, Gabriel. And, for your information, whoever you were paying to spy on me didn't deserve their fee. If they had done their work properly then they would have known that the only man I spent any time with when I was in New York was the specialist oncologist I had gone to

see. You see, unlike you, I didn't want to sit around waiting for Carlo to die when there was the remotest chance
that there could be some drug or treatment that might
have given him some extra time,' she told him con-
temptuously, before turning on her heel and following
her sons upstairs.

He didn't let her get very far, his fingers manacling
her wrist and yanking her round to face him before she
had climbed more than a couple of stairs.

'Very effective—or at least it would have been if I
did not know you so well. Has it occurred to you that
Carlo could have been ready to die? That he might even
have preferred to die peacefully in his own bed rather
than have his life eked out for a few months, days or
weeks, so that you could continue to feed off him?
While he was alive he was your passport to the life you
had always wanted, the life you sold your body to get.
He was besotted by you and you knew it—so much so
that he begged me to lend him more money at any rate
I cared to name just so he could satisfy your greed.'

'That's not true!'

Her face was as white as the marble hallway and its
curling flight of stairs. Her eyes had filled with tears.
They clouded her vision, making Gabriel's features
shimmer and break up. 'It was Carlo's pride that made
him go on borrowing, not me. I didn't even know what
he was doing.'

'Liar.'

He was still holding her wrist, and as she looked
down at him she was abruptly reminded of another time
and another set of marble stairs on which she had stood
and looked down into his face—laughed down, in fact,

with delight and teasing provocation. The stairs had been in an exclusive atelier, where he had taken her to try on the dress that she had been modelling for him, layers of black silk chiffon that sighed and whispered against her skin as she walked. She had leaned towards him, she remembered, not caring that the silk was slipping from her, in truth delighting in the fact that his gaze was caressing her semi-naked body, and that his hand was cupping her bare breast. She had still believed then that it just wasn't possible for him to mean it when he said that love and emotion had no place in his life. She had been so crazily in love with him that she had believed the sheer force of her love for him would make him love her back. Then.

But this was now. Separated from the past by the ocean of tears she had cried, and the protective wall she had thrown up around herself. That wall was impenetrable, reinforced with the bitterness of reality and the strength of her hatred, bonded together with her tears.

'I hate you so much,' she told him fiercely, her emotions darkening her eyes. She could feel the blistering hiss of Gabriel's exhaled breath against her skin as his own anger overwhelmed him and he jerked her towards him.

She had been standing awkwardly on the stair, caught in mid-step, and his angry movement made her overbalance and lurch into him. 'So you say. But my bet is that you would still go to bed with me—for a price.'

The pain inside her was instant and savage, making her recoil and fight to escape it, her nostrils flaring and the smooth muscles of her throat tightening her skin.

'You were the one who taught me to separate my

emotions from my body, to treat sex as a physical activity with no connection to any kind of emotional feelings. So yes, I dare say if I wanted to have sex with you I could detach myself enough from my emotional loathing of you as a person to enable me to do so,' she agreed thinly. 'But I do not want to, and neither do I need to use my body as currency.'

'Why? Have you found another man to replace Carlo before he is even cold in his grave?' What was that pain slicing and ripping at his guts? He didn't want her; he had stopped wanting her when she had started her unsuccessful bid for a more permanent role in his life. He could hear her voice now, soft with false emotion as she told him, 'I love you, Gabriel, and I know that you love me, even if you refuse to say the words.'

'You know wrong, then,' he had answered, and had meant it. 'I do not love anyone. The ability and the desire to love was kicked and beaten out of me by foster parents. The same foster parents who claimed to love me when they discovered that I'd become financially successful. You say you love me, but what you really mean is that you want me to keep you permanently in my life because I am rich and you are poor. What you love is what I give you.'

'That isn't true,' she had protested. But of course he had known better than to believe her.

He looked at her now as she told him fiercely, 'No. Unlike you, Gabriel, I've moved on from my past.' She lifted her head proudly. 'I have a degree now, and an MBA. I'm fully qualified to get a job that pays me enough to support myself and my sons.' She only prayed that would be true.

Gabriel had to fight against the shock of feeling that was gripping him. Why the hell should he be so angry and resentful at the thought of her working to support herself and being independent of him?

'You can't deceive me, Sasha, with your pseudo-maternal act,' he retaliated. 'Were you the mother you are trying to pretend to be, do you think for one moment that Carlo would have felt it necessary to appoint me as his sons' guardian? It's obvious that in the end he recognised exactly what you are, and that he wanted to protect them.'

Sasha had raised her hand before she could rationalise what she was doing, but just as swiftly he reacted to her action, clipping her arms to her sides. Before she could guess what he intended to do he was suddenly dragging her into his arms and kissing her in angry punishment. The pressure of his mouth ground down on her own, bruising the softness of her lips as she fought against his domination. But it was her retaliatory savage nip at his bottom lip that drew the blood she could taste on her tongue. He thrust her away so roughly that she almost fell, his eyes as dark as murder as he wiped the back of his hand across his split lip.

'Bitch,' he said brutally, before he turned and strode back down the stairs, leaving her standing watching him whilst her belly churned with ice and fire, fear and need, hatred and… And what? The opposite of hatred was love, and she did not love him. She raised the back of her hand to her eyes, shocked to see that it came away wet with tears.

Part of the charm of the hotel was that it was in many ways still very much a private house, Sasha admitted as she stood in the bedroom of the top-floor private suite that Carlo had always insisted was not to be treated as part of the hotel or occupied by anyone else.

Below this, the next floor contained another large suite and three smaller ones, with the rest of the bedrooms contained in what had once been the stable block of the house. The reception rooms were decorated and furnished as though they were rooms in a private home, and a large conservatory had been added to the rear of the house to provide a dining room that opened out onto a terrace, beyond which was the swimming pool. It would be easy enough for a man with Gabriel's wealth to turn it back into a private home. And it would certainly be more comfortable than the semi-fortress in the mountains that had been his grandfather's home.

She and Carlo had occupied separate bedrooms throughout their marriage. Hers looked out to sea, and was decorated in a palette of soft, barely-there blues and aquas and natural fabrics. She needed to speak to Maria about lunch. She picked up the telephone receiver.

Her call completed, she slipped off her linen dress and went into her bathroom to clean the cut on her leg. The time she had spent outside with the boys was giving her body a soft tan that was driving away the pallor caused by so many hours spent at Carlo's bedside. She barely glanced at her own reflection, though. Her head had begun to ache with the tension and pressure of all the morning had brought.

Why, *why* had Carlo done this? He must have known what it would do to her. He had always promised her that he would never…

But of course she knew why he had done it. It had

been his way of providing for Sam and Nico. And for her? Had he really thought she would allow Gabriel to support her? Had he believed that Gabriel would? Who knew what thoughts might have filled the head of a dying man.

Automatically she cleaned the small cut, but her mind wasn't really on what she was doing. There was a faint smear of dried blood on her dress, so she went into her dressing room and removed a pair of jeans and a tee shirt from the closet. She would have liked to have a shower before she put them on, but the boys would be hungry.

Downstairs in the kitchen, the boys and Maria, who came in to cook for them when they were in residence, were gathered around a large, well-worn and equally well-scrubbed kitchen table.

'Look, Mum, Maria is going to make a cake with these eggs from Flossie and Bessie,' Sam announced proudly.

Flossie and Bessie were the boys' bantam hens—another cornerstone of Sasha's determination to bring up her sons in a very specific way. This particular cornerstone involved active participation in becoming aware of what good food was, where it came from, and how it should be cooked.

'We're going to make chocolate brownies—but after lunch.'

'Good choice,' an unexpected male voice announced easily—unexpected and, far as she was concerned, very definitely unwanted. Involuntarily her gaze flew to his mouth. His lip had stopped bleeding but it was obviously swollen. 'Chocolate brownies are one of my favourites.'

What was happening to her? Why couldn't she make herself stop looking at his mouth? If she didn't, he would notice, and then... Could Maria and the boys feel her tension, and with it the antipathy and distrust with which she and Gabriel were filling the homey room? It appalled her that she should be reacting to him like this. She was twenty-eight now, for heaven's sake, not seventeen and vulnerable to being totally overwhelmed by his sexuality and her own immaturity.

But there was no mistaking the hot flare of her immediate arousal. It might be hidden within her body, but she could not hide from it. Anger, rejection, panic flowed through her veins like red hot lava. Why was this happening? She had lived ten whole years without him. Years during which she had been happy and secure, years during which she had privately celebrated her own freedom from the destructive emotions and needs that had tied her to him—the hungers she hadn't been able to control but he had, using them to hold her in thrall to him. There had been nothing she would not have done to please him, no pleasure more intense for her than the pleasure of pleasing him. But this ache in her body now was an unwanted reminder that, just as he had known how to compel and arouse her, he had also known how to please and satisfy her. The sex between them had been all-consuming and almost compulsive. How could one man have the power to affect her like this? It shouldn't be possible.

She tried to focus on the table in front of her. Good food should be eaten with a good digestion, and that required contentment. Already her appetite was betraying just how anxious and on edge Gabriel's presence made her feel.

What was he doing down here in the kitchen? She had already telephoned Maria to alert her to the fact that they had an unexpected guest for lunch, only to learn that Gabriel had already been to the kitchen to introduce himself to her and to explain that he would be staying.

The hotel had been officially closed from the date of Carlo's death and after the subsequent discovery of how close to bankruptcy his finances were. The Michelin-starred chef, like the imposing *maître d'* and the elegant receptionist, had left for a more secure job, and only a skeleton staff which included Maria and certain members of her family remained at the hotel.

Sasha spoke swiftly to Maria, switching automatically to the local dialect as she asked her if Gabriel had ordered lunch. Gabriel, who was fluent in several languages, had always spoken with her in English, just as he had done earlier down on the beach. He was doing so again now.

'Maria offered to serve me my lunch on the terrace, but when I discovered she was alone down here in the kitchen I told her that she need not put herself to so much trouble. She is, after all, no longer young, and the terrace is a good walk away.'

Sasha could hear the curt disapproval in his voice and knew immediately that it was directed at her.

'Actually, *I* will be the one serving you lunch, not Maria,' she corrected him. She wasn't going to tell him that it would also have fallen to her to make lunch for him as well—not because Maria was incapable of doing so, but because, contrary to what Gabriel seemed to think, she did not need him to point out to her that the elderly woman's rheumatism made it difficult and uncomfortable for her to take on too many tasks. Maria and her husband, and their extended family, were dependent on the hotel not just for their wages but also for the roof over their heads, and Sasha was already dipping into her own small reserves of cash to ensure that they did not suffer any hardship. Not that she intended to tell Gabriel any of this. Right now, what she wanted more than anything else was to have him out of her life or, failing that, at least out of the kitchen. Unable to risk looking directly at him, she told him dismissively, 'I'm sure you can find your way back to the terrace.'

'Where are you going to eat?'

A stomach-churning mixture of rejection and unstoppable, dangerous excitement held her rigid. He wasn't going to suggest that she ate with him, reprising the night they had met, was he? It was like being picked up and dropped bodily from a great height into a seething cauldron of frighteningly powerful emotions. Emotions that rightfully belonged in the past and had no place here, she tried to remind herself.

'Mum always eats down here in the kitchen with us,' Sam answered Gabriel helpfully, his youthful voice a small, still, cool rescuing hand of reality and sanity.

'As you know, the hotel is closed.' Of course he knew. He knew everything there was to know about the current state of the business because he now owned it.

She still couldn't risk looking directly at him. He, of course, was used to the very best of everything, and a chef on standby twenty-four-seven. 'The boys and I eat very simply. You'd be better off going into Port Cervo. There are plenty of restaurants there.'

'What are you having to eat?' Gabriel asked the boys, ignoring her.

'Fish,' Sam answered, adding enthusiastically, 'We chose it ourselves at the market this morning. Mum hates it when they are still flapping, but that is how you can tell they have just been landed. Pietro told us that,' he informed Gabriel importantly. 'Sometimes he even lets us go out onto his boat and see them in the net. We can ask him if you can come too if you like,' he added generously.

Just standing listening to her sons, just watching them, filled Sasha with a fiercely proud aching well of love. Tears pricked at the backs of her eyes, but she blinked them away. Boy children did not like 'soppy' displays of maternal emotion.

'Do you suppose there will be enough fish for me?' she could hear Gabriel asking Sam, treating him as an equal and not as a child—which, of course, was bound to appeal to her sons and make Gabriel instantly acceptable, she acknowledged grimly. And he knew it too. She could see that from the look he was giving her over the boys' heads. It was one of open triumph.

'If you prefer meat to fish we have some local lamb. It will take slightly longer to cook,' she told him woodenly, deliberately looking slightly past him instead of directly at him, 'but I can recommend it. We serve it in a kebab with locally grown peppers, onions and mushrooms, on a bed of wild rice. It's a local recipe—'

'I grew up here,' Gabriel cut in, and reminded her grimly. 'As you very well know. I'll have the fish,' he told her curtly.

'Mum is teaching us how to fillet it,' Nico said gravely.

'You're planning to raise two chefs?' Gabriel asked her softly, in a slightly unkind voice.

'No, I'm raising two sons to be independent and as aware of their environment and the pleasure of the simple, good things this life provides as they can,' Sasha corrected him fiercely. '*My* sons—'

'And *my* wards,' he interrupted her softly—and threateningly, Sasha recognised as small shiver ran down her spine.

Her relationship with her sons was not what he had expected, Gabriel admitted as he watched her. *She* was not what he had expected. He had anticipated a surface show of overdone pseudo-maternal concern, such as he was used to seeing from many of the wives of his peers. Women who used their children as accessories for celebrity photo opportunities and then handed them over to others to do the real hands-on caring the minute the cameras were no longer there. But, no matter how much he might wish to do so, he couldn't pretend that he hadn't seen the love in her eyes whenever Sasha looked at the twins.

He knew, of course, that the discovery that she was virtually penniless had severely curtailed Sasha's ability to live the life Carlo had given her, but he had assumed that, while her lifestyle had necessarily changed, she herself wouldn't have done so. The woman he was watching now, though, seemed perfectly at home in this kitchen environment and perfectly at ease in her role as a hands-on mother.

He looked round the comfortable, homey room, at the confident smiling faces of the two boys who were now his responsibility. He had been scarcely even allowed to enter the kitchen of his foster parents' farmhouse. It had not possessed the warmth and cleanliness, the security he could see and sense in this room. Like him, it had been dirty and neglected, tainted with the wretchedness of emotional poverty and fear. Because here in this room there was love?

Love? Automatically he lifted his hand to press his fingertips against the dull ache beneath his breastbone. He didn't believe in love. Love did not exist. And if it didn't exist then the fact that as a child he had not been given any didn't matter and couldn't hurt him. This was his private and unacknowledged inner mantra.

In the end they all had the fish, and all ate together at the kitchen table. Not that Sasha managed to do much eating. Although she had tried to position herself so that she wouldn't have to see Gabriel, she was still nerve-wrenchingly conscious of him. If he had insisted on eating with them just to torment her, he was certainly succeeding.

She could still remember the first meal they had eaten together. It had been on board his yacht, where he had taken her after he had picked her up in St Tropez. Then she had not had any trouble eating. She hadn't had a decent meal in days and had been so hungry. He had raised his eyebrows slightly when she had cleaned her plate within seconds, looking from it to her face, and then to her body.

She had thought she had been so very clever. She had been watching him all week, fantasising about him, weaving idiotic daydreams around him consisting of hopelessly implausible Cinderella themes and happy-ever-afters, in the way that only a seventeen-year-old desperately hungry for love could. She had seen him on the waterfront and had naïvely assumed that he was crewing for one of the huge yachts filling the small harbour. Having seen him striding briskly past the cafés dressed in jeans and a tee shirt, it had simply not occurred to her that he might own one. He had been the kind of man a girl like her could only dream about— tall, dark and impossibly handsome, the kind of man who had all it took to sweep a girl off her feet and carry her off with him into his life. The truth was that she had fantasised herself into being more than half in love with him before she had even spoken to him.

And she had been so very desperate for love. Her mother had died giving birth to her, and her father had been advised to have her fostered. She had been four years old when he had remarried, and although he and his new wife had attempted to make her welcome in their lives, her great need for love had led to problems—especially when her stepmother had become pregnant. She had been taken back into care and had remained there until she was sixteen, craving love but too institutionalised to know how to fit into a normal family framework.

Social Services had helped her to find a job and accommodation, but the kindly shop owners she had worked for had understandably been wary and embarrassed when she had tried to push her way into their family, desperately wanting them to be the mother and father to her that she had never had. She had received counselling after that, for her 'inappropriate attachment issues', but what good was counselling when all she'd wanted was to be loved?

Her social workers had found her another job—in a

supermarket this time—and when she and six other girls had had a small win on the Lottery it had been decided that they would have a holiday in St Tropez.

It had been one of the other girls, well endowed and twenty to Sasha's seventeen, who had struck up the acquaintanceship with the seedy 'film director' who had leeringly suggested that he feature the girls in one of his movies, claiming that he was in Cannes for the Film Festival.

An argument had raged hotly between those girls who'd wanted no truck with what they termed 'a sleazy porno merchant' and the smaller number who'd wanted fame at any price, and Sasha had found herself in the position of being pressured by Doreen, the pneumatic blonde, to join her in pornstar fame.

While the girls had been arguing amongst themselves, Sasha had been busy daydreaming about Gabriel, weaving a fantasy life for them both in which he fell head over heels in love with her and they lived happily ever after. Although, of course, she hadn't even known his name at that stage.

Now she knew that the fantasies she had created for herself as she was growing up—first that of being part of a close-knit family with loving parents, and then her desire for Gabriel to fall in love with her—had been her way of trying to give herself the love she had not received as a child. In her daydreams she could create her world as she yearned for it to be. But in reality that was impossible. No real relationship could have carried the burdensome weight of her expectations.

The night before the girls had been due to fly back

to the UK, Sasha had seized her chance to bring herself to Gabriel's attention. By what self-destructive instinct had she homed in on a man who was as emotionally damaged as she was herself? Theirs had always been a relationship doomed to failure—if you could use the word 'relationship' to describe what they had shared. Theirs had been a dangerously compulsive sexual addiction to one another coupled with an equally dangerous hunger for emotional dependency on her part and an ingrained rejection of emotional intimacy on Gabriel's. If she had deliberately set out to do so she could not have found someone less able to meet her expectations. A wiser person would have seen that. But all she had seen was the fantasy she had created.

On that first night she had truly believed that the most challenging element of her daydream future had been finding the bravado to step in front of his car with assumed studied nonchalance, mimicking the more worldly-wise girls. Miraculously, it had worked. She had inveigled her way into his car and from there to his bed. But what she hadn't known then was that there was no access from there to his heart...

The boys had finished their lunch and were clamouring to go back outside, bringing Sasha back to the present.

Today had to have been just about the longest and worst day of her life, Sasha reflected tiredly, several hours later. The boys were now in bed, but, drained of physical and mental energy, Sasha felt too emotionally wired to sleep. But sleep she must. The boys were always awake early.

Gabriel had gone up to the suite he had claimed

hours ago, saying brusquely that he had some work he needed to do and telling the boys that he would see them in the morning. It shocked her how easily he could tell them apart—something that Carlo had never been able to do.

Gabriel. She still didn't want to believe that this had happened, that he was here, she admitted as she made her way from the bathroom to her waiting bed.

Gabriel half woke up in the darkness of the unfamiliar room, so disorientated between past and present that before he could stop himself he was automatically reaching out, expecting Sasha to be there, his hand already cupping to take the warm, soft weight of her breast and rub his thumb-tip over her nipple in the caress she had told him so many times she could not resist. He had never known a woman so sexually sensitive to his touch, so immediately and uncontrollably responsive and aroused by him. But then he had also never known another time when he himself had been so equally and eagerly sexually charged. There had been times when his hunger for her had actually led him to analyse the feasibility of dismissing the yacht's crew and sailing it himself, simply so that he could have the convenience of taking Sasha wherever and whenever he wanted. She had baulked a little at first when he had suggested she wear one of his shirts over the erotically designed swimwear he had bought her instead of its matching cover-ups. But when he had told her softly and explicitly that beneath the protective cover up of his shirt he wanted her naked and ready for him, the look on her face had been one of open excitement rather than rejection.

Gabriel wasn't the type to be turned on by the thought of others witnessing their intimacy—quite the contrary—but it had become necessary for him to know that she was there, and that he could help himself to the sweetest of all fruits without hindrance. Unlike in his youth, when the basic necessities of life had been withheld from him.

He had enjoyed knowing that all it took to bring the tide of aroused colour surging up under her skin was to slide his hand beneath the hem of the shirt and stroke his way up her naked thigh. Long before his fingers had discreetly parted the soft closure of the tender outer lips of her sex she would be leaning into him, her eyes closing, her body trembling violently with the urgency of her need. There had been times when it had satisfied him more to watch her orgasm against his stroking fingers and know how completely enslaved she was by her desire for him than it had to feel his own body reaching its climax within hers. Sometimes. But his own flesh hadn't been able to go very long without hungering for the firm slide of her muscles as they gripped and caressed, and urged him deeper into her, so deep sometimes that the act of possessing her felt as if he was making her a part of himself.

Gabriel frowned when he realised that he couldn't feel the softness of Sasha's flesh at an easy arm's length from his possession. Beneath his hand the bed felt cold and empty.

Abruptly he was fully awake and even more fully aware. He cursed himself beneath his breath, and his face burned with angry determination. His pride would not be satisfied until he had brought Sasha to the point where she was begging him to take her; when nothing mattered to her other than his possession of her; when *he* was the one to walk away from her.

It was years since he had woken in the night like this, and the only reason he could be doing so now, he reasoned, was because his subconscious sensed he was close to punishing Sasha for what she had done. That was all. Nothing else. How could there be anything else?

He moved to the middle of the bed and determinedly closed his eyes. Only when his pride had been satisfied would he be able to properly address the issue of his duty toward Carlo's sons, and the need to protect them from the damage that having Sasha for a mother must be inflicting on them.

CHAPTER FIVE

A PATH led down from the house to the beach, and as he stood at the top of it Gabriel could see Sasha and her sons walking along the shore. They hadn't seen him as yet, giving him the opportunity to study them at leisure. The early-morning sun was warming the sand and glittering on the sea. Every now and again either Sasha or one of the boys paused to crouch down and pick up a shell or a pebble.

Sasha looked more like a girl than a woman, in a tee shirt, with a pair of binoculars slung round her neck, and cut-off jeans, her hair caught back off her face in a band. He could hear the sound of their conversation but not what they were saying. Occasional bursts of laughter indicated that they were all enjoying themselves. Sasha looked out to sea and said something to the boys, lifting the binoculars to her eyes and then crouching down beside them. Nico—somehow Gabriel knew without knowing how or why he knew that it *was* Nico—leaned against her, putting his arm round her and his head on her shoulder while Sam stood on her other side. As Gabriel watched she handed the binoculars to Sam and then to Nico. Gabriel shielded his eyes with his hand and looked out to sea himself. In the distance he could just about make out the shape of a small school of dolphins. Sasha had always been entranced by the creatures, he remembered.

Nico was handing the binoculars back to her. She kissed him on the top of his head as she took them from him, one arm wrapped firmly around Sam, the other around Nico.

There was a pain in his gut, a familiar dull ache that suddenly flared into a hot, stabbing sensation. As a child he had never known the tenderness of any woman's maternal embrace, never mind that of his own mother. Kicks and curses had been his lot, followed by the harsh pride of a grandfather who had tolerated him because he'd had no choice.

Down on the beach, Sasha gave her sons a final hug and then released them. These early-morning walks were a part of their traditional holiday ritual, made especially pleasurable this morning thanks to the sighting of the dolphins.

She was just straightening up when Sam called out excitedly, 'There's Cousin Gabriel!' and began to race across the sand towards him, followed by Nico.

Sam reached Gabriel first, flinging himself against him. There was no need for her to worry that her sons might object to Gabriel's presence in their lives, she acknowledged. Nico was now clinging to him as well, and their faces were turned up toward Gabriel's as they chattered non-stop, telling him about their walk and the excitement of seeing the dolphins.

'I'm going to write about seeing them in my life book,' Nico announced.

'So am I in mine,' Sam insisted, not to be outdone.

'You could do some research on them first,' Sasha suggested. 'Perhaps we'll be able to find some pictures on the Internet you can paste into your books.'

'I've already written in mine about Gabriel being our guardian,' Nico told Sasha. 'Perhaps I should put a photograph of him in my life book as well.'

'What's a life book?' Gabriel asked.

'It's a form of diary,' Sasha answered him distantly. 'The boys have kept a life book right from when they could first write. They put in their good memories—'

'And when we feel sad as well, like when Dad died,' Sam piped up. 'Race you to the house, Nico,' Sam called out to his brother.

On the face of it, Sasha was everything a good mother should be, Gabriel acknowledged. Involved with her children, concerned for them, protective of them, but at the same time encouraging them to grow towards independence. On the face of it. But the truth was that she was no more than a good actress who had played her part for so long it was almost real. He knew that.

With the boys gone, Sasha kept her distance from Gabriel. Her whole body ached with anxious tension, as though she was constantly holding her breath and tensing her muscles. She had barely slept the last three nights, since Gabriel had arrived, and she knew that her nervous system was running on empty with fear-induced adrenalin.

The twins had run on ahead of them, eager for their breakfast. Automatically Sasha increased her own walking pace, so that she could catch up with them, deliberately keeping her gaze focused on the two boys as she started to walk past Gabriel.

'You're wasting your time—you know that, don't you? You can't fool me, Sasha. I know you far too well. I know what motivates you and what drives you.'

Gabriel's low-voiced assertion was just loud enough for only her to hear, Sasha recognised. Her heart had started to thump in an unsteady, almost sickeningly heavy beat. How *could* he know about the sexual effect he was having on her? Not even the fun of her walk along the beach with the boys had had the power to silence the hammering pulse of need that had invaded her body. How was it possible for her to feel like this? She had truly believed that the long weeks she had spent after leaving him, too sick with physical and emotional longing for him to do more than gratefully allow Carlo to take care of her as though she were an invalid, had burned away that part of her that was so vulnerable to him and inoculated her against him for ever. But what if she was wrong? What if, like a drug addict or an alcoholic, she could never truly claim to be free of her old addiction to him?

She *was* free of it, she told herself fiercely. She had learned the difference between the destructive nature of the unhealthy physical and emotional need that had driven her relationship with Gabriel and the life-enhancing qualities that comprised a healthy relationship. And she still wanted him physically? *No!*

'You may think you know me, Gabriel,' she retorted, as calmly as she could. 'But the girl you knew no longer exists. Carlo gave me—'

'Carlo gave you what?' She winced at the savage

tone of his voice. 'Sexual pleasure? Sexual satisfaction? Did he make you moan in hot pleasure when he touched you with his old hands, when he filled you with his withered flesh, Sasha? Or did you close your eyes and think about his money and his ring on your finger? Did he give you *this*?' he demanded.

And then, shockingly, his fingers were digging into the soft flesh of her waist as he pulled her towards him, one hand immediately securing her flaying fists behind her back while the other slid through her hair, holding her so that she could not even turn her head to avoid the dark possession of his kiss.

The boys had disappeared inside the house, and the rhythmic sound of the waves surging against the shore mingled with the beat of her own blood surging through her veins. She was surrounded by an assault against her senses she couldn't withstand: the familiar scent of Gabriel's skin; the living, breathing male reality of him as he held her; the way her own body instantly accommodated the intimate thrust of his leg between her own; the sensation of her breasts swelling with arousal as his tongue thrust against hers in a slow, erotic dance of sensual pleasure that stripped her defences from her. Already her body was anticipating the touch of his hand. Already the ache deep inside her had become a sharply tight pang of longing.

A seagull mewed in the sky above them and immediately Gabriel released her.

'You may think you can deceive me by acting the devoted widow, Sasha, but you can't. I can see right through your little act.' Gabriel was breathing heavily, his chest rising and falling unsteadily as he spoke. Sasha focused on its movement as she struggled to make sense of what that just happened.

She badly wanted to be sick. Her stomach was churning with nausea and a guilt that was pushing her to hit back at him, to hurt him as he had done her. She lifted her head and looked at him, her eyes dark with emotion. 'Do you know something, Gabriel?' she told him shakily. 'I actually feel sorry for you. You think you're so strong, but in reality you are pitifully damaged. You can't comprehend that it's possible for a person to change because *you* can't change. You can't comprehend that it's possible for love and respect to exist within a relationship because *you* have never experienced them. All you can do is mirror the pain of your childhood and reflect it back to others. Thanks to Carlo, I have learned how to be emotionally healthy. That was his gift to me, and the most precious gift I have to give my sons. I've changed. I'm not the girl you knew any longer.'

Keeping her head held high, Sasha walked past him and into the house.

Gabriel could feel the inner explosion of his own anger in the ice-cold shards of fury that splintered through him. So Sasha pitied him, did she? Well, very soon now she was going to realise that she should have saved her precious pity for herself—because she was going to need it. He could feel the savage pulse of the tumult of emotions surging through him.

How dared she, a woman who had lived as she had done, accuse him of being damaged? And as for her having changed—that was impossible. But for some reason an image had lodged itself inside his mind of the way she had held her sons as the three of them watched the dolphins, and it refused to be deleted. Whatever she might have been, wasn't it the truth that she was now a woman with two sons whom she loved with an intensity that he could almost feel, never mind see? But if he allowed himself to accept that he was misjudging Sasha, then what might that lead to? Pain? Regret? The admission that he had lost something irreplaceable, something infinitely precious?

That could not be allowed to happen. No matter what the evidence to the contrary, he had to go on believing that Sasha was not to be trusted or believed, that she was just putting on an act. He could not forget that she had come to him from another man, from other *men,* saying openly that she preferred what he had to offer her. And she had left him for exactly the same reason. He owed it to Carlo and to Carlo's sons to be there for them against the day she chose to change again, and trade in her love for them for a new love with someone else.

No matter what she might say, he did not trust her. Sooner rather than later she was going to start looking for another rich and foolish man to take over Carlo's role in her life. She could act the doting mother all she liked now, but that couldn't alter the fact that she had already put the boys into boarding school once to suit her own needs, so she could be free to jet off to New York. How could she be the loving mother she was so successfully portraying and have done that? Especially when their father had been dying and they must have needed her more than ever? It wasn't possible.

Two hours later Gabriel looked up from his computer and out of the window of the room in the main guest suite he was using as a temporary office. The demands of his business were such that it should not have been possible for any thoughts of Sasha to surface, but somehow they had done so. For all her assumed anger and contempt, he had still felt her body's unmistakable response to him.

Had she taken lovers during her marriage to Carlo? That feeling gripping him surely wasn't really pain; it was simply anger on his cousin's behalf. When Sasha had walked out on him he had refused to think about her or what she might be doing, but now, living in such physical proximity to her, that wasn't possible. Her presence filled the house so that even when she wasn't physically visible he could feel her around him.

He looked at his computer. Several e-mails had just come through, including one from his PA in Florence whom he had instructed to find a scholarly tutor capable of evaluating the boys' strengths and weaknesses so that he could make a decision as to their future. He certainly wasn't going to allow Sasha to send them to boarding school. And one from an architect capable of turning the hotel back into a private house. He owned properties all over the world, but neither they nor his yacht were the right environment for a pair of nine-year-olds.

Quickly he opened and read the e-mails, and then instructed his PA to have the two men at the top of the list flown out to Sardinia so that he could interview them.

Sasha, of course, would not like what he was planning to do. She would no doubt much prefer to live at his expense in the kind of environment she most enjoyed: the kind of environment that went with designer shops and exclusive restaurants. No doubt she thought she had the upper hand, and that because he was allowing her to remain here in Sardinia at his expense he would continue to do so.

But there was no way he was going to underwrite her lifestyle. Even if she had easily been the best lay he had ever had. The very best. So good that no one else had ever come close to matching the intensity of the sexual chemistry they had shared. Not that he had originally planned to have sex with her the evening he had picked her up. But she had made it so obvious that she was up for it. And a quick glance at her tanned bare arms had reassured him that, unlike so many of the girls who hung out in crowded places like St Tropez in the season, her flesh showed no telltale needle marks. Nor, so far as he had been able to tell, had she been drinking.

So he had taken her back to his yacht, watching with cynical amusement as she affected round-eyed awe and excitement, squeaking breathlessly, 'You mean that it's *yours*?' For all the world as though that wasn't the main reason why she had targeted him in the first place.

Gabriel did not normally allow himself to be caught by girls like her—pretty, cheap, available, throw-away girls, used and then discarded by the men who came there. He considered himself to be above that. The women he bedded were older and more professional—more skilled, too, at concealing what their profession was. But she had jumped out of the car, and without intending to he had ended up inviting her on board the yacht. Her smile had illuminated her whole face. She had no doubt heard that men liked women who were eager or grateful, and had decided to become both.

'So what are you doing in St Tropez?' he asked her. Not that he didn't know, of course.

'I came with some friends,' she replied.

For 'friends' he mentally substituted the word 'men', but he humoured her by enquiring innocently, 'Won't they be wondering where you are?'

'Not really,' she said promptly. 'They aren't exactly friends. More just people I know.'

'Like the film director?' he suggested dulcetly.

He saw immediately that she didn't like that question. She played with the handle of her basket and refused to look at him.

'He isn't important now.'

Now *what*? Now that she thought she had found a better deal?

'But he'll be wondering where you are?' he persisted.

'I told him I wasn't interested.'

Just as the look in her eyes as she lifted her head and gazed at him told him that she was interested in him.

He stood up, about to summon one of the crew to escort her off the yacht. He was bored with St Tropez, and had already told the captain they would be leaving in the morning for Italy and the Amalfi coast. But instead, and to his own bemusement, he heard himself asking her if she wanted something to eat.

She ate quickly and hungrily, but she left the champagne he had instructed the steward to pour for her. When she had finished, he asked her if she would like to 'freshen up'. She frowned and looked confused, before bursting out breathlessly, 'Oh you mean you're going to go to bed with me?'

Had he meant that? If so, her gaucheness almost made him change his mind. He was used to women sophisticated enough to understand the rules of the game and play by them. But, on the other hand, they would not have looked at him as she was doing, with open delight and eager anticipation. No doubt because she was thinking of the money she was about to earn, he derided himself.

Down below, in the owner's suite of the yacht, he watched, leaning against the closed door to his stateroom, while she stood in the middle of the carpet and spun around, her eyes shining as she stared at the luxury surrounding her.

'It can't believe that this is really on a boat,' she exclaimed.

'It's not,' he corrected her dryly. 'This is not a boat, it's a yacht. And the bathroom is through there.'

As she started to walk towards the door he had indicated, still clutching her unwieldy straw basket, he told her impatiently, 'You can leave your bag here.'

'It's got my passport in it, and my plane ticket home.'

'Well, they'll be perfectly safe here.'

She put the basket down on one of the stateroom's silk-upholstered chairs, the basket's shabbiness incongruous against the chair's luxury.

He gave her a handful of minutes before following her into the bathroom. She was standing in the shower with her back to him. She was thin, but still shapely, with a narrow waist and softly curved hips, and long, slender legs. She had obviously washed her hair, the water making it look darker, softening the brashness of its blonde streaks. It tumbled down her back, and soap slid silkily over her naked body, caressing the smooth perfection of her skin. And then she turned around and saw him, and the slow ache that that been building from his first sight of her suddenly ignited into hard urgency.

He could barely remember removing his own clothes, or stepping into the shower with her, but he could remember the feel of her slick wet flesh beneath his hands. He could remember too what it had done to him to see her shudder with open sensual pleasure when he cupped her breasts and then played slowly with her erect tight nipples. She hadn't hidden anything from him, letting him feel and hear her immediate arousal in a way that had been uniquely sensual.

He hadn't kissed her at first. He rarely kissed his lovers on the mouth unless they demanded it; for him it was an overrated pleasure. He preferred the visual erotic stimulation of sight and touch, and watching the reactions chase one another across Sasha's face as he had stroked and caressed her naked body had been erotic. Not just her face but her whole body had registered her willingness to show him her sexual vulnerability to him. At first he had wondered if she might be faking her reaction, but he'd known that the flush of arousal staining her skin couldn't be faked.

But what had finally shattered his own control had been the way in which she had shuddered so intensely when he'd slid his hand down over her hip and stroked his fingertips from it to her pubic bone that she might almost have been on the verge of orgasm.

Then he had kissed her. Driven to do so by something deep inside himself he hadn't been able to ignore, a deep kiss, a possessing kiss, that had taken her mouth and held it whilst she'd shuddered and lain against him. He remembered how he had then lifted her hands to his own body, telling her thickly, 'My turn now.'

She had looked at him with dazed, awed eyes, before eagerly starting to massage the creamy foam against his chest with trembling hands. When the water from the shower had sluiced the suds downwards she had taken him by surprise, leaning forward and kissing his throat, and then stringing kisses along his collarbone while her hands soaped lower, causing his belly to tighten in fierce anticipation.

What he had not anticipated, though, was the soft questing touch of her lips against his nipple. Just thinking about it now was enough to make his whole body stiffen with the same confusion that he had felt then.

'I am the one who should be doing that to you.' He had stopped her, cupping her face in his hands. In response she had said nothing, merely dropping on her knees in front of him before slowly and carefully taking him into her mouth, her action piercing him with the most intense sexual pleasure he had ever known.

He hadn't understood the intensity of his response to her then, and he didn't now. Something in the soft stroke of her lips, something in the way she had touched him and looked at him, had taken him to a different level of arousal. He had picked her up and carried her to the bed, and before the water had dried from her skin he had brought her to orgasm with the touch of his hand, delaying his own completion to have the erotic pleasure of witnessing hers.

CHAPTER SIX

SHE wasn't even going to *think* about Gabriel, never mind start analyzing and brooding over that disturbing interlude on the beach path, Sasha assured herself. And then immediately destroyed her own defence system by asking herself angrily why she was so afraid to call that kiss a kiss that she had to refer to it as an 'interlude'. So Gabriel had kissed her. All that proved was exactly what she already knew—that the line she had drawn under their relationship when she had walked out on him had somehow developed a gap wide enough to allow him the power to arouse her.

She put down her hairbrush. She could see her reflection in the bedroom mirror. She was wearing the diamond earstuds that, along with the cheap plastic bangles the boys had carefully chosen and wrapped for her themselves last Christmas, were the only things that really meant something to her. Carlo had given them to her shortly after they had learned she was expecting twins. A pre-birth gift from them and their father, he had told her lovingly. She had tried to protest that at nearly two carats of flawless diamond each they were far too expensive, but Carlo had overruled her, insisting that diamond earstuds were essential for an Italian woman.

And then, when the twins had been born, both weighing in at well over eight pounds, he had told her triumphantly that to have given her anything less than two carats per earring would have been an insult to their sons.

As she shook her head at her own memories the earrings flashed white fire back at her in the mirror. She shouldn't be sitting here, wasting time. She had an important appointment in Port Cervo before lunch. As for Gabriel—once September came and the boys were back at school she wouldn't have to see him again for months.

But that was still nearly six weeks away, and after fewer than three days in his company she was already struggling to suppress her physical ache for him.

For him? How did she know that he was the cause of her sexual longing? She was twenty-eight and she had lived a celibate life since the twins' conception. A celibate life as a married woman. There had been plenty of men who had made it more than plain that they would have enjoyed helping her to break her marriage vows, but she had simply not had the need. It had been burned out of her for ever. Or so she had believed. It could simply be coincidence that Gabriel's presence was making her feel like this. Another man might have exactly the same effect on her as he did.

The trouble was, she didn't have another man to check out that theory. Of course the other way to find out was to give in to what her body was demanding and… And what? Ask Gabriel to take her to bed? Oh, yes, he would love her to do that, wouldn't he, and confirm his beliefs about her?

She picked up her hairbrush, but then put it down again.

She had known from his acid comments when she was with him that Gabriel's own childhood had been an unhappy one. He had told her that his mother had abandoned him, and how his grandfather had treated him, but aside from feeling that this gave them something in common Sasha hadn't thought to delve deeper into his past for the very simple reason that she felt so protective of her own.

She had had to work and grow through her own past before she'd had enough self-knowledge and empathy to ask Carlo more about Gabriel's.

She had been shocked by what Carlo had told her, but while it had helped her understand why Gabriel had rejected the love she had wanted to give him, she had also recognised that it needed more than another person's love to heal Gabriel's emotional wounds. It needed his own love for himself. No amount of money or success could buy him that, and no one could give it to him either.

But, even knowing what did, she still couldn't help feeling compassionate pity for the child Gabriel had been. Tears blurred her eyes now, just thinking about the neglect he had suffered—he had only been a baby, totally dependent on his mother, when she had abandoned him at her father's insistence so that she could go back to the life she missed. But he wasn't a helpless baby now. He was a very dangerous man, and she would be a fool not to remember that.

'Where are you going?'

Sasha froze in mid-step on the stairs, her colour

rising as she stared up at Gabriel, who was watching her from the landing above. She hadn't heard the door to his suite open, and now she was standing there feeling like a naughty schoolgirl caught out in some forbidden act.

'Why do you want to know?' she countered.

Gabriel's assessing gaze slid smoothly over her. She was quite obviously dressed to go out somewhere. His gaze sharpened, a feeling he didn't want to own tightening his muscles. Why the hell should he care what she did or who she did it with? It was her sons that were his concern.

'If you're planning to take the boys with you—'

'I'm not.' Sasha stopped him. She had already arranged for Maria's daughter Isabella to keep an eye on them for her. Isabella had two daughters of her own, about the same age as the twins, and Sasha knew she could trust her to keep them firmly in view and out of trouble or danger.

'No, I thought not,' Gabriel agreed. 'So much for the doting mother act.'

Sasha could feel her temper rising. 'I am going out on business—not that it is any business of yours—and that is why I am not taking the boys.'

'I wouldn't have allowed you to take them anyway,' Gabriel told her smoothly. 'I've arranged to interview a tutor for them later this afternoon, and naturally he will want to speak to them.'

Sasha opened her mouth and then closed it again as she tried to put the fiery tumult of angry objections fighting for expression inside her head into some kind of logical order.

'You don't have the right to forbid me to take my

sons anywhere,' she finally managed. 'Neither do they need a tutor. They're on holiday.'

She had seen the results of children being hot-housed by over-ambitious parents. She wanted her sons to fulfil their academic potential, of course, but she also wanted them to grow up knowing the freedoms and joys of childhood.

'They are my wards, and as such surely even you can see that in order to fulfil my responsibilities towards them I need to know more about them.'

'You could do that by being with them and talking to them, listening to them,' she said scornfully. 'They are children, Gabriel, not some new business acquisition you've bought. You can't understand how they work simply by reading a report someone else has prepared. Like…like some kind of balance sheet. What will you do if your report says that they aren't clever enough to allow you to maximise your investment? Offload them to someone else?'

'Don't be ridiculous. You always were over-emotional.'

Over-emotional! 'You are talking about my sons,' Sasha reminded him hotly. 'Not some…' She shook her head. What was the point of arguing with Gabriel like this? There weren't the words to make him understand how she felt because he himself was so incapable of feeling anything.

'You can't do this, Gabriel,' she said firmly instead. 'I won't let you. And what about the boys themselves? How do you think they are going to feel?'

'You make it sound as though they are going to be subjected to some kind of torture, when in fact you have already subjected them to pretty much the same thing yourself.'

'What?'

'They sat an entrance exam for their preparatory school, surely?'

Sasha nibbled her bottom lip. They had, of course, and with typical male confidence they had revelled in the chance to boast to her afterwards about how clever they had been.

'Professor Fennini is an extremely highly qualified educationalist, with many years' experience in his field.'

Sasha gave Gabriel a blistering look. 'You said you were interviewing a potential tutor,' she said curtly.

'If necessary he will tutor the boys, but naturally initially I want him to assess them.'

'There you go again,' Sasha exploded. 'They are children, Gabriel. *Children*. I appreciate that you never had a proper childhood—'

'Which is why I intend to make sure that my heirs are receiving everything they need to equip them.'

Sasha discovered that she needed to cling to the banister for support. Her heart was pounding nauseatingly fast, and the shock felt as if icy cold water had been poured into her veins

'Your *heirs*?' she managed to mumble. 'What…what do you mean?'

'Isn't it obvious? I mean that since Carlo's sons are my natural heirs, I would like to have some idea of how well equipped they are going to be as adults to take on that responsibility.'

The relief that surged through her was almost as physically debilitating as her fear had been.

'So I was right. This isn't just some tutor you're talking about. Well, neither you nor he are going to subject my sons to any kind of psychological tests. Has it even occurred to you that they may not *want* to be involved in your business, Gabriel? There's nothing to stop you having children of your own, you know.'

'No, there isn't, and that had been my intention. But it seems to me that since Carlo's sons are already here, and related to me by blood, it makes sense for them to be my heirs. And as for psychological tests, you are letting your imagination run away with you. The professor will simply talk with them for a little while, and then I will talk with him. And there is one thing you can be sure of: my wards will *not* be packed off to a boarding school.'

Sasha could feel the despair rising inside her. But there was no way she was going to be forced into explaining her actions to Gabriel, and no way was she going to beg for his understanding and support. Suppressing her instinct to defend herself, she said instead, 'So when is this professor supposed to be arriving?'

'After lunch. And, contrary to what you seem to think, his assessment of them is as much for their benefit as mine.'

'I'll be back by then. He is not to so much as ask them a single question unless I am there,' Sasha warned him fiercely.

She desperately needed some time to herself, to think. She still felt slightly sick and light-headed. Without another word she hurried downstairs, and then went out into the garden, where Sam and Nico were busily engaged in showing Maria's granddaughters how good they were at standing on their heads.

'*Ayeii,* boy children!' Maria's daughter laughed, but her eyes were soft with approval and affection as she watched.

Boy children, indeed, Sasha agreed, before thanking Isabella for keeping an eye on them for her and making her way around to the front of the house and the small, serviceable car Carlo had bought for her use.

It wouldn't take her long to drive into Port Cervo, the elegant resort on the Smerealda cost, with its beautiful harbour and exclusive hotels. She hoped she had dressed appropriately for the occasion. At this time of year the harbour at Port Cervo would be filled with expensive yachts, and immaculately elegant designer-clad women would be strolling its streets and shopping in its exclusive boutiques. For the purpose of her business it was important that she looked as though she was still part of that world.

Gabriel watched her leave from an upper storey window and frowned. She was wearing a taupe-coloured linen dress similar in style to the one she had been wearing the day he had arrived. A gold bracelet glinted on her wrist; large dark sunglasses with tortoiseshell frames shielded her eyes. As she slid into the driving seat of the car, he could see the natural pink gleam of her toenails in sandals that showed off the delicacy of her ankles and feet.

In the still heat of the late morning he felt as though he could almost smell the warmth of her scent. The whole house echoed subtly with it—in rooms through which she had passed and, earlier this morning, on the boys' hair, as though she had bent to kiss their heads. It was everywhere except for the rooms he had claimed for himself.

There could be only one place she was going dressed like that. And only one reason. His mouth hardened. She could give herself to as many men as she wished— once she had repaid her debt to him.

Sasha parked her car and then made her way through the elegant streets to her destination, hesitating only momentarily outside, before pressing the bell and waiting for the door to open.

The owner of the shop himself came forward to greet her, sweeping her into an elegant private office.

'Would you care for some coffee?' he asked.

Sasha shook her head and opened her handbag. When she had telephoned him earlier she had explained the purpose of her visit, to save herself any potential embarrassment. From his lack of any surprise she had guessed that he had heard about Carlo's financial problems. Placing her bag on the table in front of her, she removed the boxes she had placed so carefully inside it, opening them one by one: the necklace of diamonds and emeralds and the matching earrings Carlo had given her on their first wedding anniversary; the Cartier ring with its emerald-cut diamonds which she knew had cost over a quarter of a million euros; the huge solitaire that was her engagement ring; the yellow diamond ring surrounded by white diamonds that he had given her the Christmas before last.

Finally she reached for her diamond earstuds, and for the first time her fingers trembled.

'How much can you give me for everything?' she asked the jeweller quietly.

He picked up a magnifying glass and started to study

each item carefully. It was over half an hour before he spoke, and when he did the amount he told her he was prepared to offer her for her jewellery made her shake with relief.

It was, she suspected, nowhere near what Carlo had paid for it, but it was still enough to put a roof over their heads, and if she was careful there should be enough to pay the boys' school fees. They liked their school, and she didn't want to move them if she could avoid it.

She gave a small, terse nod of her head, her eyes widening in surprise as the jeweller pushed her solitaire earrings back across the table to her.

'I have made the calculation without including these,' he told her quietly. 'You should keep them. I am sure it is what your late husband would have wished.'

Sasha had to bite her lip to stop it from trembling. She was so overcome with emotion that it took her several seconds to put the earrings back on.

Ten minutes later she had left the jewellers and was walking purposefully into the bank, the cheque for the sale of her jewellery in her handbag.

Carlo had been kind and generous, but he had been old-fashioned as well. Sasha had never had any real money of her own. Carlo had deemed it unnecessary. She'd had an allowance and a credit card, the bills for which had been sent to him, but that was all. It felt strange to be paying such a large amount into her account. Strange, but empowering. Now she and the boys were not beholden to Gabriel. She could, if she wished, book them seats on the first flight back to London. But her sons would be disappointed to have their summer holiday cut short, she admitted, and for their sakes she would endure Gabriel's company—and his charity—for a few more weeks.

But once the boys were safely back at school...

She had it all planned out. She would rent somewhere at first, close enough to the school for her to take the boys there in the morning and collect them in the afternoon. And hopefully she would find a job quickly. Later, she would look for a small property to buy. They would not be rich, but they would manage. And her sons would be happy—she intended to make sure of that.

Now it was time for her to go back to the house—and Gabriel. Sasha closed her eyes and wished for strength. She had never imagined their paths would cross again—Gabriel and Carlo were related to one another, but they had rarely met, and she had made it plain to Carlo that she didn't want to have any contact with Gabriel. And she had certainly never suspected, not even in her darkest nightmares, that when she did see him again she would feel the way she was feeling right now.

She was almost tempted to do what he had already accused her of doing and take a lover—any lover—just to prove to herself that it was the long years without sex coupled with his presence, reactivating her memories of the sex they had had making her lie awake at night longing for him. Not Gabriel himself. Her sexual experience was limited; maybe her body had stored memories of a pleasure far in excess of that which they had actually shared. And maybe if she could show her body that it would stop tormenting her so much. Perhaps she ought to put *that* theory to the test. Sasha stopped walking and stared unseeingly before her. That was a crazy idea. Crazy and dangerous.

CHAPTER SEVEN

'YOUR sons are very fortunate in their mother,' Professor Fennini told Sasha with a warm smile. He had arrived earlier in the afternoon, shortly after the lunch which she had made following her own return from Port Cervo. And, despite her original determination to dislike him, Sasha had to admit that he had completely won her over—and not because of his flattering remarks about her parenting. The boys had taken to him immediately, and Sasha had quickly recognised how skilled he was at dealing with children and teaching them.

He had spent most of the afternoon not so much observing but joining in with the boys' activities, his questions so subtle that Sasha's maternal anxieties were quickly eased.

'I believe that school holidays should be treated as downtime for them. I don't want them hot-housed and pushed from activity to activity. I want them to learn how to learn for themselves, and how to live and enjoy life.'

'That is very obvious from the way you interact with them,' the Professor told her with another approving smile. 'I hope I have put to rest your fears regarding the term they had to board at their school,' he continued, and Sasha tensed.

She had been relieved to have the opportunity to bring this up privately with him, and she had been even more relieved when he had assured her that from his conversation with them it was quite plain to him that, if anything, the boys had rather enjoyed the novelty of being boarders and that they had certainly not suffered because of it, but she did not want her vulnerability and fear laid bare for Gabriel to see. However, there was nothing she could say now, with Gabriel standing there with her, to warn the Professor that she would prefer him to change the subject.

'Gabriel had told me of his own concerns with regard to that situation,' the Professor explained. 'It is entirely understandable that you should both have raised this issue with me, but I do assure you, Sasha, that in view of the fact that their father was dying and you were attempting to get the best medical care you could for him, you really had no other alternative. I have heard of the professor you went to see in New York. He has achieved some remarkable results with his innovative cancer care.'

'Yes. I had hoped… But, as he explained to me, Carlo's condition was too advanced for him to be able to do anything. With hindsight it would have been better if I'd stayed with Carlo.'

'You did what you believed to be in his best interests,' the Professor reassured her. 'And, as for the twins, it was far better for them to be living amongst their friends and in an emotionally familiar and secure environment than to witness the trauma of what was happening at home. I suspect there must have been many times when you wished you had them with you, for the comfort that would have given you,' he said in a kind voice.

It was hard for her to force back the tears threatening to fill her eyes. This was the first time that anyone had recognised how much she had longed for someone to lean on when Carlo had been dying.

'Yes, there were,' she admitted huskily. 'But I didn't want to turn them into an emotional support system for myself.'

'I do not see you as the kind of mother who would ever do that to her children,' the Professor said warmly. 'We can all see how well balanced and happy they are. As I was saying to Gabriel earlier,' he continued, 'since it is his wish that the boys are encouraged to take an interest in the way international politics and business interact, it would be a good idea to build on their natural interest in the environment and history, which you have already encouraged.' He was a tall man, with an earnest manner and the slightly stooped stance of an academic, and it was impossible for Sasha not to respond to his warmth and enthusiasm.

The boys were playing outside, within view of the window of the room Gabriel had turned into his office, and Sasha watched them while she waited for the Professor to finish his coffee and tell them his observations. From the noise they were making the imaginary game the boys were playing obviously involved some kind of motor racing.

She didn't see Gabriel move to stand at her side and look down at the boys with her, but she immediately sensed that he was there. She desperately wanted to move and put more distance between them, but she was too close to the window. And he was too close to her.

'I believe they are practising for Formula One.' The Professor sounded grave, but when Sasha looked at him she could see that his eyes were twinkling. 'They told me that Nico is to design the car and Sam will drive it.'

'Ferrari had better look to its laurels, then,' Gabriel said dryly.

'It is good that you have allowed them to retain the closeness of their twinship and yet at the same time encouraged them to develop their individual and different skills,' the Professor told Sasha.

'Nico is the thinker and Sam the doer,' Gabriel said abruptly.

Sasha stared at him, unable to conceal the shock it had given her to hear him describe the twins' personalities so accurately after having virtually only just met them. It made her more uneasy than she wanted to admit that he could distinguish the physical differences between them so easily, but *this*. He had always been an insightful person, of course, just so long as it wasn't *her* behaviour he was analysing. Right now, though, she was far more concerned about her sons than she was about herself.

Gabriel saw the swift, shocked look Sasha was giving him.

'What's wrong?' he demanded tersely.

'You've picked up on the differences between Sam and Nico very quickly,' she admitted reluctantly.

Gabriel gave a dismissive shrug. He didn't totally understand himself why he found it so easy to differentiate between the two boys, nor why he knew it was necessary to communicate with them in slightly different ways. He did know, though, that at some deep level they touched a part of him that he hadn't even realised he possessed. He had always had good instincts where people were concerned, he acknowledged, and he had always been able to stand back and judge their behaviour analytically. Like he had Sasha's? The Professor's revelations about her reason for boarding the twins at school had been too reasonable for him to dismiss. And no one could have faked the emotion he had just seen her trying to suppress.

He could almost feel the shift in mental focus within himself, forcing him to admit the possibility that he had deliberately chosen to view the facts from a warped angle to suit his own needs. Right now his conscience was making its feelings plain, and demanding some honest answers to some harsh questions. He *did* have to acknowledge that Sasha was a good mother, didn't he?

He would acknowledge nothing, he told himself savagely. The fierce surge of pain that came with thinking about Sasha gripped him. Out of the corner of his eye he could see the Professor moving closer to Sasha as he talked to her. Immediately Gabriel moved too, stepping close beside her.

Sasha tensed. What did he think she was going to do? Tell Professor Fennini that she wouldn't give permission for her sons to be tutored? Unlike Gabriel, she was flexible enough to change her mind. As the Professor had already said, the boys were at the stage where they were like greedy sponges, eager to soak up ideas and information and to learn new skills, provided they were delivered in the right way. She could see that with the Professor they would be. And she would be there to monitor what was going on so that she could step in if she felt it necessary.

Gabriel was obscuring her view of the boys so she stepped away, her jaw tensing slightly when she saw his mouth harden.

'I was particularly intrigued by the boys' life books,' the Professor was saying. 'It is a concept I have seen used very effectively to help troubled children, but I must admit I had not thought to use it to provide a record of a happy childhood.'

Sasha gave a small shrug. She wasn't going to tell the Professor about her own childhood, or explain that it was through her therapy that she had learned about creating life books.

'Originally I wanted to encourage the boys to keep diaries,' she explained. 'And the life books seemed a natural step. They are more interactive and fun for them. We agreed they could have private sections for their private thoughts, and open sections for what we do together.'

Gabriel listened in silence. Professor Fennini's praise for Sasha's parenting underlined everything he had already seen for himself. So why was he finding it so hard to let go of his preconceived and now unsustainable belief that she was not a good mother? Was it perhaps because *he* wanted to be part of the twins' lives? And part of Sasha's—a woman who had walked out on him? Somewhere deep inside the most private and vulnerable part of him a long-buried fear was pushing painfully through the protective layers of denial. What if the blame for Sasha leaving him lay not with her, but with him?

That deeply buried doubt, once exposed, was something Gabriel couldn't ignore. Long after the Professor had shaken hands with him and told him enthusiastically that he was looking forward to starting work with the twins the following week, and Sasha had made it clear that she intended to spend what was left of the day with her sons, Gabriel discovered that he kept returning to the question, like a man with an aching tooth, probing the sore place even though it increased his pain.

Inside his head he kept comparing the twins' childhood with his own; not, he recognised with a stab of shocked bewilderment, a material comparison, but a comparison of the love they received which he had not. Memories he had never allowed himself to acknowledge surfaced: images of himself as a child, holding out his arms to his foster mother only to retreat in bewilderment and misery when she responded with harsh words and stinging blows. He could hear his grandfather telling him how bitterly he resented him for being his only heir, that corrosive pride rasping in his voice. His grandfather had made no secret of the bitterness he felt towards him, Gabriel remembered.

'Cousin Gabriel…' There was a distinctly wheedling note in Sam's voice that caused Gabriel to give him a rueful look. 'Me and Nico were just thinking that if Mum were to ask you what we wanted for our birthday next week, you could tell her that we need proper grown-up bikes.'

It took Gabriel several seconds to properly take in what Sam was saying. 'Your birthday is next week?' he demanded. He made a swift mental calculation. Next week... That meant Sasha had conceived the twins while she had still been living with him. And that meant that she had betrayed him with Carlo when they had still been lovers. He could feel the savagery of his anger boiling up inside him, and threatening to overwhelm him.

Sam nodded his head enthusiastically, oblivious to the effect of his words. 'We'll be ten,' he told Gabriel proudly.

'Mum says that we can't have proper bikes until we're eleven,' Nico reminded his twin, but Gabriel was oblivious to the warning looks Sam was giving Nico. He needed to see Sasha and he needed to see her *now*. Leaving the two boys, he strode downstairs and found her in the living room, looking over some of the materials left by Professor Fennini.

'I want a word with you,' he told her grimly.

Sasha was tempted to tell him that she certainly did not want any words with him, but he had already manacled her arm in an almost painful grip and was forcing her upstairs to his suite.

'What are you doing, Gabriel?' she protested. 'You can't just manhandle me as though you own me. I won't have it. And where are the boys—'

'The boys are fine.' He paused and found he needed to take a deep breath before he could say, 'Sam has just told me that it's their birthday next week.'

Sasha could feel the trickle of now familiar icy-cold fear seeping into her bloodstream. She would have given anything to shake her head and say no but of course she couldn't.

'Yes, that's right,' she said instead.

'So they were conceived in December?'

Her heart jumped into her throat, her panic threatening to choke her. 'I…they…there were complications, and in the end they were delivered early.' She side-stepped his question.

'How early? Not, I take it, three months early?' he suggested sarcastically.

Sash could feel her face starting to burn.

'They were conceived while you were still with me, weren't they?' Gabriel demanded flatly.

There was no escape. She had been dreading this for so long that in some ways she was relived that it could no longer be avoided.

'Answer me, damn you, Sasha. They were conceived while you were with me, *weren't they*?' Gabriel repeated harshly. His fingers were still clamped round her arm, and as he spoke he gave her a small, almost rough shake.

Sasha was familiar with the icy coldness of his angry contempt, but she had never seen him gripped by this kind of fury before. She felt helpless against it, and very vulnerable, but she knew she couldn't conceal the truth from him any longer.

'Yes,' she admitted, bowing her head and waiting for the inevitable accusation she knew must come. Carlo had warned her this might happen, but she had told him she wouldn't let it, that she would make sure she kept the greatest distance possible between Gabriel and herself to ensure it didn't. And, foolishly, she had even begun to feel that she was safe, and that Gabriel would never challenge her deception.

'You were seeing Carlo behind my back—sleeping with him while you were sharing my bed, giving yourself to him when I thought you were only giving yourself to me. You were pregnant by him, but still claiming to love me!' Gabriel couldn't contain the savagery of what he was feeling. It had been bad enough that she had actually walked out on him without a word, but this newly discovered betrayal was more than he could endure.

Sasha looked at him uncomprehendingly.

'Don't look at me like that—as though you don't understand what I'm saying,' Gabriel raged. 'You know perfectly well! You were sharing Carlo's bed at the same time as you were sharing mine. You let him get you pregnant while you were sleeping with me. How long had it been going on? How long were you letting him sleep with you while I believed—'

'It wasn't like that!' Sasha protested sickly.

'You're lying. Of course it was like that.' Gabriel rubbed his hand over his eyes, as though it physically sickened him to look at her. 'Didn't you care about the risk you were taking, having unprotected sex with him?'

'It wasn't planned. It was an accident…a mistake!'

'You can say that again. Did Carlo know that you were telling me that you loved me when you must have known you were carrying his bastards?'

Sasha raised her hand, but Gabriel caught hold of it, forcing it back down to her side. 'Why tell me you loved me? Or can I guess…?'

'Why not? You seem to be determined to guess at everything else,' Sasha said fiercely.

'There's no guesswork involved in subtracting nine months from a year,' he told her bluntly. 'I suppose you didn't want to leave me until you were sure of Carlo. And of course knowing you were carrying his child was bound to clinch the deal for him. An old man with no children, no heir, and there you were, offering him not one but two.'

'I didn't know it was twins then—'

'Mum, Maria's here…'

Quickly Sasha pulled herself free of Gabriel's grip as she heard Sam's voice from outside the room.

Sasha looked towards the window, where the moonlight was spilling into the darkness of her bedroom. Her heart was thudding heavily and she could feel the dampness of tears on her eyelashes and face. She had been dreaming about Gabriel with such intensity that even now she was awake it was still with her.

Her nervous system could only withstand so many attacks. When Gabriel had confronted her about the boys' birthdays, she had thought…

She and Carlo had lived very quietly for the first two years of their marriage, in Carlo's apartment in New York. They hadn't made any public announcement about the birth of the twins; the Calbrini family, while extensive, wasn't close knit, and no one had ever queried the exact date of the boys' birth.

Until now.

She was wide awake now, her thoughts haunted not just by the present but also by the past.

She and Gabriel had already been enjoying the sunshine of the Caribbean island of St Lucia for several weeks on board Gabriel's yacht when Carlo had arrived, to check out a hotel he was thinking of buying. A chance meeting at a harbourside restaurant had led to Gabriel introducing her to his second cousin, and Sasha had immediately sensed the genuine kindness in the older man.

She and Gabriel had been together for over a year, and it had both frustrated and upset her that while sexually Gabriel was the most perfect lover she could ever imagine, emotionally he still held her at a distance.

'Why do you never say that you love me?' she could remember blurting out during their first Christmas together. They had been in Paris at the time, and he had taken her out and bought her the most ridiculously expensive designer clothes, plus some equally expensive and very erotic underwear.

'Because I don't,' he had replied calmly.

They had been in bed in their suite at the Georges V, and Sasha could still remember the huge cold lump that had formed inside her body and the pain that had accompanied it.

'But you must,' she had protested desperately. 'You *must,* Gabriel. You *have* to love me.' She had burst into tears, but, far from comforting her, Gabriel had simply pushed back the bedclothes and got out of bed.

'I don't do emotional scenes, Sasha,' he had told her coolly. 'I don't love you because I don't consider that love exists. Be grateful for what we have, because believe me, there are any number of women who would gladly change places with you.' He had pulled on his clothes, and then added callously, 'I'm going out now.

When I come back, I don't want to be greeted by any more of this stupidity.'

She hadn't been able to believe he could be so brutal. They had been together for months, and naïvely she had convinced herself that it was just a matter of time before he told her that he loved her. After all, he had known she loved him. She had always been telling him so, and he had never tired of having sex with her. He had spent money on her, and time with her, and in her mind she had transmuted these into the emotional bond her own neediness craved. Within half an hour she had stopped crying and convinced herself that he hadn't meant what he'd said, that as a man he was simply reluctant to admit his feelings for her.

That had been what she had told herself in Paris, and that had been what she was still telling herself months later in the Caribbean. He did love her; she was sure of it. Otherwise why would he still want to make love to her? And he *had* wanted to make love to her; there had been no doubt about that. Sexually Gabriel had not only never tired of her, he never seemed to feel he had had enough of her. She had woken in the mornings to the feel of his hands on her body, sleepily squirming in delicious pleasure beneath their roving touch, and she had fallen asleep late at night with her body soft and boneless with sexual satisfaction.

They had had a simple routine on board the yacht. More often than not Gabriel would work in the morning, and then spend the lazy heat of the Caribbean afternoons making love to her—and not always in bed. Gabriel had been an imaginative and adventurous lover, who enjoyed drawn-out, sensually erotic love-play.

She couldn't remember now when she had first been on her own with Carlo. It might have been during one of those solitary mornings when she had left the yacht to wander round the Caribbean port's expensive shops. She could remember, though, that she had quickly fallen into the habit of meeting Carlo for morning coffee, and how flattered she had been when he had suggested that she might like to see the hotel he was planning to buy.

Soon she had started confiding in him about her feelings for Gabriel, and he had told her the dreadful story of Gabriel's childhood.

'Oh, but that will bring us even closer together,' Sasha had breathed, pink-cheeked with sympathy and fellow feeling. 'I was dreadfully unhappy when I was growing up too. Poor Gabriel.'

Carlo, she remembered, had done his best to explain to her that the trauma of Gabriel's childhood had not affected him in the same way as hers had her, but she hadn't taken in what he was saying, because it wasn't what she wanted to hear.

Instead she had clung to her belief that Gabriel loved her.

She had even relayed that belief to Gabriel himself, the day before her eighteenth birthday. She had been dropping hints about her birthday to him for weeks, and finally, when they'd been in bed together that afternoon, her body still quivering in the aftermath of her pleasure, Gabriel had smoothed his hand over her stomach, causing her to tense with almost unbearable anticipation.

'So come on, then. You've dropped enough hints about this birthday of yours—what exactly is it you want?' he had demanded lazily.

She could still picture the scene all these years later: the sunlight-dappled shadows of the main cabin with its luxurious furnishings, the huge bed, its sheets tangled and pushed out of the way, Gabriel's naked body, muscled and firm-fleshed, tanned from the Caribbean sun, the familiar look of male arousal darkening his eyes. He had leaned towards her, capturing her nipple between his thumb and forefinger and teasing it so expertly that she'd writhed with renewed longing.

'I want you,' she had told him emotionally. 'I want you and your love, Gabriel, and I want us to be together for always. And—'

But before she could say any more he had released her and pushed himself away from her, getting up off the bed, his face tightening with open anger.

'What kind of game is this, Sasha?' he had demanded.

'I don't know what you mean,' she had answered him, truthfully. 'It isn't a game. I love you, Gabriel. And now that Carlo has told me about what happened when you were a child, that brings us even closer—'

She hadn't been allowed to go any further. He had leaned across the bed and roughly dragged her to her feet.

'Closer? What is all this, Sasha? The only way I want to be *close to you*, as you call it, is when I'm having sex with you. All this rubbish about love doesn't cut it with me. You know that—or you should do by now.'

She had never seen him so angry, and she had started to tremble, suddenly shocked out of her rosy fantasy into the cold sharpness of reality. But somehow she hadn't been able to stop herself from begging.

'You don't mean that. You've got to love me, Gabriel,

you've *got* to.' She had been filled with panic and fear, clinging to him and sobbing, when he forcibly removed her hands from his body. 'Tell me you love me, Gabriel…'

'*I* haven't *got* to do anything, Sasha. The onus in this relationship is on you to please me. That's the way it is—you play and I pay. Look, you're a fantastic lay,' he had continued, 'and I know I'm not the first man to have told you that. We're having a good time together, and we can continue to have a good time together, but I don't want to hear another word about love.'

Something inside her had sickened and withered when she had heard those words, but stubbornly she had ignored her own pain to protest unsteadily, 'But you must want to get married and…and have children. We would have such beautiful children, Gabriel.'

She could still see the look in his eyes as he had stared at her and said, flatly and emotionlessly, 'Children are the last thing I want, and I certainly don't want them with a woman like you.' He had left her then, and she had lain in bed, too numb to move and too afraid to let herself think.

They had gone out for dinner that evening, and she had still been in shock. She had hardly eaten anything, but she had opened her gift and dutifully admired the Cartier watch Gabriel had given her. When they had left the restaurant, he had taken hold of her in the darkness of the street, pushing aside the thin straps of her dress so that he could mould his hand around the naked warmth of her breast, caressing it with aroused urgency and kissing her so fiercely that her lips had felt slightly bruised. But she hadn't been able to feel anything. She had still been too numb, almost distanced, from what was happening.

They had gone back to the yacht and he had almost torn the clothes off her body in his need to possess her, pushing her against the door of his cabin the moment they were inside and pulling down the top of her dress, holding her hands captive behind her back, his mouth hot against her naked flesh.

He had taken her quickly, but, typically, not before speedily stretching a condom over his erection, then almost viscerally thrusting deeply into her, and coming almost immediately.

'Enjoy what we have Sasha,' he had said, still breathing heavily. 'Because I certainly intend to. This is all there is for us, and it's all there ever will be. It's called sex. Not love, sex. But you know as well as I do that you can't live without it, and you can't live without me.' His voice had held a note of undisguised triumph.

Standing silently within the circle of his arms, Sasha had known what she had to do.

It had been three o'clock in the morning when she had walked into the foyer of the hotel where Carlo was staying. At first the receptionist had refused to telephone him, but in the end she had given in.

'He says you're to go up,' she had told Sasha grudgingly.

Carlo had obviously been in bed. He'd opened the door to her wearing a monogrammed silk dressing gown, looking every inch the elderly man that he was. The contrast between him and Gabriel could not have been more cruelly underlined. Gabriel slept nude; he was a man at the height of his sexual power. There, in the harsh overhead light, Sasha saw how old Carlo was—even older than she had thought.

'I've left Gabriel,' she had said, and burst into tears.

Carlo had led her over to a chair and persuaded her to sit down. Then, quietly and compassionately, he had asked her gently, 'You're pregnant, aren't you?'

CHAPTER EIGHT

SASHA threw back the bedcovers and got out of bed. She knew she wouldn't be able to get back to sleep now, and even with the curtains closed she could see the first pale glimmer of the coming day.

It was five o'clock in the morning, and by rights she ought to be asleep, not standing here in one of the respectable nightshirts motherhood had taught her to wear, letting her emotions be ripped to pieces on the sharks' teeth of a decade-old pain.

She had broken down completely when Carlo had guessed her secret, as much because he had seen so easily what Gabriel had not as at his genuine compassion.

'I wanted him to say he loved me but he wouldn't,' she had sobbed. 'All he wants from me is sex. He doesn't care about me at all.'

The romantic happy-ever-after fantasy she had created so lovingly had not so much crashed down around her as simply evaporated in the blast of Gabriel's reaction to her pleading.

And, although she hadn't been able to say so to Carlo, a man almost old enough to be her grandfather, tonight, for the first time when Gabriel had touched her, instead of feeling desire she had felt numb despair. He didn't love her and he never would. But she had still clung tenaciously to her own need.

'Do you think he will change his mind?' she had hiccupped tearfully. 'Maybe you could speak to him for me, Carlo?'

'You want me to tell him about the baby?' he had asked, adding meaningfully, 'You must remember, Sasha, that he may not react as you would wish. He may even insist that he does not want this child and that you should…'

That was the moment when she had taken her first faltering step towards maturity, Sasha reflected. That heartbeat of time when she had placed her hand protectively on her still-flat belly and put aside her own need, recognising instead the harsh truth Carlo had just shown her and reacting to it.

'No.' She had shaken her head. 'Gabriel must never know.'

Carlo had been wonderful then, taking care of everything, chartering a private plane, marrying her before she could refuse, and insisting that it was best for everyone if he did. He was, after all, related to her child by blood. He had no children of his own, he was a rich man who would have loved to be a father, and her marriage to him would be in name only.

She could not be Gabriel's lover and the mother of his child, she had warned herself when she had felt her courage faltering. And she would never inflict the misery of her own childhood on her child. This baby was going to have all the love she could give it—all the love its father had rejected.

Fortunately, for the twins' sake, the expensive and highly qualified New York doctor whose professional services Carlo had insisted she should have had been wise enough to recognise that she had a problem. The counselling she had received both prior to and after the twins' birth had helped her to understand that the wrong kind of love could be as damaging to a child as none at all. And that, in her opinion, had been Carlo's greatest gift to them all.

By the time the twins were taking their first unsteady steps and walking unaided she too had been taking her own first emotional steps forward unaided. They had learned and grown together, she and the twins. Her love for them had healed her.

Carlo had always treated the boys as his. Everyone had. No one had ever remotely suggested that Carlo might not have fathered them. Especially not Gabriel. Carlo had told her how Gabriel had said that he was a fool to have married her. This had led to a gulf between the two men, much to Sasha's private relief. She hadn't wanted Gabriel in their lives because she hadn't felt she could trust herself around him.

The last thing she had expected to happen when Carlo was dying was that he would send for Gabriel and entrust the twins' future to him. It filled her with a mixture of anxiety and acceptance to see how easily and naturally Gabriel related to the twins, and she had thought when he'd challenged her about their birthday that he had finally guessed the truth. She had been holding her breath ever since he had arrived in Sardinia, waiting for him to look at the boys and see his own features in theirs. Her heart turned over in slow torture every time she saw him talking to them, and then again when she saw the way they looked back at him, so innocently, ready to love him even without knowing who he was.

But the fact that he was their father had obviously never even crossed his mind. The deception he believed he had uncovered was so implausible compared with the simplicity of the truth that if it had been another couple she suspected it would have made her laugh in disbelief. How could he not see that the twins were his? How could he possibly think she, or indeed any woman, could want to go from his bed, the bed of a man at his sexual height, to the bed of a man like Carlo, elderly and sexually withered? For an intelligent man Gabriel was being remarkably blind to the truth. Yes, she knew that Gabriel had always worn protection, and he would not have expected her to get pregnant, but since when had it been a fail-safe barrier to conception? Especially with a man as sexually active as Gabriel had been with her. Didn't he even question that it might be possible, knowing how much she had loved him, that the twins were his? That she had gone to Carlo in order to protect them and herself, not to exchange his body for Carlo's? Obviously not. And of course she knew why. It was because of his childhood. Because it hadn't occurred to him that he might *want* to be the twins' father.

Sasha didn't even realise she was crying until she felt the damp splash of her tears falling onto the back of her hands as she gripped the polished wood of the window.

They were his heirs, and that was enough for Gabriel. In fact that was all he wanted them to be. He felt no emotion for them, just as he didn't for her. Although that wasn't quite true, she acknowledged. He *did* feel some emotion for her: anger, contempt, bitterness, and most of all a driving need to punish her for leaving him.

So what did she feel for him? She didn't think she had the strength to let herself answer that question. Her head had begun to ache.

The sky was lightening by the minute. Sasha opened the shutters and looked out. The air smelled clean and fresh. A walk along the beach might help to clear her head. It was too early for anyone else to be up, and the beach was private enough for her to walk there safely in her nightshirt, which after all covered her to mid-thigh.

Ten minutes later she was on the shore. There was something deliciously pagan and yet somehow childlike about walking barefoot along a sandy beach, Sasha thought. She paused to watch the waves curl and fret along the shore as they welcomed the first rays of the sun.

What the hell was happening to him? There was no point trying to sleep now, Gabriel admitted grimly. And there was no point lying here tormenting himself with images of Sasha and Carlo. How could he not have known what she was doing? How could he not have sensed it, felt it every time he had touched her? He had thought she owed him a debt for walking out on him, but he had had no idea of just how great her betrayal had been. She had been pregnant with another's man's child and he hadn't even known. She had been having sex with Carlo at the same time as she was sleeping with him, and such was her skill at deceit that he had never once suspected. She had taken him for a complete fool, using him while she waited for Carlo to offer her what she really wanted.

There was an explosion of sensation in the centre of his body, a physical pain that roiled like tongues of fire, and stabbed him with deadly sharp knives.

Somewhere in the savage turmoil of his thoughts a small voice questioned how he could recognise that it was his emotions that were causing him so much pain. He didn't do emotions. Especially not where a woman like Sasha was concerned. His relationship with Sasha had merely been sexual. He felt the way he did because she had shared with someone else the sexual favours that should have been exclusively his, he told himself; that was all. He had been keeping her, and because of that surely he had had every right to expect the exclusive use of her body.

He realised suddenly that the strange noise he could hear inside his head was the sound of him grinding his own teeth. Had she enjoyed deceiving him? Had she held that pleasure to her when he was holding her? Had she lain in his arms, planning her future with Carlo? His head felt as though it was about to burst, and there was a tight feeling inside his chest; his eyes felt raw and gritty and his throat ached. He couldn't understand what was happening to him, or why, but he knew he couldn't lie here and be tormented by it any longer. He threw back the bedclothes and pulled on a pair of cut-offs.

A walk along the beach might help him calm down.

Gabriel saw Sasha before she saw him. She was standing staring out to sea, the early-morning breeze flattening the thin fabric of her nightshirt against her body. He could see her outline as clearly as though she was naked: the soft swell of her breasts contrasting with the stiff hardness of her nipples; the narrowness of her waist and the curve of her hips; the hollow indentation of her spine followed by the rounded shape of her buttocks, the thin cotton pressed against the cleft between them just as it was drawn tautly over the mound of her pubic bone.

Inside his head old images were forming, battering down his defences. Another time and another beach, as deserted as this one. Sasha standing there, naked apart from a sunhat, dipping a small fishing net into one of the rock pools, so engrossed in what she was doing that she hadn't heard him approaching her from behind until he had pulled her back into his body and then stroked his hands over her, her breasts, her belly, the inside of her thighs, over and over again until she was moaning with longing. He could still remember the slick warmth of her wetness between the silky-smooth flesh of the pouting lips no longer concealing her sex but eagerly opening to his touch. She had moved against him, as urgently eager for him as he was for her, leaning forward over the rock in front of her. He had taken her there and then, holding her hips as he thrust deep into the hot satin heat of her welcoming flesh and felt her muscles tighten greedily around him.

The erection pressed against the fabric of his cut-offs was caused by the past, not the present, Gabriel reasoned. Sasha had no power to arouse him now unless he chose to allow her to.

Suddenly Sasha turned her head and saw him. For a second she simply stared at him, and then abruptly she turned on her heel and started to run.

Gabriel's reaction was instinctive and immediate.

Sasha could hear the fierce pounding of his feet on the sand above the shocked thud of her own heartbeat. He was closing the distance between them but she still ran on, driven by the instinct of the prey to escape from the hunter.

He caught her just when the breath had started to rasp in her throat, grabbing hold of her arm and swinging her round to face him so hard that she almost lost her footing.

She could hardly breathe, and her heart was thumping erratically. She was still in shock, Sasha recognised. Her chest hurt too much for her to be able to speak. She tried to pull her arm out of Gabriel's grip, and when he refused to let her go and pulled her closer to him she lifted her free hand, intending to push him away. But the minute it came in contact with the bare warmth of his flesh her whole body was seized with a tremor she couldn't control. She gave an involuntary gasp of despair, her eyes widening. And then Gabriel's head was blotting out the light and he was kissing her with a savage passion that swept her back in time. Helplessly she closed her eyes and gave herself up to it, returning the angry fury of his kiss with her own pain, letting him take and punish her mouth while she dug her nails into the smooth flesh of his back in mute response to their mutual hostility and helpless need.

The part of her that was still capable of thought knew that he resented his desire for her as much as she did hers for him. But it wasn't enough to stop him from shaping her body with his hands as though he was repossessing it, and it wasn't enough to stop her from responding to him.

From out of nowhere, between them they had unleashed something they were both powerless to control, Sasha recognised dizzily. It was rushing through her veins, surging past her defences in a tumult of hot, urgent desire that pounded through her body.

It had been so long since she had felt like this. Too long. Sensations formed semi-conscious thoughts inside her head, instructing her body. She shuddered and moaned, arching her throat for the hot, familiar slide of Gabriel's mouth against her sensitive flesh. Each second was filled with a building intensity of aching torment. She could feel the familiar heaviness in her lower body, the slow, certain softening and opening of the thick-fleshed lips of her sex, and the urge to part her legs and lean into Gabriel so that he could feel for himself how ready she was for him. She moaned deep in her throat, a sound between a purr and a growl of female pleasure, when she felt the hard jut of his erection pressing into her. Automatically her hand dropped towards his groin, her fingertips pressing eagerly against the bulge straining against the fabric of his cut-offs. She had just enough sanity to be aware that they were out of sight of the house, protected from view by the rocks enclosing them, but she wasn't sure she would have cared if they hadn't been, Sasha realised, as Gabriel caressed her nipple through the fabric of her nightshirt.

'Gabriel…' Her need whimpered through her frantic gasp of his name and her body arched into his. She tugged impatiently at the waist of his cut-offs, sliding down the zip and closing her eyes in aching pleasure as she slipped her hand inside and discovered that he was naked beneath them. She stroked the tips of her fingers along his rigid length in breathless pleasure.

'Wait.'

The harsh command jolted her into an anguished silent protest.

Watching her, Gabriel shook his head and reached for the hem of her nightshirt. Sasha's eyes widened, the breath locking in her throat. And then she nodded and lifted her arms, so that he could pull the nightshirt free of her body.

Before she could drop her arms his mouth was on her naked breasts, tasting their familiar scented warmth, his teeth tugging erotically at the dark thrust of one nipple in the way she remembered whilst his hand cupped and caressed her other breast.

It was more pleasure than she could bear. It made her cry out aloud and rake her nails down his back as she moaned his name. Already she could feel the once familiar rhythmic force building up inside her body.

There was no need for her to say anything, or for Gabriel to ask. They seemed to move together as though their movements were pre-orchestrated.

Gabriel leaned down and lifted her bodily against himself. As she wrapped her legs around him he could feel the sharp grittiness of the sand from her feet rubbing abrasively against his skin, a reminder that intense pleasure needed to be edged with the sting of pain.

Maybe that was why he felt this overpowering need for her now. Because without her his life had been bland and dull. Maybe he needed the pain to really feel. Unconnected thoughts flashed through his head and were dismissed as Sasha wrapped her arms tightly around his neck. Bracing himself against the smooth wall of rock behind him, Gabriel thrust hotly into her.

Immediately her head dropped back, a low moan of pleasure dragging from her throat as he thrust deeper into the tight heat of the muscles holding him skin to skin so perfectly that they might have been his own.

It had always been like this with her, always, and that knowledge had haunted his dreams and savaged his pride. No other woman had ever made him feel like this. No other woman had made him want like this, driving him to break through the barrier that separated them into two different human beings. But it was only now, in the sexual extremis of his desire, that he was allowing himself to admit that to himself.

He had forgotten just how intense the pleasure of being with Sasha like this was. How could he have lived so long without it, without her?

Sasha wrapped herself as tightly around Gabriel as she could, savouring each wonderfully familiar thrust of his body. Her muscles clung to him, drawing him deeper, and she strained against him, wanting to possess all of him and be possessed by all of him. Her senses were flooded with an erotic stimulation and need that brought emotional tears to her eyes. She matched the movements of his body, taking and returning every rhythmic pulse. She pressed her lips to the base of his throat, caressing his sweat-slick skin, its taste sharp, salty and familiar.

She heard him cry out her name, and then she was gasping and shuddering wildly as she felt the first fierce spasm of her own orgasm.

Wordlessly Gabriel released Sasha, drawing great gulps of air into his straining chest. It must be lack of oxygen that was causing him to tremble from head to foot like a boy who had just had his first woman, he told himself dizzily.

Sasha couldn't believe what she had done. Her whole body was trembling so much she could hardly stand. She felt oddly weak, and yet at the same time filled with a heady sense of triumph and satisfaction.

She looked up at Gabriel.

'You owed me that,' he told her grimly, breathing hard. 'That and more.'

The rising sun dazzled her, making her turn away from its glittering light. She could see her nightshirt lying on the sand. She picked it up and pulled it on. She felt as though she was existing in some kind of void—something akin to the emotional equivalent of the golden hour after a major accident, when the victim was so traumatised that the body failed to recognise the severity of its injuries.

Without saying a word to Gabriel she started to walk back to the house.

CHAPTER NINE

FORTUNATELY it was still too early for anyone else to be up, because by the time Sasha had finally reached the sanctuary of her bedroom she was trembling with shock.

She sank down onto her bed, tears pricking her eyes. What on earth had come over her? She had behaved like…like a woman who hadn't had sex for ten years. Or like a woman who had yearned for ten years to be with the only man she could ever love.

Gabriel stood beneath the hot spray of the shower, washing Sasha's scent from his skin. Something had happened to him out there on the beach, something so precious and so illuminating that deep inside himself he wanted to reach out and hold the memory of it safe for ever. It made him want to reach out to Sasha with tenderness; it made him want to hold her for ever. But it also made him afraid. It had the potential to threaten everything he believed, everything he had built his life on.

He made himself focus on the reality of the situation: while he might not have planned what had happened on the beach, it proved that he was right about Sasha. It proved that she was no more loyal to Carlo than she had been to him. So where was the moral euphoria he should be feeling? The sense of righteousness and triumph? Why was he feeling more like an ex-addict who had suddenly and fatally been exposed to his favourite drug of choice and discovered that its pleasure was even more potent than he had remembered?

Just once, just one more time, so that this time he would be the one to walk away from her and leave her aching. That was what he had told himself, but already he knew it wasn't going to be like that. Already he was thinking about the next time…and the next. Already he was thinking about waking up in the night and reaching out to find her there next to him. Already he was filled with emotions that—

Emotions? But he didn't have emotions—especially not for Sasha. The huge discrepancy between what he had told himself to think and what was actually happening to him held him still as unwanted self-knowledge trickled through the gaps in the barriers he had thrown up, slowly but inexorably gathering force. The pain he had always denied he could feel was already squeezing his heart. On the beach, holding Sasha, completing the circle of human intimacy with her in that small, quiet moment of supreme peace after the intensity of his climax, a thought as soft as a drifting feather had brushed against his heart, telling him that here, in this private moment of time with Sasha, lay the greatest happiness he could ever know.

There were unfamiliar aches in her body that weren't caused by having spent the last three hours keeping her muscles under rigid control while she walked round the house with Gabriel and his architect as he inspected it with a view to returning it to a private home.

Now the three of them were standing outside, and the architect was delivering his opinion.

'I don't see any major problems,' he was telling Gabriel enthusiastically. 'I must say,' he added approvingly to Sasha, 'that when you originally converted the house into a hotel your architect did an excellent job of retaining its original features.'

Sasha had to force herself to at least appear to be giving her attention to what he was saying. Not because she wasn't interested. Architecture and interior décor and design were her passions, but right now she was still feeling the fall-out from this morning's very different passion. While her body might be aching with sensual lassitude, her head could hardly contain the thumping force of her mental self-flagellation. It was no use to keep on saying to herself, How could you? She had, and now she had to live with the consequences of what she had done. And right now, she acknowledged, the most unbearable of all those consequences was the way that standing anywhere within a five-yard radius of Gabriel was causing her body to go into a frenzy of sexual lust.

She would have given anything to refuse his suggestion that she join him and the architect on their inspection of the house, but her pride wouldn't let her. So now she was suffering the outcome of that pride as every nerve-ending bombarded her body with messages that were dangerously and explicitly erotic. Gabriel might be dressed now, in buff-coloured chinos and a soft white linen shirt, but all she could see in her mind's eye was his naked body, and it produced a sheeny dew of perspiration on her she was mortally afraid must carry the female scent of her desire for him.

She had kept as much distance between them as she could, standing to one side of him to keep him out of her line of vision, making sure she walked next to the architect and not Gabriel, but she was still acutely aware of him.

'One thing I would like incorporated into the grounds is a hard surface circuit for the boys.'

'For your sons' bikes and skateboards, you mean?' the architect asked. 'A good idea.'

Sasha sucked in her breath, waiting for Gabriel to correct him and tell him that Sam and Nico were not his sons but his wards, but the architect was already speaking again, telling them ruefully, 'My own sons complain that there is nowhere for them to enjoy those things since my wife says that the city traffic makes it too dangerous for them to use the roads. I must say I envy you this wonderful location you have here. You are close enough to Port Cervo to be able to enjoy its facilities without being too close, plus you have this magnificent stretch of private beach.'

'The land has been in the Calbrini family for many generations,' Gabriel told him, while Sasha writhed in inner torment as she remembered what use they had put the privacy of that beach to only this morning.

The architect was looking towards his hire car, obviously ready to leave. Sasha exhaled in relief and said a quick goodbye to him before making her escape, unaware of the way Gabriel turned to watch her walk away from them.

She found the boys on the terrace, talking excitedly

to Professor Fennini about the afternoon trip they were going to make exploring some of the island's historical sites. Even without turning around she knew that Gabriel had followed her onto the terrace.

Her hands were shaking so hard as she poured herself a glass of water from the jug that some of it spilled onto the table. In her desperation to put as much distance between Gabriel and herself she tried to step past him too quickly and missed her step. She would have collided with one of the wrought-iron chairs if Gabriel hadn't reached out and covered the metal with his hand, so that she bumped into his fingers instead.

She couldn't move. She couldn't do anything. Her body greedily soaked up the forbidden pleasure of physical contact with his. Her hand was trembling so badly she could hardly hold her glass of water, and she could see the boys looking at her. What must they be thinking? They were too young to understand what was happening to her, of course. But her face started to burn with maternal guilt.

'Mum, why don't you wear your rings any more?' Nico asked her curiously.

Her initial relief was quickly followed by fresh tension. She looked down at her left hand, bare of everything apart from her thin wedding band.

'The car is here, boys, it is time for us to leave,' the Professor announced jovially.

Sasha went with them to the front of the house, where the driver was waiting with the air-conditioned Mercedes Gabriel had hired to take them to the places the Professor wanted them to see, and gave each of the boys a quick hug and a brief kiss.

Gabriel was saying something to the Professor, and Sasha took advantage of their conversation to go back into the house. Her head was aching with the pressure of her distracted thoughts. She was still in shock from this morning, unable to truly reconcile what she had done with the reality of her true relationship with Gabriel. Gabriel despised her. He was hostile towards her, he had a grudge against her, and yet even knowing that she had still allowed him…

Allowed him? What had happened that morning hadn't happened as the result of any kind of conscious decision. Like a furious storm coming out nowhere, it had been beyond human control.

'Sasha.'

She stiffened, tempted to turn and run from him, as she had done this morning. It wasn't just her face but her whole body that was burning now.

She forced herself to turn around and look at him.

'You never answered Nico,' he said. 'Why aren't you wearing your rings?'

She took a deep breath. 'Because I've sold them,' she told him evenly. 'My jewellery was the only asset that was mine, so I took it into Port Cervo and sold it. When the boys go back to school I intend to use the money to buy a home for the three of us in London. Contrary to what you may think, Gabriel, I do not want to live at your expense.'

'You sold your jewellery?' An icy shock of angry fear sheeted through Gabriel. If she had money then she would not need him. And he needed her to need him, Gabriel suddenly recognised.

'Yes.' Sasha gave him a steady look. 'The boys need

a proper settled home. They are my sons, and there isn't anything I wouldn't do to give them that, Gabriel.'

'You could have—'

'What?' she challenged him. 'Asked you for help?' As she had once asked him for his love? 'I think we both know what your reaction to that would have been, don't we? I've got rather a bad headache, and I'm not in the mood for this conversation, Gabriel. What I choose to do with my jewellery is my own affair and no one else's.' She turned on her heel and headed for the stairs.

For some unfathomable reason Gabriel felt as though someone had just dropped a leaden weight into his chest cavity.

Sasha was walking upstairs, and for a second he was tempted to go after her and demand to know how she could reconcile her love for her sons with what she had done to him. She had, after all, told him that she loved him. She had begged him to return that love. He could still remember the intensity of the confusion and anger she had aroused in him, the strength of his desire to reject what she was saying. Yet at the same time her words had pierced him with an unfamiliar sensation—pain, even if at the time he had refused to acknowledge it. Now that long-buried memory surfaced.

His throat felt tight and his heart was hammering painfully against his ribs—because of Sasha? Because she was a mother who loved her sons? Was he *jealous* of that love?

It was like receiving a sickening sledgehammer blow out of nowhere, against which he had no defences.

One of the first things his grandfather had done when

he had taken Gabriel to live with him had been to show him the diamond and ruby necklace he had given to Gabriel's mother when she had returned home.

'This is what she sold you for,' he had taunted Gabriel, before complaining bitterly, 'She should have married the husband I chose for her in the first place, then maybe I would have the grandson the Calbrini name deserves, instead of a misbegotten nothing like you.'

After his grandfather's death Gabriel had destroyed the portrait of his mother wearing the rubies she had valued so much more than him, and he had locked the necklace itself away in the Calbrini family bank vault.

This time spent here with Sasha should have reinforced everything he thought and believed about her and her sex. It should have given him the satisfaction of a due debt paid. But instead it had thrown up such huge inconsistencies in the logic of his own thinking that he couldn't ignore them any more.

There was one thing that he could do, though. He walked out of the house and got into his car. He knew Port Cervo well enough to guess which jeweller Sasha would have visited.

The owner of the shop was reluctant to tell him at first how much he had given Sasha, but in the end Gabriel got his way. Gabriel wrote him a cheque, to which he added a substantial extra sum for 'inconvenience' and, having recovered Sasha's jewellery, made his way back to his car.

Sasha hadn't been lying about her headache. The soft roar of the Mercedes telling her that Gabriel had gone out and that she had the house to herself made her sigh shakily with relief. No need to pretend now. No need to protect herself or worry about what she might reveal for a few precious hours.

She stripped off her clothes and stepped under the shower, welcoming the cool mist of water on her tense, hot skin.

This morning on the beach...

Stop it, she warned herself. Don't think about that. But she wanted to. She wanted to think about it and relive it and relish every second of it, secretly hoarding it away...

She switched off the shower and reached for a towel, wrapping it around herself before padding into her bedroom. This hunger possessing her didn't mean anything, she tried to reassure herself. It was just a physical appetite, that was all... The needy girl who had been so desperate for Gabriel's love had gone. And the woman who had taken her place didn't need his love.

She had her sons, her self respect, a new life in front of her. What she did not need was to be dragged back into the past, to be reclaimed by a damaging relationship. Gabriel hadn't changed; he had made that obvious. He didn't want to change. He had built his whole life on the foundation stone of his mother's desertion, and without that foundation....The reality was that he wanted to despise her, Sasha acknowledged. As powerful as the sexual attraction between them was, it was built on darkness and bitterness, and that made it destructive and damaging for both of them.

She took two painkillers, and closed the shutters to block out the sunlight before crawling into her bed. Tears filled her eyes and slid down her face. They weren't just caused by the pain of her headache, she admitted, although why on earth she should cry for Gabriel, as well as herself, she couldn't understand.

The house was empty and silent. A sensation like a huge fist gripping and crushing his heart filled Gabriel's chest. Like an image on a screen, he saw himself striding through the darkness of the main cabin of his yacht, calling out irritably to Sasha, wanting to know why she wasn't in his bed.

But this time she could hardly have left with Carlo. His cousin was dead, after all, and the small car Sasha drove was parked outside. It was adrenalin-fuelled anger that was making his pulse race and his stomach muscles knot, Gabriel told himself. He checked the downstairs rooms and found them empty, then moved towards the stairs.

The sound of the Mercedes' engine purring past her window woke Sasha from her brief sleep. Gabriel was back. She pushed back the bedclothes, relieved to discover that her headache had eased. She heard Gabriel rapping on the main door to her suite, calling out her name impatiently.

'Yes, I'm here. I won't be a minute,' she called back, abandoning her attempt to get dressed when she heard him come in and cross the wooden floor to the suite's private sitting room. In another minute he would be in her bedroom. Panicking slightly, she reached for a fresh towel and wrapped it around her body, calling out to him, 'Don't come in, Gabriel, I'm not dressed.' But it was too late. He'd already pushed open the bedroom door and was standing in the middle of the room, frowning darkly at her.

'What's going on?' he demanded sharply.

Sasha frowned. His eyes were searching the room as though he was a jealous lover, expecting to find a rival. Her imagination was playing tricks on her, she decided.

'Why are the shutters closed?'

'I had a headache, so I decided to go to bed for an hour,' Sasha told him.

'On your own?'

Sasha stared at him. What on earth had got into him? Surely he didn't seriously believe that she had a lover hidden away in here?

'I had a headache,' she repeated. 'Going to bed to get rid of it is something that people do, Gabriel.'

His mouth compressed, and suddenly Sasha could almost smell the past: the sleepy afternoon air of the yacht's cabin scented with the sensuality of their sex. She could feel the heat crawling over her skin. Without a word, just by looking at her, Gabriel had taken her back to that time.

'*You* may still go to bed in the afternoon for sex,' she told him fiercely. 'But I most certainly do not.' Did she sound as though she wanted to? Was she unconsciously giving him an unsubtle message that she wanted him? 'What did you want me for?' she asked him. 'I'd like to get dressed; the boys will be back soon.'

He put down the large square package he was carrying and looked at his watch. 'They won't be back for another two or three hours yet,' he said, before picking up the package and holding it out to her.

'What…what is it?' she asked him warily.

'Why do you not open it and see?' He walked across the room to the door, but instead of going through it he closed it and turned around. 'Open it, Sasha,' he repeated coolly.

As soon as she had removed the outer wrapping paper and lifted the lid of the box inside it, to see the familiar name on the tissue paper, she knew. Her hands trembled as she removed the tissue, her mouth tightening when she found the small individual jewellers' boxes beneath it. She opened the top box, a wave of anger surging through her when she saw the familiar diamond ring. Snapping the box shut, she looked up at Gabriel.

'You'd better check that it's all there,' he told her curtly.

'What is this, Gabriel?' she demanded, ignoring his command, and somehow managing to keep her voice from cracking with anger.

'It's your jewellery. What does it look like?'

'No, it isn't.' Sasha shook her head, cramming the lid back on top of the box and thrusting it away from her. 'I sold my jewellery.'

'And I bought it back for you.'

'You had no right! Do you realise what you've done? How much did you pay for it? More than I sold it for, I'm sure.' His silence gave her the answer. An angry flush burned her face. 'How dare you do this to me, Gabriel? The reason I sold the jewellery was so I could provide a home for my sons and myself, so that we could have our independence from you. You had no right—'

'I had *every* right.' Gabriel stopped her, furious himself. Didn't she realise how lucky she was? How generous he was being? Or how controlling? an inner voice suggested. How determined to keep her in debt to you? He silenced the small, self-mocking voice. 'I have the

Calbrini name to think of. How do you think it looks to have you selling the jewellery Carlo gave you?'

'Not as gossip-worthy as you buying it back,' Sasha said bitingly. 'Everyone knows that Carlo died virtually bankrupt. I had nothing to be ashamed of in selling my jewellery, Gabriel. But now thanks to you—'

'Thanks to me, what?' he demanded dangerously.

'Do you really need me to tell you? Why did you buy it back, Gabriel? So that it would make me feel indebted to you? Grateful to you? So that you would have control over me? By buying the jewellery back you're forcing me to pay for it again, and to be left in debt for whatever extra you handed over to the jeweller. You've stolen my freedom from me, Gabriel,' she told him, white-faced with anger. 'Just like your grandfather stole your mother's freedom. But I'm not her, and I won't be bought or bullied, and I won't be forced to live in perpetual debt to you.'

She was shaking from head to foot as the true realisation of what he had done to her began to sink in. She picked up the box and thrust it towards him. 'Here— take it. I don't want it. And I don't want you. I won't let you force me into playing the role you've chosen for me, Gabriel. I'm not your mother. I'm me.'

'At least my mother didn't sleep around and share her favours with two men at the same time. You're right. You aren't her. You're a—'

It was too much for Sasha's self control. The anger inside her boiled over. She raised her hand and slapped him across his face—hard. Immediately Gabriel dropped the box and grabbed hold of her.

Sick with shock and shame, Sasha shivered with

self-disgust. This was what happened when Gabriel invaded her life. He brought with him memories from her past that aroused the kind of emotions she wasn't equipped to withstand. Even now, with anger and shame swirling through her, she still wanted him, she admitted. She had to put some distance between them.

'Gabriel, let me go,' she begged, twisting and turning in his grip, forgetting that all she was wearing was a towel. It slipped off at exactly the moment Gabriel lost his self-control and picked her up bodily to stop her struggling.

Sasha sucked in an unsteady breath as she saw the look in his eyes when his hands encountered naked flesh instead of the towel.

A thick, dangerous silence gripped the room.

'Gabriel,' Sasha pleaded again, but it was too late. He was already kicking the towel and the contents of the cardboard box out of the way and carrying her over to the bed.

'You're right,' he told her thickly. 'You are in debt to me, and I intend to claim full payment—right here and now.'

CHAPTER TEN

HELPLESSLY, Sasha looked back at him as her original anger transmuted into a sharp thrill of longing, and the hand she had lifted to push him away curled round his neck to urge him down towards her.

This, of course, was why she had needed to keep a distance between them. Because when she was near him all she could think of was how much she ached for him.

The seventeen-year-old who had gazed at Gabriel and created a fantasy world of love to enclose the two of them had had no awareness of the reality of what she would feel for him. Sex to her had been something that went hand-in-hand with love, was a mere by-product of it. She had been totally unaware of its compulsive urgency and energy, its ferocity and intensity. She had had no idea that this was how she would come to feel. That girl was not to blame for what she, as a woman, was feeling now, Sasha recognised.

She closed her eyes and ran her hands feverishly over Gabriel's torso, avidly relearning its shape, tugging buttons free of buttonholes as he kissed her, plunging her straight down into the depths of her own desire to that place where there was no reason, only the voices of her senses, whispering to her to hurry, to take what she could while she could, while there was still time.

She pushed his shirt off his shoulders, her eyes open now, as she watched him shrug it off completely, her body following his as he moved back to unfasten his belt. She leaned forward, tracing the line of his collarbone with her finger tip and then following it with small, slow kisses, breathing in the raw male scent of him as she stroked and kissed her way down his body. She was completely lost in the world of her own longing.

His belt was unfastened, his hands on the waistband of his chinos. Sasha lifted her hands and placed them against his chest, pushing him flat on the bed and then replacing his hands on his waistband with her own.

Slowly and carefully, inch by inch, kiss by kiss, she eased down his zip, relishing the sensual pleasure of slowly exposing to her touch and her gaze the plain of his belly crossed by the neat line of dark hair. She circled his navel with the tip of her tongue and then lifted her head to look, solemn-eyed, where the neat line of dark hair started to thicken. Beneath her hand, through the fabric of his chinos, she could feel his erection. A pulse quickened in her own body. She tugged impatiently at his chinos, exhaling in fierce relief when he responded to her need and stood up to remove the rest of his clothes.

On the beach there hadn't been time for her to look at him properly, but now she could. Her heart lifted and lurched against her ribs, her nipples tightening as white-hot desire—a woman's desire, not a girl's—shot through her. This too was something she hadn't known at seventeen. This fierce desire, stripped bare of the sweetness of fantasy, this real woman's need for an equally real man in the most elemental way there was. At seventeen all she had really wanted and craved from him was emotional love. Now, here, in this bed, she was fully prepared to sacrifice love for the physical satisfaction he could give her, Sasha decided fiercely. She was a woman now, with a woman's right to indulge her own sexuality and need. What had happened between them on the beach had turned the key on ten years' worth of sexual denial and repression.

But she couldn't afford this kind of self-indulgence, a warning inner voice reminded her. She was not free to do so. She was a mother, as well as a woman: a mother who needed to think first of her sons and not herself. Gabriel was their guardian, and she couldn't give him the weapons to corrupt their innocent belief in her.

As though he had guessed what she was thinking, and already sensed her withdrawal, Gabriel reached for her, telling her fiercely, 'It's too late for second thoughts now, Sasha. I mean to claim what's rightfully mine. And I intend to show you just what you gave up when you walked out on me.'

The softness of his voice, so loaded with sensual promise, made her tremble with longing. He was stroking her skin with the lightest of touches, the merest brush of his fingertips against her flesh, which suddenly burned for so much more. It was as though he was deliberately teasing her body, Sasha recognised, as he kissed her mouth lightly and then withdrew from her, only to repeat the brief kiss again and again, whilst the teasing, trailing movement of his fingertips against her skin became a form of slow torment.

Desperate for more than he was giving her, she tried to hold him closer. But he simply closed his hands round her upper arms and kept her still while he kissed her throat and then her shoulders, so briefly that she had to hold her breath so as not to miss the sensation.

'You want me,' he whispered to her. 'Don't you?'

All she could do was let the convulsions of open pleasure that seized her body give him his answer, and then moan against the liquid heat of her reward when his lips skimmed her breast, moving closer to her nipple. It was impossible to stop her body from straining eagerly towards him, or her hand, miraculously freed from imprisonment, from cupping the back of his head to urge him closer. The slow, erotic pull of his lips on the hard peak of her breast had always had the power to turn her belly liquid with erotic delight. But her memory had failed to provide a true record of the intensity, Sasha recognised weakly, when the teasing sensation of Gabriel's tongue-tip circling her eager flesh became the heat of his mouth closing on it. Pangs of pleasure so intense that they made her cry out seized her, gave her over to wave after wave of surging arousal. It flooded her and possessed her, picking her up and carrying her with it.

Without her saying a word, Gabriel found the soft wetness his touch had made ready for him. The feel of his fingers against her sex drove her desire higher, her whole body arching up to the heat of his mouth to the caress of his fingertip circling the swollen ache of the source of her female pleasure.

For a few seconds it was enough. But her body held memories of other, deeper pleasures, and it demanded that the circling fingertip become a slow, deliberate stroke over the whole length of her outer sex. Not just once, but over and over again, until she was grinding her hips and her teeth in frustration, then reaching up to grip hold of Gabriel in her need to feel him fill the waiting emptiness inside her.

'You want me?' He had moved back a little from her to position himself between her legs.

Sasha nodded her head and watched him, waiting, holding her breath as longing flooded her body.

His hands were on her hips. He was bending his head over her body, lowering it, his breath warming her belly.

Sasha drew in a defensive breath and tensed her body against an intimacy she didn't think she could survive. This wasn't what she had expected, or wanted. It was too intimate, too personal, too liable to strip her of all her defences and leave her exposed to him.

But it was too late to stop him. Gabriel's tongue-tip was already delicately stroking between the swollen pads of flesh that had opened as if in sensual offering, causing a rush of hot, shocked delight to invade her.

His tongue brushed slowly over the pulsing swell of aroused flesh it was seeking. Sasha tried, but failed to hold back her cry of pleasure. It radiated out from the place where the slow brushstrokes had become a sensually rhythmic slide. She could feel the swift assent to her climax coiling tightly inside her. It was too late now to escape. Her back arched of its own accord, her toes curling tightly as the feeling inside her soared towards its cataclysmic point of explosion. She felt Gabriel move, his weight settling against her, his heat between her thighs as he lifted her hips and thrust powerfully into her.

For the space of several strokes her body trembled on the edge of release, her muscles greedy for the sensation of his movement within them. And then the deep, gripping spasms of pleasure took over, possessing her completely as he drove through them to take her even higher. She could feel the sudden hot spill of his own climax with its added frisson of extra sensuality, and then the intensity was dying, leaving her lying defenceless and dependent on the support of Gabriel's arms in its retreating tide.

For a long time it was impossible for her to speak. All she could do was lie there, listening as the harsh sound of Gabriel's breathing softened, and accept the spasmodic after-shocks still galvanising her body.

Finally Gabriel released her and moved away from her. 'You have thrown in my face all those things Carlo gave, but we both know that he never gave you what I just have.'

His words reached her as though they had dropped like stones into deep water from a great height, disappearing from view but leaving behind them echoes of their existence that would last for ever.

'There's more to life and living than sex, Gabriel.'

'You can say that now,' he mocked her. 'But ten minutes ago—'

'I can't change the past, but I can control my future,' Sasha retaliated. 'I won't be used as your sexual plaything, Gabriel. I have my sons to consider. No amount of pleasure in bed with you can come anywhere near being worth compromising my relationship with them.'

'You say that now. But we both know that I can make you change your mind.'

Sasha closed her eyes, not wanting to watch as he gathered up his clothes, not wanting to know when he left her. But of course she did.

CHAPTER ELEVEN

HE HAD done what he had promised himself he would do. He had forced Sasha to admit that no other man could make her feel the way he could. So why wasn't he feeling elated? Why did his triumph feel so empty? Why was there this ache inside his chest? This driving need to see her smile at him with that same tender warmth with which she smiled at the twins?

Why had he allowed his need for her to overpower him to such an extent that he had had sex with her not once, but twice, without using any kind of protection? Why did he wake in the night longing for her closeness, wanting more than just the cry of her pleasure during sex?

But more of what? What exactly *did* he want from her? His heart knew the answer. His *heart*? He didn't have a heart; his mother had destroyed his emotions almost before they had been formed. He had never feared loving anyone because he had never believed he was able to love. So what, then, was this feeling that ached through him?

The truth was that Sasha was a woman any man would be a fool not to love.

Gabriel stared unseeingly at his computer screen, unable to understand where that thought had come from, and equally unable to reject the truth of it. The girl who he had once held in such bitter contempt for the damage she had done to his pride had become a woman worthy of anyone's respect, and she now had the power to inflict pain on something far more vulnerable than his pride.

Slowly, carefully, like a man lost in a tunnel without a light to guide him, Gabriel felt his way cautiously through the unknown territory of this new world of emotions he had suddenly entered, flinching when a careless movement brought him up against a sharp, painful discovery.

Was this what love was? This powerful combination of strength and weakness, of a need to have and a need to give, of wanting to protect as well as wanting to possess? When he thought back—really thought back— hadn't he felt those things for her all those years ago, even if he had denied both their existence and their meaning?

Love. He tasted the word, rolling it around his mouth, feeling its form and shape while inside his head an image of Sasha formed.

The sound of the twins' voices on the other side of the half-open door to his office broke into his thoughts.

'You ask him,' he could hear Sam saying.

'No, you ask him.' Nico was insistent.

A rueful smile tugged at his mouth as he guessed that the purpose of this unscheduled deputation was another attempt to get him on their side in the matter of their longed-for bicycles. Pushing back his chair, he got up and strolled over to the door, opening it and inviting them in.

The twins exchanged expressive looks, shuffling closer together in a way that was unintentionally endearing. They were still young enough to automatically seek the comfort of each other's physical presence, Gabriel realised as he closed the door and walked back to his chair. Having undergone some kind of radical transformation, he was now suddenly discovering that not only did he have a heart, but that it was vulnerable to the most unabashed and foolish kind of sentimentality.

'Right, so who is going to ask me whatever it is, then?' he invited.

Another eloquent exchanged look, followed by a sharp dig in Nico's ribs from Sam's elbow, seemed to decide the matter.

Nico shuffled forward a couple of inches. 'Me and Sam have been wondering if you're our real father.'

The simple question stunned Gabriel, and when he didn't answer, Nico continued in a kind voice, 'It's okay. Before Dad died he told me and Sam that he wasn't our real father.'

'Yes, but he did say, too, Nico, that he'd always be our dad and that he loved us very much,' Sam put in.

'I know that. But he didn't tell us who our real father was, did he?'

Sam, eager now to take over from Nico, gave him a scornful look.

'No, but that was because he said that one day, when we were old enough, Mum would explain it all to us, and that we weren't to tell her what he'd told us. He said that he was proud of us and that we were real Calbrinis,' Sam informed Gabriel importantly, before giving Nico another sharp nudge.

Dutifully, Nico fixed his earnest gaze on him. 'Well, me and Sam have been thinking, and we wondered…'

Gabriel watched as they exchanged more looks.

'We would really like if it you were our father,' Nico said in a rush.

'Yes, it would be really cool,' Sam agreed.

It took from the first thunderstruck realisation of what they had said to the change of his heartbeat to a sudden heavy thud of recognition for Gabriel to recognise that such a short span of time had the power to change his whole life. As though the hitherto secret combination of a complex locking mechanism had suddenly clicked into place, a series of doors opened inside his head, allowing the truth to walk freely through them.

Of course they were his. How could they not be? The wonder was not that they were, but that he had not recognised it before now.

He walked over to his sons and crouched down beside them. Their familiar features blurred slightly, causing him to blink.

'Do you really want me to be your father?' he asked. It was the first time in his life that he had thought of the emotional needs of others as something more important than what he himself might want.

The boys looked at one another and then at him, wide watermelon grins transforming their faces as they nodded their heads in unison.

'Yes.'

'We knew it was you—didn't we, Nico?' Sam said smugly.

'Yes. We both knew,' Nico told Gabriel gravely, before reaching out and tucking his hand around Gabriel's arm, leaning against him.

This was why Carlo had wanted him to be their guardian, Gabriel suddenly realised, emotion clogging his throat as he knelt there, with a child—a *son*—in each arm, hugging them both fiercely to him. No wonder he had felt so instantly at ease with them, so immediately determined to protect them. *This* was what Carlo had struggled to tell him, only to change his mind. Because he had feared that Gabriel might reject the truth?

'I think for the moment, until I've spoken to your mother, we should keep this to ourselves,' Gabriel told his sons.

'But not for too long,' Sam countered. 'Now that you're our father you'll be able to tell Mum that we can have bikes for our birthday.'

When had they thought that one up? Gabriel wondered wryly as he received a pair of happy, confident smiles. As male logic went, it seemed a reasonable exchange, but Gabriel doubted that Sasha would see it that way.

The boys went to join the Professor, sworn to secrecy and having happily assured Gabriel that they were glad he was their real father.

Against all the odds, they had the kind of sturdy emotional self-belief that he could only envy. No, not against all the odds, but because of their mother. Because *she* had given them something more precious and more valuable than any amount of money or material possessions. She had given them a mother and a father, the secure knowledge that they were loved and wanted, the loving firmness of boundaries they had been taught to respect, and most of all the emotional freedom to be themselves. Wasn't Sasha herself the most valuable gift life had given them?

And the most important gift life had given *him*?

Sasha. He needed to talk to her.

He found her in the kitchen, emptying the dishwasher. She looked up when he walked in, and then looked away again quickly. He wanted to look at her and to go on looking at her, marvelling that her body had nurtured the lives of their sons, that she was responsible for the miracle of their existence. But not solely responsible, of course.

'The boys have just been to see me.'

'They're hoping you'll persuade me to let them have bikes for their birthday,' Sasha said.

'They wanted to know if I am their real father.'

The water jug she had been holding slipped from Sasha's grasp, smashing onto the tiles in a shower of broken glass.

The look on her face told Gabriel everything he needed to know.

'Carlo was their father,' she whispered, bending down to start picking up the broken glass.

'No—leave it. You'll cut yourself,' Gabriel warned, but it was too late. Blood was dripping from her palm, where a shard of glass had slipped in her shaking hands and cut the skin.

Sasha stared numbly at the bright red blood welling from the small cut. She felt oddly separated from what was happening, as though some huge force had shunted her sideways into a place where she could only observe herself at a distance.

'But he didn't father them. He told them that himself, Sasha, so there's no point denying it.'

This couldn't be happening. She looked down at the glass.

'This needs cleaning up,' she told him. 'I—'

'I'll do it. You come and sit down.'

How had she got here, to the kitchen chair? She watched blankly as Gabriel deftly swept up the broken glass and disposed of it.

'Now, let's have a look at that hand.' Docilely she let Gabriel lead her to the sink and run cold water over her palm, before removing the first aid kit from the cupboard and putting a protective dressing over the cut.

He took her back to the table and sat her down.

'The twins are my sons; we both know that. But what I don't know is why you didn't tell me at the time.'

Shock was relinquishing its numbing hold on her now. There would be time later to worry about the effect Carlo's revelation must have had on the twins, and to wonder exactly what he had told them and why. Right now she needed to make sure that Gabriel understood that her sons were *hers*, that they were nothing to do with him.

She took a deep, steadying breath. 'Do you really need to ask that question? I'd pleaded with you to love me, Gabriel. I'd been sick virtually very morning for weeks, and I had guessed why, even if I lied to you and told you it was food poisoning. I'd even given you the opportunity to say you wanted children. I'd done everything to give you a chance to guess the truth short of spelling it out for you.

'Carlo guessed, and he hardly knew me. Carlo understood how I felt, and how afraid I was. You'd already rejected me. What if you rejected the child I was carrying—or worse? When you told me you didn't want children it made me afraid. Not afraid for me, but afraid for them. I thought you might put pressure on me to terminate the pregnancy.' Sasha closed her eyes and swallowed. 'I was afraid that I'd give in, that I'd do whatever you wanted me to do simply because you wanted it.

'Carlo made it easy for me to make the right decision. It's because of Carlo, not you or me, that the twins are here today. It was Carlo who fathered them, Gabriel. Because he was the one who gave them a father's protection and love.'

Regret, shame, and most of all pain—Gabriel could feel them crawling along his veins.

'You should have told me.'

'Perhaps *you* should have known,' Sasha retorted levelly. 'I'll never know what I did to deserve Carlo. I'll never cease to be thankful for what he gave me. Sometimes I wonder if maybe fate sent him; not for me, but for the twins. But it doesn't really matter which of us he was here to rescue, because out of his generosity and his compassion he rescued us all. Without him I would either have given in and let you persuade me to terminate my pregnancy, or ended up on the street, where my sons would have grown up in even worse circumstances than my own. They say that it passes from generation to generation, don't they? That damaged children become damaging parents. I was so lucky to be given the chance to change that pattern.'

'You're over-dramatising,' Gabriel said. 'Okay, so I said I didn't want children. But if I'd been faced with the fact that you were already pregnant—'

'You say that now, Gabriel, but the truth is that neither of us were fit to be parents. I was little more than a needy child myself, clamouring for love from a man who couldn't give it. Having the children was my wake-up call. Thanks to Carlo, I was able to take advantage of the very best kind of help. I already loved my babies, but I had to learn to love myself. I had to learn to accept my past, but to leave it as my past and not bring it into the present with me. Carlo was so proud of the boys. True Calbrinis—that's what he always called them.'

The conversation wasn't taking the course Gabriel had expected or hoped for. Sasha seemed stubbornly determined to reject his attempts to forge a bond between them via their sons. The revelations which had so awed and impressed him apparently had no impact on her. Couldn't she see that he was a changed man? That he recognised the errors of his past and was now ready to make amends for them?

'They are my sons,' he told her firmly.

Sasha shook her head. 'No. Your sons, Gabriel, would be as damaged and as tainted by your childhood as you are yourself. An adult can't find salvation through a child. You have to give to them, not take from them.'

'I made mistakes, I admit that. But it's not too late…'

'It's not too late for what?' Sasha asked.

It's not too late for us, was what he wanted to say, but instead he said, 'I know you, Sasha—'

She stopped him immediately. 'No, you don't know me, Gabriel. You never did. To you I'm a cheap tart you picked up off the street, a piece of flesh to provide you with pleasure. You believed I'd two-timed you with Carlo. You thought—'

He had made mistakes, Gabriel knew that, but he wasn't solely to blame for that. Her accusations stung and made him react defensively. 'Do you blame me?' he demanded. 'The night we met you told me—'

Sasha gave him a weary look. What did it matter now what she told him? 'The night we met I was still a virgin. *That's* how little you know me, Gabriel.' She pushed back her chair and stood up unsteadily.

'That can't be true,' Gabriel protested. 'What about that porno film director? You implied—'

Sasha gave a mirthless smile. 'Oh, yes, I certainly implied—and he certainly existed. He tried to proposition one of the girls I was on holiday with. The truth is that I was very young and even more foolish. I wanted you to think I was sexy and desirable…I was too naïve to realise you'd simply think I was used and available.'

'I don't understand any of this. You claim you were a virgin, so why the hell did you go to bed with me? You must have known—'

'What? That all you wanted was a one-night stand?' Sasha shook her head. 'Gabriel, I was seventeen. I'd been in care since I was a child. I craved love. I thought it was the answer to everything. My prince would ride into my life and sweep me up into his arms and we'd live happily ever after. That was all I wanted—to be loved. To be in love.'

He could hear the derision in her voice at her own foolishness and somehow that hurt him—for her.

'The other girls were older than me. I'd only been included in the holiday because we all worked together. I got in their way, and on their nerves, so I spent most of my time on my own. I saw you the first day we arrived in St Tropez. You were walking past the café where I was having a cup of coffee. You fitted my mental template of hero perfectly. All it took was a handful of seconds to convince myself that it was love at first sight, and that you were the only man I could ever and would ever love.' She gave a small shrug. 'That's how my neediness expressed itself.

'I started hanging around the harbour, hoping I'd see you. And I did. Coming off the yacht. I thought you must work on it. It never occurred to me that you owned it.' She smiled sadly. 'Your money was never the draw for me, Gabriel, although of course you could never believe that. It scared me half to death when I realised just how wealthy you were, but by then it was too late. I was deeply in love. So much in love and so very hungry for you that even that first time what little pain there was was far outweighed by my pleasure.'

Gabriel closed his eyes. He could remember that first time and how good it had felt, how good *she* had felt, with the close sheath of her muscles gripping him tightly. He had put that down to her experience. He should have known... And perhaps deep inside he had known, but had preferred to pretend that he did not. Shame and an acute sense of loss tightened his throat.

'And of course I'd convinced myself that you returned my feelings,' Sasha continued lightly. 'Even though you did everything possible to make it obvious that you didn't. But what did I know? All I knew was my own need. No one had ever loved me; I had no experience of what real love was. So predictably, I looked for love where I was never going to find it. I set myself the task of making myself good enough for you to reward me with your love. It's a common enough pattern. The more you withheld your love, the harder I worked to try to gain it.'

'I didn't know—'

'How could you? We never talked, we simply had sex, and I made up my foolish fantasies. Even when you did mention your mother and your grandfather, it never occurred to me that those relationships had to impact on ours. I simply thought how wonderful it was that we had both had unhappy childhoods and how it must bond us together. I convinced myself that I had been given the opportunity to give you the love you had never had. I agreed with you that your mother was cruel and selfish. I couldn't reason then that she might have been afraid and alone, that she might have found herself in a marriage that wasn't working, and that she might have been tricked by her father into returning home, only to discover too late that the price of being rescued from an unwanted marriage was the loss of her son.'

Sasha could see that Gabriel was frowning, and there was a bleak look in his eyes. 'I'm not saying that's what happened, Gabriel. I'm simply saying that there could be other explanations than the one you were given.'

Gabriel wasn't looking convinced.

'Look, I'm not trying to rewrite your family history or defend your mother. But you were too young when your mother left to know what she felt or why she did it. All you know is what you were told by others.'

Sasha gave a small tired shrug. 'We can look back to our childhoods, see the pain there and blame our parents, and then we can look back to their childhoods and see that they were damaged too. But where does it end, Gabriel? How far back do we go in loading the blame? How much of our lives do we need to spend looking for answers in the past and blaming others for our present? I had to step away from my childhood and recreate myself as the person the twins needed me to be. It was the biggest turning point in the whole of my life.'

That wasn't entirely true. But Sasha wasn't about to tell Gabriel that even now he still held a grip on her heart that no amount of counselling or anything else could release.

'So you reinvented yourself and turned your whole life around by deciding that your childhood wasn't as bad as you remembered? Unfortunately I don't have your imagination.'

The love for Gabriel that she had tried so hard to tell herself was dead filled Sasha's heart. She ached to go to him and hold him, make whole and heal all the damaged places of his past. In her mind's eye she could see him as a child—alone, afraid, and unloved; *hurting*. Tears stung her eyes. She wanted to reach into the past and snatch Gabriel the child from it, so that she could give him love. But she knew that no amount of love from her could take away his bitterness. And she knew too that she couldn't risk that bitterness flowing from him into the lives of her sons.

'Nothing more to say?' Gabriel asked grimly. 'This kind of talk is all very well, Sasha, but you can't really expect me to believe it can alter reality. Forget the past. What we need to talk about now is the present, and our sons.'

Sasha looked away from him.

'What's wrong?' Gabriel demanded. 'Or can I guess? You'd have preferred it if I'd never learned the truth, wouldn't you? That I'd continued to believe that Carlo fathered them?'

'Yes,' Sasha admitted quietly.

'Thanks for that vote of confidence.'

'I'm thinking of the boys.'

'And what you're thinking is that I'm not good enough to be their father?' Gabriel said.

Sasha dipped her head. This was so difficult, and so painful. She could remember how she had felt when she had first realised she was pregnant, her sense of excited awe that *she* was having *Gabriel's* baby. She had felt as though she'd had the greatest gift on earth bestowed on her. The pregnancy had been accidental; she had been far too much the junior partner in their relationship to think of doing something like deliberately sabotaging Gabriel's contraception. The fact that she had conceived despite Gabriel's precautions had just made her feel that her pregnancy was extra special and meant to be. She had been delirious with joy, expecting with every early-morning bout of sickness to hear Gabriel announcing that he knew she was pregnant. She had even imagined the scene, right down to his words of love and reverence as he held her and told her how thrilled he was, how much he loved her. He would insist on marrying her immediately, of course, and they would live happily ever after with their adorable baby.

Only it hadn't worked like that. Now she knew that she must have had some inner instinct warning her of what was to come. Why else would she have lied when Gabriel had commented on her sickness, saying it was food poisoning? She might have believed she wanted him to guess she was pregnant, but something deep within her had made her keep it a secret.

She had been in her second month when she had begun to feel impatient with Gabriel's lack of insight, and she had started to drop heavy hints about babies. That was when Gabriel had told her bitingly that far too many people produced children they didn't want. And he had underlined his views with explicit descriptions of his own childhood.

Remembering that time now, she took a deep breath.

'I don't think that you are whole enough to be the father I want for them. I don't want them to suffer the repercussions of your childhood, Gabriel,' she told him quietly.

It hurt her physically to see the shock in his eyes and the way he battled to conceal it from her.

'You think I'd *hurt* them, physically abuse them?' he burst out.

Sasha shook her head. 'No,' she told him honestly. 'I lived with you for long enough to know that you wouldn't hurt them that way. But there are other ways of harming those we love.'

'So you *do* accept that I love them?'

Sasha smiled ruefully. From the moment they had set eyes on one another Gabriel and the twins had formed a united male bond that had given her more cause for guilty anxiety than she wanted to admit. If he'd known right from the start they were his children Gabriel couldn't have been more of a father during these few weeks they had all spent together. He possessed an instinctive perception of what would work for them and what wouldn't, and he treated them as individuals instead of lumping them together as 'the twins'. But most telling of all was the way in which he had immediately and instinctively been able to tell them apart. Something that until now only she had been able to do. Carlo had certainly never managed to work out which of them was which.

'Yes, I do accept that. But even love can be damaging, Gabriel. It's natural for us to want to give our own children the best of everything, emotionally and materially. But that isn't always a good thing.'

'You mean you think I'd overload them with too much love and money because I'd want to give them what I never had?'

'Tell me honestly that you haven't already mentally picked out top-of-the-range bicycles for them,' Sasha asked him dryly. She could tell from the way Gabriel avoided her gaze that she was right. 'It isn't that I don't believe you love them, Gabriel, or that I doubt for one minute that you'd want the very best of everything for them. It's… I've had to learn that sometimes the best thing you can do for them is to say no.'

'So you don't want me to be part of their lives because you think I'll spoil them?'

'You are *already* a part of their lives. You're their guardian and their father.'

'Sasha.' He reached across the table and took hold of her hand before she could stop him.

'I understand what you're saying, and, yes, I accept that being a father is going to involve me in a pretty steep learning curve. But what about the other side of the equation?'

'What other side?' Sasha asked woodenly. But she already knew. This was it. She was living her worst nightmare—and her most longed-for dream.

'You and I share a history that holds a lot of pain and anger. I know that. But it also holds our sons. I know that I've let the best thing in my life slip away from me because I was too blind to see what I had. We've already proved that sexually we're not so much compatible as combustible.' Gabriel paused, and the smouldering look in his eyes made Sasha's toes curl and her heart thump with remembered pleasure. 'The best gift any parent can give their child is surely the security of a loving home life. I'd like to give that to our sons.'

It might have taken him a long time to accept that he loved Sasha, but now that he had he didn't intend to waste any more of it. There was nothing he wanted to hold back from her now; not his love, not his admission that he had deliberately made himself think the worst of her, not his heartfelt apology for his mistakes—nothing! He wanted a clean conscience, a clean fresh start, a new beginning for them all, and a life in which he could show Sasha just how much she and their sons meant to him every single day.

'You mean you want the four of us to live together

as a family?' There was a note of caution in her voice he could fully understand.

'I want us to live together as a family—yes, Sasha. And I want you and I to live as husband and wife. I want to marry you, Sasha. I want our sons to grow up with us as their parents.'

Just for a few precious seconds Sasha allowed herself to dream and believe, to think the impossible. But only for a few seconds. Because she already knew what her answer had to be.

'No,' she told Gabriel quietly.

'No? Why not? What—?'

'It wouldn't work, Gabriel. I accept that sexually we...it works between us,' she agreed hurriedly, not wanting to linger on thoughts that could only add to the rebellion inside her, threatening to overturn her hard-won decision. 'But you and I... We both may love the boys, but let's not pretend that we love one another. Because we both know that we don't.'

They were the hardest words she had ever had to say. All the more so because they were a lie. No matter what she'd told herself during the intervening years, she knew herself too well now to be able to pretend that the way he made her feel was purely sexual. But she also knew that for her sons' sake she could not afford to love him—especially not via a public relationship and a commitment that could rebound on them.

In a dream world, a perfect world, this was where she would fling herself into his arms with cries of joy that they would live happily ever after. But reality wasn't like that. Reality could be harsh and unforgiving.

'On the contrary, I know nothing of the sort,' she heard Gabriel saying softly. Her heart skipped a beat. Had he guessed that she still loved him? And if so… 'You may not love me any more, Sasha, but I do love you.'

If only she could let herself believe that. The thrill of hearing those words after so many years was threatening to sweep away all her doubts. But she mustn't let it.

'You say that now, Gabriel, but how can I believe it? How can you? Only days ago you believed that I was a bad mother, a woman who went from one man's bed to another's, a woman who was looking for a rich man to support her. Remember?'

Gabriel couldn't deny it. 'I said all those things, yes,' he said. 'And, yes, initially I was convinced that they were true. But it didn't take me very long to realise just how wrong I was, even if I was too stubborn to face up to it. I had to make myself believe them, Sasha, because my pride wouldn't let me admit how I really felt when you walked out on me that day. I'd sworn that I would never risk falling in love and I couldn't admit that I had. Besides, if you'd really wanted a wealthy man to seduce, you could have seduced me.' He smiled at her, to show that he was making a joke against himself. 'Perhaps a part of me was hoping that you would.'

Sasha didn't trust herself to say anything.

'Why didn't you tell me why you boarded the boys at their school?'

Could that really be pain she could hear in his voice? Now she *had* to speak. 'I didn't see the point. I didn't think you would believe me. It seemed to me that you were determined to think the worst of me.'

'You're right. I was. Hearing the Professor talk about the good sense you'd shown felt like being kicked in the stomach. And if that wasn't enough to jolt me out of my stupidity then the shock of discovering that you had sold your jewellery certainly was. I recognise now that deep down I've loved you all along—'

Sasha shook her head and stopped him. 'That's easy enough to say, Gabriel. But it seems to me that you've discovered you love me far too quickly after you discovered the boys were yours.'

Gabriel admitted that she had every right to throw that accusation at him—even if it wasn't true. He was thrilled to know he was the twins' father. And it had given him a distinctly male sense of satisfaction to learn that he had been her first lover. But neither of those facts could have made him love her if he hadn't done so already. *He* knew that. But how could he explain to her the slow and very painful process by which he had come to recognise what his real feelings for her were when he was still struggling to analyse them for himself? This was all such new territory to him, uncharted and untested, and no captain ever set sail on a sea he knew nothing about. Not unless he was desperate. And right now that was exactly what he was.

'I loved you before that—' he began.

'I find that very hard to believe,' Sasha told him flatly. But I want to believe you, her heart was crying. I want to believe you more than I've wanted anything in my whole life. More than the twins' emotional security? If the answer was yes, then what kind of mother did that make her? A mother just like Gabriel believed his had been? If she gave in, and then he changed his mind and discovered that he didn't love her after all, how long would it be before he was accusing her of exactly that?

'I'm ready to do whatever it takes to prove it,' Gabriel continued.

'There isn't any point.'

'There is for me. You loved me once, and I believe—'

'That wasn't love. It was a teenager's fantasy,' Sasha lied.

'So you don't love me any more—but you still had sex with me.'

'It happens,' Sasha told him evenly.

'How often?'

He was still holding her hand, and she wondered if he had felt the sudden betraying tremor that ran through it.

'Meaning what?' she sidestepped.

'Meaning how often since you left me have you had sex with men you don't love?'

'Look, Gabriel, this won't get us anywhere. I fully accept that as the twins' father you have a role to play in their lives—'

'There hasn't been anyone, has there?' he said softly, overruling her attempt to change the subject. Oh, but he wanted so badly to take her in his arms and kiss her until she clung to him as she had done in bed. Something, some instinct he hadn't even known he had, was telling him that there hadn't been anyone else in the years they had been apart. And surely that had to mean some-thing?

'I was a married woman, with two young children and a husband—a sick husband; that hardly left me any time to indulge in extra-marital sex,' Sasha pointed out.

'In other words, there hasn't been anyone?'

He didn't have to sound so damned pleased about it, Sasha thought angrily. 'So what? That doesn't mean I've spent the last ten years yearning for you!'

'Did I say it did? It does prove, though, surely, that we must have something going for us?'

This was getting out of hand. Another few minutes and she'd be drowning in the sea of counter-arguments he was throwing at her. 'So I indulged in a quick shag for old times' sake. That doesn't mean anything.'

'Now, I *know* you're lying.' Gabriel was actually laughing. 'And it wasn't just a shag. It was full-on, passionate, intimate lovemaking, and you know it.'

She couldn't take any more of this. Her defences were crumbling into nothing. 'It doesn't matter what you say or what I feel. Can't you see?' she said wildly. 'This isn't about us, Gabriel, it's about the boys. What if I gave in and agreed? And then what if a month—a year—ten years—down the line you got bored of playing happy families. What then? It's not as though I'm trying to deny you a role in the boys' lives. You are their father, and you are their guardian. You're free to form your own relationship with them. But not via my bed. I'm not doing anything that might lead to them becoming victims of a bitter broken home.'

'I could change your mind,' Gabriel warned her softly. 'I could take you in my arms right here and now and make you—'

'Make me what? Make me want you? Yes, you could do that. But it wouldn't make me change my mind.'

'Very well.' Sasha didn't know whether to be relieved

or disappointed when he removed his hand from hers and stood up. 'I understand what you're saying.'

He was starting to turn away from her, and it took every ounce of will-power she possessed not to call him back and tell him how she really felt.

'But I give you fair warning, Sasha, I don't intend to give up. I intend to do whatever it takes to convince you that you and I and the boys have a future together as a family, and that you and I have a future together as husband and wife.'

'I can't stop you from wanting that,' Sasha said. 'But what I want is what's best for the boys. You implied that you would take them away from their school. I want them to stay. They're happy there, and they're doing well.'

Was she testing him? Gabriel wondered. If so, she was going to find that he meant every word he had said to her.

'You're their mother,' he told her firmly. 'I trust your judgement as to where their best interests lie. My own suggestion would be that they should be encouraged to incorporate an awareness of their Italian heritage into their lives.'

He was giving in and agreeing that the boys could stay at their school? 'But what about the Professor?' she reminded him. 'I thought—'

'His initial role was to assess the twins' educational needs. I'm sure he'll understand when we tell him that they are going to continue at their existing school. In fact, I'm sure he will thoroughly approve.'

'And because he approves you're happy to let them stay there?' Sasha guessed. So much for thinking that Gabriel was giving in to her.

Immediately Gabriel shook his head. 'I don't need the Professor's expertise to tell me that the boys are happy at school and learning well. And, despite what you may think, I don't need an intermediary to tell me that they are well adjusted and well cared for.'

'I wasn't suggesting that you do.' Sasha tussled with her conscience, and then admitted reluctantly, 'You're very good with them, Gabriel. You understand them much better than Carlo did.' As if to make up for her weakness, she added fiercely, 'But when they go back to school I'm going back with them. I shall look for a job, and I intend to find somewhere to live close to the school and my work. That was why I sold my jewellery, so that I could do that.'

'Fine,' Gabriel agreed cordially.

Why wasn't he objecting, frowning...arguing with her, pleading with her to stay with him? And why was she disappointed that he wasn't?

'When do we leave?'

'We?' That wasn't joyful relief she was feeling— even if it felt remarkably like it.

'Of course. I meant what I said, Sasha. From now on where you and the twins go, I go. I don't care how long it takes, or what I have to do to make it happen. I am going to prove to you that we have a future together.'

'That's impossible.'

'Nothing's impossible.'

CHAPTER TWELVE

SASHA smiled as she looked at the pretty Christmas tree decorating the sitting room of her small rented flat. It was Christmas Eve, the boys had already gone to bed, and once she had placed their stockings at the end of their beds she was going to do the same. It was gone ten, and tomorrow they were spending the day with Gabriel, at his insistence, since his house was so much bigger than her flat. And then after Christmas he was going to take the boys skiing, as his Christmas present to them. He had tried to persuade Sasha to go with them, but she'd refused.

True to his word, since the boys' return to school in September, Gabriel had mounted a determined assault on her refusal to accept that they could all have a future together. It had started with some clever by-play which had resulted in the boys insisting that Gabriel was included in whatever they were doing. Even their daily journey to and from school was conducted not via public transport, as Sasha had intended, but instead via the comfort of Gabriel's Bentley.

When she had objected Gabriel had looked innocent, and reminded her that as she had refused his offer to buy her a car she couldn't do the school run herself, and since he was now based in London, and living only a few doors away, it made sense for him to take the boys to school and then drop her off at her part-time job.

Sasha had managed not to retaliate. The power of money was indeed something to be reckoned with. While she had struggled to find rented accommodation, Gabriel had obviously had no difficulty at all in buying the elegant London townhouse in which he was currently living—all four floors of it. When she had suggested that it might be rather large for him, he had replied, 'Nonsense. It's the perfect size for us.'

He had courted her, flirted with her, teased her and become the boys' hero. And not once had he overstepped the mark and tried to take her to bed…and *that* disappointed her?

Well, it certainly left her feeling frustrated, Sasha admitted ruefully. Her heart and her body seemed to be filled with one long nagging ache for Gabriel. But was satisfying that ache enough to risk the boys' happiness for?

Gabriel was being very determined and very thorough about taking apart all her arguments against them being together. At half-term he had wanted to fly them all to the Caribbean, where his yacht was berthed, but Sasha had rejected this proposition. Instead of arguing with her, Gabriel had simply and very good-naturedly suggested that instead they spend the holiday in London, having a variety of days out.

'You take the boys on your own,' she had suggested, especially when she had learned that one of the boys' chosen destinations was Madame Tussauds.

'It won't be the same without you, Mum,' Nico had complained.

'No, it won't,' Gabriel had agreed softly. And so of course she had gone, and somehow Gabriel had managed to be always at her side as they moved through the exhibits—tantalisingly close, and yet out of reach.

He hadn't caused a fuss when she had refused an allowance. Nor had he attempted to put any pressure on her to change her mind. Her job didn't pay very well, but at least it was a job—even if some evenings she felt almost too tired to move. Luckily they were close enough to Hyde Park for Gabriel to take the boys there at the weekend to give her a break.

In the months since they had left Sardinia, Gabriel had both amazed and sometimes humbled her with the effort he had put into proving how willing he was to accept that he had to make his peace with his own past. She loved him more now than she had believed possible. But she still couldn't give in and agree to marry him. Trust was the foundation stone of the kind of relationship she longed to have with him. But right now there was a growing barrier to their mutual trust. It would be easy to feel sorry for herself, to wish she could simply place herself and her future in Gabriel's arms and be held there for ever. But she couldn't. Not now.

She was just about to take the boys' stockings into the cramped bedroom they shared—so very different from the large interconnecting rooms they had in Gabriel's house—when her mobile rang.

'It's me,' Gabriel announced unnecessarily when she answered it. 'I'm outside. Come and let me in. I didn't want to ring the bell in case I woke the boys.'

Unsteadily, Sasha went to open the door. Gabriel filled the small hallway, bringing with him the smell of the cold wet streets. He was, she saw, holding a thin but quite large rectangular gift-wrapped package.

'I've brought your Christmas present,' he said, indicating the parcel he was carrying without handing it over to her.

'You could have left it until tomorrow.'

'I wanted to give it to you tonight.'

Sasha shot him a wary look, wondering if he was being deliberately provocative or if she was guilty of hoping he might be. It was probably better not to put the issue to the test by informing him that she had been on her way to bed, she decided.

'Would you like a hot drink?' she asked him instead. Gabriel shook his head, and then held out his gift to her.

'Thank you—' she began.

'Why don't you open it now?'

It looked as though it might be a calendar, and that alone was enough to make her heart thump guiltily.

'Perhaps I will have that drink after all,' he told her. 'But I'll make it.' They were talking in the low-voiced whispers familiar to all parents. 'You've no idea just how much I want to kiss you right now and then take you home with me,' he told her huskily 'All of you. Oh, God, Sasha, I want that so badly—all of you with me, under my roof and my protection.'

She could hear the emotion in his voice and see it in his eyes. She felt as though something inside her was breaking apart. Her own eyes stung with tears she couldn't allow him to see. It would be so easy to give in now to regret and self-recrimination, to rail against what was happening. But she couldn't. Gabriel turned towards the kitchen.

'Gabriel.' He stopped to look back at her. This wasn't the way she had planned to tell him, but he was waiting and looking at her, so she took a deep breath.

'I know this isn't what you want to hear, but I can't marry you.'

Gabriel shook his head. 'Open your present. We'll talk about it tomorrow.'

He disappeared into the kitchen, leaving her staring unseeingly down at her gift. It was no use. She would have to tell him.

He came back, carrying two mugs. 'I've made herbal tea for you instead of coffee—is that okay?'

'Yes. Gabriel, there's something I have to tell you.'

'No, you don't. I already know.'

'Gabriel—'

'You're pregnant. You conceived when we made love in Sardinia, and you've been worrying yourself sick about what to do ever since your visit to the doctor.'

Sasha sat down. 'You know? But how? I haven't…'

He came over to her. 'I love you. I know you. This time I recognised the signs. You've been eating avocados with every meal; I thought in the Caribbean it was just because you liked them, but this time I guessed the real reason. You've looked pale and washed out every morning, the boys have mentioned that you've been sick, you've been wearing concealing clothes and besides…' He looked down at her and then away.

'Besides, what?'

'Well, I didn't plan to score a bullseye twice over, and getting you pregnant certainly wasn't something I intended to happen when I omitted to take any precautions, but I admit the thought did occur to me that if you *had* conceived again it could make our passage down the aisle swifter and easier. But then, when you didn't tell me…'

Sasha took a deep breath. 'You sound very sure that it's yours.'

Gabriel looked at her. 'Of course it's mine,' he said quietly, and then reached for her hands, drawing her up onto her feet and into his arms before she could resist. With one hand behind her head and the other pressed gently against the carefully hidden swell of her belly, he said softly, 'How could it possibly not be mine? I love you, and you are the most loyal, faithful, trustworthy and honest person I know. Had there been someone else you would have told me, and you would not have gone to bed with me. It may have taken me far too long to realise that, but I can assure you that I know it now. I love you,' he repeated. 'We have two wonderful sons and now, between us, we've created another new life.'

Sasha looked up at him. A mistake which immediately led to him bending his head and slowly and thoroughly kissing her.

It was impossible not to kiss him back. Impossible too to deny the tell-tale lurch of her heart and the fierce, hungry tension gripping her body. Automatically she leaned into him, shivering in delicious anticipatory pleasure.

'Why didn't you want to tell me?' His question brought her back down to earth.

'It was afraid to,' she admitted. 'I knew that if you found out you'd insist on us getting married…'

'And you don't want that?'

'What I don't want—ever—is for you to feel that I

married you because of this baby,' she answered him fiercely. 'You don't know how often I've wished that I hadn't held back, that I'd told you when you asked me in Sardinia that I loved you, that I'd agreed then to marry you, before I knew about this. That way at least you would never have been able to throw it back in my face—'

'Stop right there. There is no way I will ever throw anything back in your face, Sasha. I've learned my lesson. And I've made my peace with my ghosts. Open your present—please.'

She was trembling so much it seemed to take her for ever to remove the ribbon and then the wrapping paper. Beneath it was a layer of bubblewrap, and beneath that was...

Sasha stared at what she was holding, glanced up at Gabriel, and then looked back down at his gift.

'How...?' she began, and then stopped as tears spilled down her face.

What she was holding in her hands wasn't just a painting, it was her future—their future—depicted by an artist: two boys, a man and a woman, and in the woman's arms a baby.

'I managed to work out part of what you might be thinking while I was waiting for you to tell me about the baby. I thought that maybe this would tell you how I felt about it—about you, about all of us. I was going to tell the artist to put the baby in pink, but I decided that might be tempting fate,' he added ruefully.

'Gabriel.'

There was no holding back when she went into his arms. Not the love in her heart nor the joy in her eyes.

When he kissed her she felt the fine tremor in his body and knew that it betrayed the intensity of his own emotion. He kissed her fiercely and passionately, claiming her as his. And then, very slowly and tenderly, she kissed him. When he started to ease her away, she tensed at first, and then relaxed, trading smiles with him when the door opened to admit the twins, whose imminent arrival he had obviously heard before her.

'You were kissing,' Sam accused them both sternly.

'Yes,' Nico agreed. The twins looked at one another. 'Does that mean that you're going to get married and we can go and live at Dad's house, Mum?'

'You needn't have come to collect us. You only live three streets away—we could have walked,' Sasha protested in the flurry of the boys putting on their jackets and showing Gabriel what they had found in their stockings.

'If you were really concerned about getting me out of bed early on Christmas morning you wouldn't have let me stay with you last night,' Gabriel teased her in a discreet whisper. 'Do you realise it was four o'clock when you woke me up and sent me home?'

'Do you realise that the boys were up at five?' She laughed as Gabriel ushered them out to his car.

'Did you put the turkey in the oven, like I said?' Sasha asked.

'Of course. And I turned the oven on,' Gabriel assured her, winking at the twins as he pulled away from the kerb.

Sasha nodded her head.

The house that Gabriel had bought was enough to make anyone drool with envy, Sasha admitted as she stood in front of the fire in the well-proportioned drawing room.

At Gabriel's insistence she and the twins had decorated the tree, and although its somewhat homely decorations looked out of place in the elegant room, they still brought a sheen of emotional tears to Sasha's eyes.

Her anxious inspection of the turkey confirmed that Gabriel had followed her instructions to the letter.

It had been agreed that the boys would open their presents here at Gabriel's, and now, as she listened to their excited cries of delight as they demolished hours of careful wrapping on her part, she exchanged amused looks with Gabriel.

'With any luck they'll be so tired they'll want to go to bed early tonight.'

Sasha laughed. 'I shouldn't count on it. If the boys don't wear you out wanting to ride their new bikes in the park then their sister will certainly exhaust me.'

'Isn't it time you looked at the turkey,' Gabriel suggested meaningfully.

Sasha got up, checking on the boys before heading for the kitchen, with Gabriel following her.

'When I imagined formally proposing to you it certainly wasn't in a kitchen,' he told her, as he closed the door behind them and then leaned firmly on it, taking her in his arms. 'I love you so very much. I hope you know that now. These last few months have been purgatory. Marry me, Sasha, and make me the happiest man on earth.'

'Yes,' she said. 'Yes. Yes, yes...'

He bent his head to kiss her, and then suddenly stopped to say accusingly, 'You said our *daughter*!'

Sasha laughed. 'Well, when I had my scan they said they thought it was a girl. Just as well, really,' she added.

'Why?'

She gave him a small smile. 'You didn't look carefully enough at the painting.' When he frowned, her smile broadened. 'The baby is wearing white knitted boots threaded with pink ribbon.'

EPILOGUE

Nine months later

THEY had decided not to hold the christening at the London church where they had been married shortly after Christmas, but here in Sardinia instead. The words of the service, spoken both in English and Italian, had been simple but well-chosen, and now they were back at the newly converted house, where five-month-old Celestine was the centre of attention, the guests cooing over her while the twins looked on with brotherly watchfulness.

'She's chewing her sleeve again,' Nico warned Sasha. 'I think she might be hungry.'

'No, she's not hungry. She's teething,' Sam corrected him scornfully. 'She wants to come out. She doesn't like lying there doing nothing, and it's my turn to hold her.'

'No, it's not. It's mine.'

'Actually, it's my turn,' Gabriel told them both firmly, deftly removing his daughter from her basket and expertly cradling her against his shoulder in a way that still left him free to slip his other arm around the boys.

Watching them, Sasha couldn't resist reaching for her camera.

'She's going to wind all three of you around her little finger,' she warned, as she smiled lovingly at her daughter and discreetly slid her hand down Gabriel's shirt-clad back.

'If that's an invitation for later, then the answer is yes,' he murmured softly. 'Pity we've got such a houseful, though…'

'There's always the beach,' she reminded him teasingly as she leaned closer for his kiss.

Life could not give him another gift to rival that which he now held within his arms, Gabriel thought to himself: Sasha, the twins, and now their daughter.

'I think when he made me the boys' guardian Carlo wanted this to happen and for us to be together,' he told Sasha quietly.

'Yes,' she agreed. 'He knew how much I loved you, and perhaps he sensed that you loved me—even before you acknowledged it yourself.'

'I can acknowledge it now,' he said, looking from his daughter and the twins to Sasha. He bent to kiss her. 'Now and for ever, Sasha.'

TOP THREE ROMANTIC SUMMER EVENTS IN SARDINIA

If a sizzling Sardinian affair like Gabriel and Sasha's takes your fancy, why not head off to the island for some romantic summer fun of your own? Here are three red-hot Sardinian summer events guaranteed to get your pulse racing.

- **The Cherry Festival:** Every June the beautiful town of Burcei bursts into bloom with an abundant cherry crop and each year the locals host several fun events throughout the month to celebrate this cheeky fruit. Gorgeous and tasty, the cherry festival provides the perfect excuse to paint the town red.

- **Is Fassonis:** The first Sunday in August brings with it the Is Fassonis regatta in Santa Guista – a fabulous day of waterside fun and an excellent place to bag your own smouldering Sardinian, as you watch local men sail the traditional boats they have built.

- **The Candle Holders:** The town of Sassari celebrates the festival of the candle holders in mid-August, where giant candles, supported by wooden structures, are wheeled from the town square to the church, creating a magical mood and the perfect atmosphere for love.

Million-Dollar
Love-Child

SARAH MORGAN

SARAH MORGAN'S GUIDE TO ROMANCE IN BRAZIL

An exotic, dazzling land of sensuous rhythms, a dangerously handsome billionaire, a beautiful woman in a desperate race to protect her child, and a relationship so explosive that it almost destroyed itself first time around – this is romance Brazilian style, with emotions at flashpoint, passions running at full power and a strong, macho hero determined to seduce the only woman he has ever loved back into his bed. To achieve his aim he'll use every skill he knows, without guilt or apology, and he'll use every charm that his exotic country has to offer. And nowhere has more to offer than Brazil.

Where more seductive for a setting than the ritzy, glitzy city of Rio de Janeiro? Nestled between lush mountains and sparkling sea, this is the home of the samba, breathtaking beaches and dramatic scenery. Lovers can feast on the world-famous view from the top of the Corcovado mountain, they can watch the sunset on Copacabana beach, or they can simply soak up the energy and passion that pulses through the South American people.

My hero was brought up on the streets of this vibrant city. He's the hunter, not the hunted. He's hot to handle, but when tamed he'll be the ultimate lover. He's strong, yes, and powerful; but he'll use that power to protect his woman. He's super-rich – but he would sacrifice it all for her. He demands everything from her and, in turn, gives everything to her. Many have wanted his love, but love is a gift he has only ever given to only one woman.

That's romance, the Brazilian way.

To Kim Young,
for being a great friend and fantastic editor.
Thank you.

CHAPTER ONE

SHE'D never known fear like it.

Breathing so rapidly that she felt light-headed, Kimberley stood in the imposing glass-walled boardroom on the executive floor of Santoro Investments, staring down at the throbbing, vibrant streets of Rio de Janeiro.

The waiting was torture.

Everything rested on the outcome of this visit—*everything*—and the knowledge made her legs weaken and her insides knot with vicious tension.

It was ironic, she thought helplessly, that the only person who could help her now was the one man she'd sworn never to see again.

Forcing herself to breathe steadily, she closed her eyes for a moment and tried to modify her expectations. He'd probably refuse to see her.

People didn't just arrive unannounced and gain access to a man like Luc Santoro.

She was only sitting here now because his personal assistant had taken pity on her. Stammering out her request to see him, Kimberley had been so pale and anxious that the older woman had become quite concerned and had insisted that she should sit and wait in the privacy of the air-conditioned boardroom. Having brought her a large glass of water, the assistant had given her a smile and assured her that Mr Santoro really wasn't as dangerous as his reputation suggested.

But Kimberley knew differently. Luc Santoro wasn't just dangerous, he was lethal and she knew that it was going to take more than water to make her face the man on the other side of that door.

What was she going to say?

How was she going to tell him?

Where was she going to start?

She couldn't appeal to his sense of decency or his conscience because he possessed neither. Helping others wasn't high on his agenda. He *used* people and, more especially, he used women. She knew that better than anyone. Pain ripped through her as she remembered just how badly he'd treated her. He was a ruthless, self-seeking billionaire with only one focus in his life. The pursuit of pleasure.

And for a short, blissful time, she'd been his pleasure.

Her heart felt like a heavy weight in her chest. Looking back on it now, she couldn't believe how naïve she'd been. *How trusting.* As an idealistic, romantic eighteen-year-old, she'd been willing and eager to share every single part of herself with him. She'd held nothing back because she'd seen no reason to hold anything back. He'd been the one. Her everything. *And she'd been his nothing.*

She curled her fingers into her palms and reminded herself that the objective of today was not to rehash the past. She was going to have to put aside the memory of the pain, the panic and the bone-deep humiliation she'd suffered as a result of his cruel and careless rejection.

None of that mattered now.

There was only one thing that mattered to her, *only one person*, and for the sake of that person she was going to bite her tongue, smile, beg or do whatever it took to ingratiate herself with Luc Santoro—because there was no way she was leaving Brazil without the money she needed.

It was a matter of life and death.

She paced the length of the room, trying to formulate some sort of plan in her mind, trying to work out a reasonable way to ask for five million dollars from a man who had absolutely no feelings for her.

How was she going to tackle the subject?

How was she going to tell him that she was in serious trouble?

And how could she make him care?

She felt a shaft of pure panic and then the door opened and he strolled into the room unannounced, the sun glinting on his glossy black hair, his face hard, handsome and unsmiling.

And Kimberley realised that she was in even more trouble than she'd previously thought.

She looked like a baby deer caught in an ambush.

Without revealing any of his thoughts, Luc surveyed the slender, impossibly beautiful redhead who stood shivering and pale on the far side of his boardroom.

She looked so frightened that he almost found it possible to feel sorry for her. Except that he knew too much about her.

And if he were in her position, he'd be shaking, too.

She had one hell of a nerve, coming here!

Seven years.

He hadn't seen Kimberley Townsend for seven years and *still* she had the ability to seriously disturb his day.

Endless legs, silken hair, soft mouth and a wide, trusting smile—

For a time she'd truly had him fooled with that loving, giving, generous act that she'd perfected. Accustomed to being with women who were as sophisticated and calculating as

himself, he'd been charmed and captivated by Kimberley's
innocence, openness and her almost childlike honesty.

It was the first and only occasion in his adult life when he'd
made a serious error of judgement.

She was a greedy little gold-digger.

He knew that now. And she knew that he knew.

So what could possibly have possessed her to throw herself in his path again?

She was either very brave or very, *very* stupid. He strolled
towards her, watching her flinch and tremble and decided that
she didn't look particularly brave.

Which just left stupid.

Or desperate?

Kimberley stood with her back to the wall and wondered
how she could have forgotten the impact that Luciano Santoro
had on women. *How could she ever have thought she could
hold a man like him?*

Time had somehow dimmed the memory and the reality
was enough to stun her into a temporary silence.

She was tall but he was taller. His shoulders were broad,
his physique lithe and athletic and his dark, dangerous looks
alone were enough to make a woman forget her own name.
The truth was that, even among a race renowned for handsome men, Luc stood out from the crowd.

She stared at him with almost agonizing awareness as he
strolled towards her, her eyes sliding over the glossy blue-
black hair, the high cheekbones, those thick, thick lashes that
shielded brooding, night-dark eyes and down to the darkened jaw of a man who seemed to embody everything it
meant to be masculine. He was dressed formally in standard
business attire but even the tailored perfection of his dark
suit couldn't entirely disguise a nature that bordered on the
very edges of civilised. Although he moved in a conventional

world, Luc could never be described as 'safe' and it was that subtle hint of danger that added to his almost overwhelming appeal.

His attraction to the opposite sex was as powerful as it was predictable and she'd proved herself to be as susceptible as the rest when it came to his particular brand of lethal charm.

Feeling her heart pound against her chest, she wondered whether she'd been mad to come here.

She didn't move in his league and she never had. They played by a completely different set of rules.

And then she reminded herself firmly that she wasn't here for herself. Given the choice she never would have come near Luc again. But he was her only hope.

'Luciano.'

His eyes mocked her in that lazy, almost bored way that she used to find both aggravating and seductive. 'Very formal. You used to call me Luc.'

He spoke with a cultured male drawl that held just a hint of the dark and dangerous. The staggeringly successful international businessman mingled with the raw, rough boy from the streets.

There was enough of the hard and the tough and the ruthless in him to make her shiver. Of course he was tough and ruthless, she reasoned, trying to control the exaggerated response of her trembling body. Rumour had it that he'd dragged himself from the streets of Rio before building one of the biggest multinational businesses in the world.

'That's in the past.' And she didn't want to remember the past. Didn't want to remember the times she'd cried out his name as he'd shown her yet another way to paradise.

He raised an eyebrow and from the look in his dark eyes she knew that he was experiencing the same memories. The temperature in the room rose by several degrees and the air began to crackle and hum. 'And is that what this meeting is about? The past? You want closure? You have come to beg forgiveness and repay the money you stole?'

It was typical of him that the first thing he mentioned was the money.

For a moment her courage faltered.

'I know it was wrong to use your credit cards—' she licked her lips '—but I had a good reason—' She broke off and the carefully prepared speech that she'd rehearsed and rehearsed in her head dissolved into nothing and suddenly she couldn't think how on earth she was going to say what needed to be said.

Now, she urged herself frantically, *tell him now!*

But somehow the right words just wouldn't come.

'You *did* give me the cards—'

'One of the perks of being with me,' Luc said silkily, 'but when you spent the money, you were no longer with me. I have to congratulate you. I thought that no woman had the ability to surprise me—' he paced around her, his voice a soft, lethal drawl '—and yet you did just that. During our relationship you spent nothing. You showed no interest in my money. At the time I thought you were unique amongst your sex. I found your lack of interest in material things particularly endearing.' His tone hardened. 'Now I see that you were in fact just clever. Very clever. You held back on your spending but once you realised that the relationship was over, you showed your true colours.'

Kimberley's mouth fell open in genuine amazement. What on earth he implying? It was *definitely* time to tell him the truth. 'I can explain where the money went—' She braced herself for the ultimate confession but he gave a dismissive shrug that indicated nothing short of total indifference.

'If there is one occupation more boring than watching a woman shop, it's hearing about it after the event.' Luc's tone was bored. 'I have absolutely no interest in the finer details of feminine indulgence.'

'Is that what you think it was?' Kimberley stared at him, aghast. 'You think I spent your money in some sort of childish female tantrum?'

'So you cheered yourself up with some new shoes and handbags.' He gave a sardonic smile. 'It is typically female behaviour. I can assure you I'm no stranger to the perceived benefits of retail therapy.'

Kimberley gasped. 'You are unbelievably insensitive!' Her voice rang with passion, anger and pain and her carefully planned speech flew out of her brain. He thought she'd been *shopping?* 'Shopping was the last thing on my mind! This was *not* retail therapy.' Her whole body trembled with indignation. 'This was *survival*. I needed the money to survive because I gave up everything to be with you. *Everything*. I gave up my job, my flat—*I moved in with you*. It was what you demanded.'

His gaze was cool. 'I don't recall a significant degree of protest on your part.'

She tilted her head back and struggled with her emotions. 'I was in love with you, Luc.' Her voice cracked and she paused for just long enough to regain control. 'I was *so* in love with you that being together was the only thing in my life that made sense. I couldn't see further than what we shared. I certainly couldn't imagine a time when we wouldn't be together.'

'Women do have a tendency to hear wedding bells when they're around me,' he observed dryly. 'In fact I would say, the larger the wallet, the louder the bells.'

'I'm not talking about marriage. I didn't *care* about marriage. I just cared about *you*.'

A muscle flickered in his lean jaw and his eyes hardened. 'Obviously you were planning for the long term.'

It took her a moment to understand the implication of his words. 'You're suggesting it was an act?' She gave a tiny laugh of disbelief and lifted a hand to her throat. Beneath the tips of her fingers she felt her pulse beating rapidly. 'You think I was pretending?'

'You were very convincing,' Luc conceded after a moment's reflection, 'but then the stakes were high, were they not? The prospect of landing a billionaire is often sufficient to produce the most commendable acting skills in a woman.'

Kimberley stared at him.

How could she ever have been foolish enough to give her love to this man? Was her judgement really that bad?

Tears clogged her throat. 'I don't consider you a prize, Luc,' she choked. 'In fact I consider you to be the biggest mistake of my life.'

'Of course you do.' He spread lean bronzed hands and gave a sympathetic smile, but his eyes were hard as flint. 'I can understand that you'd be kicking yourself for letting me slip through your fingers. All I can say is, better luck with the next guy.'

She stared into his cold, handsome face and suddenly she just wanted to sob and sob. 'You deserve to be alone in life, Luc,' she said flatly, battling not to let the emotion show on her face, 'and every woman with a grain of sense is going to let you slip right through her fingers. Given the chance, I'd drop you head first on to a tiled floor from a great height.'

He smiled an arrogant, all-male smile that reflected his unshakeable self-confidence. 'We both know you couldn't get enough of me.'

She gasped, utterly humiliated by the picture he painted. 'That was before I knew what an unfeeling, cold-hearted bastard you were!' She broke off in horror, *appalled* by her rudeness and uncharacteristic loss of control. What had come over her? 'I—I'm sorry, that was unforgivable—'

'Don't apologise for showing your true colours.' Far from being offended, he looked mildly amused. 'Believe it or not,

I prefer honesty in a woman. It saves all sorts of misunder-standing.'

She lifted a hand to her forehead in an attempt to relieve the ache between her temples.

It had been so hard for her to come here. So hard to brace herself to tell him the things that he needed to know. And so far none of it had gone as planned.

She had things that had to be said and she just didn't know how to say them. Instead of talking about the present, they were back in the past and that was the one place she didn't want to be. Unless she could use the past to remind him of what they'd once shared—

'You cared, Luc,' she said softly, her hands dropping to her sides in a helpless gesture. 'I *know* you cared. I felt it.'

She appealed to the man that she'd once believed him to be.

'I was very turned on by the fact I was your first lover,' he agreed in a smooth tone. 'In fact I was totally knocked out by the novelty of the experience. Naturally I was keen for you to enjoy it too. You were very shy and it was in both our in-terests for you to be relaxed. I did what needed to be done and said what needed to be said.'

Her cheeks flamed with embarrassment. In other words he was so experienced with women that he knew exactly which buttons to press. In her case he'd sensed that she needed closeness and affection. *It hadn't meant anything to him.*

'So you're saying it was all an act?' The pain inside her blossomed. 'Being loving and gentle was just another of your many seduction methods?'

He shrugged as if he could see no problem with that. 'I didn't hear you complaining.'

She closed her eyes. How could she have been so gullible? Yes, she'd been a virgin but that was no excuse for bald stupidity. Sixteen years of living with a man like her father should have taught her everything she needed to know about men. He'd moved from one woman to another, never making a commitment, never giving anything. Just using. Using and discarding. Her mother had walked out just after Kimberley's fourth birthday and from that moment on she had a series of 'Aunties', women who came into her father's life and then left with a volley of shouts and jealous accusations. Kimberley had promised herself that she was never, *ever* going to let a man treat her the way her father treated women. She was going to find one man and she was going to love him.

And then she'd met Luc and for a short, crazy period of time she'd thought he was that man. She'd ignored his reputation with women, ignored any similarities to her father, ignored her promise to herself.

She'd broken all her own rules.

And she'd paid the price.

'What did I ever do to make you treat me so cruelly?' Suddenly she needed to understand. Wanted to know what had gone wrong—how she could have made such an enormous mistake. 'Why did you need other women?'

'I've never been a one woman kind of guy,' he admitted without a trace of apology or regret, 'and you're all pretty much the same, as you went on to prove with your truly awesome spending spree.'

She flinched. This would be a perfect time to confess. To tell him exactly *why* she'd needed the money so badly. She took a deep breath and braced herself for the truth. 'I spent your money because I needed it for something very important,' she said hesitantly, 'and before I tell you exactly what, I want you to know that I *did* try and talk to you at the time but you wouldn't see me, and—'

'Is this conversation going anywhere?' He glanced at his watch in a gesture of supreme boredom. 'I've already told you that your spending habits don't interest me. And if you'd needed funds then maybe you should have tapped your other lover for the cash.'

She gasped. 'I didn't *have* other lovers. You *know* I didn't.' There'd only ever been him. Just him.

'I don't know anything of the kind.' His eyes hardened. 'On two occasions I returned home to be told that you were "out".'

'Because I was tired of lying in our bed waiting for you to come home from some other woman's arms!' She exploded with exasperation, determined to defend herself. 'Yes, I went out! And you just couldn't stand that, could you? And why not? Because you *always* have to be the one in control.'

'It wasn't about control.' His gaze simmered, dark with all the volatility of his exotic heritage. 'You didn't need to leave. You were *mine*.'

And he thought that wasn't about control?

'You make me sound like a possession!' Her voice rang with pain and frustration. She was *trying* to say what needed to be said but each time she tried to talk about the present they seemed to end up back in the past. 'You treat every woman like a possession! To be used and discarded when you're had enough! That's why our relationship never would have worked. You're ruthless, self-seeking and totally without morals or thought for other people. You expected me to lie there and wait for you to finish partying and come home!'

'Instead of which, you decided to expand your sexual horizons,' he said coldly and she resisted the temptation to leap at him and claw at his handsome face.

How could such an intelligent, successful man be so dense about women? He couldn't see past the end of his nose.

'You went out, so I went out.' Wisps of hair floated across her face and she brushed them away with an impatient hand. 'What was I supposed to do when you weren't there?'

'You were supposed to get some rest,' he delivered in silky tones, 'and wait for me to come home.'

Neanderthal man. She was expected to wait in the cave for the hunter to return.

Exasperated beyond belief, she resisted the temptation to walk out and slam the door. 'This is the twenty-first century, Luc! Women vote. They run companies. They decide their own social lives.'

'And they cheat on their partners.' He gave a sardonic lift of his brows. 'Progress, indeed.'

'I did *not* cheat!' She stared at him in outrage, wondering how such an intelligent man could be so dense when it came to relationships. *She'd loved him so much.* 'You were the one photographed in a restaurant with another woman. Clearly I wasn't enough for you.' She gave a casual shrug and tried to keep the pain out of her voice. 'Naturally I assumed that if you were out seeing other people then I could do the same. But I did not cheat!'

'I don't want the details.'

They were closing in on each other. A step here, a slight movement there.

'Well, perhaps you should, instead of jumping to conclusions,' she suggested shakily, 'and if a sin was committed then it was yours, Luc. I was eighteen years old and yet you seduced me without even a flicker of conscience. And then you moved on without a flicker of conscience. Tell me—did you give it any thought? Before you took my virginity and wrecked my life, *did you give it any thought?*'

His dark gaze swept over her with naked incredulity. 'You have been back in my life for five minutes and already you are snapping and snarling and hurling accusations. You were only too willing to be seduced, my flame-haired temptress, but if you've forgotten that fact then I'm happy to jog your memory.' Without warning he closed lean brown fingers around her wrist and jerked her hard against him. The connection was immediate and powerful.

'That first night, in the back of my car, when you wrapped that amazing body of yours around mine—' his voice was a low, dangerous purr and the warmth of his breath teased her mouth '—was that not an invitation?'

The air around them crackled and sparked with tension.

She tugged at her wrist but he held her easily and she remembered just how much she'd loved that about him. His strength. His vibrant, undiluted masculinity. In fact she'd positively relished the differences between them. His dark male power to her feminine softness. *Her good to his very, very bad.*

He was *so* strong and she'd always felt incredibly safe when she was with him. At the beginning that had been part of the attraction. Particularly that first night, as he'd just reminded her. 'I'd been attacked. I was frightened—'

And he'd rescued her. Using street fighting skills that didn't go with the sleek dinner jacket he'd been wearing, he'd taken on six men and had extracted her with apparently very little damage to himself. As a tactic designed to impress a woman, it had proved a winner.

'So you wanted comfort.' His grip on her wrist tightened. 'So when you slid on to my lap and begged me to kiss you, was that not an invitation? Or was that comfort too?'

Hot colour of mortification flooded her smooth cheeks. 'I don't know what happened to me that night—'

She'd taken one look at him and suddenly believed in fairy tales. Knights. Dragons. Maidens in distress. *He was the one.* Or so she'd thought—

'You discovered your true self,' he said roughly. 'That's what happened. So don't accuse me of seducing you when we both know that I only took what you freely offered. You were hot for me and you stayed hot—'

'I was innocent—'

His breath warmed her mouth and he gave a slow, sexy smile that made her heart thud hard against her chest. 'You were desperate.'

He was going to kiss her.

She recognised the signs, saw the darkening of his eyes and the lowering of those thick, thick lashes as his heated gaze swept her flushed face.

The tension throbbed and pulsed between them and then suddenly he released her with a soft curse and took a step backwards.

'So why are you here?' His tone was suddenly icy cold, and there was anger in the glint of his dark eyes. 'You wish to reminisce? You are hoping for a repeat performance, perhaps? If so, you should probably know that women only get one chance in my bed and you blew it.'

A repeat performance?

Erotic memories flashed through her brain and she took a step backwards, as if to escape from them. 'Let's get this straight.' Despite all her best efforts, her voice shook slightly. *'Nothing* would induce me to climb back into your bed, Luc. Nothing. That was one life experience I have no intention of repeating. Ever. I'm not that stupid.'

He stilled and a look of masculine speculation flickered across his handsome face. 'Is that a fact?'

Too late she realised that a man like Luc would probably consider that a challenge. And he was a man who loved a challenge.

She looked at him helplessly, wondering how on earth the conversation had developed into this. For some reason they were right back where they'd left off seven years before and it wasn't what she'd planned.

She'd intended to be cool and businesslike and to avoid anything remotely personal. Instead of which, their verbal exchange had so far been entirely personal.

And still she hadn't told him what she needed to tell him. Still she hadn't said what needed to be said.

He prowled around her slowly and a slightly mocking smile touched his firm mouth. 'Still so much passion, Kimberley, and still trying to hold it in check and pretend it doesn't exist. That it isn't a part of you and yet how could your nature be anything else?' He brushed a hand over her hair with a mocking smile. 'Never get involved with a woman who has hair the colour of dragon's breath.'

Kimberley lifted her chin and her green eyes flashed. 'And never get involved with a man who has an ego the size of Brazil.'

He laughed. 'Ours was never the most tranquil of relationships, was it *meu amorzinho?*'

Meu amorzinho. He'd always called her that and she'd loved hearing him speak in his native language. It had seemed so much more exotic than the English translation, 'my little love'.

His unexpected laughter released some of the throbbing tension in the room and she felt the colour flood into her face as she remembered, too late, that she'd promised herself she wasn't going to fight with him. She couldn't afford to fight with him. 'We both need to forget the past.' Determined not to let him unsettle her, she took a deep breath and tried to find the tranquillity that usually came naturally to her. 'Both of us have moved on. I'm not the same person any more.'

'You're exactly the same person, Kimberley.' He strolled around her, like a jungle animal assessing its prey. 'Inside, people never really change. It's just the packaging that's different. The way they present themselves to the world.'

Before she could guess his intention, he lifted a lean bronze hand and in a deft, skilful movement removed the clip from her hair.

She gasped a protest and clutched at the fiery mass that tumbled over her shoulders. 'What do you think you're doing?'

'Altering the packaging. Reminding you who you really are under the costume you're wearing.' His burning gaze slid lazily down her body. 'You come in here, suitably dressed to teach a class of schoolchildren or sort books in a library, that hot red hair all twisted away and tamed. On the outside you are all buttoned up and locked away, yet we both know what sort of person you are on the inside.' His dark eyes fixed on hers and his voice was rich and seductive. 'Passionate. Wild.'

His tongue rolled over the words, his accent more pronounced than usual, and she felt her stomach flip over and her knees weaken.

'You're wrong! That's not who I am! You have no idea who I am.' Despite her promise to herself that she'd remain cool, she couldn't hold back the emotion. 'Did you really think I'd be the same pathetic little girl you seduced all those years ago? Do you really think I haven't changed?'

Despite her heated denials, she felt a flash of sexual awareness that appalled her and she squashed it down with grim determination.

She wasn't going to let him do this to her again. She wasn't going to feel anything.

She'd come here to tell him something she should have told him seven years ago, not to resurrect feelings that she'd taken years to bury.

'You weren't pathetic and neither,' he said softly, touching a curl of fiery red hair, 'did I seduce you, determined though you seem to be to believe that. Our passion was as mutual as it was hot, *meu amorzinho*. You were with me all the way.' He said the words 'all the way' with a smooth, erotic emphasis that started a slow burn deep within her pelvis. 'The only difference between us was that you were ashamed of how you felt. I assumed that maturity would allow you to embrace your passionate nature instead of rejecting it.'

To her horror she felt her body start to melt and her breathing grow shallow and she shrank away from him, desperate to stop the reaction.

How?

How, after all these years and all the thinking time she'd had, could she still react to this man?

Did she never learn?

And then she remembered that she *had* learned. The hard way. And it didn't matter how her body responded to this man, this time her brain was in charge. She was older and more experienced and well able to ignore the insidious curl of sexual desire deep in her pelvis.

'This isn't what I came here for.' She lifted a hand to her hair and smoothed it away from her face. 'What happened between you and me isn't important.'

'So you keep saying. So what *is* important enough to bring you all the way back to Rio de Janeiro when you left and swore never to return, I wonder? Our golden beaches? Our dramatic mountains?' His rich accent rolled over the words. 'The addictive beat of the samba? I recall that evening that we danced on my terrace...'

He flicked memories in front of her like a slide show and she looked away for a moment, forcing herself to focus on something bland and inanimate, trying to dilute the disturbing images in her head. The chair drew the full force of her gaze while she composed herself and plucked up the courage to say what she had to say.

'I want us to stop talking about the past.' She paused for a moment and felt her knees turn to liquid. It was now. It had to be now. 'I'm here because—' Her voice cracked and she licked dry lips and tried again. 'I'm trying to tell you—w-we had a son together, Luc, and he's now six years old.' Her heart pounded and her body trembled. 'He's six years old and his life is in danger. I'm here because I need your help. I've no one else to turn to.'

CHAPTER TWO

How could silence seem so loud?

Was he ever going to speak?

Relief that she'd finally told him mingled with apprehension. What was he going to say? How was he going to react to the sudden discovery that he was a father?

'Well, that's inventive.' His tone was flat and he sprawled in the nearest chair, his eyes veiled as he watched her, always the one in control, always the one calling the shots. 'You certainly know how to keep a guy on his toes. I never know what you're going to come up with next.'

Kimberley blinked, totally taken aback.

He didn't believe her?

She'd prepared herself for anger and recrimination. She'd braced herself to be on the receiving end of his hot Brazilian temper. She'd been prepared to explain why she hadn't told him seven years before. But it hadn't once crossed her mind that he might not believe her.

'You seriously think I'd joke about something like that?'

He gave a casual shrug. 'I admit it's in pretty poor taste, but some women will stoop to just about anything to get a man to fork out. And I presume that's what you want? More money?'

It was exactly what she wanted but not for any of the reasons he seemed to be implying.

Her mouth opened and shut and she swallowed hard, totally out of her depth. She hadn't even entertained the possibility that he wouldn't believe her and she honestly didn't know what to say next. She'd geared herself up for this moment and it wasn't going according to her script.

'*Why* wouldn't you believe me?'

'Possibly because women don't suddenly turn up after seven years of silence and announce that they're pregnant.'

'I didn't say I was p-pregnant,' she stammered, appalled and frustrated that he refused to take her seriously. 'I told you, he's *six*. He was born precisely forty weeks after we had—after you—' She broke off, blushing furiously, and his gaze dropped to her mouth, lingered and then lifted again.

'After I had my wicked way with you? You're so repressed you can't even bring yourself to say the word "sex".' His dark eyes mocked her gently and she bit her lip, wishing she was more sophisticated—better equipped to deal with this sort of situation. Verbal sparring wasn't her forte and yet she was dealing with a master.

He'd wronged her and yet suddenly she felt as though she should be apologising. 'You're probably wondering why I didn't tell you this before—'

'The thought had crossed my mind.'

'You threw me out, Luc,' she reminded him in a shaky voice, 'and you refused to see me or take my calls. You treated me *abominably*.'

'Relationships end every day of the week,' he drawled in a tone of total indifference. 'Stop being so dramatic.'

'*I was pregnant!*' She rose to her feet, shaking with emotion, goaded into action by his total lack of remorse. 'I decided that you ought to know about your child. I tried to tell you so many times but you cut me out of your life. *And you hurt me.* You hurt me so badly that I decided that no child of mine was going to have you as a father. And *that's* why I didn't tell you.' She broke off, waiting for an angry reaction on his part, waiting for him to storm and rant that she hadn't told him sooner.

Instead he raised an eyebrow expectantly. 'Seven years and this is the best you can come up with?'

She stared at him blankly, unable to comprehend his callous indifference. 'Do you think I made that decision lightly? *Have you any idea what making a decision like that does to a person?* I felt screwed up with guilt, Luc! I was depriving my son of a father and I knew that one day I'd have to answer to him for that.' She broke off and dragged a shuddering breath into her starving lungs. 'I have felt guilty every single day for the last seven years. *Every single day.*'

'Yes, well, that's another woman thing—guilt,' Luc said helpfully, 'and I suppose that all this *guilt* suddenly overwhelmed you and that's why you've suddenly decided to share your joyous news with me?'

She shook her head. 'I can't *believe* you're behaving like this. Do you *know* how hard it was for me to come here today? *Have you any idea?*' He was even more unfeeling than she'd believed possible. How could she feel guilt? She should be *proud* that she'd protected her son from this man. But the time for protection had passed and, unfortunately for everyone, she now needed his help. She couldn't afford the luxury of cutting him out of her life. 'What do I have to do to prove that I'm telling the truth?'

Luc turned his head and glanced towards the door expectantly. 'Produce him.' He lifted broad shoulders in a careless shrug. 'That should do the trick.'

She looked at him in disbelief. 'You seriously think I'd drag a six-year-old all the way to Brazil to meet a man who doesn't even know he's a father? This is a huge thing, Luc. We need to discuss how we're going to handle it. How we're going to tell him. It needs to be a joint decision.'

There was a sardonic gleam in his dark eyes. 'Well, that's going to be a problem, isn't it? I don't do joint decisions. Never have, never will. I'm unilateral all the way, *meu amorzinho*. But in this case it really doesn't matter because we both know that this so called "son" of yours, oh, sorry—' he corrected himself with an apologetic smile and a lift of his hand '—I should say son of *"ours"*, shouldn't I?—is a figment of your greedy, money-grabbing imagination. So it would be impossible for you to produce him. Unless you hired someone to play the part. Have you?'

Kimberley gaped at him.

He was an utter bastard!

How could she have forgotten just how cold and unfeeling he was? What a low opinion of women he had? How could she have thought, even for a moment, that she'd made a mistake in not persisting in her attempts to tell him that she was expecting his child? At the time she'd decided that she could never expose a child of hers to a man like him and, listening to him now, she knew that it had *definitely* been the right decision.

People had criticised her behind her back, she knew that, but they were people who came from safe, loving homes—homes where the father came home at night and cared about what happened to his family.

Luc wasn't like that. Luc didn't care about anything or anyone except himself.

He was *just* like her father and she knew only too well what it was like to grow up with a parent like that. She'd been right to protect her child from him and if it hadn't been for her current crisis she would have continued to keep Luc out of his life.

But fate had intervened and she'd decided that she had no choice but to tell him. He *had* to help her. He *had* to take some responsibility, however distasteful he found the prospect of parenthood.

But at the moment he didn't even believe that his son existed—

He seemed to think that their child was some sort of figment of her greedy imagination.

She sank on to the nearest chair, bemused and sickened by his less than flattering assessment of her. 'Why do you have such a low opinion of me?'

'Well, let's see—' he gave a patient smile, as if he was dealing with someone very, *very* stupid '—it could have something to do with the volume of money you spent after we broke up. Or the fact that you're now stooping to depths previously unheard of in order to sue me for maintenance. *Not* the actions of someone destined for sainthood, wouldn't you agree?'

She stared at him blankly. Her mind didn't work along the same lines as his and she was struggling to keep up. 'I'm not suing you for maintenance.'

He gave an impatient frown. 'You want me to pay money for the child.'

She licked her lips. 'Yes, but not to *me* and it's nothing to do with maintenance. I can support our son. I took the money from you because I was pregnant, alone and very scared and I couldn't think how I could possibly bring a child into the world when I didn't even have somewhere to live. I used your money to buy a small flat. If I hadn't done that I would have had to find a job and put the baby into a nursery, and I wanted to care for him myself. And I bought a few essentials.' She gave a tiny frown, momentarily distracted. 'I had no idea how many things a baby needed. I bought a cot and a push-chair, bedding, nappies. I didn't use any of the money on myself. I *know* that technically it was stealing, but I didn't know what else to do so I told myself it was maintenance. If I'd chased you through the courts you would have had to pay a lot more to support Rio.'

One dark eyebrow swooped upwards. *'Rio?'*

She blushed. 'I chose to name him after the city where he was conceived.'

'How quaint.' Luc's tone was a deep, dark drawl loaded with undertones of menace. 'So if I've already paid for the pushchair and the nappies, what else is there? He needs a new school coat, perhaps? His feet have grown and his shoes no longer fit?'

He still didn't believe her.

'Last week I received a kidnap threat.' Her voice shook as she said the words. Perhaps the truth would shake him out of his infuriating cool. 'Someone out there knows about our son. They know you're a father. And they're threatening Rio's life.'

There was a long silence while he watched her, his dark eyes fixed on her pale face.

They were sitting too close to each other. *Much too close.*

Her knee brushed against his and she felt the insidious warmth of awareness spread through her body. Against her will, her eyes slid to the silken dark hairs visible on his wrist and then rested on his strong fingers. *Those long, clever fingers—*

Her body flooded with heat as she remembered how those fingers had introduced her to intimacies that she'd never before imagined and she shifted slightly in her chair. His eyes detected the movement. Instantly his gaze trapped hers and the temperature in the room rose still further.

'Show me the letter.'

Did she imagine the sudden rough tone to his voice? Relieved that she could finally meet one of his demands, she delved into her bag and dragged out the offending letter, dropping it on the table next to him as if it might bite her.

He extended a hand and lifted the letter, no visible sense of urgency apparent in his movements. He flipped it open and read it, his handsome face inscrutable.

'Interesting.' He dropped the letter back on the table. 'So I'm expected to shell out five million dollars and then everyone lives happily ever after? Have I got that right?'

She stared at him, stunned, more than a little taken aback that he didn't seem more concerned for the welfare of his son. Still, at least now he'd seen the evidence, he'd know she was telling the truth.

'Do you think paying is the wrong approach? You think we should go to the police?' She looked at him anxiously and rubbed her fingers across her forehead, trying to ease the pain that pulsed behind her temples. She'd gone over and over it in her head so many times, trying to do the right thing. 'I have thought about it, obviously, but you can see from the letter what he threatened to do if I spoke to the police. I know everyone always says you shouldn't pay blackmailers, but that's very easy to say when it isn't your child in danger and—' her voice cracked '—and I can't play games with his life, Luc. He's everything I have.'

She looked at the strong, hard lines of Luc's face and suddenly wanted him to step in and save her the way he'd saved her that first night they'd met. He was hard and ruthless and he had powerful connections and she knew instinctively that he would be able to handle this situation if he chose to. He could make it go away.

'I think involving the police would *not* be a good idea,' he assured her, rising to his feet in a lithe, athletic movement and pacing across the office to the window. 'Police in any country don't generally appreciate having their time wasted.'

Her eyes widened. 'But why would this waste their time?'

He shot her an impatient look. 'Because we both know that this is all part of your elaborate plan to extract more money from me. I suppose I should just be grateful it took you seven years to work your way through the last lot.' His voice was harsh and contemptuous. 'It was a master stroke suggesting we contact the police because it does add credibility to the situation, but we both know that would have proved somewhat embarrassing if they'd agreed to be involved.'

She stared at him in stunned silence. 'You still think I'm making this whole situation up, don't you?'

'Look at it from my point of view,' he advised silkily. 'You turn up after seven years, demanding money to help a child I know nothing about and whose existence you cannot prove. If he's my child, why didn't you tell me you were pregnant seven years ago?'

'I've already explained!' She ran a hand over the back of her neck to relieve the tension. 'Over and over again I rang and came to your office and you refused to see me. You wouldn't even *talk* to me.'

He'd cut her dead and she'd thought she'd die from the pain. She'd missed him *so* much.

'Our relationship was over and talking about it after the event isn't my forte.' Luc gave a careless shrug. 'Talking is something else that's more of a woman thing than a man thing. A bit like guilt, I suppose.'

'Well, just because you're totally lacking in communication skills, don't blame me now for the fact you weren't told about your child!' Her emotions rumbled like a volcano on the point of eruption. 'I *tried* to tell you, but your listening skills need serious attention.'

His eyes hardened. 'It's a funny thing, but I always find that I become slightly hard of hearing when people are begging me for money.'

She stared at him helplessly. 'He's your *son*—'

He held out a hand. 'So show me a photograph.'

'Sorry?'

'If he exists, then at least show me a photograph.'

She felt as though she was on the witness stand being questioned by a particularly nasty prosecutor. 'I—I don't have one with me. I was in a panic and I didn't think to bring one.' *But she should have.* Should have known Luc would ask to at least see a picture of his child. 'I wasn't expecting to have to prove his existence, so no, I don't have a photograph.'

One dark eyebrow swooped upwards and his hand fell to his side. 'What a loving mother you must be.' His tone was dangerously soft. 'You don't even carry a photograph of your own child.'

She exploded with exasperation. 'I don't *need* to carry a photograph of him because I'm with him virtually every minute of every day and have been since he was born! I used your money to buy a little flat so that I could stay at home and look after him. And now he's older I work from home so that I don't miss a single minute of being with him. I don't need photographs! I have the real thing!'

He inclined his head and a ghost of a smile touched his firm mouth. 'Good answer.'

She shook her head slowly, helpless to know what to do to convince him. 'You think I'm making all this up just to get money for myself?'

'Frankly?' The smile vanished. 'I think you're a greedy, money-grabbing bitch who wants five million dollars and is prepared to go to most distasteful lengths to achieve that goal.' His eyes scanned her face. 'And you can abandon the wounded look—it's less convincing once you've already ripped a guy off big time.'

Her mouth fell open and her body chilled with shock. '*Why* would you think that about me?'

'Because I already know you're greedy,' he said helpfully, checking his watch. 'And now you'll have to excuse me because I have a Japanese delegation waiting in another meeting room who are equally eager to drain my bank account. If they're even half as inventive as you've been then I'm in for an interesting afternoon.'

She stared at him in horrified disbelief.

Was that it?

Was he really going to walk out on her?

She knew instinctively that if he left the room now, she wouldn't see him again. Gaining access to Luciano Santoro was an honour extended only to a privileged few and she sensed that she was on borrowed time.

'No!' She stood up quickly and her voice rang with panic. Her feelings didn't matter any more. Nothing mattered except the safety of her son. 'You can't just send me away! I'm telling the truth and I'll prove it if I have to. I can get Rio on the phone, I can arrange for you to talk to the school, I'll do anything, *absolutely anything,* but you have to give me the money. I'm *begging* you, Luc. *Please* lend me the money. I'll pay you back somehow, but if you don't give it to me I don't know what else to do. I don't know where else to turn—'

She broke off, her slim shoulders drooped as the fight drained out of her, and she slumped into a chair.

He wasn't going to help her. The responsibility of being a single parent had always felt enormous, but never more so than now, when her child's safety was threatened.

She wanted to lean on someone. She wanted to share the burden.

Luc stilled and his dark eyes narrowed. 'For five million dollars you'd do *absolutely anything*?'

There was something in his tone that made her uneasy but she didn't hesitate. 'I'm a mother and what mother wouldn't agree to anything if it meant keeping her child safe?'

'Well, that's a very interesting offer.' His eyes scanned her face thoughtfully. 'I'll think about it.'

She bit her lip and clasped her hands in her lap. 'I need an answer quickly.'

'This is Brazil, *meu amorzinho,*' he reminded gently,

stretching lean muscular legs out in front of him, 'and you of all people should know that we don't do anything quickly.'

She caught her breath, trapped by the burning heat in his eyes and the tense, pulsing atmosphere in the room. All at once she was transported back to long, lazy afternoons making love on his bed, in the swimming pool—afternoons that had stretched into evenings that had stretched into mornings.

She swallowed as she remembered the slow, throbbing, intense heat of those days.

No, Brazilians certainly didn't rush anything.

'The deadline is tomorrow night.'

His eyes gleamed. 'So many shoes, so little time. You think I will just give you the money and let you go? Is that what you think?'

She swallowed, hypnotised by the look in his eyes. 'Luc—'

'Let's look at the facts, shall we?' Lean bronzed fingers beat a slow, menacing rhythm on the glass table. 'You clearly hold me responsible for seducing you seven years ago. You come into my office ignoring the past as though it is a vile disease that you could catch again if you stay close to me for long enough.' His gaze swept over her. 'Everything about you is buttoned up. You are wearing your clothes like armour, protecting yourself and the truth is—' he leaned towards her, his dark eyes mocking '—you are afraid of those things I made you feel, are you not? You are afraid of your own response to me. That is why you deny your feelings. It is so much easier to pretend that they don't exist.'

The breath she'd been about to take lodged in her throat. 'I don't feel anything—'

He gave a lethal smile. 'You forget, *minha docura*, that I was once intimately acquainted with every delicious inch of you. I know the signs. I recognise that flush on your cheeks, I recognise the way your eyes glaze and your lips part just before you beg me to kiss you.'

Completely unsettled by his words, Kimberley rose to her feet so quickly she almost knocked the chair over. 'You're insufferably arrogant!'

Her heart was pounding heavily and everything about her whole body suddenly felt warm and tingly.

'I'm honest,' he drawled, swivelling in his seat so that he could survey her from under slightly lowered lids, 'which is more than you have ever been, I suspect. It is so much easier to blame me, is it not, than to accept responsibility yourself? Why is it that you find sex so shameful, I wonder?'

She couldn't catch her breath properly. 'Because sex should be part of a loving relationship,' she blurted out before she could stop herself and he gave a smile that was totally male.

'If you believe that then clearly maturity has added nothing to your ability to face facts.'

Tears pricked her eyes. 'Why are you so cynical?'

He shrugged. 'I am realistic and, like most men, I don't need the pretence of love to justify enjoying good sex.'

How had she ever allowed herself to become involved with this man?

They were just so different. 'I—I hate you—'

'You don't hate me—' his relaxed pose was in complete contrast to her rising tension '—but I know you think you do, which makes this whole situation more intriguing by the minute. You would so much rather be anywhere else but here. Which makes your greed all the more deplorable. You must want money very badly to risk walking into the dragon's den.'

'I've told you why I need the money and this situation has nothing to do with us—we've both moved on.' Her fingers curled into her palms. 'I know you're not still interested in me, any more than I'm still interested in you.'

'Is that a fact?' His voice was a deep, dark drawl and he lounged in his seat with careless ease, contemplating her with lazy amusement. 'And what if you're wrong? What if I *am* still interested in you?'

Her mouth dried. 'You're being ridiculous.'

'A word of advice—' His voice was suddenly soft and his eyes glittered, dark and dangerous. 'When you're trying to relieve someone of an indecent sum of money, don't accuse them of being ridiculous.'

She swallowed. How could she ever have thought she was a match for this man? She was a different person around him. Her brain didn't move and her tongue didn't form the right words.

She should never have come, she thought helplessly. 'If you won't lend me the money then there's no more to be said.'

She'd failed.

Panic threatened to choke her and she curled her fingers into her palms and walked towards the door.

'Walk out of that door and you won't be allowed back in,' he informed her in silky tones. 'Come back and sit down.'

Would he be ordering her to sit down if he had no intention of lending her the money?

Hope mingled with caution and she turned, her hand on the door handle and her heart in her mouth.

'I said, sit down.' His strong face was expressionless and, with barely any hesitation, she did as he ordered and then immediately hated herself for being that predictable. For doing exactly what he said.

Wasn't that what her whole life had been like for that one month they'd spent together? He'd commanded and she'd obeyed, too much in love and in lust to even think of resisting. Completely overwhelmed by him in every way. And here she was, seven years on, in his company for less than an hour and still obeying his every command.

Well, it wasn't going to happen that way again.

She wasn't that person any more, and being in the same room as him didn't make her that person.

Her expression was defiant as she looked at him. 'It's a simple question, Luc. Yes or no. It doesn't matter whether I sit or stand and it doesn't matter whether I leave the room. All the information you need is in that letter in front of you.'

The letter he clearly thought was a fake.

She watched in despair as he gave a casual shrug and pushed it away from him in a gesture of total indifference. 'I have no interest in the letter or in your stories about phantom pregnancies. What *does* interest me, *meu amorzinho*, is the fact that you came to me.'

She froze. 'I already told you, I—'

'I heard—' he interrupted her gently, 'you came to me to tell me you would do *absolutely anything* for five million dollars and now I simply have to decide exactly what form *absolutely anything* is going to take. When I've worked it out, you'll be the first to know.'

CHAPTER THREE

BACK in her hotel room, Kimberley dragged off the jacket of her suit and dropped on to the bed, fighting off tears of frustration and anxiety.

She'd blown it. She'd totally blown it.

She'd planned to be calm and rational, to tell him the facts and explain the reasons for having kept Rio's birth a secret from him for so long. But from the moment he'd walked into the room her plans had flown out of the window.

She'd been catapulted back into the past.

And she had less than twenty-four hours before the deadline came and went. Less than twenty-four hours in which to persuade a man with no morals or human decency to deposit five million dollars into the blackmailer's bank account.

The blackmailer he didn't even believe existed.

She took several deep breaths, struggling to hold herself together emotionally. It had been the hardest thing in the world to leave her child at this point in time, when all her instincts as a mother told her to keep him close. But she had known that to bring him on this trip would have been to expose him to even greater danger. And she'd hoped that she would only be in Rio de Janeiro for two days at the most. And after that—

She closed her eyes briefly and took a deep breath. She

hadn't dared think further than this meeting. Hadn't dared think what would happen if Luc refused to lend her the money.

Even now, with the letter still lurking in her handbag, she couldn't quite believe that this was happening. Couldn't believe that someone, somewhere, had discovered the truth about her child's parentage. She'd been so careful *and yet somehow they knew.*

And she'd left her son with the only person in the world that she trusted. The man who was a father figure to him.

As if by telepathy the phone in her bag rang and she answered it swiftly.

'Is he all right?'

Jason's voice came back, reassuringly familiar. 'He's fine. Stop fussing.' They'd agreed not to discuss any details on the phone. 'How are you? Any luck your end?'

Kimberley felt the panic rise again. 'Not yet.' She couldn't bring herself to tell Jason that Luc didn't believe her. Part of her was still hoping for a miracle.

'But Luc agreed to see you this time? You met with him?'

Kimberley's fingers tightened on the phone. 'Oh, yes.' And her whole body was still humming and tingling as a result of that encounter. 'But he won't give me an answer. He's playing games.'

'Did he fall on bended knee and beg your forgiveness for treating you so shoddily?'

Kimberley tipped her head back and struggled with tears as she recalled every detail of their explosive meeting. 'Not exactly—'

'I don't suppose "sorry" is in his vocabulary.' Jason gave a short laugh that was distinctly lacking in humour. 'Hang in there. If he doesn't come banging on your door in the next hour then he isn't the man I think he is.'

Banging on her door? Why would he do that?

Kimberley gave a sigh. She knew only too well that Luc Santoro didn't go round banging on women's doors. Usually they fell at his feet and he just scooped them out of his path and dropped them in his bed until he'd had enough of them.

'I wish I had your confidence. What if he refuses?'

'He won't refuse. Have courage.' Jason's voice was firm. 'But I still think we should talk to the police.'

'No!' She sat bolt upright on the bed and swept her tangled hair out of her eyes. '*Not* the police. You saw the note. You *know* what that man threatened to do—'

'All right. But if you change your mind—'

'I won't change my mind.' She wouldn't do anything that would jeopardize the safety of her child. 'All I want is to deposit the money in his account as he instructed. I don't want to do anything that might upset him or give him reason to hurt Rio.'

Limp with the heat and exhaustion, Kimberley snapped the phone shut and lay back on the bed and closed her eyes. For a moment she questioned her decision to stay in this small hotel with no air-conditioning in a slightly dubious part of Rio de Janeiro. At the time it had seemed the right thing to do because she didn't want to squander money, but now, with the perspiration prickling her skin and her head throbbing, she wished she'd chosen somewhere else. She was hot, she was miserable and she hadn't eaten or slept since the letter had arrived two days previously.

Instead she'd spent the time pacing the floor of her London flat, planning strategy with Jason. It had been hard to act as if nothing was wrong in front of her little boy. Even harder to board a plane to Rio de Janeiro without him, because apart from the time he spent at school or playing with friends, they were hardly ever apart.

She'd stayed at home when he was little and, with the help of Jason, a top fashion photographer who she'd met when she was modelling, she'd started working from home, selling her own designs of jewellery. She'd managed to fit her working hours around caring for her new baby and she'd worked hard to push all thoughts and memories of Luc Santoro out of her system.

And she'd dealt with the enormous guilt by telling herself that there were some men who just weren't cut out to be fathers and Luc was definitely one of them. He was a man like her father—a man who shifted his attention from one woman to the next without any thought of commitment—and she vowed that no child of hers was ever going to experience the utter misery and chronic insecurity that she'd suffered as a child.

Finding the heat suddenly intolerable, Kimberley sprang to her feet and stripped off the rest of her clothes before padding barefoot into the tiny bathroom in an attempt to seek relief from the unrelenting humidity.

The shower could barely be described as such, but it was sufficient to cool her heated flesh and she washed and dried herself and then slid into clean underwear and collapsed back on to the bed, wishing that the ceiling fan worked.

'Presumably this is all part of your plan to gain the sympathy vote, staying in a hotel with no air-conditioning in a part of town that even the police avoid.' His deep, dark drawl came from the doorway and she gave a gasp of shock and sprang off the bed.

She hadn't even heard the door open.

'You can't just walk in here!' She made a grab for her robe and dragged it around herself, self-conscious and just horrified that he'd caught her in such a vulnerable state. Her hair was hanging in dark, damp coils down her back and she wasn't wearing any make-up. She felt completely unprepared for a confrontation with a man like him. 'You should have knocked!'

'You should have locked the door.' He strolled into the room and closed the door firmly behind him, turning the key with a smooth, deliberate movement. 'In this part of town, you can't be too careful.'

Hands shaking, she tied the robe at the waist, still glaring at him. 'What are you doing here?'

'I was under the impression that you wanted an urgent answer to your request for funds.' He strolled across the cramped, airless room and stared out of the smeared window into the grimy, litter infested street below. His broad shoulders all but obliterated the light in the room and she couldn't see his face. 'If your finances are in this bad a state, perhaps you ought to be asking me for more than five million.'

She didn't answer. She couldn't. She could hardly breathe, trapped in this tiny, airless room with Luc Santoro, who dominated every inch of available space with his powerful body. He was still wearing the sleek business suit and the jacket moulded to his shoulders, hinting at masculine strength and power. His glossy hair brushed the collar of his white silk shirt, just on the edges of what would be considered respectable in the cut-throat world of corporate finance. His hard jaw betrayed the tell-tale signs of dark stubble and at that precise moment, even dressed in the suit, he looked more bandit than businessman.

He was wickedly, dangerously attractive and with a rush of horror she felt her nipples harden and push against the soft fabric of her robe.

Mortified by her own reaction, she wrapped her arms around her waist and tried to remind herself that none of that mattered. It didn't matter how her body reacted to this man. This time around, her brain was running the show and all that mattered was her child.

Would he agree to the loan? Would he have come in person if he was going to refuse to help her? Surely he would have sent a minion—one of the thousands of people who worked into the night to ensure that the Santoro empire kept multiplying.

'I've already told you that the money isn't for me.' Nervous and self-conscious, she blurted the words out before she could stop herself. 'I don't know what else to do to convince you.'

He turned to face her, his voice soft. 'To be honest, I'm not particularly interested in your reasons for wanting the money. What does interest me is what you intend to give me in return for my—' he lingered over the word thoughtfully '—let's call it an *investment*, shall we?'

There was something in his eyes that made her suddenly wary and nerves flickered in her stomach, her feminine senses suddenly on full alert. 'I don't understand—'

'No?' He moved away from the window. 'Then allow me to give you a basic lesson in business.' His voice was smooth and he watched her with the unflinching gaze of a hunter studying its prey for weakness. 'A business deal is an exchange of favours. No more. No less. I have something you want. You have something I want.'

Feeling as though she was missing something important, her heart beat faster and she licked dry lips with the tip of her tongue. 'I have nothing that you can possibly want. So I assume you're saying no.'

He lifted a hand and trailed a lean, strong finger down her cheek. 'I'm saying that I'm willing to negotiate.' His finger lingered at the corner of her mouth and his smile was disconcerting. 'I will give you money but I want something in return.'

Not his son.

Dear God, please don't let him ask for his son.

Trying to ignore the sudden flip of her stomach, she stared at him helplessly, hardly daring to breathe. 'What?' What else did she have to offer that could possibly be of interest to him? Her flat in London was ridiculously modest by his standards and she had few other assets. 'What is it you want?'

Not Rio. Please, not Rio—

His hand slid into her hair and his eyes didn't shift from hers. 'You.' He said the word with simple clarity. 'I want you, *minha docura*. Back in my bed. Naked. Until I give you permission to get dressed and leave.'

There was a stunned silence. A stunned silence while parts of her body heated to melting point under the raw sexuality she saw in his dark gaze.

She couldn't believe she'd heard him correctly.

He wanted *her?*

Relief that he hadn't mentioned Rio mingled with a shivering, helpless excitement that she didn't understand.

Somehow she managed to speak, but her voice was a disbelieving croak. 'You *can't* be serious.'

'I never joke about sex.'

'But why?' The blood pounded in her ears and she felt alarmingly dizzy. She wished he'd move away from her. *He was too close.* 'Why would you want me in your bed? We've been there, done that—'

His eyes burned into hers. 'And I want to do it again.' He gave a lazy, predatory smile. 'And again. *And again—*'

The air jammed in her lungs. 'You can have any woman you want—'

'Good,' he said silkily, withdrawing his hand from her hair slowly, as if he were reluctant to let her go. 'Then that's settled.'

He stood with his legs planted firmly apart, in full control mode, completely confident that he could manipulate any situation to his advantage.

'Hold on.' She wished desperately that she hadn't taken off the crisp business suit. It was hard to maintain an icy distance dressed in a virtually transparent robe, especially when the conversation was about sex. 'Are you saying that you'll give me the money if I agree to—' she broke off, having difficulty getting her tongue around the words '—sleep with you?'

'Not sleep, no.' His mouth curved into a slow smile that mocked her hesitation. 'I can assure you that there will be very little sleeping involved.'

Her mouth dried and she hugged the robe more closely around herself, as if to protect herself from the feelings that shot through her body. 'It's a ridiculous suggestion.'

Winged dark brows came together in a sharp frown. 'What's ridiculous about it? I'm merely renewing a relationship.'

'A relationship?' Her voice rose. 'We did *not* have a *relationship*, Luc, we had *sex!*' Relentless, mindless, incredible sex that had neutralized her ability to think straight.

Someone in the next room thumped on the wall and Kimberley closed her eyes in embarrassment.

Luc didn't even register the interruption, his handsome face as inscrutable as ever. 'Sex. Relationships.' He shrugged broad shoulders. 'It's all the same thing.'

Her eyes flew wide and she stared at him in appalled dismay. 'No! It is not the same thing, Luc!' She was so outraged she could hardly breathe and she barely remembered to lower her voice. 'It is not the same thing at all! Not that I'd expect a man with your Neanderthal, macho tendencies to understand that.'

He clearly hadn't changed a bit!

Luc shrugged, supremely indifferent to her opinion. 'Women want different things from men, it's an acknowledged fact. I don't need fluffy romantic to make me feel OK about good sex, but if fluffy romantic makes you feel better then that's your choice.'

Her jaw dropped. He just didn't have a clue. 'I can't believe you'd think I'd even *consider* such a proposition. What sort of woman do you think I am?'

'One who needs five million dollars and is willing to do *"absolutely anything"* to get it.' He was brutal in his assessment of the situation. 'I have something you want. You have something I want. This is a business deal at its most basic.'

It was typical of Luc that he viewed sex as just another commodity, she thought helplessly. Typical that he thought he could just buy whatever he wanted. 'What you're suggesting is immoral.'

'It's honest. But you're not that great at being honest about your feelings, are you?' His gaze locked on hers with burning intent. 'Tell me that you haven't lain in your bed at night unable to sleep because you're thinking about me. Tell me that your body doesn't burn for my touch. *Tell me that you're not remembering what it was like between us.'*

Her breathing grew shallow. She didn't want to remember something she'd spent seven years learning to forget.

Kimberley licked dry lips and her stomach dropped. 'You're prepared to pay to go to bed with a woman, Luc?' She struggled to keep her tone light, not to betray just how much he'd unsettled her. 'You must have lost your touch.'

'You think so?' He smiled. 'There is nothing wrong with my touch, *meu amorzinho*, as you will discover the moment you say yes. And, as for paying—' he gave a dismissive shrug '—I can be a very generous lover when I want to be. The money is nothing. Call it a gift. Only this time I will pay you for your services up front to save you the bother of taking the money afterwards.'

Her desperate need for the money warred with her own powerful sense of self-preservation. It had taken her years to recover from the fallout of their relationship. Years to rebuild her life. How could she even contemplate putting herself back in that position?

She knew from bitter experience that he was incapable of connecting with a woman on any level other than the physical. He was incapable of showing or even *feeling* emotion. *He'd break her heart again if she was foolish enough to let him.*

Except that this time she wasn't an idealistic teenager, she reminded herself. Her expectations were realistic. This time round she knew the man she was dealing with. Understood his shortcomings. Understood that he wasn't capable of a relationship.

And, most of all, this time she would have more sense than to fall in love with him.

She almost laughed at her own thoughts. She was weighing up the facts as if she had a decision to make but the truth was there was no decision to make. What choice did she have?

Given the circumstances, how could she say no?

The only thing that mattered was her son.

So what were Luc's reasons? Why would he want her back when he'd been so determined to end their relationship all those years before?

'Why do you want this when our relationship was over years ago?' She just couldn't bring herself to refer to it as sex, even though that was what it had been. 'I just don't understand.'

'Don't you?' His gaze dropped to her mouth and his dark eyes heated with molten sexuality. 'We have unfinished business, *meu amorzinho*, as you well know.'

Her heart thudded hard against her chest. 'I need time to think about it.' *Time to talk herself into doing something that left her almost breathless with panic.*

'You can have ten seconds,' he offered in a smooth tone, glancing around the basic, threadbare room with an expression of appalled distaste. 'And then we're leaving.'

'Ten seconds?' How she wished she'd booked a room with air-conditioning. It was too hot to think properly and she *needed* to think. Just in case there was an alternative—'That's ridiculous! You can't expect me to make a decision that quickly!'

'And yet it was you who said that you needed the money immediately,' he reminded her, thick dark lashes shielding his expression, 'you who told me there was no time to linger over this decision. The blackmailer is waiting, is he not?'

His tone dripped sarcasm and she stared at him helplessly, looking for a hint of softness, a chink in that solid armour plating which might suggest that for him this arrangement was about something deeper than just animal hunger.

But there was nothing soft about Luciano Santoro and no break in the armour. He was hard, ruthless and he took what he wanted.

And it seemed that he wanted her.

'Why?' The words fell from her lips like a plea. 'Why do you want me back? You yourself said that women don't get a second chance with you. It doesn't make sense.'

'It will make perfect sense when you're naked and underneath me,' he assured her in the confident tone of a man who knew a negotiation was all but over. 'Your thinking time is up, *meu amorzinho*. Yes or no?'

She looked at him with loathing, wondering how he could be so cold and detached. Was he capable of feeling *anything*? All her instincts were warning her to say no and run a mile. But then she thought of her son— 'You leave me no choice.'

'How typical of you to pretend that this isn't what you want. Again I'm cast in the role of big bad wolf.' His smile was faintly mocking and he lifted a hand and gently drew his thumb over her lower lip. 'You can always refuse.'

She stared at him, hypnotised by the heat in his eyes.

How? How could she say no, knowing what that would mean for her child?

And yet how could she say yes, knowing what it would mean for her?

'Unfortunately I cannot refuse.' Her voice didn't sound like her own. There was a cold, bitter edge to it that she didn't rec-

ognise. 'Unlike you, my commitment to our child is absolute.
And to keep him safe I need the money in my account by tonight.'

'My, we are desperate.'

She lifted her chin. 'I'll climb back into your bed, Luc, if
that's what it takes, but you'd better be warned. I'm not the
same innocent girl you seduced seven years ago. I'm a very
different person now. Be sure you know what you're getting.
You may not be able to handle me.'

Having agreed to his terms, a tiny part of her refused to let
him have it all his own way. Where in their contract did it say
that she had to be nice to him?

She didn't feel nice. She didn't feel nice at all.

She was boiling inside and *angry*.

His eyes gleamed dark and his voice lowered to a sexy purr.
'I can handle you with both hands tied behind my back.'

She lifted her chin and her eyes flashed in blatant challenge. 'You can force me into your bed, Luc, but you can't
make me enjoy the experience.'

'You think not?'

He moved remarkably quickly for such a powerfully built
man, his mouth coming down on hers with a fierce, driving
compulsion which shocked and thrilled in equal measure.

It was savage and basic and he stole, plundered and seduced with the warm promise of his mouth and the hot slide
of his tongue until her head swirled and her senses exploded.

He kissed with a sexual expertise that made the pleasure
roar in her head and she kissed him back, greedy, starved and
desperate for more.

And he gave her more. Gave her exactly what he knew she
needed.

With a grunt of masculine satisfaction he kissed her
deeper, harder, his hands sliding down her back and anchor-
ing her hard against the proud thrust of his arousal. Her

starved body melted and hungered for the virile male feel of him and she pressed closer still, her movements feminine and instinctive.

She shivered with wicked excitement and then gave a soft gasp of protest as he dragged his mouth away from hers, leaving her shaking and gasping. She felt the roughness of male stubble graze the soft skin of her cheek and then he released her so suddenly that she almost fell.

'As I said,' he drawled softly, spreading his hands like a magician who had just performed an incredible trick for the benefit of a rapt audience, 'I can handle you with both hands tied behind my back if necessary. No problem.'

Dazed and still fighting the explosion of sensual fireworks that his touch had released, she struggled to bring herself back to the present. Her insides were spinning and her brain was foggy.

If she'd needed proof that she was still vulnerable to Luc Santoro's particular brand of macho sex appeal, then she had it now and she found the knowledge that he could still make her forget everything, just by kissing her, deeply humiliating.

'Thank you for reminding me that I really, *really* hate you.'

'I think I've just proved that you don't.' He gave a shrug that suggested that her feelings were a matter of complete indifference to him. 'And stop pretending that this deal is going to be a hardship to you when we both know you're going to be sobbing and begging the moment I get you back in my bed.'

Goaded past the point of self-control, she lifted a hand and slapped him hard across his lean bronzed cheek—so hard that her palm stung. Shocked and mortified, her hand fell to her side and she stepped back with a gasp of horror.

Never before in her life had she struck anyone or anything, but the image he'd painted of the person she'd been in his bed had been so agonisingly embarrassing that she'd been unable

to control herself, and her cheeks flamed at the less than subtle reminder of how eager she'd once been for his caresses.
Instantly she vowed that, no matter what happened, *no matter what he did to her,* the next time he touched her she
wouldn't respond. She wasn't going to give him the satisfaction. *Whatever it took,* she was going to just lie there.

'You're so wrong about me. I *do* hate you—' Her passionate declaration fell from her lips like a sob. 'I truly hate you
for turning me into a person that I don't even recognise.'

'That's because you've conveniently forgotten the person
you really are.' He touched long fingers to the livid red streak
that had appeared high on his cheek, his expression thoughtful. 'I look forward to reminding you. Over and over again,
meu amorzinho.'

She stared at him, her chest rising and falling as she struggled to contain the emotion that boiled inside her. 'You're
about to discover the woman I really am, Luc, and I just hope
it doesn't come as a shock because there's no refund.' She
lifted a hand to her throat, struggling to calm herself. 'How
long do you expect this charade to last?'

'Until I've finished with you.'

She felt a shaft of maternal panic. 'I have to get home to
my son.'

'I don't want to hear any more about this "son",' Luc
growled, 'and, just for the record, next time you decide to pin
a paternity suit on a guy, don't wait seven years to do it.'

If she'd had a gun she would have shot him for his total
insensitivity. Instead she stared at him, angry and frustrated,
wondering what she had to do to convince him of Rio's existence. But then she realised that she really didn't *need* him
to believe her. All she needed was the money, and it seemed
he was willing to give her that.

Providing she agreed to resume their relationship.

She closed her eyes and allowed herself one last frantic attempt to find an alternative, but there wasn't one. And she knew there wasn't one because he had always been her last resort. If there'd been any other conceivable way of raising the money, then she would have found it, but who else could give her five million dollars as easily as blinking?

Her son would be fine without her for a short time, she assured herself firmly, trying to ignore the maternal anxiety that twisted inside her. Jason was like a father to him. Jason would make sure that no harm came to her child. As for her—*she couldn't escape the feeling that she was now in more danger than her child.*

She opened her eyes. 'Two weeks. I can stay no more than two weeks.' She needed to put a time frame on it. Needed to know when she was going home. 'And I didn't pack for a long stay so I'll need to buy something to wear.'

She was proud of her flat, practical tone but he merely smiled in that maddening fashion that never failed to raise her pulse rate. 'Dress by all means, because I have no desire to share your more private attractions with the rest of Brazil, but you don't need to buy anything to wear. For what I have in mind,' he purred softly, 'you're not going to need clothes.'

Her eyes widened. 'But—'

'My car is parked outside and drawing attention even as we speak,' he said smoothly, 'so, unless we wish to begin the second chapter of our relationship the way we began the first, with a brawl on the streets, I suggest we make a move.'

He was no stranger to violence, she knew that from the way he'd handled himself the first night they'd met. And he was no stranger to the darker, rougher side of Rio de Janeiro. But the rumours that he had taken himself from the poverty of the *favelas*, the famed slums of Rio, to billionaire status, had never been confirmed, because Luc Santoro flatly refused to talk about his personal life.

He would talk about the money markets and business in

general, but questions of a more personal nature were skilfully deflected. Luc Santoro remained something of an
enigma, which simply served to increase his fascination for
the media. *And for women.*

Grabbing her clothes, Kimberley took refuge in the bathroom and dressed quickly. She twisted her hair back on top
of her head, buttoned the jacket of her suit and gave her reflection a grim smile. This was a business deal. Nothing more.
She was not going to scream or beg. And, most of all, she was
not going to fall in love.

She almost laughed at the thought.

That was the one aspect of this deal of which she could be
entirely confident. There was absolutely *no* risk of her falling in love with him. This time she'd be walking away from
the relationship with both her heart and her head in perfect
working order.

Drawing confidence from that fact, she opened the bathroom door, picked up her bag and walked towards the door.
'Shall we go?'

Luc cast a disparaging look at the lift and took the stairs.
'If we risk climbing into that thing we may find ourselves
stuck for the foreseeable future. Why did you pick this hotel
when Rio de Janeiro has so much better to offer?'

Because she'd been saving money.

'It has charm,' she said blithely and his eyes gleamed with
appreciative humour.

'If this is the standard that is required to win your approval then I'm not going to have to work very hard to impress you.'

Momentarily transfixed by his smile, her heart gave a tiny
flip and then she remembered that Luc used charm like a
weapon when it suited him.

'Nothing you do could ever impress me, Luc.'

She'd never been particularly interested in material things.

For her, the true attraction had been the man himself. Luc Santoro approached life with a cool confidence in his own ability to win in every situation. To him, obstacles existed to be smashed down and the greater the problem then the bigger the challenge. And he was a man who loved a challenge. His belief in himself was nothing short of monumental and that, combined with his indecent wealth and staggering dose of sex appeal, made him a prime target for every single woman on the planet.

And he'd chosen her.

There were mornings she'd woken up in his enormous bed, limp and exhausted after a night of relentless sensual exploration, and feasted her eyes on his bronzed male perfection, unable to believe that he was really her man and that this was actually *her life*.

But it hadn't been her life for anywhere near long enough and yet how could anything so perfect ever be anything but ephemeral?

Real life wasn't like that, she reminded herself gloomily as they arrived in the foyer of the hotel. Sixteen years of living with her father had taught her that.

Luc gestured towards the long silver limousine that was parked at the front of the hotel. A driver stood by the open door while a bodyguard stood eyeing the streets around them.

Kimberley frowned. Because Luc was so obviously capable of looking after himself physically, it hadn't really occurred to her that he was a target for crime, but of course he must be, and she gave a little shiver, once more reminded of the letter that lay in her bag.

'Let's go.' His hand was planted firmly in her back but she tried to stop, still reluctant to relinquish her independence.

'I need to settle my bill.'

'You mean they charge to stay in this place?' There was a glimmer of humour in his dark eyes as he urged her into the limousine without allowing her time to pause. 'My staff will deal with it. We need to get out of here before the press arrive, unless you wish to find yourself plastered all over tomorrow's newspapers as an object of speculation for half the world. I have a feeling that *"Woman sold to highest bidder"* would make a very appealing headline for the tabloid press.'

She ignored his sarcasm and frowned slightly. She'd forgotten that Luc Santoro was always an object of press attention and so was any woman seen with him. As one of the richest, most eligible bachelors in the world, it was inevitable that he attracted more than his fair share of media interest and attention.

Out on the street in the sun several flash bulbs went off in her face and Kimberley froze, dazzled and taken by surprise.

'Get into the car,' Luc ordered harshly, just as his bodyguard leaped forward to deal with the photographers.

CHAPTER FOUR

KIMBERLEY slid into the luxurious interior of the vehicle, grateful for the darkened windows that afforded a degree of privacy for those inside.

'How did they know you were here?' She stared at the group of photographers, watching as Luc's bodyguard ushered them out of the way.

'The press follow me everywhere and they also follow anyone who is linked to me in any way,' Luc reminded her in a grim tone, his lean, handsome face taut as he leaned forward and issued a string of instructions to his driver, who promptly accelerated away, leaving the photographers scrambling for their own transport.

'Perhaps if you didn't drive around in a car that shrieks "look at me" you might escape their attention,' she muttered, knowing even as she said the words that it would be virtually impossible for Luc Santoro to be incognito. Everything about him was high profile. He headed up a hugely successful global business and was no stranger to controversy. Added to that, his continued status as a rich playboy meant that he was a constant source of fascination for the world's media. Every woman he was seen with provided days of speculation in the newspapers. *Was this the one? Had a woman finally tamed the Brazilian bad boy?*

It had been the same when she had been with him. They hadn't even been out in public, she recalled bitterly, and yet still the press had managed to snap photos of her climbing into his car. And it had been the media that had alerted her to the fact that he'd left her bed to spend an evening with another woman. *And the media who'd printed pictures of her on the day he'd had her driven to the airport, her expression traumatised, her eyes huge and bruised from too much crying.*

Luc lounged back in his seat, indifferent to what was happening outside the confines of his car. 'I hardly need to remind you that you were the one who chose to book into a hotel in one of the seedier parts of Rio. At least the car is air-conditioned so we can indulge in conversation without risking heatstroke.'

'You were born here. You don't feel the heat.'

He reached across the back of the seat and twisted a coil of her hair around lean bronzed fingers, his eyes trapping hers. 'Whereas you, *minha docura,*' he breathed softly, 'with your blazing hair and your snowy white skin, were designed to be kept indoors in a man's bed, well away from the heat of the sun.'

Her heart thudded against her chest and she felt a vicious stab of sexual awareness deep inside her. 'I prefer the more traditional approach of a hat and sunscreen. And your attitude to women is positively Neolithic.'

The truth was, the heat that could do her the most damage, *the heat that she feared most,* didn't come from the sun.

She felt the gentle pressure on her scalp as he twisted the hair around his fingers and felt her stomach tumble. For a moment she just gazed at him helplessly, captivated by the burning masculine appraisal she saw in his eyes.

It had always begun like this—with his hands in her hair. He'd used her hair as a tool in his seduction. How many times had he murmured that it was the sexiest part of her? How many times had he raked his fingers through the thick copper waves and then wound the strands round his hands to hold her head still for his kiss? Her hair had become an erotic, sensual part of their lovemaking.

Hypnotised by the memories and by the look in his eyes, Kimberley felt a curl of heat low in her pelvis. Her breath jammed in her throat and for a brief, crazy moment her body swayed towards his, lured by the look in his partly veiled eyes and the almost irresistible draw of his hard mouth.

She remembered only too well what that mouth could do to her. *How it felt to be kissed by him.*

And then she also remembered what a cold-hearted, unfeeling man he was and she lifted a hand, removing her hair from his toying fingers with a determined jerk.

'*Don't* touch me—'

'I'm paying you for the privilege of doing just that,' he reminded her in soft tones, 'but I'm prepared to wait until there are no camera lenses around.'

She waited for him to slide back across the seat but he didn't move, his powerful shoulders only inches from hers.

'It's strange that you're so flushed,' he observed in a soft purr, his eyes raking her face. 'Why is that, I wonder?'

She tried to move further away from him but she was trapped against the door of the car with nowhere to go. 'As you yourself pointed out, I'm not great in the heat,' she stammered hoarsely and he gave a knowing smile.

'The car is air-conditioned and we both know perfectly well that it isn't the heat that's bothering you. You want me, *meu amorzinho*, every bit as much as I want you and eventually you're going to stop playing games and admit it.'

Her heart lurched. 'You have an exaggerated opinion of your own attractions,' she said witheringly and he gave a laugh of genuine amusement and slid back across the seat, finally giving her the space she'd thought she craved.

Alarmingly, it didn't seem to make any difference to the growing ache deep in her pelvis. Trapped within the confines of his car, she was still agonizingly aware of his lean, muscular body, sprawled with careless ease in the leather seat.

His phone rang and he gave a frown of irritation as he answered it in his native tongue, switching to rapid, fluent Italian once he identified the caller.

Kimberley watched helplessly, trying not to be impressed by the apparent ease with which he communicated in yet another language, wondering what it was about this man that affected her so deeply. She'd met plenty of handsome men in her time and plenty of clever, successful men. But none of them had once threatened her equilibrium in the way that Luc Santoro did. What was it that made him different? What was it that made her respond to him even though she knew he was so bad for her?

They were *completely* unsuited. They didn't want the same things out of life.

Luc didn't do relationships. Luc just did sex. And the really appalling thing was that he didn't believe there was a difference.

Not for the first time, she wondered what had happened in his life to bring him to that conclusion, but she knew better than to ask. Luc didn't talk about his past. In fact, in the short time they'd spent together, they'd barely talked at all. All their communication had been physical. As a result, she knew next to nothing about him.

He ended the call, snapped the phone shut and she cast a speculative look in his direction.

'Just how many languages do you speak?'

'My business is global, so enough to ensure that everything runs smoothly and I don't get fleeced.' As usual he gave nothing away and she rolled her eyes in exasperation.

'Your conversation skills are so limited that I don't suppose you need a very extensive vocabulary,' she muttered sarcastically. 'You just need to be able to boss people around. You're definitely fluent in He-man.'

He dropped the phone back into his pocket with a laugh. 'It was interesting,' he observed smoothly, 'that you were in my bed for almost a month and only at the end did I see that glorious temper. The signs were always there, of course, only your passion was otherwise directed.'

Kimberley felt a stab of pain as he dropped in yet another reminder of just how uninhibited she'd been during the month they'd spent together. The truth was she'd been so deliriously, ecstatically in love with him that she hadn't seen any reason to hold back. Hadn't realised what sort of man Luc Santoro really was. *Hadn't understood how totally different they were.*

'I hadn't been to bed with a man before,' she said tonelessly. 'It was the novelty factor.' It was a feeble attempt to defend herself and it drew nothing but a mocking gaze from her tormentor.

'The novelty factor?'

Breathing was suddenly a challenge. 'Of course. I was young and I discovered sex for the first time. What did you expect? It would have been the same with anybody.'

'You think so?' His eyes gleamed dark and dangerous as he leaned towards her, his gaze disturbingly intense. 'We barely touched the surface of sensuality,' he drawled huskily, 'but now I think you're ready to be moved on to the next level, *meu amorzinho.*'

Her mouth dried, her heart thudded hard against her chest and suddenly everything around her seemed to be happening in slow motion. She felt a flicker of alarm, mixed with a tinge of an intense excitement that horrified her. 'What do you mean, the next level?'

'Seven years ago you were a virgin. I was your first sexual experience, so naturally I was very careful with you.' His firm mouth curved into a smile of masculine anticipation. 'Now, as you keep reminding me, things are different. The girl is grown up. It's time to discover the woman. This time there will be no holding back.'

Holding back?

Recalling the fierce intensity of their lovemaking, Kimberley wondered exactly what he'd been holding back. She remembered how they'd hungered for each other. She remembered the burning desperation as they slaked their need time and time again. She remembered the heat and the explosive passion. But she didn't remember anything that could have been described as holding back.

Her stomach clenched.

So what exactly did he have in mind this time?

She tore her gaze away from his, horrified by the sexual awareness sizzling through her body. She wanted so badly to feel nothing, to be indifferent, and yet she felt *everything* and the knowledge just appalled her.

She'd spent the last seven years concentrating on making a good life for her child and never once during that time had she experienced even the smallest inclination to become involved with another man.

Her experience with Luc had put her off men completely. It had taken her so long to piece herself back together that she'd assumed she was no longer capable of experiencing such depth of feeling. The discovery that she *was* shocked and horrified her.

It was just physical, she told herself firmly, nothing more than that.

She'd denied herself for so long that it was hardly surprising that her body had reawakened. And so what? She gave a mental shrug. As he rightly said, she was a woman now. She wasn't a naïve girl. She knew that Luc wasn't capable of love and she no longer expected it. They could have sex and then she could walk away back to her old life.

'The question is, can you cope with the woman, Luc?' She threw him a cool, challenging look. 'As you rightly said, the girl has grown up. And, like I said, be careful you don't find yourself with more than you can handle.'

'We've already established that I can handle you.' His dark eyes narrowed. 'And the mere fact that you've agreed to this shows that you are as eager as me to renew our relationship.'

'We didn't have a relationship,' she said flatly. 'We had sex, and I agreed to this because you left me no choice.'

'We always have choices.' For a brief second his expression was bleak and then the moment passed and his eyes held their customary mocking expression. 'It's just that some of them are more difficult than others. That's life.'

She stared at him with mounting frustration. He really thought she was willing to go to bed with him just to satisfy an indecent lust for retail therapy? Did he really have such a low opinion of her?

For a wild moment she was tempted to try one more time to convince him about the existence of his child, but she knew there was no point. 'You're paying me to sleep with you,' she reminded him coldly, 'not to indulge in conversation. That's going to cost you extra.'

Far from being annoyed, he laughed. 'I believe my bank balance will remain unthreatened. You still don't know men very well, *meu amorzinho*. Talking is something that women want, not men. I have no intention of paying you to talk. To be honest, I couldn't care less if you don't speak at all for the next two weeks.'

His gaze shimmered with molten sexuality and suddenly the luxurious interior of the car seemed hotly oppressive. She shifted in her seat, trying desperately to ignore the wicked curl of her stomach.

'Where are we going, anyway?'

He threw her a predatory smile. 'My lair.'

The smooth intimacy of his tone was more than a little disturbing and she felt her breath catch. 'Which one?'

'To my office and from there we'll fly to the island.'

Her fingers curled into her palms. His island. West of Rio was the beautiful Emerald coast, littered with islands, some of them owned by the rich and privileged.

'You mean you're prepared to abandon work?'

'Some things are worthy of my full attention.'

The fact that he was planning to sequester her somewhere secluded increased her tension.

As an impressionable eighteen-year-old, she'd fallen in love with the stunning scenery of this part of Brazil, the forests and the mountains and most of all the beaches. And she'd been overwhelmed by the sheer indulgence of staying on Luc's private island, with all the accompanying luxury and privacy.

During the time they'd spent there, she'd been cocooned in a romantic haze, so sexually sated and madly in love with Luc and the exotic beauty of her surroundings that she couldn't imagine ever wanting to live anywhere else. All her memories of him were tied up with that one special place and she had no desire to return there.

It was just too raw.

'You have other homes,' she croaked. 'Can't we stay somewhere else?'

Somewhere that wouldn't remind her of the past—*of the humiliating completeness of her surrender.* Somewhere that wasn't brimming with memories.

She knew he had an apartment in New York and homes in Paris and Geneva. In fact, one of the reasons she'd chosen to settle in London was because it was the one place where Luc didn't have a home so she was unlikely to bump into him.

His eyes gleamed with masculine amusement. 'For what I have in mind, I require privacy and the island is perfect for that. And anyway—' he gave a careless shrug '—I'm still close enough to the office to be able to fly back if necessary.'

'Business. Business. Business.' She stared at him in exasperation, her nerves jumping and her senses humming. 'Is that all you ever think of?'

'No.' His reply was a sensual purr. 'I also think about sex. Like now, for instance.' He leaned his head back against the seat, his expression inscrutable. 'I'm cursing the need for me to return to the office to sign some papers when all I want to do is fly straight to the island and strip you naked.'

His words should have shocked her, but instead a wicked thrill flashed through her and her tummy muscles tightened. Suddenly she was aware of every masculine inch of him and just hated herself for feeling excitement when what she wanted to feel was indifference. 'You have a totally one track mind, do you know that?'

She told herself that it didn't matter what she felt as long as she didn't reveal those feelings to him. Last time she'd offered every single part of herself and he'd rejected her. This time she would give nothing except her body.

'If by "one track mind" you mean that I know what I want and I make sure that I get it, then yes—' he gave a lethal smile '—I have a one track mind. And as soon as these papers are signed, my mind is going to be on you, *meu amorzinho,* and you're going to discover just how fixed on one track my mind can be.'

His gaze slid down her body in a leisurely scrutiny and she struggled and fought against the wicked excitement that burned low in her pelvis.

He was the sexiest man she'd ever encountered, Kimberley thought helplessly, dragging her eyes away from his shimmering dark eyes and staring out of the car window in quiet desperation. She didn't want to notice anything about him, but instead she found herself noticing *everything*.

Determined not to sink under his seductive spell a second time, she tried to talk some sense into herself.

Sexy wasn't enough.

She reminded herself that this man was a control freak who was incapable of feeling or expressing normal human emotions.

She reminded herself that he'd taken her heart and chopped it into a million tiny pieces.

She reminded herself that she'd spent years building a new life after their scorching, intense, but all too brief relationship had ended.

Suddenly aware that the car had stopped, she realised that she'd barely even noticed the journey. All her attention had been focused on Luc.

A perfectly normal reaction, she tried to assure herself as she unfastened her seat belt. She hadn't seen him for years and he was the father of her child. They shared plenty of history. It was understandable that she'd find him impossible to ignore.

His driver held the door for her and she stepped out. For a wild moment she was tempted to turn and run along the sun-baked pavement and lose herself in the streets of Rio, but her bag was on her shoulder and in her bag was the letter.

The letter that had changed her life.

She wasn't in a position to run anywhere.

She needed five million dollars and the only man who could give her that was Luc Santoro.

And perhaps he read her mind because he paused for a moment on the pavement, watching her with those amazingly sexy dark eyes. Then he placed a hand firmly in the small of her back and walked her into the building.

'Loitering on pavements is not an occupation to be commended,' he observed dryly, striding towards the express lift without looking left or right, very much the king of his domain.

He urged her inside, hit a button and the doors slid together, closing out the outside world. A tense, intimate silence folded around them. Suddenly she was breathlessly, helplessly aware that she was alone in this confined space with the one man capable of turning her perfectly ordered life upside down.

Struggling to control the tiny tremors that shook her body, Kimberley stared at the floor but she felt the attraction pulsing between them like the pull of a magnet.

With a quiet desperation she risked a glance at him, expecting to find him watching the passage of the lift upwards. Instead their eyes locked and the last of her sanity fizzled out, torched by the sexual awareness that flared between them.

His handsome features grim and set, he gave a harsh curse and powered her back against the wall of the lift, his mouth hard and hungry as he kissed her with unrelenting passion.

Driven to fever pitch by the tension that had been mounting between them since she'd walked back into his office less than twenty-four hours earlier, she kissed him back, their tongues blending, her desperation more than matching his.

Her arms slid round his neck and her fingers jammed into his dark hair as he took her mouth with erotic expertise, exploring and seducing until her body was humming with unrelieved sexual need and her mind was numb. Every rational thought slid from her brain and she ceased to be a thinking, intelligent woman. Instead she responded with almost animal desperation, her head swimming with a wild hunger that was outside her control.

His eyes still burning into hers, he released a throaty groan of masculine appreciation and, without lifting his mouth, he yanked her skirt upwards and his hands slid down to her bottom. He hauled her hard against him and she gave a gasp of shock as she felt the unmistakable thrust of his erection against her.

The last of her resistance fell away to be replaced by a driving need so basic and powerful that she was completely controlled by its force. Her body throbbed and ached and cried out for satisfaction while her heart raced madly in a flight of excitement.

She forgot all her resolutions. Forgot all the promises she'd made to herself.

Instead she yanked at his shirt and slid her hands underneath, needing to touch, *to feel*, just desperate to get closer to him. Her seeking fingers found warm flesh, male body hair and hard muscle and she moaned her pleasure against his mouth as her starved senses leapt into overdrive and her body awakened.

She'd denied herself for so long that there was no hope of denying herself now. Not when what she needed so badly was standing right in front of her.

She felt every male inch of him pumped up and hard against her, and then his hands tore aside her panties and he lifted her, crashing her back against the wall with a thud as he took the weight of her body, his fingers digging hard into her thighs.

The lift gave a muted 'ping' but he merely reached out and thumped a button with an impatient hand, his eyes never leaving her eyes, his mouth never lifting from her mouth.

Helpless with excitement, Kimberley curled her legs around him, driven by an urgency that she didn't understand, her body throbbing with almost agonising excitement.

'Luc, please—' She sobbed his name into his mouth and moved her hips in a desperate plea for satisfaction and he gave a low grunt and cupped her with his hand.

Immediately Kimberley exploded into a climax so intense that she could hardly breathe. And still he kissed her, trapping her wild cries and sobs with his mouth as he slid his fingers deep inside her, his touch so shockingly intimate and amazingly skilled that the agonizing spasms just went on and on. She trembled and gasped, trapped on a sexual plateau until finally her body subsided.

Only then did he lift his mouth from hers, his breathing harsh and ragged as he scanned her flushed cheeks.

Gradually her own breathing slowed and her vision cleared and she became aware of exactly what she'd just done. *What she'd let him do to her.* In a public place.

'*Meu Deus*—' As if realising the same thing, he lowered her to the floor, streaks of colour highlighting his stunning bone structure as he lowered her to the floor. 'I don't know myself when I'm with you.'

His breathing was far from steady and his dark hair was roughened where her fingers had tugged and pulled. Still without uttering a word, he gently freed himself from the twisting, clinging coils of her fiery hair.

Tangled and wild from his hands and her own frantic movements, it tumbled in total disarray over her shoulders, half obscuring her vision.

Which was just as well, she reflected miserably as she ducked her head and tried frantically to straighten her clothing, because she couldn't bring herself to look at him and her hair provided a convenient curtain.

Deeply shocked by her own behaviour, she wanted to slink into a dark hole and never re-emerge.

She'd done it again.

For the past seven years she'd had absolutely no trouble resisting men. And it hadn't been for a lack of invitations. In fact she'd been so uninterested in the opposite sex that she'd assumed that her relationship with Luc had killed something inside her. And she'd been hugely relieved by that knowledge. It meant that her one all-consuming experience of love had rendered her immune to another attack of a similar nature. It meant that she was never again at risk of experiencing that out of control burning desire for a man, which had left her broken-hearted and soaked with humiliation.

How wrong could she have been?

Five seconds in an enclosed space with Luc was all it had taken for her to revert to her old self. She responded to him in the most basic animal fashion and no amount of logic or reason seemed to quell the burning need she had for him. The searing attraction between them was more powerful than common sense and lessons learned. So powerful that it outweighed all other considerations.

Like the fact that they were in a public lift.

Suddenly aware of their surroundings and the risk they'd just taken, various scenarios flashed across her brain and she lifted her head and stared at him in horror. 'Someone could have called the lift—'

For a long pulsing moment he didn't speak and she had a vague feeling that he was as stunned as she was, but then he stepped away from her and gave a casual shrug.

'Then they would have had a shock,' he drawled, adjusting his own clothing with a characteristic lack of concern for the opinion of others.

'You may be into public displays, but I'm not.'

In response he stroked a leisurely finger down her burning cheek. 'As usual you appear to be blaming me, but face it, *meu amorzinho*, you were as hot for it as I was. You didn't know where you were or what you were doing.' As if to prove his point, he stooped to retrieve something from the floor. 'These are yours, I believe.'

Kimberley stared down at the torn panties he'd given her and wanted to sink to the bottom of the lift shaft. Before she had a chance to comment, he stretched out a hand, hit a button on a panel on the wall and the lift doors opened.

Furious with him for not giving her more time to compose herself and still shrinking with mortification,

Kimberley was forced to stuff the remains of her underwear into her handbag. She stared after him with growing frustration and anger as he strolled out into his suite of offices without a backward glance in her direction, and for a wild moment she was tempted to take the lift back down to the ground floor and make a run for it. How could he seem so indifferent? He was totally relaxed and in control, as if indulging in mind-blowing sex in a lift was an everyday occurrence for him.

And perhaps it was, she reflected miserably as she reminded herself of the reason she was here and forced herself to follow him, her heels tapping on the polished marble floor. Women threw themselves at Luc Santoro wherever he went. She was sure there were endless numbers of females only too eager to indulge in a spot of elevator-sex with a drop dead gorgeous billionaire, given the opportunity.

Spotting a door marked 'Ladies', Kimberley took the opportunity to slip inside and do what she could to rectify her appearance.

When she emerged she saw that Luc was talking to the same personal assistant who had brought her the water and shown her such kindness.

She possessed the same exotic dark looks as her boss, but she was about twenty years older than Kimberley would have expected. Somehow she'd assumed that his personal assistant would be young and provocative.

The woman ended a phone call and gave her boss a wry smile. 'Well, you've stirred them all up as usual.'

'Is everything arranged?'

'You just need to check these figures, sign these because the fifth floor lot almost passed out with horror when I told them that you were planning to be out of the office—' she pushed some papers in his direction '—and everything else I can cope with. I'll speak to Milan about rescheduling that presentation and Phil will be over from New York next Wednesday as you requested. All sorted.'

'The helicopter?'

'Your pilot is waiting for you both.'

Horribly self-conscious and uncomfortably sure that, despite her attempts to freshen up her make-up, the evidence of their passionate encounter must be somehow visible, Kimberley hovered in the background, wondering how Luc could make the shift from hot lover to cool-headed businessman with such casual ease.

There was no trace of the hungry, passionate, out of control man who'd driven her to vertiginous heights of sexual pleasure only moments earlier.

Instead he seemed icy cold and more than a little remote and detached, his mind well and truly back on business as he scanned the papers and held his hand out for a pen.

Sex and business—the only two things that interested him in life.

Clearly their steamy encounter in the lift hadn't affected him in the same way it had affected her, Kimberley thought, and the knowledge depressed her more than she cared to admit. Even in the bedroom their relationship was one-sided. He turned her into a shivering, sobbing wreck, willing to do *anything* for his touch, while he was perfectly capable of walking away from their steamy encounters with equanimity.

She had a horrid lowering feeling that she could have been anyone.

Glancing at his lean, handsome profile, she decided that there was nothing to suggest that he'd shared anything but polite conversation with the woman who had been his companion in the lift. In total contrast, her own body was still throbbing from the intimacies they'd shared. Her heart was pounding and her lips were sore and swollen from his touch and she was sure that it must be completely obvious to anyone who cared to look at her that their trip in the lift hadn't involved a single moment of conversation.

Having handed Luc another file, the older woman looked across and gave her a slightly harassed apologetic smile. *'Como vai você?* How are you? I'm Maria. Sorry to hold you up but we weren't expecting him to be out of the office next week. He just needs to take a look at these figures for me, then you can go off and spoil yourselves.'

Spoil themselves?

Kimberley looked at her in consternation, not sure how to respond. Just how much did his PA know about their deal? She made it sound as though they were going to take a holiday. And Luc's proposed absence was clearly causing no end of problems for everyone. She glanced back at him but he had his eyes on the screen, scanning the figures.

He made a few comments, signed the rest of the papers and then glanced at his watch in an impatient gesture. Restless energy pulsed from his powerful frame and he closed lean, strong fingers around her wrist and hauled her against his side in a proprietary gesture.

'Enough. Let's go.' Like a man on a mission, he virtually dragged her across the floor and through the glass doors that led directly to the roof of the building and the helicopter pad.

His pilot and another man who Kimberley assumed to be another bodyguard immediately snapped to attention as Luc strode towards them, a look of purposeful intent in his shimmering dark gaze.

'There's no need to drag me,' she muttered, stumbling to keep up with him and he flashed her a smile that was nothing short of predatory.

'I'm in a hurry. It's either this or we go straight back in that lift. Take your pick.'

She shot him a look of naked exasperation. 'Your behaviour is well and truly locked in the Stone Age, do you know that? Have you ever even heard of the feminist movement and equal opportunities?'

'You will certainly have equal opportunity to experience pleasure once you're in my bed,' he assured her in silky tones, nodding to the pilot as he urged her into the helicopter with an almost indecent degree of haste.

Left with no choice, she slid into the nearest seat and shot him a look of helpless disbelief. 'You're unbelievable. Do any women actually agree to work for you?'

'Of course.' He loosened his tie and gave a tiny frown, clearly thinking it an odd question. 'You just met Maria.'

'Yes, she wasn't at all what I expected.' Kimberley's fingers tightened on her bag. She was horribly conscious of his proximity and the quivering, aching response of her own body, which seemed to be totally outside her control. No matter what she thought or what she wanted, it seemed she was destined to be fatally drawn to his raw male sex appeal.

Dangerous black eyes gleamed with amusement as he fastened his seat belt. 'And just what were you expecting?'

Kimberley looked away from him and focused on a point outside the window. 'I don't know. Someone younger? More glamorous. You're addicted to beautiful women.' *As she'd discovered to her cost.* For a short blissful time, she'd thought he was addicted to *her* and then she'd discovered just how short his attention span was. He'd cured his addiction to her all too easily.

'The secret of success in business is to be clear about the job description and then select the right person for the job,' he informed her in cool tones. 'The attributes I require in a PA are not the same as those I require in my bedroom. I never confuse the two roles and I never mix business with pleasure.'

This evidence of his ruthless self-discipline was in such stark contrast to her own dismal lack of control when she was around him that she felt her frustration slowly mounting. Was he really able to be that detached?

Recalling the way he'd strolled out of the lift and clicked his mind into business mode, she decided that he clearly was and the realisation wasn't flattering.

Evidently the effect she had on him was less than overwhelming.

She glanced across at him. 'So what would you do if you wanted a relationship with someone who worked for you?'

'Fire them and then sleep with them,' he replied without hesitation. 'But I don't understand why that would interest you. You're not working for me, so there's absolutely no barrier to our relationship.'

'Apart from the fact that we can't stand the sight of one another.'

'Cast your mind back to the lift,' he suggested silkily, dark lashes lowering as he studied her with blatantly sexual intent. 'And if that doesn't jog your memory, then try asking yourself why you're not currently wearing underwear.'

She gave a tiny gasp of shock and her heart skipped a beat. 'You didn't give me the opportunity to put them back on, they were in tatters,' she murmured, trying without any confidence of success to emulate the cool indifference that he constantly displayed.

'That's because I believe in economy of effort and I don't see the point in removing them twice.'

'Aren't you ever interested in anything other than sex?' she blurted out suddenly. 'Don't you want to know a single thing about me?'

'I know that you excite me more than any woman I've ever met,' he responded instantly, night-black eyes raking her tense, quivering body with raw masculine appreciation. 'What else would I want, or need, to know?'

She gazed at him helplessly, both fascinated and appalled by his total lack of emotional engagement. He was a man who operated alone. A man who appeared to need no one.

Luc didn't have a single vulnerable bone in his body.

Then she thought of Rio and she was stifled by a maternal love so powerful that it almost choked her.

In a sudden rush of panic, she fumbled for her seat belt and unclipped it. 'I can't do this, Luc, I'm sorry,' she stammered. 'You have to take me to the airport. I have to go home now. I need to be there for my son. I've never left him before, not for this long, and he's in danger—'

Luc lounged in his seat, watching her with interest. 'Drop the act, *meu amorzinho*,' he advised gently. 'The money is already paid. The deal is done.'

Her breathing quickened. 'But what if it isn't enough?' She bit her lip. 'Don't blackmailers often come back for more?'

Luc paused, his eyes glittering dark in his handsome face. 'I think it will take our "blackmailer" a little while to work her way through five million dollars, don't you?' His tone was mocking and she flushed with anger and frustration.

'You're making *such* a big mistake.'

'I don't make mistakes. I make decisions and they're always the right ones,' he said in a cool tone, 'and my decision on this is to pay you what you've asked for. It's done. Now you have to play your part and I don't want to hear any more mention of blackmailers or sweet, vulnerable children who need you at home.'

What could she do?

The helicopter was already in mid-flight and, if what Luc said was correct, then the money was already in the hands of the blackmailer.

Kimberley turned her head so that he couldn't see the tears in her eyes.

This was about *her,* not her son, she acknowledged helplessly. She'd always been hideously over-protective. From the moment Rio was born, her love for him had been absolute and unconditional. She'd tried hard not to smother him but she found it incredibly hard. She just loved him *so* much and she couldn't bear the thought that anything might make him unhappy, even for a moment.

But Rio would be fine, she told herself firmly. He adored Jason and Jason adored him back and would never let anything happen to him.

It was she who was going to suffer by not being close to her child.

Two weeks. She straightened her narrow shoulders and forced herself to get a grip on her emotions. Just two weeks and then her life would be back to normal again.

No blackmailer and no Luc.

Would it really be that hard? What was he asking for? Sex without love?

Well, she could do that.

She was just going to lie there, she vowed fiercely to herself. She wasn't going to sob and she wasn't going to beg.

And when eventually she bored him and he decided to let her go, she was going to walk away without a backward glance, as emotionally detached as he was.

CHAPTER FIVE

THE helicopter had barely settled on dry land before Luc was out of his seat. If he was aware of the mystified glances exchanged between his bodyguards and his pilot then he gave no sign, his darkly handsome face a mask of cool indifference as he strode the short distance to the villa with Kimberley clamped firmly by his side.

For a man who prided himself on his rigid self-discipline and self-control, he was suffering from no small degree of discomfort and irritation because at that precise moment he'd never felt *less* in control. Only once before in his life could he remember acting in such a wild and impulsive manner and that was seven years before when Kimberley had first entered his life.

The knowledge did nothing to soothe his volatile and uncertain mood.

He was frustrated, exasperated and more than a little disturbed by his own behaviour, and he didn't need to read the body language of his clearly stunned staff to confirm that his behaviour was totally out of character.

It wasn't just the incident in the lift, he mused grimly as he walked with single-minded purpose through the grounds of the villa, indifferent to the visual temptation presented by the lush gardens. His fingers were still clamped around her slender wrist as he headed directly for the master suite, skirting round the tempting blue of the pool, which sparkled and shimmered in the sunlight.

No. It definitely wasn't about the lift. What did that prove, apart from the fact that he was a normal red-blooded guy with a healthy appetite for an attractive woman and an ability to make the most of the moment?

He could even have dismissed the more seedy aspects of seducing a woman in a public place if the experience had left him clear-headed and sated and with his sanity fully restored. But that wasn't the case. Like an alcoholic who had allowed himself the dark indulgence of just one drink, that one taste of the forbidden had left him with a throbbing, nagging need for still more and he had an uncomfortable feeling that even a gawking crowd wouldn't be enough to tempt him to exercise restraint should the situation arise again.

And that was what he found uncomfortable about the whole situation in which he now found himself.

He never lost control. In fact he prided himself on his ability to remain cool when others around him were reaching boiling point. He prided himself on his ability to maintain a rational approach to decision making when others around him became emotional. It was his ability to think, unencumbered by the emotional baggage that seemed to trouble some people, which was a major contributor to his current success.

And, although women played an important part in his life, never *ever* had a woman compromised his business decisions.

Until now.

From the moment Kimberley had re-entered his life, all that mattered to him was getting her back in his bed and keeping her there until his body was sufficiently sated for him to be able to think clearly again.

His behaviour since Kimberley had walked back into his

life had been so completely out of character that he was not in the least surprised that his bodyguards and pilot were looking at him strangely. Even Maria, who knew more about him than most, had been openly shocked by his sudden request that she completely rearrange his diary in order to accommodate his need to be absent from the office for the foreseeable future. In fact he was entirely sure that a large proportion of his staff would be huddled together at this very moment discussing the question of their boss's personality transformation.

And he was asking himself the very same question.

Given the delicate stage of the business deal he was currently negotiating, it was nothing short of reckless to cancel meetings and leave the office at a time when his presence was mandatory.

But that was exactly what he'd done and he was ready to ignore the consequences.

He was ready to ignore everything except the building sexual tension that nagged at his body. Their torrid encounter in the lift had succeeded in heating his blood to intolerable levels and, if it hadn't been for the fact that halting the lift for any longer would have attracted the attentions of a maintenance team with embarrassing consequences, he would have satisfied his baser urges and taken her there and then, against the mirrored wall of his express lift.

The knowledge would have disturbed him more had he not been grimly aware that there had never been a woman who had succeeded in holding his attention longer than a few weeks. Given that knowledge, he was entirely confident that, with the right degree of dedication to the task in hand, he could easily work Kimberley out of his system.

She really was pushing her luck, he mused, trying to slap him with a paternity suit seven years after their relationship had ended. Did she think he was entirely stupid? Still, her greed had thrown her back into his path and for that he was grateful. He'd been given the chance to get her out of his system once and for all.

This time he was going to take the relationship to its inevitable conclusion.

Despite the number of corporate headaches bearing down on him from all sides, he'd decided to dedicate the next few weeks of his life to becoming bored by Kimberley. He owed it to his sanity and his ability to concentrate. And all he required to fulfil that task was privacy and an extremely large double bed, both of which were very much available in his villa. It was the one place in the world where he was guaranteed not to be disturbed. The one place where the press and the public were unable to gain any sort of access.

The one place where he could be truly alone to concentrate on Kimberley.

And, if the episode in the lift was anything to go by, they really, *really* needed to be alone.

Hot, sticky and thoroughly overheated by factors far more complex than a tropical climate, Kimberley glanced longingly at the cool water of the pool, but Luc didn't alter his pace as he strode towards the bedroom suite that she remembered all too well.

Her pulse rate increased and her mouth dried.

During the time they'd spent on the island she'd hardly left that room and going back there now simply intensified the shame she already felt at the uninhibited way she'd responded to him all those years ago.

She wanted to dig her heels in and resist but the tight grip of his strong fingers on her wrist and the grim, set expression on his face were warning enough that any argument on her part was futile.

And anyway, she reasoned helplessly, how could she argue?

She'd agreed to this.

For the sum of five million dollars and to protect her child, she'd agreed to it and she just wanted to get the next two weeks over with as quickly as possible and get home.

She wanted to be with her son. She missed him dreadfully.

And she was afraid. Desperately afraid that she might turn back into the helpless, needy woman Luc had seduced all those years before.

When she'd met him she'd been a hard working, successful model. She'd never missed a shoot or been late for an appointment in her life. Then she'd met Luc and all that had changed.

One hot glance from those dark eyes and she'd been dazzled, unable to see anything except *him.* She'd abandoned her job, forgotten her responsibilities and ceased to care about anything except Luc.

She'd been so drunk on her love for him that she'd failed to see that, for him, their relationship was all about sex. Even when he'd left her in bed to date other women, she hadn't truly accepted that their relationship had no future. Only when she'd discovered that she was pregnant, only when she'd turned to him for help and been rejected, had she finally accepted that it was over.

And now here she was, about to walk back into Luc Santoro's bedroom again. *About to risk everything.*

Last time he'd hurt her so badly with his cruel indifference that it had taken years for her to piece her life back together again, but she'd done it and she was proud of the woman she'd become. Proud of her son and the small business she'd built. Proud of her life. And she'd been very careful to preserve and protect that life.

But this wasn't like the last time, she reminded herself firmly. The last time she'd been young, naïve and hopelessly in love with the man she'd wanted Luc to be. Now she was a very different person and, no matter how powerful the sexual attraction, she wasn't going to lose sight of the man he really was. She had no intention of making that mistake a second time in her life.

She knew now that Luc didn't have an emotional bone in his perfectly put together body and he was never going to change.

She lifted her chin. He'd proved to her time and time again that he was capable of enjoying sex without emotion, so why shouldn't she be able to do the same thing? In many ways he was the perfect man for the task, she thought, sneaking a sideways glance at his hard, handsome profile. Whatever criticisms could be levelled at him in the emotional stakes, his bedroom technique was surely unsurpassed.

Remembering the wild, mindless encounter in the lift, her breathing hitched in her throat and a sudden flare of delicious, forbidden excitement scorched her body.

She would approach the next two weeks with the same emotional detachment that he did, she vowed silently, ignoring the bump of her heart as he all but dragged her into the bedroom that opened directly on to the pool area.

In front of her was a huge bed, *the* huge bed that she remembered well. She should do, she thought wryly, because she had barely left it for the entire time they'd spent at the villa.

Covered with sheets of the finest Egyptian cotton, it faced both the pool and the sea, but Kimberley recalled with a lowering degree of clarity that on the previous occasion she'd lain in that very bed and been totally unaware of the view. When she had been with Luc, for her the outside world had ceased to exist.

Well, not any more.

This time she was going to enjoy the pool and the sea along with any other hidden delights that his private island had to offer.

She'd enjoy the sex for the two weeks, just as she'd agreed, but this time everything else would be different. She'd enjoy his incredible body in the most superficial way possible. She wasn't going to fall in love and she wasn't going to pretend that Luc might fall in love with *her*.

That way she'd be sure of being able to walk away with her heart completely intact.

If he could do it, so could she, and just to prove that fact she turned to him with a cool smile on her face.

'Well—' She waved a hand towards the bed in an almost dismissive gesture. 'We seem to have everything we need, so shall we make a start?'

Wasn't that what it was all about? Practicality versus romance.

She just needed to learn to play by different rules. *His rules.*

His dark eyes sharpened on her face. 'Sarcasm doesn't suit you. It isn't part of your personality and it isn't part of who you are.'

'You have no idea who I am, Luc, and we both know that it isn't my personality that interests you.' She kept her tone casual as she strolled towards the bed and dropped her bag on the cover. 'And you're the one who keeps reminding me that you didn't pay five million dollars to indulge in conversation.'

She saw the flicker of incredulity cross his handsome face and suddenly felt like smiling.

He'd expected her to stammer and protest. He'd been prepared to control and dominate in his usual fashion. But this time she wasn't going to allow it. This time, she was the one with the upper hand. Instead of fighting against the tide she was swimming with it.

She'd surprised him and it felt *good*.

With a sense of power and confidence that she couldn't ever remember feeling before in his company, she casually undid the buttons of her shirt and strolled towards the luxurious bathroom. 'I'll just take a shower and I'll meet you in the bed in five minutes.'

She was doing brilliantly, she told herself gleefully as she stripped her clothes off and stepped under the power shower. Even though this situation wasn't of her choice, there was no reason why she had to allow Luc to call all the shots.

The spray was the perfect temperature and she closed her eyes and gave a soft moan of pleasure as the cool water drenched her heated flesh.

For a moment she just stood there, humming softly to herself, revelling in the feel of the water on her skin and the knowledge that, for once, she was the one in control.

Her feeling of smug satisfaction lasted all of eight seconds.

'I never knew you had such a good singing voice,' came a dark male drawl from directly next to her and with a soft gasp of shock she opened her eyes and brushed the water away from her face to clear her vision.

Luc stood only inches away from her, gloriously naked and unashamedly aroused, his body as close to male physical perfection as it was possible to get.

'I must congratulate you.' The water clung to his thick, dark lashes and he watched her with a slumberous expression in his wicked dark eyes. 'A shower together was the perfect idea, *meu amorzinho*. I more than approve.'

Her new-found confidence vanished in an instant.

He wasn't supposed to approve. He was supposed to be feeling deflated and frustrated and slightly at a loss by the fact she'd taken control.

Instead he looked like a man who was well and truly in command of the situation.

Remembering her promise to herself not to play the part of the shrinking maiden, she resisted the temptation to flatten herself against the wall of the shower.

'You didn't need to join me,' she said in a cool voice, averting her eyes from the tantalising vision of curling black hair shadowing a bronzed, muscular chest. She didn't dare look lower. Her one brief glimpse when she'd opened her eyes had been more than enough to remind her of his undeniable masculinity. 'We have a contract and I intend to honour it. You don't need to worry about me escaping.'

'Do I look worried?' His eyes gleamed dark with amusement and he lifted a hand and smoothed her damp hair away from her face. 'Why would I worry when I know you can't say no to me?'

She gritted her teeth and tried to ignore the tiny spasms of excitement that licked through her body. 'You need a private island to accommodate your ego.'

He gave a soft laugh and reached out to pull her closer in a gesture that was pure caveman. 'I love the fact that you pretend you can resist me. It's going to make your final surrender all the more satisfying. You present me with a challenge and I *love* a challenge.'

She stared at him helplessly, appalled by his arrogance and yet fascinated by his undiluted masculinity. 'What you're saying is that you just can't take no for an answer.'

'Perhaps my English isn't always perfect.'

'Your English is f-fluent,' she stammered, heat piercing through her pelvis as the roughness of his thighs brushed against her bare legs. 'It's just that you always have to get your own way in everything.'

'And what's wrong with that?' He gave a casual shrug and curved an arm around her narrow waist, bringing her hard against him. 'Especially when we both want the same thing.'

Her heart was thumping so hard that she could hardly breathe and as she felt him reach for the soap and slide his hands down her bare back she couldn't hold back the moan.

'You have an amazing body,' he said hoarsely, turning her round and sliding his strong hands down her spine.

Her eyes closed and she forced herself to think about something else. But the only thing in her mind was Luc and when she felt his hands move to her hair she gave a shudder of approbation.

He lathered her hair, his fingers delivering a slow, sensual massage to her scalp, and she closed her eyes, unable to resist the amazingly skilful pressure of his fingers. It had always been like this, she thought helplessly as she sank into his caress. He knew exactly how to touch her. Exactly how to melt resistance. *Exactly how to drive her wild.*

He washed the rest of her body, lingering in some parts just long enough to make her squirm and then moving on to concentrate his attentions elsewhere.

He carried on until her entire body was quivering with anticipation. *Until she was desperate to explore him the way he was exploring her.* Unable to wait a moment longer, Kimberley reached out and slid a hand over his chest and then lower still, following the track of dark hair that led downwards.

But he caught her wrists in his hands and drew her arms round his neck, refusing her the satisfaction of touching him.

Need and frustration pounding in her veins, she tried to free her arms but he held her firm, a glimmer of mockery in his dark eyes as he lowered his mouth to hers.

But he refused to kiss her properly.

Still in teasing mode, he licked at the corners of her mouth, played with her lower lip and kissed his way down her neck until she was gasping and writhing against him, but still he wouldn't give her what she craved.

Her whole body throbbed and ached with an intensity that approached pain, but there was nothing she could do to relieve the mounting frustration. Only he could do that and he was careful to give her just enough to build the excitement while withholding the ultimate satisfaction that she craved.

He teased her and seduced her until every nerve in her body was throbbing and humming, until she was unable to think about anything except the man in front of her. Her mind ceased to function and she was driven entirely by her senses to the point where she wasn't even aware that he'd switched off the shower until she felt herself wrapped in a soft towel and lifted into his arms.

Somewhere in the back of her mind something nagged at her. Something about him being the one in control once more. But she couldn't hold on to the thought long enough to examine it, let alone act on it, so she lay still in his arms, drugged and dizzy from his slow, expert seduction.

He laid her on the bed, removed the towel with a gentle but determined tug and then came down on top of her, a gleam of masculine purpose in his dark eyes.

Almost breathless with desperation, she ran her hands down the sleek muscle of his back and shifted her body under his in an attempt to gain access to the male power of him. He slid away from her in a smooth movement and she gave a sob of frustration, her hips writhing against the sheets.

'You touch me—why can't I touch you?'

'Not yet—' He anchored her wrists in his hands and held them above her head and then finally he lowered his head to hers.

His mouth took hers in a kiss so hot and sexual that the room spun around her and she thought she might actually lose consciousness.

His tongue explored every inch of her mouth with erotic expertise and she was so drugged by his skilful touch that she didn't realise that he'd tied her wrists until she tried to slide her arms round his neck and discovered that she couldn't.

Her hands were firmly secured to the head of the bed.

He gave a low laugh of masculine satisfaction and slid down her body. 'Now I have you *exactly* where I want you, *meu amorzinho*.'

A flicker of alarm penetrated the sensual fog that had paralysed her brain and she tried to tug at her wrists but he chose that precise moment to flick his tongue over her nipple and she gave a gasp as sharp needles of sensation pierced her body.

She writhed and shifted on the bed, trying desperately to rediscover her powers of speech and demand that he let her go, when he sucked her into his mouth and proceeded to subject her to the skill of his tongue.

It was maddeningly good and she felt the burning ache in her pelvis increase to almost intolerable levels but he was in no hurry, his seduction slow and leisurely as he skilfully caressed first one breast and then the other.

She squirmed and gasped and tugged at her bound wrists and just when she thought she couldn't stand it any longer he slid down her body.

Barely able to form the words, she gave a moan of protest, horribly embarrassed. 'Untie me, Luc, please—'

He lifted his dark head, 'Not yet. You still have too many inhibitions. You think too much. I want to show you what your body can feel when the freedom of choice is removed. You are quite safe, *meu amorzinho*. All that is going to happen is that I intend to torture you with pleasure and you will be totally unable to resist.'

Horror and disbelief mingled with a sense of wicked anticipation as he slid further down the bed and closed his strong hands round her trembling thighs.

Realising his intention, she tried desperately to keep her legs together, but he gave a low laugh and ignored her feeble resistance, opening her to his hungry gaze with the gentle pressure of his hands.

She'd never felt so exposed before, so vulnerable, and her face burned hot under his probing, masculine gaze. Her whole body tensed as she felt his fingers slide through the fiery curls at the apex of her thighs and then he was parting her and she felt the damp flick of his tongue exploring her intimately.

She gave a gasp of shock and tried to free herself but her hands were securely tied and she had no way of protecting herself from his determined seduction. And soon the very thought of protecting herself vanished from her brain because what he was doing to her body felt so impossibly, exquisitely good she thought there was a very strong chance that she might pass out.

When he slid his fingers deep inside her, Kimberley shot into a climax so intense that she cried out sharply in almost agonised disbelief. The sensation went on and on, his fingers and his mouth witness to the sensual havoc he was creating within her body.

It was so wild that she lost touch with reality, lost touch with everything, controlled entirely by erotic sensation caused by one man.

Finally the spasms eased and he slid up her body in a smooth movement and ran his fingers through her damp, tangled hair.

Limp and dazed, she stared up at him blankly, slowly registering the triumphant expression in those night-black eyes as they raked her flushed cheeks.

Without shifting his gaze from hers, he reached up and freed her in one simple movement, trailing the scarlet silk ribbon that had held her captive to his sexual whims over one hardened nipple.

'*Now* you can touch me,' he informed her in silky tones and she wished she had the energy or the inclination to smack the smug smile from his indecently handsome face. He was all too aware of his own abilities to drive a woman to the edge of sanity, but unfortunately she was suffering such an overload of excitement that she could think of nothing but her own need for him.

She reached for him urgently, closing her slender fingers over the impressive throb of his erection with a moan of feminine approval.

With a grunt deep in his throat, he slid an arm under her hips, positioned her to his satisfaction and thrust deeply into her shivering, quivering body and it felt so shockingly good to have him inside her again that she gave a sob of relief. Wrapping her legs around him, she moved her hips instinctively and he muttered something against her mouth before driving into her hard and setting a rhythm that was pagan and primitive and out of control.

She raked her nails down his back and he dug his fingers into her thighs, bringing his mouth down hard on hers, connecting them in every way possible until the inevitable sensual explosion engulfed her, suspending thought and time.

Kimberley felt her mind go blank, felt her body come apart as fierce excitement gripped her. For a moment, everything was suspended and exaggerated and she struggled to breathe as her body convulsed around the plunging, primal force of his. Dimly she registered a masculine groan and knew that her climax had driven him to the same peak. She felt the liquid force of his own release, felt him thrust hard as he powered into her, felt the rasp of male chest hair against her sensitised breasts as his body moved against hers. The spasms went on and on and she clung to him, overpowered by sensation, riding the storm, waiting for the world around her to settle.

And eventually it did. Her senses cleared and calm was restored. She opened her eyes and saw a bronzed male shoulder, became aware of the slick heat of his body against hers, the harshness of his breathing against her cheek and the weight of him pressing down on her.

And then he rolled on to his back, taking her with him. Her hair tumbled and slid across his chest and he gave a satisfied groan and brushed it gently away from her face so that he could kiss her mouth.

'That was amazing.' His tone was slightly roughened and Kimberley shifted her head slightly so that she could look at him, her eyes trapped by his slumberous dark gaze. 'You are so wild in my bed. And, just in case you're tempted to pretend that you didn't enjoy it, then I ought to warn you that you'd be wasting your time,' he drawled lazily, smothering a yawn. 'You were completely mad for me and I still have the wounds on my back to prove it.'

His less than subtle reminder of just how uninhibited she'd been horrified her and she pulled away from him, suddenly realising that, despite her best intentions, he'd taken all the control right back. And, judging from the satisfied macho smile on his sickeningly handsome face, he knew it.

Ignoring the fact that her limbs felt weak and her body ached and throbbed, she sprang out of bed. It was the only way she could fight the impulse to snuggle against him. And their relationship wasn't about affection.

'Well, I thought that five million dollars required an above average performance on my part.' Her casual tone drew a quick frown from him but she turned and strolled into the bathroom with what she hoped was a convincing degree of indifference.

Inside the palatial bathroom she bolted the door and then slid in a boneless heap on to the marbled floor and covered her face with her hands.

She remembered his words as he'd untied her with a whimper of horror.

'Now you can touch me.'

Even in the middle of lovemaking, he'd still been the one in control and she'd been so desperate for him that she hadn't even noticed. In fact she'd ceased to care about anything else except satisfying the maddening, almost intolerable ache in her body. He'd orchestrated every second of her seduction, without once allowing her the same privileged, unlimited access to his body. And, although he'd clearly enjoyed their encounter, at no point in the proceedings had he appeared to lose control or been consumed by the same degree of sexual abandon.

She remembered how pleased she'd been with herself earlier when she'd taken control back for a few moments. And she remembered the surprise in his eyes. But it hadn't lasted. From the moment he'd stepped into the shower with her, he'd been in full command mode. The truth was that in the bedroom he would always be in charge. And his skills in that department were such that he could turn her into a mindless squirming mass within seconds and she just hated herself for being unable to resist him.

Dragging herself over to the mirror, she gazed at her reflection, seeing flushed cheeks and a soft, bruised mouth.

What had happened to her?

In the last seven years she'd raised a child and built a successful business from scratch. She considered herself to be competent and independent. She was proud of the woman she'd become.

And yet in Luc Santoro's bed that woman vanished and in her place was the same clingy, needy, desperate girl that she'd been at eighteen.

Two weeks, she reminded herself grimly as she splashed her face with cold water and tidied her hair. She just had to get through two weeks and then she could return home to her child and put Luc Santoro back in the past where he well and truly belonged.

CHAPTER SIX

STRETCHED out in the shade by the exquisite pool almost two weeks later, Kimberley decided drowsily that she'd undergone a complete personality change. Far from being an independent thinking woman, she now felt more like a sex slave, ready and willing to obey the commands of her master.

Luc only had to cast a burning glance in her direction and she fell into his arms with an enthusiasm as predictable as it was humiliating.

Underneath the sensual addiction that fuelled her every move she was secretly *appalled* at herself and she didn't know which was worse—the knowledge that she'd reverted to her old self the moment he'd brought his extremely talented mouth down on hers, or the fact that she was actually enjoying herself and she was far too honest a person to pretend otherwise. How could she when she couldn't take her eyes off him? *Couldn't stop wondering when he was going to reach for her next?*

If it hadn't been for the fact that she was missing Rio horribly, she would have been completely and totally happy.

Even though Luc had assured her that the money had immediately been transferred into the right account, as per her instructions, and that her surreptitious calls to Jason had assured her that everything seemed fine at home, she couldn't stop worrying.

It made no difference that she'd sneaked off at least once a day, and sometimes twice, to phone her son and chat about what was happening in his life. It made no difference that he'd sounded happy and buoyant and didn't seem to be missing her at all.

She missed him.

Desperately.

And she wanted to go home.

Which just left her to finish her part of the deal with Luc.

And so far he'd certainly been getting his money's worth. They'd barely left the bed.

Maybe it was being back in this villa, she thought helplessly as she glanced across the pool to the lush gardens that led down to the beach. It had such powerful associations with the first time they'd met that it was impossible for her to remember how much she'd changed since those days.

She'd regressed to the girl she'd been at eighteen.

'You are dreaming again.' Luc lifted himself out of the swimming pool in a lithe, powerful movement and ran a hand over his eyes to clear the water from his face. He reached for a towel and flashed her a predatory smile. 'There is no need to dream when you have the real thing. If you wish to return to the bedroom, *meu amorzinho*, then you only have to say the word.'

His arrogant assumption that her dreams had all been about him should have made her slap his face or at least deliver an acid comment about the size of his ego. But she was prevented from speaking because it was true. Her dreams *were* all about him.

And that was the most annoying thing of all, she mused as she stretched out a hand and reached for her drink. Apart from being with her child, there was no place in the world she'd rather be than in Luc's bed and she just hated herself for feeling like that. It might have been different if the relationship had been equal, but it wasn't.

He was *always* the one in control. He decided when they ate, when they slept, when they made love, even *how* they made love. Any attempt on her part to take the lead was always brushed aside.

It wasn't that Luc didn't enjoy the sex, because he clearly did, but she was humiliatingly aware that he never lost control in the way that she did. He orchestrated every move in the bedroom.

He strolled over to her, the towel looped over his broad shoulders, water clinging to the hairs on his chest and the hard muscles of his thighs. He had a body designed to scramble a woman's brain and she felt her stomach clench. No wonder she couldn't resist him. What woman could? He was as near to masculine perfection as it was possible to get.

'You've been out here for almost an hour.' He dropped the towel, a frown in his eyes as he studied her semi-naked body. 'Go back inside before you burn.'

She opened her mouth to point out that he was being controlling again, when she realised that it would give her the perfect opportunity to call home again.

She could have been open about phoning her son but, given that Luc hadn't mentioned the subject since they'd arrived on the island, it seemed more sensible to let the matter drop.

Suddenly she missed Rio so acutely that the pain was almost physical.

She needed to hear his voice.

Trying to look suitably casual, she swung her legs over the edge of the sunbed and stood up. 'You're right, I'm burning,' she stammered quickly, reaching for her bag and sliding her feet into her sandals. 'I'll go inside for a while and lie down. I'm feeling a little tired.'

It was true. Unlike Luc, who seemed possessed of almost supernatural energy levels and stamina, she found it hard to go through an entire night with virtually no sleep without then dropping off to sleep at various intervals throughout the day.

Ignoring the hot slide of his gaze over her body, she hurried into the bedroom, reaching into her bag for her mobile phone.

With a quick glance over her shoulder, she checked that Luc was still safely on the terrace by the pool and then dialled the number.

Rio answered. 'Mum?' He sounded breathless with excitement and older than his six years. 'You have to buy me a fish!'

She closed her eyes and felt relief flood through her. He sounded so normal. *And so like his father.* Life with Rio was one long round of commands and orders.

'What sort of fish?'

'Like the one we've just got at school; it's *really* cool.'

Kimberley smiled. To her six-year-old son, everything was cool.

They talked for a few more minutes and then she cut the connection reluctantly, feeling as though she was tearing her own heart out.

But as she dropped the phone back into her bag she saw the letter and remembered the reason she was doing this. *She was keeping her baby safe.*

Something glinted underneath the envelope and she gave a slight frown and delved into the bag again, this time removing a set of handcuffs. She gave a disbelieving laugh and then remembered that her son had borrowed a policeman's outfit from one of his friends and had been dressing up on the day before she'd flown out to Brazil. He must have dropped the cuffs into her bag. How they hadn't been detected by the airport authorities, she had no idea.

She fingered the handcuffs thoughtfully and a wickedly naughty idea suddenly shot through her brain.

Did she dare?

Before she could lose her nerve, she quickly looped them round the bed head and covered them with a pillow.

'I've decided that I'm risking sunstroke by staying outside and that I'm also in serious need of a rest.' Luc's sardonic masculine drawl came from the doorway and she gave a start and quickly jumped off the bed, her heart thumping, convinced that the guilt must be written all over her face.

Had he noticed what she'd just done?

Her eyes clashed with his and her stomach dropped in instinctive feminine response to the masculine intent she read in his eyes. He hadn't noticed. He was too busy looking at her legs and other parts of her openly displayed by the almost non-existent bikini that had been part of her newly acquired wardrobe.

'The sun doesn't bother you and you never get tired,' she reminded him, watching him stroll towards her in a pair of swimming trunks that did nothing to conceal his rampant arousal. 'And anyway, we only got up an hour ago.'

Her mouth dried and wicked excitement curled deep in her pelvis as she stared at him helplessly.

He was unbelievably good-looking and it was no wonder he affected her so strongly.

'An hour is a long time,' he said silkily, reaching for her and dragging her to her feet. 'Especially when you are wearing that particular bikini.'

His eyes dropped to her mouth and suddenly breathing seemed difficult. 'You chose the bikini.' It had been one of a selection of clothing that had been waiting for her at the villa. 'I didn't bring any clothes, remember?'

He gave a predatory smile. 'And so far, *minha docura*, you haven't needed any.'

'When it comes to sex, you're insatiable,' she said breathlessly. 'Do you know that?'

'When it comes to *you*, I'm insatiable,' he informed her and then frowned slightly as if the thought made him uncomfortable.

'Why are you frowning?'

'I'm not.' The frown on his brow lifted as he clearly dismissed the thought with his customary single-minded determination.

She felt his hand slide down her back and gave a shiver of response. Her reaction to him was so predictable, she thought helplessly. He only had to touch her and she surrendered.

Except that this time—

He slid his hand into her hair and tugged gently, exposing the smooth skin of her neck for his touch. She gasped as she felt the burning heat of his mouth and then she was tumbled back on to the bed with Luc on top of her, his seductive gaze veiled by thick, dark lashes.

'I can't get enough of you,' he raked hoarsely as he quickly stripped her of her bikini and then fastened his mouth on hers again.

He rolled on to his back, taking her with him, and she dragged her mouth away from his. She couldn't think straight when he was kissing her. Couldn't concentrate. *And she needed to concentrate because she had a plan.*

For once she was determined to take control. She was determined to torture him the way he always tortured her. *Payback time.*

Knowing that she had to act quickly, she drew his hands above his head, moving the pillow to reveal the handcuffs she'd already looped round the bed. Heart thumping, she snapped the cuffs on his wrists before he had time to realize her intentions.

He stilled and a look of stunned incredulity illuminated his dark gaze. *'What* do you think you are doing?'

She held her breath, watching as the muscles of his shoulders bunched as he jerked his wrists in an attempt to free himself. *Would the handcuffs hold?*

Deciding that she needed to use more than one method of

holding him captive, she bent her head and teased the corners of his mouth with her tongue. 'You said you could handle me with both hands tied behind your back,' she reminded him in a husky voice, 'so I thought I'd give it a try. Both of your hands are well and truly behind your back, or above your head if you want to be precise. I'm all yours, Luc.' Her tongue slid between his lips in a teasing, erotic gesture and she saw his eyes darken. She lifted her head and licked her lips slowly, savouring the taste of his mouth. 'Or perhaps you're all mine. Let's find out, shall we?'

She saw the shock flicker across his handsome face and for the first time in her life had the pleasure of seeing Luc Santoro out of his depth. She saw him struggling to shake off the raw desire so that he could think clearly and almost smiled. *How many times had she tried to do the very same thing in his bed and failed?*

'No woman has ever done this to you before, have they?' She slid her body over his, soft woman over hard man, felt the power of his erection brush against her abdomen and immediately moved away. *She wasn't ready to touch him there yet.* 'You're about to discover what it's like to be ruled by the senses and to be totally at the mercy of another person.'

His dark eyes were fierce. '*Meu Deus*, Kimberley. Let me go, now!'

With agonising slowness she dragged a slender finger through the hairs on his chest, her mouth curving into a smile as he shuddered.

'You're not in a position to give orders,' she pointed out in a husky voice, 'so you might just as well relax and go with the flow. Who knows, you might find that you enjoy having someone else in the command position for a while.'

His aggressive jaw hardened. 'Kimberley—' his tone was hoarse and he jerked at his hands again '—I demand that you let me go.'

'Order—' she bent her head and trailed her tongue along the hard ridge of his jaw '—demand—' her tongue snaked upwards towards his ear '—they're not the words I want to hear,' she informed him huskily, enjoying herself more and more. 'By the time I've finished with you, you're going to scream and beg, Luc. In exactly the same way that you make me scream and beg.'

'That's *different*—'

'How is it different?' She lowered her mouth again and trailed hot kisses over his bronzed muscular shoulder. *She just adored his body.* 'Because you're a man and I'm a woman?' Her teeth nipped his shoulder and she heard the hiss of his breath as he fought for control. 'You told me that you believed in equal opportunities, Luc. Let's find out whether you were telling the truth, shall we? I've just turned the tables on you.'

For the first time in their relationship she had the chance to admire his body the way he insisted on admiring hers. *She could take her time.* And she had every intention of doing just that.

Registering his stunned and slightly dazed expression with a sexy, satisfied smile, she slid her hands down his body and removed his swimming trunks in a smooth movement, sliding them down his legs and exposing him fully to her gaze.

He was hard and proud and totally ready for all the dark, sensual exploits she had in mind.

For a moment she just stared and he swore fluently in his own language and shifted his lean hips on the bed.

'Release me, now! This is *not* funny—'

'It isn't supposed to be funny.' The atmosphere in the room crackled and throbbed as the tension mounted. *He was magnificent,* she thought to herself. Hot, aroused and more of a man than he had a right to be. And she wanted him badly.

But she was going to make herself wait.

And, more to the point, she was going to make *him* wait.

With a low laugh of triumph and a heated glance that was pure seductress, she slid her fingers down his body until her hand lingered teasingly on his taut abdomen, just short of the straining shaft of his manhood.

'Release me!' He swore softly and pulled hard at the handcuffs but they held firm and Kimberley lifted her head and smiled a womanly smile, her confidence and power increasing by the minute.

'No way.' Her hand slid to the top of his thigh. 'For once I've got you exactly where I want you and you're going to stay there until I've finished with you.'

'You can't do this—'

'I *am* doing it. It's time you learned that you can't always be the one in control. I'm going to show you what it feels like to be tortured by sensual pleasure.'

He gave a soft curse and jerked at the handcuffs again but still they held fast and Kimberley bent her head, her glorious fiery hair trailing over his body as she used her tongue to trace the line of hair that ran below his navel. Her touch was slow and teasing and she saw the muscles of his abdomen tense viciously. He wanted her to touch him, badly, but she was determined not to. Not yet. She wasn't ready. And neither was he.

She had never been given unrestricted access to his body before and suddenly she needed to touch and taste all of him. To know him in every way possible.

Dimly she heard the harshness of his breathing, but she was too caught up in the sensual feast she'd made for herself to be distracted. She licked and nibbled and tasted him everywhere except his throbbing, pulsing masculinity.

Once, her fingers brushed against him fleetingly and she heard his guttural groan and felt him jerk his body towards her but she pulled back and slid up his body, raking her fingers through his chest hair and using her tongue to tease his nipples.

His breathing was harsh in her ears and she saw the muscles in his shoulders bunch as he pulled at the restraints, but he failed to free himself and cursed again, his eyes burning dark in his handsome face.

He muttered something in his own language and she lifted her head and gave him a mocking smile.

'If you expect me to understand what you're saying, you're going to have to speak English.' Her voice was smoky and softened by desire. 'What is it you want, Luc?'

For a moment he just stared at her, obviously unable to form the words, his eyes glazed and fevered. Then he licked his tongue over his lips. 'I want you to touch me,' he muttered hoarsely. 'Touch me now.'

There was no mistaking just how much he wanted her and she felt a flash of womanly triumph. 'Not yet. I'm not ready, and neither are you.'

He closed his eyes and beads of sweat appeared on his brow. 'Kimberley, please—'

A feeling of power spread through her veins and she gave a slow womanly smile. 'When I'm ready, I'll touch you,' she told him in a husky, smoky voice. 'All you have to do is lie there.' She shifted up the bed and teased the corner of his mouth with her tongue. Instantly he moved his mouth to capture hers but she was too quick for him, moving just out of reach and smiling as he swore fluently.

'This isn't a joke, Kimberley!'

'I know that. I never joke about sex.' She saw from the flash in his eyes that he recognised the words that he'd spoken to her. 'Just relax, Luc. It may have escaped your notice, but this time *I'm* the one in control. I've got you exactly where I want you and you're not going anywhere until I've finished with you.'

He swore under his breath but she saw him harden still further and gave a low laugh of satisfaction. He wanted her every bit as much as she wanted him and the knowledge thrilled her. Suddenly aware of her own power, she raked a nail down his chest and ran her tongue over her lips.

'I'm going to make you sob and beg, Luc,' she said softly, leaning forward and tracing the line of his rough jaw with her tongue. 'I'm going to make you so desperate that you can't even remember who you are or what you're doing here.'

She slid a hand slowly down his taut body and rested her palm just millimetres away from his straining manhood.

His hard jaw clenched and his eyes glittered dangerously. 'I will make you suffer for this.'

'You're the one who's suffering, Luc.'

But the truth was that she was suffering too. Her body ached and throbbed with a need that she hadn't experienced before. She was supposed to be the one doing the seducing but having his perfect masculine physique stretched out for her enjoyment was a temptation too great to resist.

She proceeded to lick her way down his body, exploring him everywhere except that one place that was straining to be touched. Her long hair fell forward, sliding over his naked, straining body like a sensual cloak.

'Kimberley—' His hoarse plea made her lift her head and she gazed at him, her mouth damp and her eyes shimmering with need.

'Not yet—' Desire curled low in her pelvis but she held it in check, determined to delay his satisfaction the way he always delayed hers. 'You haven't begged.'

'*Meu Deus*—' he cursed softly and closed his eyes, thick dark lashes brushing his bronzed skin as he struggled against his body's natural desire for satisfaction.

Her gaze slid down his body and her mouth dried. He was rock-hard and so aroused that she felt her mouth dry in anticipation. Why hadn't she thought of doing this before? she wondered.

For the first time she felt strong and powerful.

For the first time she felt like his equal.

For the first time she was able to torment him the way he always took pleasure in tormenting her.

She waited until every muscle was straining in his powerful body, until she couldn't wait any longer.

'Kimberley—' His voice shook and his lean hips thrust upwards. 'I'm begging—'

And then she touched him.

With the hot slide of her mouth, she took him and tasted, his harsh moans of pleasure fuelling her own sense of power and need. She explored every part of him with her fingers, with her tongue until she could no longer bear the ache deep in her body.

Only then did she lift her head and slide on top of him. She positioned herself over him, her hair trailing over his chest, her eyes fixed on his face as she allowed only the tip of his manhood to touch her intimately. With a soft curse he strained upwards trying to fill her, trying to take her breast in his mouth, but she held herself slightly away from him and leaned forward to kiss him.

'I'm still the one in control, Luc,' she whispered against his lips, but she knew that, strictly speaking, it wasn't true. She wanted him every bit as desperately as he wanted her.

But still she was going to make him wait.

She made him wait until the beads of sweat gathered on his brow, until he could no longer see straight, *until she wanted him so badly that she couldn't hold herself back a moment longer.*

And then finally she took him. Deep inside her so that she could feel the hard throb of his erection with every pulse of her body, so that she forgot that they were supposed to be separate, man and woman. Instead they were one.

And when the inevitable explosion came it was so blisteringly intense that for a moment she was afraid of what she'd unleashed. It was a beast that couldn't be tamed. A beast that savaged both of them. A beast that had to be allowed to run riot until finally it burned itself out.

Which it finally did. In a riot of soft cries, harsh groans, gasps and sobs and slippery flesh, the beast finally left them.

Struggling to breathe, Kimberley slid sideways, her arm over his chest, her leg over his leg.

Eventually her senses settled and she dared to lift her head.

He lay with his eyes closed, dense dark lashes brushing his perfect bone structure, his arms still locked above his head.

Suddenly, in the aftermath of such intimacy, she felt ridiculously shy and self-conscious. 'Luc?'

He didn't respond and she gave a frown and reached up and undid the handcuffs.

Instantly strong arms came around her and he rolled her on to her back, his eyes burning into hers. 'I can't believe you just did that—'

She felt the power and strength of his body pressing into her and gave a soft gasp. 'Are you angry with me?'

'Angry?' He groaned and brushed his mouth over hers in a lingering kiss. 'How could I be angry with you for giving me the best sex of my life? And anyway I don't have the energy to be angry. I don't have the energy for anything.'

She smiled, feeling clever and beautiful and every inch a woman. 'It was good, wasn't it?'

He rolled on to his back, taking her with him. 'It was amazing,' he said huskily, stroking her tangled hair away from her flushed cheeks with a gentle hand. '*Where* did you get those handcuffs?'

She tensed. That was a question she hadn't anticipated and she didn't want to spoil the moment by mentioning Rio. 'Someone I know was playing a joke on me,' she muttered vaguely, hoping that he wouldn't delve further.

Fortunately he didn't. Instead he hauled her closer still, snuggling her against him.

She felt a flicker of surprise. Luc tolerated a cuddle after sex but she could never recall him initiating that kind of contact before.

Luc did sex. He didn't do the emotional stuff.

He kissed the top of her head. 'I can't believe you just did that. And I can't believe I just let you.'

She gave a low laugh, more than a little pleased with herself. 'You didn't have any choice. For the first time in your life, you weren't the one in control. I was.'

To her surprise, he laughed. 'You're right, you are a different woman now,' he said in husky tones as he slid a hand over her heated flesh with undisguised masculine appreciation. 'You never would have had the courage to do what you just did seven years ago. In fact, you were pretty shocked by me.'

'You were my first lover,' she reminded him. 'I hadn't done any of those things before and you were totally controlling.'

'Necessary,' he assured her arrogantly, 'because you were too tied up with your inhibitions to let go. You were only able to do so when you could convince yourself that I was the one who seduced you. It was all my fault, isn't that right, *meu amorzinho*?'

There was laughter in his voice and she lifted her head and gave him a reproachful look. 'I was a virgin.'

He gave a macho, self-satisfied smile. 'I *know* that. And being the only man who had ever slept with you gave me an incredible high. Now, go to sleep.' He tightened his grip. 'You need to get some rest and recover your energy.'

Having delivered that command, he closed his eyes and promptly fell asleep himself, his arms locked firmly around her.

And it felt so good that Kimberley hardly dared move in case he woke up and changed his mind about the cuddle.

Being held by him made her feel safe and secure. *And it felt totally right.*

Which was ridiculous, she told herself, because there was nothing right about a relationship based on nothing more than sex.

Slowly, the happiness drained out of her as realisation dawned.

For her it was so much more than sex, and it always had been. She'd dismissed what she'd felt for him at eighteen as childish infatuation. Who wouldn't have been dazzled by a man as sophisticated as Luc? But the truth was that she'd loved Luc almost from the first moment she'd set eyes on him and time had done nothing to dilute her feelings. What she'd felt as a girl was no different to what she felt now, as a woman. Love was the reason she was so vulnerable to Luc. Love was the reason she hadn't looked at another man in the last seven years. It didn't matter that he was controlling and that he revealed nothing of himself. *It didn't matter that he was totally the wrong man.*

It didn't even matter that he didn't love her.

She still loved him.

She closed her eyes tightly, refusing to allow her bleak thoughts to spoil the moment. It would be over soon enough because they were almost at the end of their two weeks.

Luc woke several hours later to find the sun setting and Kimberley gone.

He felt a flicker of something that he didn't recognise. *Disappointment*, he decided immediately, rejecting the opportunity to examine his emotions in more detail.

The most explosive sex of his entire life had left him feeling refreshed and invigorated and more than ready to appreciate the woman who had been part of the experience.

Was it surprising that he felt disappointed that she wasn't still lying in his arms?

He sprang out of bed, noted the abandoned handcuffs with an appreciative male smile, and reached for a pair of casual trousers.

He found her by the pool, her expression pale and strained, her mobile phone in her hand.

The tension in her slender frame stopped him dead. 'Is something wrong?'

After what they'd shared, he'd expected to find her relaxed and smiling, recovering her energy levels in the sun, ready for the next bout of lovemaking. Instead she gave a start and shot him a guilty look before stuffing the phone back in her bag. 'Nothing's wrong.'

More unfamiliar emotions boiled up inside him. 'Who were you calling?'

She dipped her head, her long fiery hair concealing her expression from him. 'Just a friend.'

A friend?

Luc felt the sharp claws of jealousy dig into his flesh. What sex was the 'friend'? Had she been talking to another man? What was her life like when she was at home? Did she date? *Had she tied another man to the bed and rendered him unable to think?*

He realised with no small degree of discomfort that, although he'd spent weeks in bed with this woman, he knew next to nothing about her, and suddenly he was driven by a burning desire to discover *everything*.

'We're dining on the terrace tonight,' he said firmly as she glanced up at him, clearly as startled by hearing this unusual announcement as he had felt making it. 'And we're going to talk.'

She blinked and her lips parted. Those perfectly shaped lips that had driven him wild only hours earlier.

Resolutely Luc pushed the thought away. He wasn't going to think about that now. The same instincts that had made him an unbeatable force in business were currently telling him that something wasn't right about this situation. And he intended to make it right. He had a sudden burning need to see her smiling again. The reason *why* he should suddenly feel the urge to make a woman happy outside the bedroom didn't occur to him as he searched his brain for an answer.

Obviously she wasn't short of sex, so the problem couldn't possibly lie there. Just to confirm that fact, his mind ran speedily through the time they'd spent together and he concluded with a warm feeling of masculine satisfaction that she *definitely* couldn't be feeling unappreciated in that department.

Which meant that the problem must lie elsewhere.

Romance.

With a sudden burst of clarity, he identified the reason for her long face.

Perhaps the last two weeks had been a little too bedroom focused, he conceded. Wasn't it true that women needed different things to men? Apparently whole books had been written on the subject. For some inexplicable reason women needed to *talk* and certainly during the past two weeks he and Kimberley hadn't indulged much in the way of conversation. Acknowledgment of that fact would normally have left him nothing short of indifferent, but for some reason that he didn't entirely understand he suddenly felt a driving need to give her everything she wanted. *He wanted to make Kimberley happy.* And if conversation was what it took, then he was willing to make that sacrifice.

Convinced that he'd found the solution to the white, pinched look on her face, he waved a hand towards the bedroom with the smug look of a man who knew he had all the answers when it came to women.

'There are clothes in the wardrobe,' he informed her silkily. 'Choose something and meet me out here when you're dressed.'

She stared at him blankly, as if he'd just delivered a command that was nothing short of incomprehensible.

'What's the point of getting dressed when you're just going to strip me naked again?' she asked him and there was a hint of wariness in her tone that triggered his male early warning system.

Telling himself that he could exercise restraint when there was a higher purpose, he gave a smile. 'Because tonight I'm more interested in your mind than your body. We're going to *talk, meu amorzinho,* and I'm going to find out everything there is to know about you.'

That soft mouth, *the same mouth that had taken him to paradise and back,* curved into a wry smile. 'And what about you, Luc? Are you going to talk too? Or am I going to be the one doing all the giving? Perhaps I want to know everything there is to know you too.'

Luc gave a brief frown but recovered himself in time. If she wanted him to talk too, then he could do that. True, it wasn't his favourite pastime, but he dealt with inquisitive journalists on a daily basis and was used to talking about a wide range of subjects. He was more than confident that he could maintain conversation over dinner with an attractive woman if the incentive was great enough.

'I look forward to telling you everything you want to know,' he said diplomatically, urging her back towards the villa with the palm of his hand. 'Change and I'll ask the staff to serve dinner by the pool.'

She walked away from him with the fluid, graceful movement of a dancer. Luc's eyes automatically slid down her slender back and he struggled briefly against a powerful impulse to forget this whole 'romantic' approach and indulge the caveman that was threatening to burst out from inside him.

Remembering the desolate expression on her face, he reminded himself that a small investment could often yield surprising results and that might well be the case with Kimberley.

He was entirely confident that exercising physical restraint for a short time would pay dividends in the bedroom.

All he needed to make his investment complete were pretty flowers, good wine and plenty of delicious food and the smile would soon be back on her face.

Easy, he thought to himself as he strode purposefully towards the kitchen to brief his chef and his housekeeper. Handling women was no different from any other business negotiation. It was just a question of identifying their weakness, and then moving in for the kill.

Before the evening was out, she'd be smiling again.

And he could satisfy the caveman inside him.

CHAPTER SEVEN

'So why did you give up modelling?'

Luc lounged across from her, his face bronzed and lethally handsome in the flickering candlelight. The setting couldn't have been more romantic. The pool was illuminated by what seemed like hundreds of tiny lights, the evening was warm and the air was filled with the heady scent of exotic flowers. It was a setting fit for seduction and yet he'd already seduced her. More times than she cared to count.

So why the exotic arrangement of flowers on the table?

Why the tablecloth and the sparkling crystal?

And why was he dressed in a pair of tailored trousers and an exquisite silk shirt when he'd barely bothered to get dressed for the past two weeks?

If it hadn't been Luc sitting across from her, she would have thought that the setting had been designed for romance.

But Luc didn't do romantic. Luc did white-hot sex. Luc did blistering, uncontrollable passion. Luc did control and domination. He most certainly, *definitely* didn't do romantic.

So why was he doing it now?

And why the sudden desire to acquaint himself with her every thought and feeling? Ever since she'd emerged on to the terrace he'd been openly solicitous about every aspect of her comfort and asked her endless questions about herself until she felt like a candidate in an interview. Especially because it was impossible to relax in case she gave the wrong answers and revealed too much.

Kimberley concentrated on her food, wondering what had sparked Luc's sudden uncharacteristic desire for conversation. Had he guessed that she was hiding something? Had he overheard her on the phone?

'Modelling gave me up,' she said dryly, 'when I chose not to turn up for any of the swimwear shots on the beach because I was in your bed. It was a lucrative account for the agency and I lost it for them. They took me off their books and made sure I wasn't given work again.'

Luc's eyes hardened. 'Give me the name of the agency.'

She blinked. 'Why?' Amusement lit her eyes. 'Are you going to close them down?'

He didn't smile. 'Maybe.'

'There's no need. I was glad to give up modelling. The lifestyle never suited me. You know I was never comfortable with the partying, the drugs—any of that.'

'I know you were incredibly naïve and innocent when I met you,' he drawled softly, leaning across to top up her glass. 'Why else would you have been walking along the beach in Rio de Janeiro at midnight in a non-existent dress with your hair dazzling like an Olympic torch? I couldn't believe my eyes. You were like some sort of virgin sacrifice, left out for the lions to consume.'

She gave a wry smile, acknowledging how stupid she'd been. 'The other girls persuaded me to go to a party but I hated every moment. I just wanted to get back to my hotel and there were no taxis,' she said simply, remembering that evening with a small shudder. If Luc hadn't come along when he had—

'It had been a long time since I'd been required to test my skills against a flick-knife,' Luc observed lightly, his eyes resting on her face in an intense male scrutiny that she found more than a little disturbing.

'You were impressive,' she conceded, wondering if the moment when he'd taken on a gang of six thugs, all with knives, had been when she'd fallen in love with him.

But even dressed in a shockingly expensive designer suit Luc Santoro looked like a man who could handle himself. And she'd be less than honest if she didn't admit that his spontaneous demonstration of physical skill and courage had been one of the elements that had initially drawn her to him. When in her life, before that moment, had anyone ever defended her? Never, and the novelty of meeting a man prepared to risk his life to extract a female from a situation that had been entirely of her own making had proved more than a little intoxicating.

In the single second it had taken him to identify the leader of the gang, he'd moved with such speed and skill that Kimberley had wondered for a moment whether her rescuer might not be more dangerous than her attackers.

Where exactly had he learned those street-fighting tactics that he'd used to extricate her from danger that night?

Kimberley fingered her glass and glanced across at him, remembering the gossip that she'd heard about his past. Nothing specific. Just speculation.

Her eyes hovered on his blue-shadowed jaw and the hard male perfection of his bone structure. No one with a grain of common sense would mess with Luc Santoro.

'Where did you learn to fight?' She asked the question before she could stop herself and she saw his hand still en route to his glass.

'*Não entendo*. I don't understand.' He frowned at her. 'What do you mean, "fight"?'

She swallowed. 'The night you rescued me, you took on six men. How did you learn to do that? *Where* did you learn?'

He picked up his glass. 'I'm a man. Fighting is instinctive.'

'I don't believe that.' Something made her push the point. 'You were outnumbered six to one and you anticipated all their tricks. As if you'd been trained in the same school of fighting.'

There was the briefest pause. 'The school of fighting I attended is called life,' he said dryly. 'I learned a great deal and I learned it early on.'

'What was it about your life that made it necessary for you to learn those skills? I've never learned them. If I had, perhaps I wouldn't have got myself into trouble that night,' she admitted. 'I wasn't very streetwise. To be honest, there wasn't any need to be where I was brought up.'

He gave a short laugh and drank deeply. 'You once told me that your home was a leafy English village where everyone knew everyone. Very middle class. Perhaps it's hardly surprising that you didn't find yourself learning self-defence.'

Maybe that was why he fascinated her. He was a man of contradictions. On the one hand he had great wealth and sophistication and he moved in the highest, most glittering social circles. But that veneer of sophistication didn't entirely hide the dark, dangerous, almost primitive side of his nature that she'd sensed from the very first moment they'd met. There was nothing tame or safe about Luc Santoro.

Which was one of the reasons he was so irresistible to women.

'I take it your upbringing wasn't middle class,' she ventured. 'Were you born in Rio de Janeiro?'

'Yes.' His smile was slightly mocking. 'I'm a genuine *Carioca.*'

She knew that was the name given to someone born or living in Rio de Janeiro.

'So how did you make it from *Carioca* to billionaire tycoon?' she asked lightly and he delivered her a smile that both charmed and seduced.

'Motivation and hard work.' He leaned forward, his eyes fixed on her face. 'If you want something badly enough, *meu amorzinho*, you can have it. It's just a question of careful planning and letting nothing stand in your way.'

His cold, ruthless approach to life, so different from her own, made her shiver. 'Just because you want something you can't just go out there and take it!'

His gaze didn't shift from hers. 'Why not?'

'Because you have to consider other people.'

A slightly mocking smile touched his beautifully shaped mouth. 'That's a typically female approach.' The smile faded. 'I, on the other hand, believe that trusting people is a hobby for fools. You decide what you want in life and then you go for it. You build something up until no one can take it away from you.'

There was such passion and volatility in the sudden flash of his dark eyes that Kimberley found that she was holding her breath. For one brief tantalising moment she felt she'd been given a glimpse of the real Luc—the man underneath that cool, emotionless exterior.

Sensing the sudden turbulence in his mood, she reached across the table in an instinctive gesture of comfort. 'Is that what happened?' Her voice was soft. 'Did someone take something away from you?'

He removed his hand from hers and leaned back in his chair, dark eyes veiled. 'Why do women always search for the dramatic? Everyone's character is formed by events in their lives.' He gave a dismissive shrug. 'I'm no different.'

'But you shut everyone out,' she said passionately and he gave a cool smile.

'I'm a man, *meu amorzinho*, and like most men I hunt alone. And I don't allow another male to poach on my territory. The friend you were speaking to earlier—' the warmth of his tone dropped several degrees '—was it a man?'

His slick change of subject took her by surprise and she answered without thinking. 'Yes.'

She saw his eyes glint dangerously and his lean, strong fingers tighten on his glass. Suddenly the atmosphere changed from comfortable to menacing.

His mouth was set in a grim line and his body held a certain stillness that raised the tension several notches. 'And have you been together long?'

'It isn't like that—'

'Evidently not,' he delivered with ruthless bite, 'if he allows his woman to spend two weeks in another man's bed. Or doesn't he know?'

She bit her lip. 'He's just a friend—'

'How good a friend?'

'The very best!' Loyalty to Jason made her tell the truth. 'He's stood by me through everything.'

'I'm sure he's done far more than stand.' The sardonic lift of his dark brow stung her more than his sarcasm.

She dropped her fork with a clatter. 'Not everyone is like you, Luc! Some people have proper relationships.' She rose to her feet, so angry and upset that she almost knocked the chair over. 'Relationships that aren't all about sex and nothing else. But you're so emotionally stunted you couldn't possibly understand that.'

'*Meu Deus*, what is this about?' He rose to his feet too, six-foot-four of powerful, angry male. Tension throbbed and pulsed between them. 'I am *not* emotionally stunted.'

She lifted her hands in a gesture of exasperation. 'Then *tell* me something about yourself! Anything.'

'Why? What does the sharing of past history bring to a relationship?' His eyes burned dark with temper. 'Does it change things between us if I tell you that I was born in the *favelas*, the slums of Rio, so poor that food was a luxury? Does it change things between us if I tell you that my father and mother worked like animals to take themselves and me away from that place? *Does it help you to know that they succeeded, only to lose everything and be forced back into the lifestyle they'd fought so hard to leave behind?'* He paced round the table and dragged her hard against him, his face grim and set as he raked her shocked face with night-black eyes. 'Tell me, *meu amorzinho*, now that you know the truth of where I came from, now that you know that I have emotions, has our relationship improved?'

Somehow she found her voice. 'That's the first time you've ever told me anything about yourself.'

'Then savour the moment,' he advised silkily, raking lean bronzed fingers through her silky hair in an unmistakably possessive gesture, 'because mindless chatter about past events doesn't rank as my favourite pastime.'

Had she been in any doubt, one breathless glance into his dark eyes enlightened her as to exactly what constituted his favourite pastime.

'I thought tonight was about conversation and getting to know each other.'

'You now know more about me than almost any other person on the planet,' he delivered in husky tones, tugging at her hair gently and fastening his mouth on the smooth pale skin of her neck. 'Let's leave it at that.'

His tongue flickered and teased and she felt her stomach shift and her eyes drifted closed. 'Luc—'

'A man can only stand so much talking in one night,' he groaned against her skin, sliding his hand down her back and bringing her hard against him. 'It's time to revert to body language.'

With that he scooped her up and carried her through to the bedroom.

She stared up at him in a state of helpless excitement, part of her simmering with exasperation that his ability to sustain a conversation about himself had been so short-lived and part of her as desperate for him as he clearly was for her.

They'd made progress, she thought, as he stripped off his shirt and dropped it on the floor with indecent haste and a careless disregard for its future appearance. Small progress, perhaps, but still, it was progress.

They'd dressed. They'd shared a meal. They'd talked—sort of.

And that was her last coherent thought as he stripped her naked with ruthless precision and brought his mouth down on hers.

Kimberley waited for all the usual feelings to swamp her but this time something was different. He was different. More gentle. More caring?

The thought popped into her head and she pushed it away ruthlessly. No! She wasn't going to do that again—make the mistake of believing that Luc was interested in anything other than her body. She'd done that once before and allowing herself to dream about something that could never happen had almost broken her heart.

But it *was* different.

Instead of dominating or being dominated, they *shared* and when they finally descended from an explosive climax he held her firmly against him, refusing to let her go.

As the delicious spasms died and they both lay spent and exhausted, he still refused to let her go, curving her into his body and locking his arms tightly around her as if he was afraid she might leave.

Which was ridiculous, she told herself sleepily, because they both knew that she was leaving and they both knew he wouldn't care.

The two weeks was almost up.

But she was too sleepy to make sense of any of it and eventually she stopped wondering and asking herself questions and drifted off to sleep in the warm, safe circle of his arms.

The day before she was due to fly home, Kimberley awoke late and found the bed empty.

Her heart gave a thud of disappointment and then she noticed that the French doors on to the terrace were open and she heard the rhythmic splashing of someone swimming in the pool.

She lay there and smiled.

Obviously Luc had decided on an early swim. Or maybe not that early, she thought ruefully as she cast a glance at her watch.

Now would be a good time to phone home for the final time, to check on the arrangements for the following day.

She scraped her tangled hair out of her eyes, flinched slightly as her bruised aching body reminded her of how they'd spent most of the night, and reached for her phone.

Jason answered and they talked for a bit and then she spoke to Rio, a soft smile touching her mouth as she listened to his excited chatter.

She couldn't wait to see him.

'I miss you, baby.'

'Are you coming home soon, Mummy?' Suddenly he sounded very young. 'I miss you.'

Tears clogged her throat. 'I'll be home tomorrow. And I miss you too.'

She heard a noise behind her and, with a horrified premonition, she turned round to see Luc standing there. A towel was looped carelessly around his waist, his breathtakingly gorgeous bronzed body was glistening with water and his expression black as thunder.

She said a hasty goodbye to Rio, cut the connection and turned to face the music.

'So your "*friend*" is missing you.' His tone was icy cold

as he padded towards her, all simmering anger and lethal menace. 'Next time you can tell the "*friend*" that he's poaching on my time.'

She couldn't understand why he was so angry.

'Our two weeks are up tomorrow, Luc,' she reminded him, trying to keep her tone reasonable, 'and I was making arrangements.'

He stopped dead and stared at her blankly, as if she'd told him something that he didn't already know. Something flitted across his handsome face. Surprise? Regret?

'It was just a phone call—' If she hadn't known better she would have said that he was jealous, but how could he be jealous of a phone call?

For a moment her heart skittered slightly and then she remembered that in order to be jealous you had to care, and Luc didn't care about anything except sex. He enjoyed the physical side of their relationship but nothing more.

'This is ridiculous,' she said, trying to keep her voice steady. 'You were the one who negotiated the terms. You agreed to two weeks, Luc, and those two weeks are up today.'

'I didn't agree to two weeks. You really can't wait to get home to him, can you?'

She gaped at him in disbelief. 'Why are you behaving like this? It doesn't make sense. Especially as we don't even have a proper relationship.'

His breath hissed through his teeth. 'We *do* have a relationship. What do you think the last two weeks have been all about?'

'Sex,' she replied in a flat tone. 'The last two weeks have been all about sex.'

The anger faded and he eyed her warily, like a man who knew he was on extremely rocky ground. '*Not* just about sex. Last night we talked.'

'*I* talked,' she pointed out wryly. '*You* questioned me.'

His hard jaw clenched. 'I told you about my past.'

'You yelled and shouted and lost your temper,' she reminded him in a calm voice, 'and then reluctantly disclosed a tiny morsel of your experiences in childhood! Prisoners under torture have revealed more!'

'Well, I'm not *used* to talking about myself,' he exclaimed defensively, pacing across the floor and throwing her a simmering black look. 'But if that's what you want, we'll have dinner on the terrace again tonight and we'll talk again.'

She stared at him, stunned into silence by his uncharacteristic offer to do something that was so completely against his nature.

Why would he bother?

'I have to go home, Luc,' she said quietly and he stopped pacing and simply glared at her.

'*Why?*'

'Because I have a child,' she said flatly, 'a child who I love and miss and need to be near. We've carefully avoided mentioning it for the past two weeks but the fact that we haven't mentioned it doesn't change the facts. My *life* is in London and tomorrow I'm going home.'

A muscle flickered in his lean jaw. 'You have a *lover* in London.'

Was he ignoring the issue of Rio once again?

She rose to her feet, totally bemused. 'Why are you acting in this jealous, possessive fashion when we both knew that this was just for two weeks?'

'I'm *not* jealous,' he refuted her accusation in proud tones, the disdainful look he cast in her direction telling her exactly what he thought of the mere suggestion that he might suffer from such a base emotion. 'But I don't share. Ever. I told you that once before.'

Kimberley closed her eyes briefly and decided that if she

lived to be a hundred and read every book written on the subject, she'd never understand men.

'My flight leaves tomorrow afternoon,' she reminded him steadily and his eyes narrowed.

'Cancel that flight,' he advised silkily, 'or I will cancel it for you.'

She'd done it again, she thought helplessly as she dragged her eyes away from his magnificent body. Given herself to him, heart, body and soul. And now she was going to have to find a way to recover.

How could she ever have thought she'd be able to walk away from him and feel nothing?

They had clinics for coming off drugs and drinks, she reflected with almost hysterical amusement. What she needed was a clinic for breaking her addiction to Luciano Santoro. Otherwise she was going to live the rest of her life craving a man she couldn't have.

Jealous?

Luc powered through the swimming pool yet again in an attempt to drive out the uncomfortable and unfamiliar thoughts and feelings that crowded his brain. The fact that he'd spent an unusual amount of time in the pool in pursuit of calm that continued to elude him hadn't escaped him.

If he was totally honest, then he didn't exactly know what was happening to him at the moment. Certainly he'd never felt the same burning need to keep a woman by his side as he did with Kimberley.

But was that really so surprising? he reasoned. She was *incredible* in bed. What normal sane man would want to let her go? It had nothing to do with jealousy and everything to do with sanity, he decided as he executed a perfect turn and swam down the pool again.

The fact that the agreed two weeks hadn't been enough to

get her out of his system troubled him slightly, but he was entirely sure that a week or two more would be sufficient to convince him of the merits of moving on to another willing female, this time someone less motivated to discover everything about him.

He'd simply work out a way of persuading Kimberley to extend their deal, he decided, confident that the problem was now all but solved.

With his usual limitless energy, he sprang out of the pool and reached for a towel.

The fact that she appeared to be determined to fly home the following day didn't trouble him in the slightest. He would simply talk her out of it. How hard could that be for a man who negotiated million dollar deals before breakfast on virtually a daily basis? He dealt with hard-nosed businessmen all the time. One extremely willing woman would be a piece of cake, even if she did have red hair, an extremely uncertain temper and what could almost be termed as a conversation disorder.

He had one more night.

He'd start by proving to her that he could talk as much as the next man when the situation called for it. Then he'd take her to bed.

By the end of the night he was entirely confident that she would be the one calling the airline to cancel her flight.

The following morning Kimberley checked her flight ticket and her passport and tucked them carefully back into her handbag. A small piece of hand luggage lay open on the bed. She'd found the case in her dressing room and, since it was clearly for her use and the clothes had been purchased specifically for her, she'd decided that she might as well take her favourites. Probably none of Luc's other girlfriends ever wore the same outfit twice, she thought wryly as she slipped the silk dress off the hanger and placed it carefully in the case, trying not to think too hard about what leaving would mean.

The previous evening they'd dined on the terrace again, and this time Luc had made what could only be described as a heroic effort to talk about himself. In fact he hadn't stopped talking and if she hadn't been so touched she would have laughed.

It was such an obvious struggle for him to discuss anything remotely personal but he'd tried extremely hard, sharing with her all manner of snippets about his childhood and the way his office worked.

The question of *why* he was trying so hard slid into her mind, but she dismissed it because the answer was so obvious. He wanted her to stay because he wanted more sex and for some reason he'd worked out that the way to change her mind about leaving was to start talking.

But of course her mind hadn't been changed, even by what had followed. Before last night she'd thought that she'd already experienced the very best in sex. But Luc had been relentless in his determination to drive her to the very pinnacle of ecstasy, proving once again that he was a skilled and sophisticated lover.

And she couldn't imagine living without him.

She was *desperate* to go home and be with her son, but she wanted to be with Luc too.

At that moment he walked out from the bathroom, his dark jaw freshly shaved, his hair still damp from the shower. Despite his almost total absence of sleep, he looked refreshed and invigorated and sexier than any man had a right to be.

Her eyes feasted on him, knowing that it would probably be the last time.

If she didn't have her son to think of, would she have stayed?

No, because she wasn't going to get her heart broken a second time in her life, she told herself firmly as she dropped a bikini into the case.

His gaze fastened on the case and he gave a sharp frown. 'Why are you packing?'

'Because I'm going home,' she reminded him, slightly bemused by his question. He knew she was going home that afternoon. 'I'm presuming your pilot will take me to the airport.'

'He certainly will not.' The Rolex on his bronzed wrist glinted as he reached out to remove the bag from her hand in a decisive movement. 'Because you're not going home. I thought we both agreed that.'

Kimberley racked her brain and tried to recall having said anything that might have given him that impression. 'We didn't agree that.'

He stepped closer to her and slid a possessive hand into her hair. 'Did we or did we not,' he enquired in silky tones, 'spend the entire night making love?'

Her face heated at the memory and the breath caught in her throat. 'Yes, but—'

His dark head lowered towards hers, an arrogant smile on his sexy mouth. 'And was it, or was it not, the most mind-blowing experience of your life?'

The flames flickered higher and higher inside her. 'It was amazing,' she agreed huskily, 'but I still have to go.'

The arrogant smile faded and blank incomprehension flickered across his handsome face. 'Why?'

'Because I have to go home.'

His brow cleared. 'Easily solved. Your home is now here. With me.'

She stared at him in amazement and a flicker of crazy hope came to life inside her. 'You want me to live with you?' She was so stunned that her voice cracked and he gave a smile loaded with an abundance of male self-confidence.

'Of course. The sex between us is simply amazing. I'd have to be out of my mind to let you go. So you stay. As my mistress. Until we decide that we've had enough of each other.'

The hope disintegrated into a million tiny pieces, blown away by his total lack of sensitivity, and she stared at him in disbelief.

'Your *mistress?* Are we suddenly living in the Middle Ages?'

'Mistress, girlfriend—' He gave a casual lift of his broad shoulders to indicate that he considered the terms both interchangeable and irrelevant. 'Choose whatever title you like.'

'How about "mug" or "idiot"?' Kimberley suggested helpfully, her temper starting to boil, 'because that's what I'd be if I accepted an invitation like that from a man like you.'

How could she have allowed herself to think for one single solitary minute that he might care for her just a little bit?

Luc wasn't capable of caring for anyone.

He raked long fingers through his dark hair, his expression showing that he was holding on to his patience with visible effort. 'I don't think you understood,' he said stiffly. 'I'm suggesting that you move in with me on a permanent basis, at least for the foreseeable future—'

'That's semi-permanent, Luc, and I understood you perfectly. Sex on tap, until I bore you.' Kimberley reached for the nightdress she'd worn before he'd stripped it from her quivering, pliant body. 'Very convenient for you—very precarious for me. So no thanks. These days I have more self-respect than to accept an offer like that.' She stuffed the nightdress in the case, as angry with herself as she was with him.

How could she have been so stupid as to fall for this man again?

How could she have been that shallow?

'No thanks?' Night-black eyes raked her flushed cheeks

with a lethal mixture of naked incredulity and stunned amazement. 'Do you realise that I have never made that offer to a woman before in my entire life? I will need to start visiting the office occasionally but believe me, *meu amorzinho*, we will be spending plenty of time together.' His voice dropped to a sexy drawl as he clearly dismissed her refusal as a misunderstanding. 'From now on I'll be extremely motivated to finish my working day early.'

Clearly he thought that was sufficient inducement for her to empty the contents of the case back into the drawers.

'You're unbelievable, do you know that?' She stared at him with a mixture of amazement and exasperation, wondering whether a sharp blow to the head would be of any help in bringing him to his senses. 'It is *not* a compliment to know that someone wants you just for sex!'

He frowned. 'If you're pretending the sex isn't amazing between us then you're deluding yourself again and I thought we'd moved past that point.'

'There's nothing wrong with the sex. The sex is great. The sex is amazing.' She spoke in staccato tones as she turned back to the bed and continued to stuff and push things into the tiny bag. 'But there are other things that are just as important as sex and there's *everything* wrong with those.'

'What do you mean, other things? What other things?' There was a hint of genuine confusion in his handsome features, as if he couldn't for one minute imagine there being anything more important than sex. And for him there probably wasn't, she conceded helplessly, flipping the lid of the case shut.

She scraped her hair back from her face and lifted her chin, her eyes challenging as she met his scorching dark gaze. 'Sharing a life, for one thing. Everyday activities. But you wouldn't understand about that because you're well and truly stuck in the Stone Age. For you, a woman's place is flat on her back, preferably stark naked, isn't that right, Luc?' She dropped the bag and spread her hands in a gesture of pure exasperation. 'Do you realise that you've never actually taken me out, Luc? Never. I mean, what exactly was the point of buying me a whole wardrobe full of flashy clothes when I have no need to dress up?'

'Because I like stripping them off you and because I can't see you naked without wanting to be inside you,' he admitted with characteristic frankness and she gave a gurgle of exasperation and fought the temptation to stamp her foot.

'Sex again! Do you realise that once again we haven't actually left this island?'

His dark brows came together in a sharp frown. 'There was no reason to leave. Everything we need is here.'

'Of course it is.' Her voice shook. 'Because all you need when a relationship is based on nothing but sex is a very large bed and maybe not even that if there happens to be a comfortable lift handy.'

His dark eyes narrowed warily. 'You're becoming very emotional—'

'Dead right I'm emotional.' She flung her head back and her hair trailed like tongues of fire down her back. 'I'm a woman and I like being emotional. Believe it or not, I *like* being able to feel things because feeling is what makes us human. You should try it some time; you might find it liberating.'

A muscle flickered in his lean cheek and he gritted his teeth, hanging on to his temper with visible difficulty. 'I can't talk to you when you're like this.'

'You can't talk to me whatever I'm like, Luc.' She dragged the case off the bed and dropped it on the floor. 'You *try* and talk to me but it's such an effort, such an act, that I feel exhausted for you. And you always treat me like a journalist. Giving me sound bites. Things that you're happy for me to hear. Things that sound good. I never get near to the real you.'

'You have been naked underneath the real me for the best part of two weeks,' he reminded her silkily. 'How much nearer could you get?'

Suddenly the fight drained out of her.

He just didn't get it. And he never would. And the sooner she gave up trying to make him understand, the better it would be for both of them.

They were so different it was laughable.

'And those two weeks are now finished,' she reminded him flatly, picking the case up and taking it to the bedroom door. 'You don't know the meaning of the word compromise. There's a flight leaving for London this afternoon. I'd be grateful if you'd ask your pilot to fly me to the airport so that I can catch it. I'm going home to my child. The child you still don't believe exists.'

He stared at her in stunned silence, his expression that of a man trying to comprehend the incomprehensible. Then he muttered something in his own language and turned on his heel, striding out of the room without a backward glance.

Exhausted and drained, Kimberley stared after him, her heart a solid lump of misery in her chest. What had she expected? That he'd argue with her? That he'd make her stay?

That he'd suddenly have a personality transplant and they'd live happily ever after?

She gave herself a mental shake and decided that she was losing her mind.

The two weeks were over and Luc was never, ever going to change. And neither was she. The truth was that the physical attraction between them was so breathtakingly powerful that it blinded her to the truth.

He wasn't what she wanted in a relationship and that was the end of it.

She was never going to share anything other than passion with Luc, and it wasn't enough for her.

She'd done what was needed. Her son was safe. It was time to get on with her life.

Time to go home.

CHAPTER EIGHT

LUNCHTIME came and went with no sign of Luc and Kimberley glanced at her watch with increasing anxiety, afraid that she was going to miss her flight. By mid-afternoon she was sure of it. There was no sign of the helicopter and no sign of Luc.

Short of swimming or flagging down a passing boat, there was no other way off the island.

Feeling hot and tired and furious with Luc for blatantly sabotaging her plans, she was on the point of picking up the phone and seeing whether she could arrange a helicopter taxi to take her to the airport when she finally heard the distinctive sound of a helicopter approaching.

She breathed a sigh of relief. There was no way she'd make it to the airport in time to catch her flight to London, but at least she'd be at the airport ready to take the first available flight the following day.

Keen to leave the island as soon as possible, Kimberley picked up her bag and walked quickly through the lush gardens towards the helicopter pad, wondering whether Luc was even going to bother to say goodbye.

The late afternoon sun was almost unbearably hot and she exchanged a few polite words with the pilot before climbing into the helicopter, eager to protect herself from the heat.

Moments later Luc came striding towards her and he looked so staggeringly handsome that she caught her breath. The casual trousers, swimming trunks, bare torso were gone to be replaced by a designer suit that outlined the male perfection of his body.

There was more to a relationship than the physical, she reminded herself firmly, gritting her teeth and glancing in the opposite direction in an attempt to break the sensual spell his presence cast over her.

He exchanged a few words with one of the bodyguards who was hovering and then joined her in the helicopter, seating himself beside her.

Surely he wasn't coming with her?

She looked at him in surprise, trying not to notice the way his immaculate grey suit showed off the impressive width of his shoulders. He looked every inch the sophisticated, successful tycoon, cool and more than a little remote.

'What are you doing?'

'Exploring the meaning of the word compromise,' he informed her in silky tones, fastening his seat belt in a determined gesture. 'Showing you that I can be as flexible as the next guy when the need arises. If you won't stay here, then I'll come with you.'

She gaped at him.

Luc? Flexible?

He was about as flexible as a steel rod. But, on the other hand, he was sitting next to her, she conceded, feeling slightly weakened by that realisation.

'You're seriously coming with me?' Delight and excitement mingled with sudden panic. Was he coming to see his son? Was he seeking the proof he'd demanded? Or was there another reason? 'Do you have business interests in London?'

'I have business everywhere,' he informed her in a lazy drawl, 'and London is no exception, although perhaps it's only in the last few hours that I developed this burning need to give that particular area of my business my personal attention.'

He leaned forward and issued some instructions to his pilot before relaxing back in his seat.

'Well, I hate to tell you this but we won't be going anywhere today because we've missed the flight,' she informed him and he threw her an amused look.

'The flight leaves when I give orders for it to leave. Not before. We most certainly won't miss it.'

'It takes off in—' she glanced at her watch and pulled a face '—ten minutes, to be precise. And even you can't command a commercial airline.'

'But we're not flying by commercial airline,' he informed her in lazy, almost bored tones as he stretched his long legs out in front of him. 'My private jet is already refuelled and waiting for our arrival.'

His private jet? She blinked at him. 'You have your own plane?'

'Of course.' A dark eyebrow swooped upwards and the amusement in his eyes deepened. 'I have offices all over the world which require my presence on an all too frequent basis. How else did you think I travelled? Flying carpet?'

She blushed and gritted her teeth, feeling ridiculously naïve. 'I've never thought about it at all,' she admitted, 'but I suppose if I had I would have naturally assumed you caught a flight like other people.'

His smile widened. 'But I'm *not* like other people—' he leaned forward, his dark gaze burning into hers '—and two weeks naked in my bed should have convinced you of that fact.'

Vivid, erotic images burst into her brain and she struggled with a ridiculous impulse to slide her arms round his neck.

He was an addiction, she reminded herself firmly, *and no one cured an addiction by continuing to enjoy the addictive substance.*

'Luc—' she cleared her throat and wished he wasn't quite so close to her '—we agreed two weeks and the two weeks is finished.'

'And the next two weeks are just beginning,' he told her helpfully and she looked at him in exasperation.

'Do you know the meaning of the word no?'

He gave a careless shrug of his broad shoulders. 'I'm not that great with "no" or "maybe",' he admitted without a trace of apology, 'but I'm working on "compromise" and "conversation" so who knows?'

She didn't know whether to laugh or hit him. And, no matter how much the rational part of her brain told her that having Luc in London would complicate her life in the extreme, another part lifted and floated with sheer excitement that he'd changed his plans for her. That he was coming to London to be with *her*.

In desperation she tried to stifle that part of herself but failed dismally and spent the entire helicopter flight in a dreamy haze, trying not to read too much into his actions, *trying to drag herself back down from the clouds.* He was still Luc, she reminded herself firmly, and he was never going to change.

At the airport they transferred on to his private jet and Kimberley found it hard to appear cool and indifferent as she was greeted on to the aircraft like royalty.

Once inside, she eyed the luxurious seating area in amazement. 'It's bigger than the average house. And more comfortable, come to that.'

'I do a lot of travelling, so comfort is essential.' He urged her forward into the body of the plane. 'There's a bathroom, a meeting room, a small cinema and an extremely large bedroom.' The sudden gleam in his eyes warned her that they'd be making use of the latter and hot colour touched her cheeks as she gazed around her in amazement.

'Just how rich are you?'

'Shockingly, indecently, *extravagantly* rich,' he assured her calmly, amusement lighting his dark eyes as he registered her ill-disguised awe at this visual demonstration of his wealth, 'which is presumably why you came to me for the five million dollars you needed to pay for your—er—*expenses*.' He waved a hand at the sofa. 'Sit down. We missed lunch and I'm starving and there's an extremely good bottle of Cristal waiting for our attention.'

She sank into the soft embrace of a creamy leather sofa and wondered what it was like to have so much money that you never, ever had to worry again.

They were served by a team of staff who discreetly tended to their every need and then vanished into a different part of the plane, leaving them alone.

'I didn't know you had an office in London.' She sipped her champagne and tucked into spicy chicken served with a delicious side salad.

'I have offices in most of the major cities of the world,' he observed in dry tones, the amusement back in his dark eyes. 'And I didn't know that you had such a burning interest in the detail of my business.'

'That's because we never talk,' she reminded him and he gave her a mocking smile.

'You wish to spend our evenings discussing fourth quarter sales figures?'

She sipped her champagne and realised that she was only just appreciating the true size of his business empire. The truth was that when she was with him she never saw further than the man himself and she'd somehow managed to remain oblivious to the power he yielded. 'And what will you be doing while you're in London?'

One dark eyebrow lifted in abject mockery. 'If you have to ask me that question then I obviously haven't made the objective of my visit clear enough,' he drawled and she felt her heart skitter in her chest.

She shouldn't be flattered. She really shouldn't. *But she was.*

'You're seriously travelling to London to be with me?' She just couldn't contain the little jump in her pulse rate.

'You thought I required a change of scenery?'

Remembering the beauty of his island, she gave a smile. 'Hardly. I just can't quite believe that you changed your plans to be with me.'

Hope flared inside her.

Maybe she'd got him wrong.

Would he cross an ocean just for physical satisfaction? Or was there something more to their relationship, after all?

'The sex between us is truly amazing, *meu amorzinho*,' he replied, 'and in any relationship there must be compromise. You taught me that.'

Hope fizzled out. 'So what you're saying is that you're willing to change countries in order to carry on having sex with me.'

So much for believing that he actually wanted to spend time with her.

'If you're about to pick a fight then I ought to warn you that there is sufficient turbulence outside the plane without causing more on the inside.' He stretched long legs out in front of him, infuriatingly relaxed in the face of her growing tension. 'As you yourself pointed out, I have never before changed my plans for a woman. It's a compliment.'

She bit her lip and refrained from lecturing him on the true definition of the word compliment. It was true that she didn't want to pick a fight. What was the point? He was never going to change and the sooner she accepted that, the happier she'd be.

'Well, we won't be able to spend much time together. I have a business that needs my attention,' she said flatly. And a son. *A son who Luc still didn't believe existed.* 'Unlike you, I don't have a massive staff willing to do the work in my absence. Having been away for two weeks, I have lots of catching up to do.'

'My hotel suite comes complete with my own staff and full office facilities, which you are welcome to use,' he offered smoothly and she felt herself tense.

'I don't need office space,' she said quickly. 'I've been away for two weeks, Luc. There are people I need to see.'

There was a sardonic gleam in his dark eyes as he studied her. 'But presumably your evenings and nights will be available.'

She should say no. She should tell him that their relationship was over. 'Possibly.' She put down her fork, leaving her food untouched. Being with Luc unsettled her stomach so much that she couldn't face food. 'I'll meet you for dinner.'

Once Rio was tucked up in bed and asleep.

What was wrong with that? she asked herself weakly. She was already crazily in love with Luc. What did she have to lose by spending more time with him?

They landed in the early morning in time to get stuck in the commuter traffic that crawled its way into London on a daily basis during the week and Luc had plenty of opportunity to contemplate the distinct possibility that he'd suffered a personality change.

Never in his life before had he suffered an impulse to adjust his plans for a woman, least of all follow one halfway across the world. The fact that he was now in London, a city that hadn't featured as part of his immediate plans, left him suffering from no small degree of discomfort.

And if he needed any confirmation of the fact that he

was acting out of character, then he simply had to look at Kimberley's face.

It was hard to say who was more shocked, he mused with wry amusement as he cast a sideways look at the woman who had wrought this miraculous change in him. She was clearly wondering what on earth was going on and he could hardly blame her. He was still telling himself that it was just about great sex and certainly the night they'd spent on his plane had given him plenty of evidence to support that assumption. The fact that he'd never gone to similar lengths for any woman before was something he preferred not to dwell on.

'I haven't even asked you where you live.'

The way she looked at him reminded him of a small vulnerable animal trapped in the headlights of an oncoming car. 'I bought a small flat with your money,' she reminded him calmly. 'If you just drop me at your office I'll make my own way home and meet you at your hotel later.'

Luc watched her intently. *Was she planning to meet her lover?*

'Fine.' He agreed to her terms, taking the way she immediately relaxed as confirmation of his suspicions.

She'd assured him that she didn't have a man in her life, but the evidence appeared to suggest otherwise, he thought grimly.

It started to rain heavily as they approached the London office of Santoro Investments, which was situated in Canary Wharf along with many of the other leading merchant banks.

'My driver will take you home,' he informed her smoothly, leaning across to give her a lingering kiss on the mouth. 'I'll order dinner for eight.'

After which he intended to drive all thoughts of other men clean out of her mind.

His relationship with women was the one area of his life

where he'd never before encountered competition but he was entirely confident that he was more than up to the task.

Having issued a set of instructions to his driver in his native language, Luc stepped out of the car and contemplated the degree of havoc he was about to cause in an office unprepared for his imminent arrival.

Flanked by members of his security team, who had been in the car behind, he strode towards the building, trying to recall exactly how he'd intended to justify his unexpected visit to his London office to his amazed staff.

Kimberley spent the day catching up on some urgent business issues, talking to Jason and watching the clock, anxious for the moment when she could pick her son up from school.

When his little figure finally appeared at the school gates she was struck by his powerful resemblance to his father. He had the same night-black hair and the same dark eyes. Perhaps it was because she'd just spent two weeks with Luc that the similarity was so marked, she thought as she swept him into her arms and cuddled him close. *She'd missed him so much.*

They chatted non-stop all the way home to the tiny flat she shared with Jason and carried on chatting while she made tea.

Kimberley had just cleared Rio's plate when the doorbell rang.

'I'll get it.' Jason stood up and gave her a smile. 'You two still have a lot to talk about.'

He strolled out of the room to answer the door but was back only moments later, this time without the smile.

'Who was—?' Kimberley broke off as she caught sight of the tall, powerfully built figure standing beside him. Her heart dropped like a stone.

'Luc.' She stood up quickly, her chair scraping on the tiled floor of the kitchen, her knees shaking and the breath suddenly trapped in her lungs. *What was he doing here?* 'I was going to come to you at eight.'

'I finished in the office early and decided to surprise you.' There was an edge to his voice that alerted her to danger and she lifted a hand to her throat.

'But you didn't know my address—'

He gave a cool smile. 'You were careful to keep it a secret. I wanted to know why.' His eyes slid to Jason and then he noticed the child. A slight frown touched his dark brows and then his expression shifted swiftly from cool to shattered.

'*Meu Deus*, it can't be—' His voice was hoarse and his handsome face was suddenly alarmingly pale under his tan. He looked totally shell-shocked.

Kimberley suddenly found she couldn't move. She made a nervous gesture with her hand. 'I *did* tell you—'

His gaze fixed on her, his dark eyes fierce and hot and loaded with accusation. 'But you *knew* I didn't believe you—'

She stared at him helplessly. 'We should go outside to talk about this—'

For a long moment he didn't respond. Appeared to have lost his ability to speak. Then, finally, he found his voice.

'Why?' He didn't shift his gaze from the child. 'If this is really how it appears, then *why* am I discovering this now? *After seven years!*'

Kimberley held her breath, trapped by the anger and emotional tension that throbbed in his powerful frame. She was on the verge of sweeping Rio into her arms, afraid that he'd pick up the same vibes as her, afraid that he'd be upset. But, far from being upset, he was staring at his father in blatant fascination.

'You look like me.'

Luc inhaled sharply and his proud head jerked backwards as if he'd been slapped. 'Yes.'

Kimberley closed her eyes and asked herself why her child couldn't have been born with red hair. As it was, the resemblance between father and son was so striking that there could be absolutely no doubt about the boy's parentage.

She felt Luc's tension build. Felt his anger, his uncertainty, *his agony*, and guilt sliced through her like the blade of the sharpest knife.

For the first time since she'd known him, all his emotions were clearly etched on every plane of his handsome face for all to read, and the vision of such a private man revealing himself so completely deepened her guilt still further.

She held her breath, not knowing how to rescue the situation, just praying that he wouldn't say anything that would upset their child.

He didn't.

Instead he hunkered down so that his eyes were on the same level as the boy's. 'I'm Luc.'

Her son's eyes fixed on his father for the first time in his life. 'You look cross. Are you cross?'

'*Not* cross,' Luc assured him, his voice decidedly unsteady and his smile a little shaky. 'I just wasn't expecting to meet you, that's all.'

'I'm Rio.'

Luc closed his eyes briefly and the breath hissed through his teeth. 'It isn't a very common name.'

'I'm named after a very special city,' Rio confided happily, sliding off his chair and walking over to a wall of the kitchen which was covered in his paintings, photos and cards. 'This is it.' He tugged a card from the wall and handed it to Luc with a smile. 'That's where I get my name. That's the mountain Corcovado with the statue *Cristo Redento*—' he pronounced it perfectly '—doesn't it look great? I'm going to go there one day. Mum's promised. But it's a long way away and we don't have enough money yet. We're saving up.'

There was a long painful silence as Luc stared down at the postcard in his hand and then he lifted his gaze and looked straight at Kimberley, raw accusation shimmering in his dark eyes.

She stood totally still, unable to move, paralysed by the terrifying anger she sensed building inside him. But this was like no anger she'd ever encountered before. This wasn't a raw red anger, quick to ignite into flames of vicious temper. This was a blue cold anger, a simmering menace that threatened a far more lethal outcome.

Her courage shifted and, for no immediate reason that she could identify, she felt afraid. 'Luc—'

'Not now and not in front of the child,' he growled before dragging a deep breath into his lungs and turning his attention back to Rio.

Kimberley watched in a state of breathless tension, marvelling at the change in him, at how much he softened his attitude when he looked at their son. The anger seemed to drain away to be replaced by a gentle fascination. 'It's a lovely picture. A great city.' His voice was soft and he smoothed a bronzed hand over Rio's dark curls in a surprisingly tender gesture. 'Those paintings on the wall—did you do them?'

'I'm going to be an artist,' Rio confided, slipping his hand into Luc's and dragging him towards the wall where the paintings were proudly displayed. 'That's my favourite.' He pointed to one in particular and Luc nodded.

'I can see why. It's very good.' His expression was serious as he studied every childish brushstroke with enormous interest.

Kimberley felt her heart twist with guilt.

She'd made the wrong decision.

She'd robbed him of the right to know his son. And her son of the right to know his father. Suddenly she could hardly breathe. But what else could she have done? she reasoned.

She'd *tried* to tell him. She'd wanted, *needed*, his support right at the beginning. But he'd made it clear that the relationship was over. And she'd seen a man like her father.

'You can have it if you like,' Rio offered generously and there was a long silence while Luc continued to stare at the painting. Then he swallowed hard and cleared his throat.

'Thanks.' He glanced down at his son and the roughness of his tone betrayed his emotion. 'I'd like that.'

He carefully removed the painting from the wall and held it as if it were priceless. Then he crouched down again and started to talk to his son. He asked questions, he listened, he responded and all the time Kimberley watched, transfixed by what she was seeing.

How could he be so good with children?

He had absolutely no experience with children. He should have been at a loss and yet here he was, totally comfortable, talking to a six-year-old boy about football, painting and any other subject that Rio chose to bring up.

Eventually he glanced at his Rolex and brought the conversation to a reluctant halt. 'Unfortunately, I have to go now.'

Rio frowned. 'Will I see you again?'

'Oh, yes.' Luc's voice was still gentle but his broad shoulders were rigid with simmering tension. 'You'll definitely see me again. Very soon.'

Kimberley's heart kicked hard against her chest as she was forced to face the inevitable. 'Luc—'

Finally he looked at her, his gaze hard and uncompromising. 'Eight o'clock.' His tone was icy cold. 'I'll send my driver for you. We'll talk then. I think you might find it's a skill I've finally mastered.'

CHAPTER NINE

KIMBERLEY paused outside the door to Luc's suite and took a moment to compose herself.

Was he still as angry as he'd been when he'd left the house?

She took a deep breath and felt dread seep through her like a heavy substance, weighing her down. Whichever way you looked at it, this wasn't going to be an easy meeting.

And she didn't feel at all prepared. For the past seven years she'd convinced herself that even if she *had* managed to get close enough to Luc to tell him about her pregnancy then he would have completely rejected the prospect of fatherhood. This was a man who couldn't sustain a relationship for longer than a month, whose lifestyle was so far removed from that of a family man that it was laughable. There had been nothing about him to suggest that hearing the word 'pregnancy' would have stimulated a reaction other than panic and after he'd flatly refused to see her she'd managed to convince herself that it was all for the best.

But today, seeing him interacting with his son, she'd asked herself the same question she'd been asking herself for the past seven years. *Had she done the wrong thing by not persisting in her attempts to contact Luc and tell him the truth?*

Certainly Luc had appeared far from horrified by the realisation that he actually did have a son. Shocked, yes. Angry with her, yes. But horrified? No. In fact, his reaction had been so far from what she'd predicted all those years ago that it merely confirmed, yet again, how little she knew him. *He'd surprised her.*

And now he was expecting an explanation.

She was shown into the enormous living room of the suite by one of the security guards, who immediately melted into the background, leaving her alone with Luc. He was standing with his back to the window, facing into the room.

Waiting for her.

He watched her in silence, his handsome face cold and unsmiling, his long legs planted firmly apart in an attitude of pure male aggression.

The silence dragged on and on and in the end she was the one to break it, unable to bear the rising tension a moment longer.

She curled her fingers into her palms. 'Luc—'

'I don't even want to talk about this until we have resolved the issue of the blackmailer. Evidently someone really is threatening my child. I want that letter and I want it now.' He held out his hand and she delved in her handbag and produced it.

'There are absolutely no clues as to who sent it, he—'

'It isn't your job to look for clues.' Luc spoke into his mobile phone and moments later a man who Kimberley recognised as his head of security walked into the room.

He spoke briefly to Luc, took the letter and then walked out of the room, pausing only to give a reassuring smile to Kimberley, who stared after him in surprise.

'Doesn't he want to ask me anything?'

Luc gave a cool smile. 'I don't micromanage my staff. I appoint people based on their skills to do the job and then I leave the job up to them. Ronaldo is the best there is. If he feels the need to question you then doubtless he'll do so. In the meantime I have arranged for Rio to have twenty-four hour security both inside and outside the home.'

She gaped at him and her stomach curled with fear. 'You think he's still in danger?'

'He's my son,' Luc pointed out coldly, 'and that alone is enough to put him in danger. He'll be under guard here until I can arrange to take him back to Brazil.'

The room spun. 'You're *not* taking my child to Brazil! I know you're angry about all this, but—'

'*Our child,* Kimberley. We are talking about *our* child and angry doesn't even *begin* to describe what I am feeling at this precise moment,' he informed her in dangerously soft tones, every muscle in his powerful body pumped up and tense as he struggled for control. 'I am waiting for an explanation and I don't even know why, because frankly there *is* no explanation sufficient to justify your failure to inform me that I have been a father for the past six years.'

'I told you two weeks ago—'

'Because you needed my help! If it hadn't been for the blackmail letter the chances are I *never* would have found out, isn't that right?' He paced the floor of the hotel suite, his anger and volatility barely contained. 'I can't believe you would have kept my son from me!' His eyes flashed bitter condemnation and she stiffened defensively, his total lack of self-recrimination firing her own anger.

The fact that he hadn't even considered his own behaviour in the whole situation filled her with outrage.

He was laying the blame squarely on her and yet she knew that had he agreed to see her when she'd tried to contact him she would have told him immediately.

'I don't have to justify anything, Luc.' Her voice shook but she carried on anyway, determined not to let him bully her. 'You treated me abominably.'

'And this was my punishment?' He stared at her in derision. 'Because I ended our relationship, you decided that I'd forfeited the right to know about my child?'

'No.' Her own temper exploded in the face of his accusing look. 'But you're supposed to take responsibility for your actions. You were eager enough to sleep with me but considerably less eager to find out whether I was pregnant, weren't you, Luc?'

The faintest flicker of a frown touched those strong dark brows. 'I did *not* ignore the possibility,' he gritted, 'but I used protection. There was no reason for you to become pregnant.'

'And that's it? Your responsibility ends there? Well, I'm sorry to be the one to point out that you're not infallible,' she said bitterly, 'and your so-called "protection" didn't work. I discovered I was pregnant the day after I left your house.'

'You were still in Rio de Janeiro when you discovered your pregnancy?' His gaze changed from startled to scornful and he swept a hand through the air in a gesture of disgust. 'Then it would have taken *nothing* for you to come and find me and tell me.'

His condemnation was the final straw. 'You have a selective memory. It's so easy for you to stand there now and say that, but at the time you wouldn't let me come *near* you!' Her body trembled with outrage and her hair tumbled over her shoulders, emphasising the pallor of her face. 'You'd had enough of me, Luc. Remember? You went out partying, just to prove that you were bored with me. And when I did the same you lost your temper. We hardly parted on good terms.'

His gaze was ice-cold. 'This wasn't about us. It was about a child. You had a responsibility to tell me.'

'*How?*' She almost choked on the word. 'How was I supposed to tell you? Do you realise how *impossible* it is to get near to you unless you give permission? It's easier to see royalty than get an audience with you!'

He frowned. 'You're being ridiculous—'

'*Not* ridiculous, Luc.' She smoothed her hair away from her face and forced herself to calm down. 'You are totally inaccessible to the public and you should know that because you made yourself that way.'

'But you were not the public.' His gaze raked her face with raw anger. 'We had a relationship.'

'But once that relationship was over I had no better access to you than anyone else. I couldn't get through the walls of bodyguards and frosty-faced receptionists to exchange a single word with you.'

'You obviously didn't try hard enough.'

The injustice of the suggestion stung like acid in an open wound. 'Cast your mind back, Luc.' She wrapped her arms around her waist to stop the shivering. It was a warm June evening but suddenly she felt cold. 'Twice I rang asking to see you and twice you refused to take my call. You thought I'd left Brazil and then suddenly, two weeks after our relationship had ended, I made a final attempt to tell you I was pregnant. This time I turned up in your office asking to see you. I thought that if I came myself then it would be harder to send me away. Your response was to arrange for your driver to take me to the airport, just to make sure that this time there could be no doubt that I'd left the country. It was what you wanted, Luc, so it was what I did.'

He stiffened but had the grace to look uncomfortable. 'I assumed you wanted to talk about our relationship.'

'No. I wanted to tell you I was *pregnant*. But you wouldn't listen. So I went home and did everything by myself. You thought I was a gold-digger—' Shaking with anger and the sheer injustice of it all, she dug a hand into her bag and pulled out a sheaf of papers. 'Here are the receipts, Luc. Everything I spent is itemised there, down to the last box of nappies, and there isn't a single pair of shoes on the list. Just for the record, I *hated* having to use your money and I only did it for Rio.'

She stuffed the papers into his hand and had the satisfaction of seeing him speechless.

He stared at the papers for a moment, his handsome face unusually pale. 'I did *not* know you were pregnant.'

'You didn't give me a chance to tell you! You'd already made up your mind that our relationship was over.' She felt tears clog her throat. 'And it *was* over. Maybe it's a good thing I didn't manage to tell you the truth. What would have happened? You'd never stayed with a woman for more than a month, Luc.'

He threw the papers on to the nearest sofa and paced the length of the suite until he ran out of room. Then he turned to face her, his eyes glittering dark and fierce. 'I would *not* have abandoned a child—'

'But the child would have come with a mother,' she reminded him flatly. 'Complicated, isn't it? Would you have abandoned your playboy lifestyle to give your son a home?'

He jabbed long fingers through his sleek dark hair, clearly driven to the edges of his patience. 'I do not know what I would have done—but finding out this way, it is very difficult—'

Goaded past the point of noticing that his usually fluent English was less than perfect, she turned on him. '*You're* finding it difficult? Try discovering you're pregnant at the age of eighteen when you're unemployed and on your own in a foreign city. I was totally alone, scared, jobless and homeless. *That's* difficult, Luc!'

His broad shoulders tensed. 'You must have had family who could help you—'

'Well, I didn't exactly meet their parental expectations.' She tried to hide the hurt because the truth was that she still couldn't quite believe that her parents had both turned away her pleas for help. She couldn't imagine any situation where she would refuse to help her son. 'They didn't approve of my modelling career but they approved even less of my career as your mistress and the fact that I'd abandoned *everything* to be with you.'

From the moment she'd laid eyes on him she'd been dazzled. Everything else in her life had become inconsequential. *Nothing* had mattered except Luc.

His eyes meshed with hers and she could see that he too was remembering the sensual madness of the time they'd spent together.

Disapproval emanated from every inch of his powerful frame. 'They should have supported you—'

'Perhaps. But you don't always get what you deserve in life and people don't always behave the way they should.' She shot him a meaningful look and had the satisfaction of seeing two spots of colour appear high on his cheekbones. 'The only support I had were your two credit cards, so don't talk to me about difficult, Luc, because I've been there and done that. And don't keep telling me that I did the wrong thing. I tried to tell you. Yes, I failed, but some of the responsibility for that failure lies with you, so don't give me that self-righteous, I'm-so-perfect look! Maybe you should rethink the way you run your life. Ex-girlfriends who think they might be pregnant should be given priority when your staff are handing out appointments to see you.' She picked up her bag and walked towards the door, suddenly feeling a desperate need for fresh air and space. The past was closing in on her and she had to get away.

His voice stopped her. 'You're *not* walking out of here.'

'Watch me!' She turned to look at him, her hair tumbling past her shoulders, her gaze challenging him to stop her if he dared. 'This conversation is clearly going nowhere and I'm tired.'

'Then we will continue the conversation sitting down.' He gestured towards the nearest sofa. 'We have much to discuss still.'

'But we're not discussing,' she pointed out tightly, 'we're arguing, and I've had enough for one night. I've had enough of your accusations and your total inability to see the situation from anyone's point of view but your own. So I'm going home. And when you've calmed down enough to think properly, then maybe we'll talk.'

His hard jaw clenched. 'I have arranged dinner.'

'I'd rather starve than eat dinner with you.' Driven by hurt and frustration, she yanked the door open, ignoring the startled gaze of the bodyguard stationed outside the door. 'And if you've got an appetite at this particular moment in time, then you're even more insensitive than I thought.'

After a sleepless night spent reliving every moment of their conversation, Kimberley was drinking strong coffee at the kitchen table when the doorbell rang.

It was Luc and judging from the shadows under his eyes and the growth of stubble on his hard jaw, his night hadn't been any better than hers.

But he still managed to look devastating, she thought helplessly, running her eyes over his broad shoulders.

His eyes were wary, as if he wasn't sure what reaction to expect. 'Can I come in?'

'What for?' She lifted her chin. 'More recriminations, Luc? More blame?'

A muscle flickered in his hard jaw. 'No recriminations or blame. But you have to admit that we do have things to talk about.'

'I'm not sure that we do.'

His eyes flashed, dark and angry. *'Meu Deus*, I am doing my best here but you won't even meet me halfway!'

'It isn't you or I that matter in this, Luc! It's Rio. I won't have him upset. And I don't trust your temper.'

'There is nothing wrong with my temper!' Luc inhaled deeply and dragged long fingers through his hair, visibly struggling for control. 'I admit that I was angry last night but I'm over that now and I would never upset Rio. Did he look upset yesterday, when he met me?' His voice was a masculine growl. 'Did he?'

She forced herself to stand her ground. 'No. But he didn't know who you were. It isn't just about your temper, Luc, although you definitely need to work on that. You're about to upset his life and I won't let you do it.'

Luc's jaw clenched. 'I have no intention of upsetting anyone.'

'No?' Her tone was cold. 'The way you didn't upset me last night?'

A muscle flickered in his jaw. 'I may have been slightly unfair to you—' he conceded finally and she fought a powerful temptation to slap his handsome face.

'Slightly?'

He shrugged broad shoulders and looked distinctly uncomfortable. 'All right, very possibly more than slightly—' his accent was more pronounced than usual '—but that is all in the past now and we have to talk about the future.'

'That's it?' Kimberley gave an incredulous laugh. 'That's your idea of an apology? Push it into the past and forget about it? How very convenient.'

He swore under his breath. 'It is true that there are many things I regret about what has happened but the past is history and the most important thing is that we concentrate on the future.'

'That's it?' Kimberley shook her head in weary disbelief. 'You need to add "apology" to your list of things you're going to work on, along with "no", "compromise" and "conversation".'

'*Meu Deus, what* do you expect me to do?' He displayed all the explosive volatility of a man well and truly wedged in a tight corner. 'I can't change what happened but I *can* make it right now. But we need to talk.'

'We said everything that needed to be said last night,' Kimberley said stiffly and he gave a driven sigh.

'We were both in a state of shock last night and we have both had time to do some thinking,' he muttered, glancing over his shoulder to where his car and driver waited. 'This is all new territory for me and I certainly don't want to explore it in public. Are you going to let me come in or are we going to provide headlines for tomorrow's newspapers?'

What was the point of refusing? She'd known when she'd walked away from him the night before that she was only postponing the inevitable.

She opened the door a little wider and he strode past her and made straight for her kitchen.

'This is a nice room—' His eyes drifted to the French windows that opened on to the tiny garden. 'It has a nice atmosphere. You chose well.'

Given that her entire flat would have fitted into one room of the villa, she took his words as a sign that he was at least attempting to be conciliatory.

'Thanks.'

He tilted his head and scanned the four corners of the room. 'Its value must have increased considerably since you purchased it.'

She stared at him with undisguised incredulity. 'Do you only ever think about money and return on investment?'

'No, sometimes I think about sex and now I also have a child to think about.' His eyes were cool as he glanced around him. 'Has Jason lived with you from the start? It was Jason you were talking to on the phone?'

'Yes.' She made a pot of coffee. 'He was the only friend I had.'

'It's good that I'm aware that Jason's sexual preferences don't run to beautiful female models,' Luc drawled and something in his tone made her glance at him warily.

'Why's that?'

'Because it saves me having to knock his teeth down his

throat,' he said pleasantly, the gleam in his dark eyes making her catch her breath.

'You and I were no longer an item, Luc,' she pointed out, pouring them both a coffee and taking the mugs to the table, 'so jealousy on your part is nothing short of ridiculous. I could have been with any number of men quite legitimately.'

The atmosphere in the room instantly darkened.

'And were you?' His voice was a threatening male growl and she gave an impatient sigh.

'No, Luc, I wasn't. I had a baby, I was struggling to build a business and I was always exhausted. The last thing I needed was the additional mental strain of a man. And, frankly, my experience with you was enough to put me off men for life.'

'Not exactly for life,' he said softly, lifting his mug to his lips and sipping his coffee. 'I seem to recall you displaying no small degree of enthusiasm over the past two weeks. Not exactly the reaction of a woman who has gone off men.'

Her eyes met his and she swallowed hard. 'That's different.'

'*Not* different.' He looked at her thoughtfully, his gaze curiously intent. 'Perhaps what you're saying, *meu amorzinho*, is that you failed to find another man who made you feel the way I did. Perhaps what you're saying is that being with me put you off other men for life because none of them matched up.'

Her jaw dropped at his arrogance even while a tiny voice in her head told her that he was absolutely right. No man had ever come close to making her feel what she felt for Luc and she doubted that any man ever would. 'Your ego is amazing—'

'I'm merely telling the truth.' He was cool, confident and totally back in control. It was as if that split second moment of regret and apology had never happened. 'It is time to be totally honest with each other. It's essential if our marriage is to work.'

If she'd been holding her coffee she would have dropped it. 'Our marriage?' She almost choked on the word. 'What marriage?'

'It's the obvious way forward.' He gave a dismissive shrug as if marriage had frequently featured in his plans in the past. 'We share a child. It makes sense for us to share the other aspects of our lives as well.'

She gaped at him and struggled to find her voice. 'We share nothing.'

He gave a smug male smile. 'I think the last two weeks have proved that isn't true.'

'You're talking about sex again, Luc!' Kimberley rose to her feet, resisting the temptation to scream with frustration. She couldn't believe what she was hearing. 'You cannot possibly base a marriage on what we have!'

His smile faded. 'We have a son,' he said coldly, 'and that's more than enough of a basis for a marriage.'

She flopped back down on to her chair. 'You're delusional,' she said flatly and he stared at her with naked incredulity.

'Is that any way to respond to a proposal of marriage?'

'Possibly not, but you didn't make a proposal of marriage,' she said bitterly, standing up again and pacing round her tiny kitchen in an attempt to work off some of her anger and frustration. 'You marched in here and announced that we're getting married because we have a child.'

Jaw clenched, he stood up too. 'I have never proposed to a woman before—'

'Then trust me, you need more practice.' She lifted an eyebrow in his direction. 'Perhaps by the fourth or fifth attempt you might get it right.'

He reached out and grabbed her, his lean strong fingers gripping her arms as he forced her to look at him. 'Stop pacing and listen to me. I mean that you should be flattered. Do you know how many women have wanted to hear me say those words?'

'What words exactly?' She stared at him in helpless frustration. '*"We share a child. It makes sense for us to share the other aspects of our lives as well"*? That certainly wasn't in any of the fairy tales I read as a child.'

'*Stop* making a joke—'

'Do I look as though I'm laughing?' She tried to wriggle away from him but he held her firmly. 'Believe me, Luc, I've never been as far away from laughing. You've just insulted me beyond belief.'

'*Meu Deus*, how have I insulted you?' He stared down at her with ill-concealed exasperation. 'I am asking you to marry me.'

She tilted her head to one side, significantly unimpressed. 'And why would I want to do that? Because it's an honour bestowed on so few?'

'Because it is the best thing for our child,' he growled with a dangerous flash of his dark eyes. 'And because it's what women always want from men.'

And the stupid thing was it was exactly what she wanted. *But not like this.*

'You think so?' Her tone dripped sarcasm. 'Well, not this woman, Luc. I can't think of anything worse than tying myself to you.'

'You are not thinking straight.'

'I'm thinking perfectly straight. Marriage to you would be a nightmare. I'd never be able to go out because you're so hideously possessive, we wouldn't have any sort of social life because your idea of an evening with me is to be naked in bed. You probably wouldn't allow me to get dressed!'

He inhaled sharply, his face unusually pale under his tan. 'You're becoming very emotional.'

'Too right I'm emotional! *"We share a child. It makes sense for us to share the other aspects of our lives as well."* What about the things that matter, Luc, like love and affection? I grew up with a man like you. My father felt the need to go to bed with every woman who smiled at him! Our house was filled with "aunties" and, believe me, there is absolutely no way I'd inflict a similar childhood on a child of mine.'

'That is *not* the way I would behave.' His hand sliced through the air in a gesture of outrage. 'It's true that there is no love between us but marriage can be successful based on other things.'

'Like what? Sex?' She threw him a derisory look. 'For a marriage to work a couple at least have to be able to spend time in each other's company, preferably dressed. That's the bare minimum, Luc, especially when there's a child involved.'

Luc studied her thoughtfully. 'So if we spend time together, then you'll say yes? Those are your terms?'

Terms?

'You make it sound like another of your business negotiations.'

He gave a slight shrug. 'And in a way it is. We each have something that the other wants.'

'You have nothing that I want.'

He leaned back in his chair, his eyes holding hers. 'You want Rio to grow up not knowing his father?'

She bit her lip and shifted slightly. 'No, but—'

'So if we can find a way of sharing an existence amicably then it would be what you would want for him?'

'Well, yes, but—'

'Name your terms.'

She stared at him in stupefied silence. *Name your terms?* Was he that desperate to get his hands on Rio?

'It isn't that simple. I—'

'It is exactly that simple.' As usual he was arrogantly confident of his ability to manoeuvre the situation to his advantage. 'Tell me what it is you want and I will give it to you.'

Love. She wanted him to love her.

She bit back a hysterical laugh, imagining Luc's reaction

if she were to deliver that as her ultimatum. He thought that he could deliver anything she asked, but of course he couldn't. And she would be asking the impossible.

'So I tell you what I want, you say yes and then we get married.'

'That's right.' He gave a confident smile, evidently relieved that she'd finally understood.

'And then you revert to your old ways.'

He frowned. 'I want this marriage to work—'

'But you've never exactly excelled at commitment before, have you, Luc? What's your longest relationship up until now? A month? Two months?'

'There has never been a child involved before—'

'Maybe not, but two months to a lifetime is still rather a stretch,' she muttered, 'and I think it might tax your staying power.'

'I will do whatever it takes to make it work.'

'Really?' She looked at him curiously. 'You'll do whatever it takes?'

'Whatever it takes.'

What did she have to lose?

'All right, this is what it's going to take.' She folded her arms and tilted her head to one side. 'For the next month all our meetings will take place fully clothed. You're going to take me out and you're going to take Rio out. We're going to behave like a family, Luc. And every evening you're going to have me home by ten o'clock. No overnight stays and no sex. And no sex with anyone else, either. If I see one incriminating photograph of you in the press, the deal is off.'

The air throbbed with sudden tension. 'No sex?'

It was hard not to laugh at his tone of utter disbelief.

'No sex. I'm sure you'll be able to hold yourself back for the greater good of proving that being a good father to your child is what really matters to you. And it will give us a chance to find out whether we can stand being together when there is no sex involved. If we can—' she shrugged her slender shoulders '—then I'll marry you.'

She smiled placidly, safe in the knowledge that he was about to leap to his feet and reject her terms as totally unreasonable.

He was a red-blooded highly sexed male in his prime. He was *never* going to agree to her terms.

And that was fine by her. She didn't want to marry Luc. He didn't love her and he never would, and spending every day with him, knowing that he was only with her because of their child, would be torment.

'All right.'

She was so busy smiling to herself that at first she thought she'd misheard him. 'Sorry?'

'I said all right.' He rose to his feet and walked towards her, a slightly dangerous glint in his dark, sexy eyes. 'I accept your terms.'

She looked at him dubiously. 'All of them?'

'All of them.'

'You do?' She stared at him in confusion and a slight smile touched his hard mouth.

'I do. And pretty soon I'll be saying those words in a marriage ceremony, *meu amorzinho*, because you are going to enjoy spending time with me, and so is Rio.'

Kimberley gaped at him. Did anything dent his confidence?

He'd never manage it, she told herself firmly.

Deprived of sex and forced to communicate on a daily basis would soon put an end to his desire for marriage, she thought wryly, and then perhaps her life could return to normal. Obviously Luc would need access to his son, but that could be easily arranged.

'Fine,' she said airily. 'It's a deal.'

* * *

Luc strode away from the house, wondering at exactly what point he'd lost his sanity.

He'd just agreed to a month without sex with a woman who made him think about nothing but sex.

What sort of normal healthy guy would agree to terms like that?

Had he gone totally and utterly mad?

For a man who'd made a point of avoiding commitment at all costs, he was more than a little disturbed by how far he was prepared to go to persuade Kimberley to marry him.

And she *would* marry him, of course, because he would meet all her terms.

How hard could it be? Conversation? Easy—he was getting better at it by the day. Family trips out—easy. No sex—not so easy, he conceded ruefully, ignoring the waiting car and striding purposefully in the opposite direction. But perhaps if she was fully clothed the whole time they were together and he took lots of cold showers, he might just be able to manage it.

Which meant that the deal was as good as done.

One month, that was all it was, he reminded himself as he crossed the road without noticing the cars.

And then he could be a proper father to his son.

Because that was what this marriage was all about.

What other possible reason could there be?

CHAPTER TEN

ONE month later Kimberley sat in the pretty, airy sitting room of her flat, wondering what had happened to her life.

The room was filled with the scent of yet more fresh flowers, which had arrived from Luc that morning, and around her neck lay a beautiful necklace, which he'd given her only the night before as they'd shared another intimate dinner on her patio.

If she'd thought he wasn't capable of sustaining a relationship outside the bedroom then she'd been proved more than wrong.

She stared down at her sketch-book, which lay in front of her, open and untouched. She'd promised herself that today she was going to do some rough designs of a necklace for a very wealthy French client, but so far she hadn't as much as glanced at the page in front of her. She was too distracted.

She couldn't stop thinking about Luc.

It was ironic, she mused as she gazed out of the window without so much as a glance at the sketch-pad in front of her, that the first time she and Luc had spent time together fully clothed and without a double bed in sight had been on a visit to London Zoo with their son.

And the ridiculous thing was that *they'd felt like a family.*

It didn't matter how many times she reminded herself that

he didn't love her and that this amazing, romantic month was all about him trying to manipulate her into marrying him so that he could have full access to his son, she still couldn't stop feeling ridiculously happy.

The almost agonizing anxiety she'd felt over the kidnap threat had finally vanished, partly because she'd heard nothing more from the man and partly because Luc's security team were now part of her everyday life.

But the real reason for her happiness was that she just adored being with Luc. And today she was missing him. That morning he'd been forced to fly to Paris for an urgent business meeting and already she was watching the clock, anticipating the time when his flight would land.

She'd been fast discovering that as well as being amazing in bed, Luc was also incredibly entertaining company when he wanted to be and she was enjoying seeing a completely different side of him.

From the moment he had announced his intention of marrying her, his entire focus had been on her and Rio. He'd contacted lawyers, changed his will, signed countless documents and presented her with countless documents to sign, all designed to ensure that Rio was well provided for. And he'd spent endless hours with his son, waiting at the school gates to collect him at the end of the school day and then taking him on trips, giving him treats and just *talking*.

With the insensitivity of youth, Rio was always asking him questions and Luc had started to relax and respond, gradually becoming more open about himself and his past. And that willingness to reveal intimate details about himself had extended into the evenings, when Rio was safely tucked up in his bed. London was experiencing a heatwave and Luc and Kimberley had fallen into a habit of eating dinner in the tiny walled garden that led from her kitchen and the intimacy of their surroundings had somehow stimulated conversations of a deeply personal nature.

In the past few days alone she'd learned that both his parents had died when he was thirteen and that he'd been given a home by Maria, the woman who was now his personal assistant. And in return he'd given her a job. And she'd been with him for over twenty years.

Maybe Luc *was* capable of commitment, Kimberley mused as she picked up her pencil and attempted to translate the design in her head into a drawing that would provide the basis of her first discussion with her client. After all, he was obviously committed to Maria. And he was showing all the signs of being equally committed to his son.

Committed enough to make an effort in his relationship with her.

She was far too realistic to pretend, even for one unguarded minute, that all this effort on his part was driven by anything other than a desire to secure unlimited access to their child.

With her agreement, he'd revealed his identity to Rio immediately and if she'd harboured any doubts about the sense of marrying a man who clearly didn't love her, then they had dissolved once she'd seen the undiluted excitement and delight on her child's face when he'd finally realised that this vibrant, energetic, exotic man was his father.

How could she deprive her child of the chance to grow up in a normal family? Particularly as Luc himself was so clearly determined to be the very best father possible.

And he'd met every one of her terms. All too easily, it would seem.

Was she the only one who was sexually frustrated? she wondered ruefully.

Evidently the answer was yes. Luc hadn't made one single move in her direction in the past month. He kissed her on both cheeks when they met and when they parted and that was the limit of their physical contact. Very formal. Very restrained.

The desperate need to touch him and be touched by him was driving her mad.

And they were getting on well, she conceded as her pencil danced over the page, creating a stunning individual design. She enjoyed the time they spent together. Enjoyed spending time with him, even though she knew he was doing it with a distinct purpose in mind.

All right, so their relationship wasn't perfect, but what relationship was? She'd learned at eighteen that fairy tale endings didn't happen in real life and at least she was with Luc and Rio had a father. The fact that Luc didn't love her had almost ceased to matter.

As long as she was careful not to reveal the strength of her feelings, careful to do nothing which might frighten him off, what could go wrong?

Kimberley glanced at the clock again. She'd arranged to pick Rio up from school half an hour early so that they could go and meet Luc at the airport. Wasn't that what families did?

The phone rang and, expecting Luc's call, she lifted the receiver and tucked it under her ear, leaving her hands free to gather up her sketches.

But it wasn't Luc and her face turned pale as she immediately recognised the voice.

'So—this time you've really hit the jackpot.'

The papers slid from her nerveless fingers and her knees shook so much she sank on to the nearest chair. It was that or slide to the ground.

Anxiety and panic slammed through her with the force of an express train. 'What do you want?'

'If you have to ask that then you're a lot stupider than you look.'

'W-we already paid you.' Her confidence fell away and her fingers clenched on the phone. 'A fortune. You promised that would be it—'

'Well, let's just say that circumstances have changed. You're a wealthy lady. This time I want ten million.'

She closed her eyes briefly. 'That's ridiculous.'

'You've snagged the attentions of a billionaire.'

'It isn't my money. I can't—'

'Bad decision.' The voice was harsh. 'Goodbye.'

'Wait!' She stood up, panic and anguish in her tone. 'Don't hang up!'

'Are you going to be reasonable?'

What choice did she have? Her eyes filled and her voice was little more than a whisper. 'Yes. I—I'll do anything—'

There was a cold laugh from the other end of the phone. 'Now you're being sensible. And because I'm in a generous mood I'll give you twenty-four hours to get the money. Then I'll contact you again. And if you tell the police or Santoro, then the deal is off.'

Twenty-four hours?

How was she going to get the money in twenty-four hours? *It wasn't long enough.* She couldn't possibly—

'I won't tell Luc, I promise I won't tell Luc, but—' She broke off as she realised that the connection was dead.

'So what exactly are you not going to tell me?' An icy voice came from the doorway and the phone fell from her fingers with a clatter to join the papers on the floor.

She stared at Luc in horror, wondering just how much he'd heard. 'You're early—'

'Clearly ploughing through obstacles in order to spend more time with my family wasn't a sensible move,' he said flatly, walking into the room and pushing the door shut behind him, hostility and condemnation pulsing from every inch of his powerful frame. 'I have spent the last month jumping through hoops to be the sort of man you want me to be. You accuse me of not being able to communicate and yet time and time again the person with the secrets in this relationship is *you*.'

She could hardly breathe, but her panic was all for Rio. 'I don't have secrets—' She couldn't handle this now. She just needed to be left on her own to think and plan and yet how could she do either when her mind was full of anxiety for her child?

Luc planted himself in front of her, his powerful frame a wall of tension. 'So what is it that you've promised not to tell me and who were you making that promise to?'

For a moment she stared at him, sickened by the icy remoteness she saw in his eyes and the disdainful slant of his beautiful mouth. She wanted to defend herself but how could she when the blackmailer had insisted she didn't tell Luc? What if she told him and something happened to Rio?

She tried to comfort herself with the knowledge that Luc had security staff watching Rio, but she still couldn't relax.

'I can't talk about this now.' She needed to talk to Jason. She needed to go to the school. She needed to pick up her child. Urgently. In a complete fluster, she dropped to her knees to gather up the papers she'd scattered but her hands were shaking so badly she immediately dropped them again. Tears pricked her eyes and she blinked them back. 'Can we go back to Brazil this afternoon?' she blurted out impulsively, tilting her head to look at him. 'All three of us? Please?'

Luc lifted stunned dark eyes from the mess on the floor and stared at her with unconcealed amazement. 'The school term isn't ended yet. You said you wanted to wait until the summer holidays. Those were your terms. Remember?'

'I kn-know what I said,' she stammered, gathering up the sketches she'd dropped and then promptly dropping them again. Her hands were shaking so much she couldn't hold anything. 'I've changed my mind. I want us to go now. As soon as we can.'

If she took Rio out of school, then they could go to the island and he'd be safe there, she reasoned desperately. He'd be surrounded by water and Luc's security team. In a place like that they'd be able to protect him, *keep him safe*.

Luc studied her with a visible lack of comprehension. 'Suddenly you want to fly to Brazil. Why?'

She started picking up papers again, her brain paralysed by terror. 'Why must you always ask so many questions?'

'Perhaps because you're not giving me anything that looks even remotely like an answer,' he ground out, reaching for her and hauling her against him. '*Stop* picking up papers and dropping them again, *stop* avoiding my gaze and stand still for just one minute so that we can *talk*.'

'I can't. Not now.' Not ever. She didn't dare think what might happen to Rio if she told Luc the truth. 'And anyway, there's nothing to say.' Her voice was barely audible and he took such a long time to react that for a moment she wondered whether he'd even heard her.

Then he released her so suddenly that she almost fell. 'Fine.' His tone was ice-cold. 'Clearly I was the one who was crazy to even think we could have a relationship. Go and do whatever it is you have to do that I mustn't find out about. I'm going to the office. I'll be back later to pick Rio up and take him for tea. And then my lawyer will contact you to discuss arrangements for the future. Finally I agree with you. Marriage is not on the agenda. I can't marry a woman whose behaviour I'm not even *close* to understanding.'

She wanted to hurl herself into the safety of his arms.

She wanted to tell him *everything* and let him sort it out the way he'd sorted everything out. But she didn't dare.

So instead she stood there, watching through a haze of tears as he strode out of the room like a man with no intention of ever coming back.

Kimberley wanted to break down and just sob and sob until her heart was empty of emotion and her body was dry, but she knew she couldn't allow herself that luxury. She had to get to her son. *Before anyone else did.*

She made it just as far as the door when the phone rang again.

This time it was the school and they were ringing to say that Rio had gone missing.

Luc strode towards his car, struggling to contain the fierce rage of jealousy that threatened to consume his usually cold and rational approach to life. The guilt on Kimberley's face when she'd dropped the phone had ignited feelings inside him that he had never before experienced. For a wild, primitive moment he'd been tempted to throw her over his shoulder, carry her to his nearest property and lock all the doors so that she could have no contact with the outside world.

No contact with other men.

Because he was completely and utterly sure that it was a man who was causing her to be so secretive.

Hadn't she already told him on several occasions that there was no reason why she shouldn't have another man in her life?

And hadn't he spent the last month trying to prove to her that she didn't *need* another man in her life?

Was that why she'd put that ridiculous ban on sex? Because she was spending her nights with another man?

He uttered a soft curse and wondered why he should be suddenly experiencing a depth of insecurity hitherto completely alien to him.

He'd left Paris earlier than planned, overwhelmed by a sudden inexplicable need to be with Kimberley, only to find her white-faced and clearly horrified to see him. His dreams of an ecstatic romantic reunion had dissolved on the spot. The rare diamond that he'd chosen with such care and hidden securely in his pocket until such time as he deemed it appropriate to present it to his future wife, had remained in his pocket, a cruel reminder of how life with Kimberley never turned out the way he expected.

In fact *nothing* had gone the way he'd planned.

For a man used to nothing short of adulation from the female sex, Kimberley's less than flattering reaction to his arrival had come as a severe shock. But over the past month he'd been convinced on several occasions that she was actually enjoying their time together.

Which simply went to prove that a desperate man was a deluded man, he thought grimly as he strode towards his car.

How had he expected her to react to his early arrival?

So surprised by his unexpected appearance that she'd drop her guard, throw herself into his arms and declare her love?

That she'd show him the same unquestioning devotion she'd offered him at the age of eighteen?

Hardly. As she kept reminding him, she wasn't that person any more. Instead of warmth and affection, she displayed nothing but cool reserve and nothing in her body language suggested that she was missing the physical side of their relationship.

Was that because her affection was given elsewhere?

He ground his teeth at the very thought and wondered what it was that she was hiding from him. Whatever it was had been enough to drain the colour from her cheeks and put a look of raw terror into her green eyes.

As the first punch of jealousy receded and his brain once more clicked into action he frowned, recalling her extreme pallor and the papers scattered over the floor.

He stopped dead, oblivious to the curious glances of his security staff and his chauffeur, who was poised to take him to his next appointment. *The papers had already been on the floor before he'd entered the room.*

With the same single-minded focus and ruthless attention to detail that characterised all his business dealings, Luc applied his mind to every moment of their meeting, searching for clues and answers.

She had been pale from the moment he'd walked into the

room, he reminded himself. He hadn't caused the pallor. The papers had already been on the floor. His unexpected arrival hadn't caused her to drop them.

The only thing she'd dropped when she'd seen him had been the phone.

He frowned as he mentally ran through the exact sequence of events.

Like a woman who was desperate, she'd begged him to take them back to Brazil, even though she'd been the one to insist that Rio needed stability and should finish his term at school before they considered travelling.

Why would she want to go back to Brazil if she had another man in her life?

Something didn't feel right.

Like so many men before him, he cursed fluently and wished that women didn't have to be so extremely complicated and perverse in their behaviour.

At that moment his mobile phone rang and he answered the call immediately, all his senses on full alert when he saw that it was Kimberley's number displayed on the screen.

She whispered three words. 'I need you.'

Where was Luc and when would he come?

Kimberley was huddled on the floor, shaking so badly that she couldn't speak.

Her worst nightmare had come true.

'Calm down and tell me again what the school said—' Jason held a glass of brandy to her lips but she pushed it away, her eyes wild with fear. For a moment she thought she might be swallowed up by panic and then she heard the firm, determined tread of Luc's footsteps on the wooden floor and almost wept again with relief because she needed him badly, even though she knew she wasn't supposed to need him.

He strode into the room, his expression grim as his dark

eyes swept the room. He took in Jason holding the glass and then registered her tear-stained face with a soft curse.

In two strides he was by her side. 'From the beginning,' he commanded in rough tones as he lifted her easily and sat in the nearest chair with her on his lap, 'and this time you're going to leave nothing out.'

For a brief moment Kimberley rested a hand against his chest, feeling the solid strength of hard male muscle under her fingers, allowing herself the luxury of comfort. And then she remembered that she didn't have time for comfort.

'I have to go—' She went to slide off his lap but his arms tightened around her waist, preventing her from moving.

'You're going nowhere.'

'You don't understand—' Almost whimpering with fear, she pushed at his arms, trying to free herself. 'He's been taken.'

Luc stilled. 'Who has been taken?'

'Rio.' Her eyes were frantic. 'He was supposed to give me twenty-four hours to get the money but the school just phoned and he's disappeared.'

'You are making absolutely no sense.' Luc narrowed his eyes as he tried to decipher her garbled statement. Then he inhaled sharply, his expression suddenly grim. 'The black-mailer has contacted you again? Is that what you're saying?'

Kimberley turned to Jason for support, not knowing what to do or say.

'You want my opinion?' Her friend gave a helpless shrug. 'You need to tell him everything. He might be able to help. We both know that Luc's a nasty bastard when he's crossed.'

'Thanks.' Luc cast an ironic glance at the other man, who gave an apologetic shrug.

'Take it as a compliment. You have assets that we need at the moment.'

'They made me promise not to tell you. What if they find out?' Kimberley was shivering with fear but Luc was totally calm, his handsome face an icy mask as he reached for his phone. Without providing them with any explanation, he made three calls in rapid succession, his tone cold and unemotional as he issued what she assumed to be a string of instructions in his own language. Then he slipped the phone back into his pocket and gave her a gentle shake.

'You should have told me. Do you know nothing about me? Do you think I would allow anyone to take our child?' His tone was rough and his fingers tightened on her arms and she looked at him blankly, too afraid to think straight.

'I suppose not—' Suddenly there was a glimmer of light in the darkness. She'd forgotten how strong Luc was, even though she'd seen the evidence of that strength on several occasions. Even now he was strong. Unlike her, he was showing no sign of panic. Instead he was cold and rational and very much in control.

Jason dumped the glass down on the table. 'How can a child of six go missing from a school?'

Despite the warmth and safety of Luc's arms, Kimberley couldn't stop shivering. 'Because someone took him.'

'Calm yourself, *meu amorzinho*,' Luc urged roughly. 'No one has taken him. It isn't possible. My team have not left his side since I discovered his existence.'

His phone rang suddenly and he answered it immediately, his expression revealing nothing as he listened and responded. He ended the call with a determined stab of one bronzed finger. 'As I thought—all is well. Rio is safe. One of my security team picked him up two minutes ago, just to be on the safe side. You can relax, *minha docura*.'

'They've found him?' Kimberley's voice was a strangled whisper and Luc gave a soft curse and stroked her tangled hair away from her blotched face.

'He had crossed the road to the sweet shop,' he said gruffly, 'apparently to buy me a present to take to the airport. He had much to say to my driver about your plans to surprise me.'

Kimberley blushed. 'We were going to meet you, but you were early—'

His dark eyes were unusually penetrating. 'A mistake I will remember not to make again,' he said softly, pushing her gently off his lap but maintaining a firm grip on her hand as they stood up. 'My team are taking Rio straight back to my hotel. He'll be safe there. I'll take you to him, but first you need to wash your face and practise your smile. We don't want him to know that anything is wrong.'

'But what about the man? He's still out there and he gave me twenty-four hours—'

'It is not your problem,' Luc informed her with the cool confidence of a man totally comfortable in the command position. 'He slipped up when he called you here. We now have his identity and his whereabouts. He'll be dealt with.'

For once she was more than willing to let him take control of the situation.

Something in the grim set of his mouth made her feel almost sorry for the blackmailer but then she reminded herself that the man had threatened her child and deserved to be on the receiving end of Luc's wrath.

She splashed her face in the bathroom and when she came out there were two security staff waiting to escort her to the hotel.

Luc had gone.

CHAPTER ELEVEN

KIMBERLEY spent the rest of the afternoon and evening playing with Rio in the safety of the hotel suite. Despite the comforting presence of Luc's security staff, she didn't let him out of her sight, all too aware that the threat to his safety still remained.

And as the hours passed and there was still no sign of Luc, she suddenly discovered that her anxiety wasn't only confined to the safety of her child.

What if something had happened to Luc?

Finally, long after Rio had been tucked up in bed asleep, Luc walked into the suite and she dropped on to the nearest sofa, worn out with worrying and almost weak with relief.

'Thank goodness—I was *so* worried and no one would tell me where you were.'

'Why were you worried?' His shirt was undone at the collar and he strolled towards her, as cool and unconcerned as ever. 'You have Rio safe with you.'

'I know, but I thought something might have happened to *you*,' she confessed and then almost bit her tongue off as she realised what she'd revealed.

He didn't want her love or affection.

He just wanted their son. And suddenly she knew that she couldn't marry him, no matter how much she wanted to. It wouldn't be fair on Luc. Eventually he would find someone he could love and she didn't want to stand in the way of his happiness.

They'd have to come to some other arrangement.

He stopped in front of her and dragged her gently to her feet.

'I think it's time you learned to trust me, *meu amorzinho*,' he urged, sliding a hand under her chin and forcing her to look at him. 'You accuse me of being controlling, yet there are times when it is good to allow another to take charge and this was one of them. You have proved time and time again that you are capable of running your own life, but I think when it comes to dealing with blackmailers you can safely leave the work to others. You need to learn to delegate.'

His eyes hardened and she caught her breath, hardly daring to ask the question. 'Did you find him?'

His hand dropped to his side and he gave a smile that wasn't altogether pleasant. 'Of course. The problem is solved.'

'Thank you,' she breathed, almost weak with relief. She suddenly discovered that she didn't even want to know what had happened. She was just glad that it was over. 'Thank you so much.'

Luc released her abruptly and raked long fingers through his sleek, dark hair as he paced away from her. 'Before you bestow your gratitude in my direction I should probably tell you that the whole situation was my fault.' His voice was harsh as he turned back to her. 'He made your life a misery because of me, *minha docura*. I am entirely to blame for your recent trauma so you might want to hold on to your thanks.'

She frowned. 'I don't understand—'

'He was an employee of mine. One of my drivers.' Luc's hands dropped to his sides and he walked towards the window, his expression grim and set, his tone flat. 'I fired him.

He was dishonest and I won't tolerate dishonesty in my employees. That was seven years ago.'

Kimberley stared at him. 'I was with you seven years ago.'

'That's right.'

She looked at him blankly, still not understanding. 'But what does that have to do with me?'

He let out a driven sigh. 'He wanted to make money the easy way. You presented him with the opportunity to do that.'

'But *how*? How did he even know about Rio?'

Luc loosened more buttons of his shirt. 'He was my driver. I suspect he overheard something which he then used to his advantage.'

'But I never—' Kimberley broke off and Luc gave a wry smile.

'You never?' he prompted her gently and she lifted a hand to her mouth.

'Oh, God—the very last time I tried to see you, I came to the office and you arranged for a car to take me away. I was terribly upset—I called Jason to ask him if I could stay with him—'

'And naturally you told him why,' Luc finished for her with a dismissive shrug of his broad shoulders. 'I think you have your answer.'

'Then it's *all* my fault,' she whispered in horror and Luc frowned sharply.

'Not true. If it is anyone's fault it is mine, for sending you away that day without even giving you the courtesy of a hearing. And on the other occasions.' He hesitated, his bronzed face unusually pale as he surveyed her stricken expression. 'I am very much to blame for everything that has happened to you and for that I am truly sorry. My only defence is that you were so very different from every other woman I've ever met.'

She gaped at him, so startled and taken aback by the previously unimaginable vision of Luc Santoro *apologising* that she wasn't aware that he'd even taken her hands until he pulled her against him.

'But the thing that makes me most sorry is that I didn't believe you when you said you were being blackmailed. I'm truly sorry that you've had so much worry to cope with alone,' he said roughly, his dark eyes raking her pale face. 'That day you came to my office and asked me for five million dollars; I should have believed you, but I've never been able to think clearly around you. The truth is that I wanted to believe that you were a cold-hearted little gold-digger.'

'But *why?* Why would you want to think a thing like that about someone?' She stared at him in amazement and he spread his hands, as if the answer should be obvious.

'Seven years ago it was the only way I could keep myself from following you and bringing you back. But I should have known better. You were never interested in possessions. It wasn't until recently that I realised that you truly had no idea just how wealthy I am—'

She bit her lip, more than a little embarrassed that she'd been so naïve. 'To be honest, I'd never really given it any thought.'

She'd never been interested in Luc the businessman. *Only Luc the man.*

'Unlike every other woman I've ever been with, all of whom thought about little else,' he informed her, a hard edge to his voice. 'In contrast, the only thing you've ever asked me for is conversation. You're not interested in material things, so I should have known that when you told me about Rio you were telling the truth. I should have listened to you but unfortunately my temper is as hot as my libido.'

She blushed. 'I can understand that you were still angry with me,' she conceded hastily, more than willing to forgive him. 'I did spend a great deal of your money. Which was probably wrong of me, but I was very upset and scared about the future and I badly wanted to be able to stay at home and look after our baby.'

'You spent next to nothing compared to your predecessors,' he informed her in a dry tone and she blinked in astonishment.

'I bought a *flat*.'

'Which has turned out to be an excellent investment,' he pointed out with some amusement. 'I have had girlfriends who have spent a similar amount expanding the contents of their wardrobes. It appears that the flat has more than trebled in value since you first bought it.'

It was typical of Luc to have already discovered that fact, she thought dryly. 'But if you truly thought I was a gold-digger, why did you want me back in your bed? I never understood that. You'd so obviously had enough of me when we parted seven years ago.'

He grimaced. 'I wish that was the case, but sadly the complete opposite was true.'

She stilled. 'But you drove me away.'

'That's right.'

'You'd *definitely* had enough of me—'

'I doubt I would ever have enough of you, *meu amorzinho*. And that was the very reason I had to make you leave.'

She felt thoroughly confused. All these years she'd made certain assumptions and it seemed now that she'd been wrong. 'You knew I'd leave?'

'Of course—' His smile was self-mocking. 'You were very possessive. I knew that if I was photographed with another woman that would be the end for you. And us.'

'I can't believe you did that.' She struggled to find her voice. 'I was *so* hurt.'

He flinched as though she'd hit him. 'I know and for that I am truly sorry. If it makes it any better, it was all staged. I let the photographer do his stuff and then spent the rest of the evening getting blind drunk. I never touched another woman when we were together.'

She lifted a hand and rubbed the frown between her eyes. 'You hated the fact I was so affectionate, hated the fact that I loved you—because you didn't feel the same way about me.'

He gave a short laugh that was totally lacking in humour. 'You're wrong. I felt *exactly* the same way about you and those feelings scared me.'

Luc, *scared*?

There was a long painful silence while she stared at him. 'You felt the same way I did?'

'That's right.'

Her heart thudded against her chest. 'I *loved* you.'

He tensed slightly. 'I know.'

She licked her lips. 'You accused me of acting—'

'Some men will say anything rather than accept that he's been well and truly hooked by a woman.' Luc ran a hand over the back of his neck, visibly discomfited by the admission. 'I guess I'm one of those men. I didn't know how to handle the situation. For the first time in my life I found myself seriously out of my depth.'

She stared at him. 'You're saying you felt the same way about me?'

'Why do you think I refused to see you on those three occasions? I've always considered myself to be a self-disciplined man but that went out of the window when I met you. I didn't trust myself to turn you away. I was relieved when you spent all that money because it meant that I was finally able to bracket you with all the other women I'd ever been with. It made it easier to push you away.'

'I don't understand.' Her voice was little more than a whisper as she tried to comprehend what he was telling her. 'If you loved me, why did you want to push me away?'

He inhaled sharply. 'Because I didn't want to be in love. I've spent my life avoiding emotional entanglements and I succeeded very well until you came along. I was always careful to pick the same type of woman. Cold, hard and with an eye set firmly on my money. I suppose, in a way, it was a guarantee. I knew there was no chance that I'd ever fall in love with a woman like that so I was perfectly safe. But I made a mistake with you. A big mistake.'

'What's wrong with being in love if it's mutual?' She stared at him in confusion. 'I *adored* you.'

There was a long silence and she saw a shadow cross his hard, handsome face.

He paced over to the window, keeping his back to her as if speaking was suddenly extraordinarily difficult. 'My father loved my mother so much and when she died his entire life fell apart. I watched it happen. I saw a strong man shrivel to nothing and become weak. He no longer wanted to live and he lost interest in everything, including me.' Luc's voice was flat. 'I was thirteen years old and it certainly wasn't a good advertisement for the benefits of love. My father ceased to function. His business folded. We lost our home. And finally he died.'

Kimberley stilled, appalled and saddened. And her heart ached for how he must have suffered as a boy, losing both his parents at such a young, impressionable age. She looked at the stiff set of his broad shoulders and wanted to go to him. *Wanted to hug him tight.* But she sensed that he didn't want her comfort. 'How did he die?'

Luc didn't turn, his eyes still fixed on a point outside the window. 'To be honest, I think he just didn't care enough to live. He gave up.'

She stared at his back helplessly, for the first time feeling as though she'd been given some insight into what made him the person he was. 'And you vowed that was never going to happen to you—'

'And it never did.' He turned, his dark eyes fixed on hers with shimmering intensity. 'Never even came close until I met you. And what I felt for you frightened me so much I refused to acknowledge it, even to myself.'

She swallowed. 'I wish I'd known about your childhood. I wish you'd *talked* to me—'

'I didn't want to talk. I just wanted to run a mile. I'd vowed that it was never going to happen to me. *That I would never make myself that vulnerable.* My father went from being a man with energy and drive to little more than a shell. We lost everything virtually overnight. Maria gave me a home. She was like a mother to me.'

And she guessed that he'd repaid that debt many times over.

'I still think you should have told me.'

He gave a wry smile. 'I didn't tell anyone anything, *meu amorzinho*. That's how I kept myself safe.'

She curled her fingers into her palms. 'So when I turned up at your office six weeks ago—'

'I couldn't resist the temptation to see you one more time and, having seen you, I couldn't resist the temptation to get you into my bed one more time,' he confessed with brutal frankness. 'I convinced myself that two weeks would be enough to cure me. Then I convinced myself that just a little longer would do the trick. I'm not good at being without you, *meu amorzinho*.'

She gazed at him, unable to suppress the bubble of happiness inside her. 'I never even guessed you felt that way.'

'I followed you to England,' he pointed out dryly, 'which should have told you something.'

'I thought it was just sex—'

'*Not* just sex,' he assured her, 'and the last month should have proved that. But if you still don't believe me you can talk to my board of directors, who are currently wondering if I'm ever going to work again. I have been absent from the office for so long they're all becoming extremely jittery.'

She chewed her lip, hardly daring to ask the question that needed to be asked. 'And what about now—' her voice cracked '—are you cured, Luc?'

Luc fixed her with his dark, possessive gaze. 'You really have to ask me that?' His accent was strangely thick, as if he couldn't quite get his tongue around the words that needed to be said. 'In the past month I have thought only of you and what you need in a relationship. I have talked until my throat is sore and told you *everything* about myself. I have expressed thoughts that I didn't even know I was thinking. But, most of all, I have ignored the fact that you only have to walk into a room and I want to strip you naked. You have stayed fully clothed for an entire month and I haven't so much as kissed you on the lips. I have done for you what I've never done for any woman before. And yet *still* you ask me if I love you?'

Suddenly Kimberley just wanted to smile and smile. 'I thought you just wanted to marry me because of Rio—'

'I want to marry you because I love you and because I can't live without you,' he confessed with a groan, pulling her against him. 'And if I was a decent sort of guy I'd be saying that I love you too much to marry you unless you love me. But, as you've pointed out so many times in the past, I'm ruthless and entirely self-seeking and don't understand the word no, so I'm going to keep on at you until you say yes.'

He sounded so much like his usual self that she laughed. 'Controlling again, Luc?' Her eyes twinkled suggestively. 'The handcuffs are still in my bag. Perhaps I should use them again. It isn't good for you to have everything your own way.'

'If it's any consolation, I am suffering badly for the way I treated you,' he confessed in a raw tone. 'It tortures me to think of how alone and afraid you were and that I was the cause of it. I don't know how you managed—'

'Well, your credit cards certainly helped,' she muttered and he gave an agonized groan.

'And you even kept the receipts for everything you bought. Do you know how that made me feel? To know that you felt the need to itemise everything?'

'I'm used to watching what I spend,' she said simply and then gave a rueful smile. 'And, I suppose, deep down I felt guilty spending your money. But you'd called all the shots and it was a way of taking some of the control back.'

His own eyes gleamed dark in response. 'Once we're safely married you can take control any time you like,' he assured her huskily, sliding his hands into her hair and tilting her face to his. 'But, in the meantime, I need you to put me out of my misery. I never dreamt that asking a woman to marry me could be so traumatic. No wonder I've avoided commitment for so long.'

'I didn't know you were asking—I thought you were telling.'

'I'm *trying* to ask; it's just that asking is all very new to me,' he confessed in a smooth tone that suggested that he had absolutely no intention of changing his ways in the near future.

'Like compromise and conversation,' she teased and he gave a tortured groan.

'*Don't* tease me—just give me an answer.' His dark head lowered and his mouth brushed against hers. 'Are you going to say yes or do you have still more challenges and tests for me to pass before you'll agree to tie yourself to me for ever?'

For ever.

How could two words sound so good?

'I think you've more than passed the test,' she whispered as she slid her arms round his neck. 'And the answer is yes.'

'And do you think, if I really concentrate on compromise and conversation, that you might manage to love me back one day, the way you used to love me?'

'I already do,' she said softly, standing on tiptoe and kissing him again. 'You were absolutely right when you said that no other man had ever matched up to what we shared. I've never found anyone who made me feel the way you do.'

'Seriously?' He looked stunned, as if he couldn't quite allow himself to believe what she was saying. 'You still love me?'

'I've never stopped loving you. Although I'm worried about what such a confession will do to your already massively over-inflated ego.'

He gave a delighted laugh and pulled her hard against him. 'So if I put a ring on your finger straight away, can we drop the "no sex" routine because, frankly, abstinence is something else that I don't excel at.'

'Me neither,' she confessed breathlessly, her cheeks heating at the hard, male feel of him against her, 'and there's no need to wait for a ring.'

'You're going to wear the ring,' he told her in his usual tone of authority, reaching into his jacket pocket and removing a velvet box. 'The ring says "hands off, she's mine" to any other man who happens to glance in your direction. I want you well and truly labelled so that there can be no mistake.'

'Not possessive at all then, Luc,' she teased and then gasped as he flipped open the box and the stunning diamond winked and sparkled at her. 'Oh, it's *beautiful*—'

'It's worth a small fortune, not that you care about things like that,' he added hastily. 'I bought it in Paris when I decided that I absolutely wasn't going to take no for an answer.' He slid it on to her finger and then pulled her back into his arms.

'And if I *had* said no?'

He stroked her hair away from her face. 'I don't understand no,' he reminded her in husky tones as he bent his head to claim her mouth again. 'I had a *very* limited education.'

She felt her head swim and her legs turn to liquid and forced herself to pull away briefly before she completely lost the ability to communicate. 'In that case I'd better say yes—' the look in his eyes made her breathless '—but you have to promise not to be too controlling or I might be forced to handcuff you to the bed again so that I can have my own way.'

His eyes gleamed. 'In that case, *meu amorzinho*,' he murmured huskily, 'it's only fair to warn you that I'm planning on being controlling any moment now.'

Her heart missed a beat and she ran her tongue over her lower lip. 'So perhaps we ought to move this conversation through to the bedroom.'

Luc gave a low, sexy laugh and scooped her into his arms. 'I'm finding the whole concept of conversation increasingly more appealing with practice.'

And he walked through to the bedroom and kicked the door closed behind them.

TOP THREE SUMMER ROMANCE
EVENTS IN RIO

Brazilian billionaire Luc certainly knows how to woo a woman, but here are three *other* hot Rio attractions that make the city *the* place to escape for a summer fling:

- **The June Bonfire Festival:** Fireworks and moonlight right in the heart of the city – a perfect recipe for romance.

- **The Rio Boat Show:** Taking place in May each year the Rio Boat Show has some of the world's most spectacular yachts on display. Where else would a lady look to find her very own tycoon?

- **Platforma 1 Samba Show:** Looking for a man with sensual Latin moves? Head on down to the daily samba show, performed at Platforma 1 (Rua Aadalberto Ferreira 32) from 10pm throughout the summer.

Jet-Set Seduction

SANDRA FIELD

SANDRA FIELD'S GUIDE TO
JET-SET ROMANCES

A simple enough request, you'd think — put together a short guide to romance in the main destination of your book.

The problem? Although Clea meets Slade in San Francisco, their romance leads them in quick succession to Monaco, Copenhagen, Florence, Paris, Manhattan, Kentucky, Chamonix, back to San Francisco, and finally to the rugged coastline of Maine.

Their chosen rendezvous aren't always the epitome of romance. Paris in a pre-Christmas downpour? A building site in San Francisco in January? Mind you, put Clea and Slade within twenty feet of each other and you're guaranteed heat.

Still, perhaps you should wander San Francisco's Japanese Tea Garden in spring, when the cherry trees and azaleas are in glorious bloom. Then fly to Paris; in a café on a cobblestone street by the Seine order wine the colour of rubies and gaze into your lover's eyes...

Your body aching pleasurably from a day on the slopes, rest your head on his shoulder by fire-light in your chalet in Chamonix...together, find Botticelli's Venus in the Uffizi, her shell-pale skin, the ripples of her long blonde hair...gaze at the forlorn statue of the mermaid in the harbour of Copenhagen and know you'll never make her mistake, you'll never lose yourself for love...but in Monte Carlo, where everyone goes to gamble, understand that risk is inseparable from romance. Lastly, no matter how romantic it sounds to make love beneath the tall pines of Maine to the fall of the waves, there are some risks you shouldn't court

– ants and mosquitoes, to name two. No, tumble into your bunk on a yacht moored in a moonlit cove...

But maybe you're not able to jet-set to Paris or Monaco or Maine. So do you know what I really believe? Romance is a state of mind – or of heart – and you can find it wherever you are.

CHAPTER ONE

A GARDEN party. Not his usual scene.

Slade Carruthers had stationed himself in one corner of the garden, a palm tree waving high over his head, his back flanked by California holly. The sun was, of course, shining. Would it dare do anything else for Mrs. Henry Hayward III's annual garden party?

He was here on his own. As he preferred to be.

He was in between women right now; had been for quite a while. Maybe he'd grown bored with the age-old game of the chase, and the inevitable surrender that led, equally inevitably, to the end of yet another affair. Certainly for quite a while he hadn't met anyone who'd tempted him to abandon his solitary status.

Casually Slade looked around. Belle Hayward's guests were, as usual, an eccentric mixture of extremely rich, well-bred socialites and artistic mavericks. But every one of them knew the rules: suits and ties for the gentlemen, dresses and hats for the ladies. The two large men stationed at the iron gates had been rumored to turn away a famous painter in acrylic-spattered jeans, and an heiress in diamond-sprinkled capri pants.

The Ascot of San Francisco, Slade thought, amused. His

own summerweight suit was hand-tailored, his shoes Italian leather, his shirt and tie silk. He'd even combed his unruly dark hair into some sort of order.

A young woman strolled into his field of view. Her head was bent as she listened to an elderly lady who looked familiar to Slade, and who was wearing a mauve gown that looked all too recently resurrected from mothballs. He searched for her name, realizing he'd met her here last year. Maggie Yarrow, that was it. Last of a line of ruthless steel magnates, possessor of a tongue like a blunt ax.

The young woman had broken both Belle's rules. She was hatless and she was dressed in a flowing tunic over wide-legged pants.

Her wild tangle of red curls shone like flame in the sunlight.

Slade left his post under the palm tree and started walking toward her, smiling at acquaintances as he went, refusing a goblet of champagne from one of the white-jacketed waiters. His heart was beating rather faster than he liked.

As he got closer, he saw she had wide-spaced eyes of a true turquoise under elegantly arched brows; a soft, voluptuously curved mouth; a decided chin that added character to a face already imbued with passionate intelligence.

And with kindness, Slade thought. Not everyone would have chosen to pass the afternoon with a rude and dotty ninety-year-old. His nose twitched. Who did indeed smell of mothballs.

Then the young woman threw back her head and laughed, a delightful cascade of sound that pierced Slade to the core. Her hair rippled over her shoulders, gleaming as a bolt of silk gleams in the light.

He stopped dead in his tracks. His palms were damp, his heart was racketing in his chest and his groin had hardened. How could he be so strongly attracted to someone whose name he didn't even know?

It looked as though his long months of abstinence were over. If he didn't meet her, he'd die.

Where the hell had that thought come from? Cool it, he told himself. We're talking lust here. Plain old-fashioned lust.

As though she sensed the intensity of his gaze, the young woman looked straight at him. Her smile faded, replaced by a look of puzzlement. "Is something wrong?" she said. "Am I supposed to know you?"

Her voice was honey-smooth, layered like fine brandy; she had the trace of an accent. Slade said, "I don't believe we've met, no. Slade Carruthers. Hello, Mrs. Yarrow, you're looking well."

The elderly lady gave an uncouth cackle. "Watch out for this one, girl. Richer than you by a city mile. Money and machismo—he's one of Belle's favorites."

"Why don't you introduce me anyway?" Slade said.

"Introduce yourselves." Maggie Yarrow hitched at the shoulder of her gown. "Look at the pair of you—an ad for Beautiful People. California Chic. I need more champagne."

Slade ducked as she swished her ebony cane through the air to get the attention of the nearest waiter. After grabbing a glass from his tray, she tossed back its contents, took another from him and walked in a dead-straight line toward her hostess.

Trying not to laugh, Slade sought out those incredible turquoise eyes again. "I'm not from California. Are you?"

"No." She held out one hand. "Clea Chardin."

Her fingers were slender, yet her handclasp was imbued with confidence; Slade always paid attention to handshakes. It also, he thought shakily, carried a jolt like electricity. He opened his mouth to say something urbane, witty, erudite. Instead he heard himself say, "You're the most beautiful woman I've ever met."

Clea tugged her hand free, to her dismay feeling desire

uncoil in her belly; every nerve she possessed was suddenly on high alert. Danger, she thought. This man wasn't her usual fare. Far from it. Taking a deep breath, she said lightly, "I read an article recently that said beauty is based on symmetry. So you're complimenting me because my nose isn't crooked and I'm not wall-eyed."

Pull out all the stops, Slade thought. Because this is a woman you've got to have. "I'm saying your eyes are like the sea in summer when it washes over a shoal. That your hair glows like the coals of a bonfire on the beach."

Disconcerted, Clea blinked. "Well," she said, "poetry. You surprise me, Mr. Carruthers."

"Call me Slade…and I can't imagine I'm the first man to tell you how astonishingly beautiful you are." He smiled. "Actually, your nose is slightly crooked. Adds character."

"You mean I'm imperfect?" she said. "Now your face is much too strong to be called handsome. Compelling, yes. Rugged, certainly." She smiled back, a smile full of mockery. "Your hair is the color of polished mahogany, and your eyes are like the Mediterranean late on a summer evening—that wonderful midnight-blue."

"You're embarrassing me."

"I can't imagine I'm the first woman to tell you how astonishingly attractive you are," she riposted.

"You know what? Your skin's like the pearly sheen inside a seashell." And how he longed to stroke the hollow beneath her cheekbone, its smooth ivory warmth. Fighting to keep his hands at his sides, Slade added, "A mutual admiration society—is that what we are?"

"From the neck up only," Clea said, deciding the time had come for a solid dose of the truth. "I'm not going near your body."

He dropped his iron control long enough for his gaze to

rake her from head to toe, from her softly shadowed cleavage to the seductive flow of waist, hip and thigh. On her bare feet she was wearing jeweled sandals with impossibly high heels. My God, he thought, I'm done for. "That's very wise of you," he said thickly, and looked around the crowded garden. "Given the circumstances."

"I meant," she said clearly, "that I'm literally not going near your body."

"Scared to?"

"Yes."

His choke of laughter was involuntary. "You're honest, I'll say that for you."

She gave him an enigmatic smile; at least, she hoped it was enigmatic. "Where's home for you, Slade?"

Tacitly accepting her change of subject, he answered, "Manhattan. And you?"

"Milan."

"So your accent's Italian?" he said.

"Not really. I grew up in France and Spain."

"What brings you here?"

"I was invited."

An answer that wasn't an answer. He glanced down at her aqua silk trousers. "How did you get past the dragons at the gate? Belle's dress code is set in concrete."

She said demurely, "I arrived earlier in the day and changed in the house."

"So you know Belle well?"

"I'd never met her before yesterday…nor had I met Maggie Yarrow. Just how rich are you, Slade Carruthers?"

"I could ask the same of you."

"Carruthers…" Her eyes widened. "Not Carruthers Consolidated?"

"The same."

"You're doing all that cutting-edge research on environmentally sustainable power sources," she said with genuine excitement, temporarily forgetting that Slade represented nothing but danger. She asked a penetrating question, Slade answered and for ten minutes they talked animatedly about wind power and solar systems.

Although she was both informed and interested, it was he who brought the conversation back to the personal. "How long are you staying in the area? I could show you the project we're working on outside Los Angeles."

"Not long enough for that."

"I have a house in Florence," he said.

She smiled at him, her lips a sensual curve. "I spend very little time in Italy."

He couldn't invite her for dinner tonight; it was a yearly ritual that he have dinner with Belle after the garden party so she could dissect all the guests and savor the latest gossip. "Have dinner with me tomorrow night."

"I already have plans," she said.

"Are you married? Engaged?" Slade said, failing to disguise the urgency in his voice. He had a few inflexible rules as far as women were concerned, one being that he never had an affair with a woman who was already taken.

"No and no," she said emphatically.

"Divorced?" he hazarded.

"No!"

"Hate men?"

Clea smiled, her teeth even and white, her eyes laughing at him. His head reeled. "I like the company of men very much."

"Men in the plural."

She was now openly laughing. "In the plural overall, one at a time in the specific."

Didn't he operate the same way with women? So why did

he hate her lighthearted response? He said, "I'm not inviting you for dinner tonight because Belle and I have an annual and long-standing date."

Clea's lashes flickered. For her own reasons, she didn't like hearing that Slade Carruthers and Belle were longtime friends. She said calmly, "Then perhaps we aren't meant to talk further about windmills."

"Meet me tomorrow morning at Fisherman's Wharf," Slade said.

"Why would I do that?"

Because you're so beautiful I can't think straight. "So I can buy you a Popsicle."

"Popsicle?" She stumbled over the word. "What's that?"

"Fruit-flavored ice on a stick. Cheap date."

She raised her brows artlessly. "So you're tight with your money?"

"I don't think you'd be overly impressed were I to splash it around."

"How clever of you," she said slowly, not altogether pleased with his small insight into her character.

"Ten in the morning," he said. "Pier 39, near the Venetian carousel. No dress code."

"Beneath your charm—because I do find you charming, and extremely sexy—you're ruthless, aren't you?"

"It's hard to combine raspberry Popsicles with ruthlessness," he said. Sexy, he thought. Well.

"I—"

"Slade, how are you, buddy?"

Slade said, less than enthusiastically, "Hello there, Keith. Keith Rowe, from Manhattan, a business acquaintance of mine. This is Clea Chardin. From Milan. Where's Sophie?"

Keith waved his glass of champagne somewhat drunkenly in the air. "Haven't you heard? The Big D."

Clea frowned. "I don't understand."

"Divorce," Keith declaimed. "Lawyers. Marital assets. Alimony. In the last four months I've been royally screwed—marriage always boils down to money in the end, don't you agree?"

"I wouldn't know," Clea said coldly.

Slade glanced at her. She was pale, her eyes guarded. But she'd never divorced, or so she'd told him. He said, "I'm sorry to hear that, Keith."

"You're the smart one," Keith said. "He's never married, Chloe. Never even been engaged." He gulped the last of his champagne. "Evidence of a very shu—oops, sorry, Chloe, what I meant was superior IQ."

"Clea," she said, even more coldly.

He bowed unsteadily. "Pretty name. Pretty face. I've noticed before how Slade gets all the really sexy broads."

"No one gets me, Mr. Rowe," she snapped. "Slade, I should be going, it's been nice talking to you."

Slade fastened his fingers around the filmy fabric of her sleeve to stop her going anywhere. Then, in a voice any number of CEOs would have recognized, he said, "Keith, get lost."

Keith hiccuped. "I can take a hint," he said and wavered across the grass toward the nearest tray of champagne.

"He's a jerk when he's sober," Slade said tightly, letting go of Clea's sleeve, "and worse when he's been drinking. Can't say I blame Sophie for leaving him."

Heat from Slade's fingers had burned through her sleeve. Danger, her brain screamed again. "So you condone divorce?" Clea said, her voice like a whiplash.

"People make mistakes," he said reasonably. "Although it's not on my agenda. If I ever get married, I'll marry for life."

"Then I hope you enjoy being single."

"Are you a cynic, Clea?"

"A realist."

"Tell me why."

She gave him a lazy smile that, Slade noticed, didn't quite reach her eyes. "That's much too serious a topic for a garden party. I want one of those luscious little cakes I saw on the way in, and Earl Grey tea in a Spode cup."

Much too serious, Slade thought blankly. That's what's wrong. I'm in over my head, drowning in those delectable blue-green eyes. When have I ever wanted a woman as I want this one? "I'll get you whatever you desire," he said.

Her heart gave an uncomfortable lurch in her chest. "Desire is another very big topic. Let's stick to *want*. What I want is cake and tea."

Visited by the sudden irrational terror that she might vanish from his sight, he said, "You'll meet me tomorrow morning?"

He wasn't, Clea was sure, a man used to being turned down; in fact, he looked entirely capable of camping out on her hotel doorstep should she say no. Better, perhaps, that she meet him in a public place, use her usual tactics for getting rid of a man who didn't fit her criteria, and then go back to Belle's on her own.

"Popsicles and a carousel?" she said, raising her brows. "How could I not meet you?"

"Ten o'clock?"

"Fine."

The tension slid from his shoulders. "I'll look forward to it." Which was an understatement if ever there was one.

She said obliquely, "I leave for Europe the next day."

"I leave for Japan."

Her lashes flickered. "Maybe I'll sleep until noon tomorrow."

"Play it safe?" He grinned at her. "Or do I sound incredibly arrogant?"

"I only take calculated risks," she said.

"That's a contradiction in terms."

She said irritably, "How many women have told you your smile is pure dynamite?"

"How many men have wanted to warm their hands—or their hearts—in your hair?"

"I don't do hearts," Clea said.

"Nor do I. Always a good thing to have out in the open."

She looked very much as though she was regretting her decision to meet him, he thought. He'd better play it cool, or Clea Chardin would run clear across the garden path and out of his life.

"Tea and cake," he said, and watched her blink. Her lashes were deliciously long, her brows as tautly shaped as wings. Then she linked her arm with his; the contact surged through his body.

"Two cakes?" she said.

"A dozen, if that's what you want," he said unsteadily.

"Two is one too many. But sweets are my downfall."

"Clams and French fries are mine. The greasier the better."

"And really sexy broads."

He said flatly, "Let's set the record straight. First, I loathe the word *broad*. Secondly, sure I date. But I'm no playboy and I dislike promiscuity in either sex."

So her tactics were almost sure to work, Clea thought in a flood of relief. "This is a charming garden, isn't it?" she said.

For the first time since he'd seen her, Slade looked around. Big tubs of scented roses were in full bloom around the marquee, where an orchestra was sawing away at Vivaldi. The canopy of California oaks and palm trees cast swaying patterns of shade over the deep green grass, now trampled by many footsteps. The women in their bright dresses were like flowers, he thought fancifully.

Because Belle's garden was perched on one of the city's hilltops, a breeze was playing with Clea's tangled curls. He reached over and tucked a strand behind her ear. "Charming indeed," he said.

Her eyes darkened. Deliberately she moved a few inches away from him, dropping her hand from his sleeve. "Do you see much of Belle?" she asked.

"Not a great deal. I travel a lot with my job, and my base is on the East Coast...how did you meet her?"

"Through a mutual friend," Clea said vaguely; no one other than Belle knew why she was here. "Oh look, miniature éclairs—do you think I can eat one without getting whipped cream on my chin?"

"Another calculated risk," he said.

"One I shall take."

Had he ever seen anything sexier than Clea Chardin, in broad daylight and surrounded by people, licking a tiny patch of whipped cream from her lips? Although *sexy* was far too mundane a word for his primitive and overwhelming need to possess her; or for the sensation he had of plummeting completely out of control to a destination unknown to him. Every nerve on edge, every sense finely honed. For underneath it all, wasn't he frightened?

Frightened? Him, Slade Carruthers? Of a woman?

"Aren't you going to eat anything, Slade?"

"What? Oh, sorry, of course I am." He took a square from the chased silver platter and bit into it. It was a date square. He hated date squares. He said, "The summer my mother learned how to make chocolate éclairs, my father and I each gained five pounds."

"Where did you grow up?"

"Manhattan. My parents still live there. My mother's on a health kick now, though. Soy burgers and salads."

"And what does your father think of that?"

"He eats them because he adores her. Then at least once a

week he takes her out for dinner in SoHo or Greenwich Village and plies her with wine and decadent desserts." Slade's face softened. "The next day it's back to tofu and radicchio."

"It sounds idyllic."

The sharpness in her voice would have cut paper. "You don't sound amused."

"I'm not a believer in marital bliss, whether flavored with tofu or chocolate," she said coldly. "Ah, there's Belle…if you'll excuse me, I must speak to her before I leave. I'll see you tomorrow."

She plunked her half-empty cup on the linen tablecloth so hard that tea slopped into the saucer. Then she threaded her way through the crowd toward Belle, her hair like a beacon among the clusters of pastel hats. Slade watched her go. *Prickly* wasn't the word for Clea Chardin.

Although she claimed never to have been married, some guy had sure pulled a dirty on her. Recently, by the sound of things, and far from superficially.

He'd like to kill the bastard.

Maybe Belle would fill him in on the details at dinner tonight. After a couple of glasses of her favorite Pinot Noir.

He wanted to know everything there was to know about Clea Chardin.

CHAPTER TWO

THAT evening, Slade waited until he and Belle were halfway through their grilled squab, in a trendy French restaurant on Nob Hill, before saying, "I met Clea Chardin at your party this afternoon, Belle."

Belle's fork stopped in midair. While her hair was unabashedly gray, her shantung evening suit was pumpkin-orange, teamed with yellow diamonds that sparkled in the candlelight. Her eyes, enlarged with lime-green mascara, were shrewd: Belle harbored no illusions about human nature. Slade was one of the few people who knew how much of her fortune went to medical clinics for the indigent.

"Delightful gal, Clea," she said.

"Tell me about her."

"Why, Slade?"

"She interests me," he hedged.

"In that case, I'll leave her to do the telling," Belle said. "The sauce is delicious, isn't it?"

"So that's your last word?"

"Don't play games with Clea. That's my last word."

"I'm not in the habit of playing games!"

"No? You're thirty-five years old, unmarried, hugely rich and very sexy...why hasn't some woman snagged you before now?" Belle answered her own question. "Because you know all the moves and you're adept at keeping your distance. I'm telling you, don't trifle with Clea Chardin."

"She struck me as someone who can look after herself."

"So she's a good actor."

Belle looked distinctly ruffled. Choosing not to ask why Clea was so defenseless, Slade took another mouthful of the rich meat and chewed thoughtfully. "Maggie Yarrow was in fine form," he said.

Belle gave an uncouth cackle. "Don't know why I invite her, she gets more outrageous every year. Nearly decapitated one of my waiters with that cane of hers…which reminds me, did you see what the senator's wife was wearing? Looked like she ransacked the thrift shop."

He knew better than to ask why Belle had slackened her infamous dress code for Clea. "Will your lawn recover from all those stiletto heels?"

"A whole generation of women crippled," Belle said grandly. "What's a patch of grass compared to that?"

He raised his glass. "To next year's party."

She gave him the sweet smile that came rarely and that he cherished. "You be sure to be here, won't you, Slade? I count on it."

"I will."

His affairs never lasted more than six months; so by then, he'd no longer be seeing Clea. Game over.

Oddly, he felt a sharp pang of regret.

The next morning Slade was walking along Pier 39 past the colorful moored fishing boats. It was October, sunniest month in the city, and tourists still thronged the boardwalk, along with buskers joking raucously with the crowds. The tall spire of the carousel beckoned to him, the lilt of its music teasing his ears. Would Clea be there? Or would she have thought the better of it and remained in her hotel?

He had no idea where she was staying. Added to that, she was going back to Europe tomorrow. If she was determined not to be found, Europe was a big place.

He walked the circumference of the fence surrounding the carousel, his eyes darting this way and that. No Clea. She'd changed her mind, he thought, angered that she should trifle with him. But underlying anger was a depth of disappointment that dismayed him.

Then movement caught his eye. A woman was waving to him. It was Clea, seated on the gold-painted sidesaddle of a high-necked horse, clasping the decorated pole as she went slowly up and down. He waved back, the tension in his shoulders relaxing.

She'd come. The rest was up to him.

The brim of her huge, flower-bedecked sun hat flopped up and down with the horse's movements. Her legs were bare, pale against her mount's dark flanks. Bare. Long. Slender.

As the carousel came to a stop, she slid to the floor. She was wearing a wildly flowered skirt that fell in soft folds around her thighs, a clinging top in a green so vivid it hurt his eyes and matching green flat-heeled sandals. The skirt should be banned, Slade thought. Or was he even capable of thought through a surge of lust unlike any he'd ever known?

Clea walked toward Slade, her heart jittering in her chest. He was so overpoweringly male, she thought. Tall, broad-shouldered, long-legged, with an aura of power that she was almost sure he was unaware of, and which in consequence was all the more effective. She came to a halt two feet away from him. *"Buon giorno."*

"Come sta?"

"Molto bene, grazie." She gave him a dazzling smile that

reduced his brain to mush. "This is a fun place, Slade, I'm glad you suggested it."

"Popsicles," he said firmly, and led her to the little booth decorated with big bunches of rainbow-hued balloons.

She chose grape, he raspberry. Sucking companionably, they wandered in and out of the boutiques and stands, Slade purposely keeping the conversation light. Belle was no fool, and had, in her way, only confirmed his own suspicions: Clea had been badly burned and it behooved him to take it slow.

Slow? When she went back to Europe tomorrow?

Slow. He made frequent trips to Europe.

They watched a very talented mime artist, and a somewhat less talented musician, tossing coins into their hats. Out of the blue Clea said, "Did you enjoy your dinner with Belle?"

"I did, yes. We go back a long way—she's known my parents for years."

"Ah yes, your estimable parents."

"I like my parents and I'm not about to apologize for it," Slade said, a matching edge to his voice.

"It's none of my business how you feel about them."

He reached over and wiped a drop of purple from her mouth with his fingertip. "Why don't you believe in marital harmony?"

As she bit her lip, it was as much as he could do to keep his hands at his sides. "I told you—I'm a realist. Oh look, what gorgeous earrings."

She dragged him over to a kiosk selling abalone earrings that shimmered turquoise and pink. Lifting one to her ear, she said, "What do you think?"

"They clash with your sweater. But you could wear anything, and you'd still look devastatingly beautiful." Anything, he thought. Or nothing.

She laughed. "Oh, you Americans—so direct. The earrings, Slade, the earrings."

"They match your eyes. Let me buy them for you."

"So I'll be indebted?"

"So I'll have the pleasure of knowing that perhaps, occasionally, you'll think of me."

"I promise that perhaps, occasionally, I will," she said, removing the gold hoops she was wearing and tucking them in her purse. Increasingly, she was finding it difficult not to like Slade. Didn't that make him all the more of a threat?

"Let me," Slade said, and with exquisite care inserted the silver hooks into her lobes. Her skin was as smooth as he'd imagined it. Deep within him, desire shuddered into life.

Her irises had darkened, as though a cloud had covered the sea. He stepped back, reaching for his wallet and paying for the earrings. "They look great on you."

She struggled to find her voice. "Thank you."

"My pleasure," he said formally.

Between them, unspoken, crackled the electric awareness of sexual attraction. Slade said abruptly, "You know I want you. You've probably known it from the first moment we met."

"Yes, of course I know—which doesn't mean we do anything about it…other than enjoy each other's company on a sunny morning in October." She fluttered her lashes at him in deliberate parody. "Are you enjoying my company?"

"Very much. Don't fish, Clea."

"Where better than on Fisherman's Wharf?" As he chuckled, she went on calmly, "We're talking about sex between two total strangers here. Possibility is so often more interesting than actuality, wouldn't you agree?"

"Not when one of the strangers is you."

"You have a pretty way with a compliment."

He said, fixing her with his gaze, "Possibility's on a par

with fantasy. Nothing wrong with fantasy—last night I had a few about you I'd be embarrassed to describe. But actuality is real. Real and risky. That's the catch, isn't it?"

She said through gritted teeth, "I don't sleep with someone I don't know."

"That's easily fixable. We can get to know each other."

"Slade, I've been told I'm beautiful, and I know I'm rich. Consequently I've learned to choose my partners carefully. I already told you that you scare me—you're the last man I'd have an affair with."

He shouldn't have been so direct. But he had a horrible sense of time running out, along with the even worse sense that nothing he was saying to her was making any real or lasting impression. Welcome to a new experience, Slade thought wryly. He'd never before had to work at getting a woman interested in him; fighting them off was his area of expertise.

"There's a bakery a couple of blocks from here that sells crusty sourdough bread," he said. "I always take some home with me."

He heard the tiny puff as she let out her breath. "Let's go," she said agreeably. "Do you like to cook?"

"I do. Sheer self-defense. I eat out a lot, and it's relaxing to stay home and cook for myself. My specialties are bouillabaisse and pumpkin pie. I'll make them for you sometime."

"Perhaps. Occasionally," she said, her eyes full of mockery.

"For sure. At least once."

"You don't like opposition."

"Neither, dear Clea, do you."

She laughed. "Who does? Tell me about sourdough bread—it doesn't sound very appetizing."

Impatient of small talk, suddenly desperate for details beyond the superficial, Slade said, "How old are you, Clea?"

"Old enough to enjoy flirtation without—how do you say

it?—strings attached." She stepped off the boardwalk onto the sidewalk at the end of the wharf. "As for—"

Shouting and swearing, a gang of teenagers surged around the nearest building. Three of them collided head-on with Slade. Automatically he threw his arms around Clea, pulling her close to his body for protection, his feet planted hard on the tarmac.

"Sorry!" one of the kids yelled. Another gave a loud whoop. None of them stopped.

Slade stood very still. Clea's body was crushed to his, her breasts jammed against his chest. One of his arms encircled her hips, the other her waist; for a heart-stopping moment he felt her yield to him.

Her floppy hat had been shoved to the back of her head. He bent his own head and found her lips in a kiss that he wanted to last forever.

And again she yielded to him, a surrender all the more potent for being unexpected. He brought one hand up, tangling it in her hair, so silky and sweet-scented, and deepened the kiss, his lips edging hers apart. Her fingers were digging into his nape; her tongue was laced with his, teasing him, tasting him, driving him out of his mind.

As animal hunger surged through him, he forgot he was on a city sidewalk; forgot all Belle's warnings and his own advice. Robbed of any vestige of caution, he muttered, "I feel as though I've been waiting for you my whole life...God, how I want you!"

His words sliced through the frantic pulsing of Clea's blood, and brought in their wake an ice-cold dash of reality. She stiffened, then pushed hard against Slade's chest. "Stop!" she gasped. "What are we thinking of?"

"We're not thinking at all, which is just the way it should be," he said thickly, lifting her chin with his fingers and bending to kiss her again.

"Slade, stop—you mustn't, I don't want you to."

His gaze bored into hers. "Yes, you do."

She sagged in his embrace, her forehead resting on his chest. He was right. She had wanted him, in the most basic of ways, her body betraying her into a response that, in retrospect, appalled her. "You took me by surprise, that's all," she said weakly.

Keeping one arm around her waist, he said, "We're going into a restaurant on the pier, we're having lunch together and we're talking this through. No perhaps, no opposition."

All the fight had gone out of her; she looked both frightened and defenseless. Slade hardened his heart and headed back along the pier to a restaurant that specialized in seafood. Because they were early for lunch, he was able to get a table in one corner, overlooking the bay. A table with a degree of privacy, he thought, and sat down across from her.

She picked up the menu; to his consternation, he saw how she had to rest it on the table to disguise the trembling of her hands. But by the time she looked up, she had herself under control again. Unsmiling, she said, "I'll have the sole."

Quickly he ordered their food, along with a bottle of Chardonnay from a Napa Valley vineyard. The service was fast; within minutes he was raising his glass of chilled pale golden wine. "To international relations," he said with a crooked smile.

Her mouth set, she said, "To international boundaries," and took a big gulp of wine. Putting her glass down, she said, "Slade, let's get this out of the way, then maybe we can go back to enjoying each other's company. What happened out there on the sidewalk—it frightened me. I don't want a repeat, nor do I want to discuss the reasons you frighten me. And, of course, it simply confirmed what I've already told you—I'm not available. No sex. No affair. Is that understood?"

Banking his anger, Slade said curtly, "Of course it's not understood—how could it be when I have no idea why I frighten you? It's certainly not my intent to do so."

"I didn't say it was." She took another reckless gulp of wine. "We're strangers—and strangers we'll remain. That's all I'm saying."

"I want far more than that."

"We don't always get what we want. You're old enough to know that."

"You kissed me back, Clea. And I'm going to get what I want."

Heat flushed her cheeks. "No, you're not." Quickly she reached for her purse. It was time to produce her usual line of defense with a man who wouldn't take no for an answer. Hadn't she known when she'd left the hotel this morning that she'd need it with Slade Carruthers?

Taking out an envelope, she plunked it on the table. "You should take a look at this."

"Are you about to ruin my appetite?" he said.

"Just look at it, Slade."

The envelope was full of clippings from various tabloids and newspapers the width of Europe. Clea was pictured in every article, hair up, hair down, in evening gowns and jewels, in skimpy bikinis, in jeans and boots. Accompanied by, Slade saw, a succession of men. Aristocrats, artists, businessmen: none of them looking at all unhappy to be escorting the rich, the elegant, the charming Clea Chardin.

"What are you trying to tell me?" he said carefully.

"What does it look like?"

"Like you date a lot of different men."

"Date?" she repeated, lifting one brow.

"Are you trying to tell me you've slept with all of them?"

"Not all of them, no," she said. It was the truth, but not the entire truth. She should have said, "With none of them." But a reputation for flitting from man to man was, at times, extremely useful; right now she needed every weapon she could lay her hands on.

The waiter put their plates in front of them, said, "Enjoy," and left them alone again.

Clea said, as if there'd been no interruption, "If you want to take me to bed, you should know what you're getting into. I date lots of men and that's the way I like it."

Her hair shimmered in the light. Slade flicked the clippings with his finger. "So I'd be just one more guy to add to the list."

"You don't have to keep on seeing me if you don't like the way I operate," she said mildly.

He didn't like it. At all. "Are you saying if we had an affair, you wouldn't be faithful to me for its duration?"

"That's the general idea," she said, wondering why she should feel so ashamed of her duplicity when she was achieving her aim: to send Slade Carruthers in the opposite direction as quickly as she could.

Slade looked down at his *cioppino*. He wasn't the slightest bit hungry. Picking up his spoon, he said, "I happen to have a few standards. I'm not into long-term commitment or marriage, but when I have a relationship with a woman I expect fidelity, and I promise the same."

She shrugged. "Then let's enjoy our lunch and say goodbye."

He said with dangerous softness, "Perhaps I could change your mind. On the subject of standards."

"You're not going to get the chance."

"I make frequent trips to Europe. If we exchange e-mail addresses, we can keep in touch and arrange to meet some time."

She was attacking her sole as though she couldn't wait to

be rid of him. "No. Which, as I'm sure you know, is spelled identically in English and Italian."

He'd never begged a woman for anything in his life. He wasn't going to start with Clea Chardin. "Commitment is what you're really avoiding. Why?"

Clea put down her knife and fork and looked right at him, her remarkable eyes brilliant with sincerity. "I don't want to hurt you, Slade. And hurt you I would, were you to pursue me, because—as you just pointed out—our standards are different. So I'm ending this now, before it begins."

He said sharply, "I don't let women close enough to hurt me."

Her temper flared. "Why am I not surprised?"

"You must have hurt some of those other men."

"They knew the score and were willing to go along with me."

Cut your losses, Slade thought. Get out with some dignity. What's the alternative? Grovel?

Not your style.

Biting off his words, anger rising like bile in his throat, Slade said, "So you're going to play it safe. Ignore that kiss as if it never happened."

With a huge effort Clea kept her eyes trained on his. "That's right."

"Then there's nothing more to say." Picking up his spoon, he choked down a mouthful of the rich tomato broth.

She was eating her fish as fast as she could. She hadn't lost her appetite, Slade thought sourly. Why should she? He didn't matter a whit to her.

Rationally he should be admiring her for turning her back so decisively on all his money. Unfortunately he felt about as rational as a shipwrecked sailor brought face-to-face with Miss America.

Clea drained her wine. "You're sulking."

He put his spoon down with exaggerated care. "If you

don't know the difference between sulking and genuine passion, you're worse off than I suspected."

She paled. Surely he hadn't guessed that she'd never known genuine passion? Reaching in her purse, she extracted a bill, tossed it on the table and said coldly, "That's to pay for my lunch. Goodbye, Slade."

Pushing back her chair, she walked away from him, her hips swaying in her flowered skirt. With an effort that made him break out into a cold sweat, Slade stayed where he was, his fingernails digging into the chair. Be damned if he'd chase after her.

He picked up his glass, tossed back the contents and addressed his seafood stew. He would never in his life order *cioppino* again.

He'd never go to bed with Clea Chardin, either: if it came to a battle of wills, he was going to be the one in control. Not her. So he'd better forget the highly erotic fantasies that had disturbed his sleep all night.

The empty chair across from him was no fantasy, nor was the twenty-dollar bill lying beside Clea's plate. The money felt like the final insult.

He'd give it to the first panhandler he met.

Through the plate glass window, Slade watched the waters of the bay sparkle in the sunshine. He felt as though he'd been presented with a jewel of outstanding brilliance. But before he could touch it, it had been snatched from his reach.

CHAPTER THREE

AT THREE o'clock that afternoon in his hotel room, Slade was on the telephone punching in Sarah Hutchinson's extension. Sarah was Belle's cook, whom Slade had known for years, and whose chocolate truffles he liked almost as much as he liked her. When she answered, he said, "Sarah, it's Slade Carruthers."

"Mr. Slade, what a nice surprise…how are you?"

They chatted for a few minutes about the garden party, then Slade said easily, "I've mislaid my appointment book—Mrs. Hayward's having dinner with Clea Chardin tonight, isn't she?" He waited for her reply, his heart thumping so loudly he was afraid she'd hear it over the phone.

"That's right. Seven o'clock."

"Just the two of them?"

"Private, that's what Mrs. Hayward said."

"Great—I'll call Belle in the morning, then. No need to mention this, Sarah, she'll think I'm having a memory lapse. How are your grandchildren?"

He patiently listened to their many virtues, then hung up. All he had to do now was decide on a course of action. Gate-crash Belle's place? Or find a bar, get royally drunk and cut his losses?

Slade started prowling up and down the room, as restless as a caged tiger. Why had he phoned Sarah Hutchinson? Why couldn't he—for once in his life—accept that a woman didn't want to go to bed with him?

The answer was simple: because he wanted Clea as he'd never wanted a woman before.

Or was it that simple? Clea had been so ardent in his arms, then so frightened by her own response. Neither reaction had been fake, he'd swear to it. By touching her physically, he'd touched her emotions in a way that had terrified her.

So she'd very cleverly produced the clippings, refused any prospect of fidelity and taken her leave. She'd played him, he thought. And he'd fallen for it.

It wasn't going to happen again. Be damned if he was going to sit back and let Clea Chardin vanish from his life. He wanted her and he was going to have her. On his terms.

All of which meant he'd better have a plan of action in mind before nine-thirty tonight.

At nine-thirty, however, when Slade pressed the heavy brass bell on the Hayward front door, he felt devoid of anything that could be called a plan. He'd have to wing it. But this time he'd be the one in control.

Carter, the butler, let him in and left him in the formal parlor, where family photographs in sterling silver frames covered every available surface. The furniture represented, in Slade's opinion, the very worst of Victorian excess. Over the elaborate wrought-iron fireplace, a stuffed stag's head gazed down its aristocratic nose at him.

There was a painting by the fireplace, a small dark oil. Curious, he wandered over to look at it. A man in chains, head bowed in utter defeat, was being led by three armored guards into the black maw of a cave. Slade knew, instantly, that the prisoner would never emerge into daylight again.

It was his own lasting nightmare, he thought, his palms damp, his fingers curled into fists: the nightmare that had tormented him ever since he was eleven. His limbs heavy as lead, he turned away from the painting, staring instead at an innocuous watercolor of a sunny meadow.

"Slade," Belle exclaimed, "is anything wrong? Your parents? You look terrible!"

He fought to banish the nightmare where it belonged, deep down in his psyche. While Belle knew the reason behind it, she had no idea of its extent, and he wasn't about to enlighten her. "I didn't mean to frighten you," he said with real compunction. "My parents are fine. I'm here because I need to see Clea."

Her smile vanishing as if it had been wiped from her face, Belle said, "How did you know she's here?"

"I got it out of Sarah and you're not to blame her. Clea and I had lunch today, Belle. But we left some loose ends about our next meeting. I head off to Japan tomorrow and she's going back to Europe, so I figured it was simplest if I turned up on your doorstep and gave her a lift back to her hotel."

Tonight Belle was wearing a rust-brown linen dress that did little for her complexion. Rubies gleamed in her earlobes. She looked like a highly suspicious rooster, Slade thought with a quiver of amusement, and said truthfully, "I don't want Clea to disappear from my life—there's something about her that really turns my crank."

Belle said flatly, "If she doesn't want to drive to the hotel with you, I'm not pushing her."

He hesitated. "She dates a lot of men, so she told me. But when I kissed her, she acted like a scared rabbit. Do you have any idea why?"

"If I did, do you think I'd tell you?"

"I'm not out to hurt her, Belle."

"Then maybe you'd better head right out the front door."

He said tightly, "You've known me since I was knee-high to a grasshopper. Have you ever seen me chase after a woman before?"

"I've seen you treat women as though they're ornaments sitting on a shelf—decorative enough, but not really worth your full attention."

He winced. "Clea gets my full attention just by being in the same room. So she's different from the rest."

"That's what they all say."

"You're an old friend, and I'm asking you to trust me," Slade said, any amusement long gone. "Clea's knocked me right off balance. No other woman's ever come close to doing that. All I want is the chance to drive her back to her hotel—I'm not going to jump on her the minute she gets in the car!"

"And if she says no?"

"She won't."

Belle snapped, "If you hurt that gal, I'll—I won't invite you to next year's garden party."

It was a dire threat. "Belle, I'll go out on a limb here. I want Clea, no question of that, but I have this gut feeling she's not really running away from me, she's running from herself. And I don't give a damn if that sounds presumptuous."

For a long moment Belle simply stared at him. Then she said, "I'll ask her if she wants a drive back to her hotel."

The massive oak door swung shut behind her. The stag's upper lip sneered down at him. Turning his back on the dark little oil painting, Slade jammed his hands in his pockets and stared down at the priceless, rose-embroidered carpet. He felt like his life were hanging in the balance.

How melodramatic was that? Sex was all he wanted. Nothing more. Nothing less.

Five minutes later—he timed it on his watch—the door was pushed open. Clea marched through, followed by Belle in her rust-brown dress. Clea's dress was ice-pale turquoise, calf-length, fashioned out of soft jersey; her hair had been tamed into a coil on the back of her head. With a physical jolt, Slade saw she was still wearing the earrings he'd given her earlier in the day.

Clea said crisply, "I said goodbye to you this morning."

"It wasn't goodbye. More like *au revoir.*"

"My hotel is exactly four blocks from here—I can walk."

"If you won't go with me, you're going in a cab."

Clea glared at him, then transferred that glare to Belle. "This man is your friend?"

Belle said calmly, "If he wasn't, he wouldn't have made it past the front door."

Clea's breath hissed between her teeth. When had she ever felt as angry as she did now? Angry, afraid, cornered and—treacherously, underneath it all—ridiculously happy to see Slade. Happy? When the man threatened to knock down the whole house of cards that was her life? "All right, Slade, you can drive me to my hotel," she said. "But only because I don't want to waste my time arguing with you."

"Fine," he said, unable to subdue his grin.

She said furiously, "Your smile should be banned—lethal to any female over the age of twelve."

Belle smothered a snort of laughter. "You've got to admit he's cute, Clea."

"Cute?" Slade said, wincing.

"Cute like a high voltage wire is cute," Clea snapped.

"Certainly plenty of voltage between the two of you," Belle remarked, leading the way to the front door, where she took a lacy shawl from the cupboard and passed it to Slade. Dry-mouthed, he draped it over Clea's shoulders.

Belle leaned forward to kiss Clea on the cheek. "We'll talk next week."

"Monday or Tuesday." Clea's voice softened. "Thank you, Belle."

"Slade's a good man," Belle added.

Clea's smile was ironic. "Maybe I prefer bad men."

Slade said in a voice like steel, "Good, bad or indifferent, I really dislike being discussed as though I don't exist."

Belle said lightly, "Indifferent wouldn't apply to either one of you. Good night."

Slade and Clea stepped out into the cool darkness, which was still scented with roses, and the door closed behind them. He reached over and plucked a pale yellow bloom; she stood as still as one of the marble statues flanking the driveway as he tucked it into her hair. "I think that'll stay," he said, tugging on the stem.

Her eyes were like dark pools. "You're a hopeless romantic."

"You're still wearing the abalone earrings," he retorted. "Doesn't that make you one as well?"

"They go with my dress."

"We're arguing again."

"How unromantic," she said. As he helped her into his rented car, a speedy silver Porsche, the slit in her skirt bared her legs in their iridescent hose. Taking her time, she tucked her feet under the dash, straightened her skirt and smiled up at him. "Thank you," she said with perfect composure.

Slade took a deep breath, shut her door and marched around to the driver's seat. His next job was to convince her that he was going to become her lover. And by God, he was going to succeed.

"I'll buy you a drink at the hotel," he said, and turned onto the street.

By now, Clea had managed to gather her thoughts. It was time for her second line of defense, she decided. One she would have no scruples using with Slade. She called it, privately, The

Test, and it had rarely failed her. She was certain it would work with Slade Carruthers, a man used to wielding power and being in command. "A drink would be nice," she said.

"That was easy."

"I dislike being predictable."

"You don't have a worry in the world."

He'd made it past the first hurdle, Slade thought, and concentrated on his driving. After leaving the car with the hotel valet, he led her into the opulent lobby. Marble, mahogany, oriental carpeting and a profusion of tropical blooms declared without subtlety that no expense had been spared. He said, "I would have thought something less ostentatious would have been more to your liking."

"Belle made the reservations."

It was definitely Belle's kind of place. In the bar, a jazz singer was crooning, her hands wandering the keys of the grand piano. They made their way to a table near the dark red velvet curtains with their silken tassels. The ceiling was scrolled in gold, the walls layered in damask of the same deep red.

Waiting until the waiter had brought their drinks, Slade said, "The clippings you showed me this morning threw me, Clea, as no doubt you intended. Nor did I like your terms. But I gave up much too easily."

She took a delicate sip of her martini. "You're used to women chasing you."

"I have a lot of money—it's a powerful aphrodisiac."

She raised her brows. "Now who's the cynic?"

He leaned forward, speaking with all the force of his personality. "Clea, I want you in my bed...and I'm convinced that you want to be there, too. I travel a lot, we can meet anywhere you like."

Clea said evenly, hating herself for the lie, "I play the field, I have a good time and move on. That's what I told you this morning, and it hasn't changed. You can give me your phone number, if you like—and if I'm ever at a loose end, I'll call you."

So she was lumping him together with what she called, so amorphously, *the field.* Slade said, lifting one brow, "I dare you to make a date with me. More than that, I dare you to get to know me. In bed and out."

Her nostrils flared. "You're being very childish."

"Am I? If we stop taking risks, something in us dies."

"Risks can kill!"

"I assure you, I don't have homicide in mind." *Kill,* he thought. That's a strong word.

Her breasts rising and falling with her agitated breathing, Clea said, "Men don't stick around long enough for women to get to know them."

"Generalizations are the sign of a lazy mind."

"The first sign of trouble, you'll be gone faster than I can say *au revoir.*"

"You're being both sexist and cowardly," he said.

Her chin snapped up. "Who gave you the right to stand in judgment on me?"

"Deny it, then."

"I'm not a coward!"

Slade said softly, "Prove it to me. More important, prove it to yourself."

Toying with the olive in her glass, Clea said raggedly, "You're talking about us getting to know each other. Yet you never let any of your women close enough to hurt you."

He said grimly, "You may be the exception that proves the rule."

And how was she supposed to interpret that? "I like my life the way it is," she said. "Why should I change?"

"If you didn't want to change, we wouldn't be sitting here having this conversation."

He was wrong. Completely wrong. "Do you do this with every woman you meet?"

"I've never had to before."

"So why are you bothering now?"

"Clea, I don't want to play the field," he said forcibly. "Right now it's you I want. You, exclusively. Because deep down I don't really believe you are a coward."

"Just sexist," she said with a flare of defiance.

"Don't you get bored playing the field?"

She said nastily, "I've not, so far, been bored with you."

"Then I'll make another dare—date me until you do get bored." Slade pushed a piece of paper across the table to her. "My personal assistant's phone number in New York. His name's Bill and he always knows where I can be reached."

She stared down at the paper as if it might rear up and bite her. Her second line of defense, she thought wildly, what had happened to it? Hadn't Slade jumped in ahead of her, daring her to date him? Worse, to go to bed with him? "I'm not interested in your money," she blurted, trying to collect her wits. "I have plenty of my own."

"I never thought you were."

The Test, she thought. Now's the time. Do it, Clea. She glanced up, her accent pronounced, as it always was when she was upset. "Very well, Slade...I also can make dares."

"Go ahead."

"Meet me in the Genoese Bar in Monte Carlo, three weeks from now. In the evening, anytime after seven-thirty. Wednesday, Thursday or Friday."

"Name the day," he said.

"Ah," she said smoothly, "that's part of the dare. I'm not telling you which evening. Either I'm worth waiting for, or I'm not—which is it?"

"But you will turn up?"

Her eyes flashed fire. "I give my word."

"Then I'll wait for you."

"It stays open until 2:00 a.m., and the music is deafening," she said with a malicious smile. "You won't wait. No man would. Not when the world's full of beautiful women who are instantly available."

"You underrate yourself," he said softly. Reaching over with his finger, he traced the soft curve of her mouth until her lip trembled. "I'll wait."

Fear flickered along her nerves. He wouldn't wait. Not Slade Carruthers, who—she'd swear—had never had to wait for a woman in his life. Tossing her head, she said, "If you're unfamiliar with Monte Carlo, anyone can direct you to the Genoese—it's well known."

"Monte Carlo—where life's a gamble and the stakes are high."

"High stakes? For you, maybe—not for me." Which was another barefaced lie.

"I wouldn't be where I am today if I didn't know how to gamble, Clea...tomorrow I'll give Bill your name. You have only to mention it, and he'll make sure I get any messages from you."

She said, so quietly that the drifting jazz melody almost drowned her out, "I must be mad to have suggested a meeting between us. Even one you won't keep."

She looked exhausted. Slade drained his whisky. "Finish up," he said, "and I'll take you back to the lobby. Then I'll be on my way—my flight's early tomorrow."

Her face unreadable, she said, "So you're not putting the moves on me tonight?"

His jaw tightened. "I don't gamble when the deck's stacked against me—that's plain stupidity."

"At any table, you'd make a formidable opponent."

He pushed back his chair. "I'll take that as a compliment. Come on, you look wiped."

"Wiped? I don't know what that means, but it doesn't sound flattering."

He took her hand and brought her to her feet. Standing very close to her, his eyes caressing her features, he said huskily, "It means tired out. In need of a good night's sleep. When you and I share a bed, sleep won't be the priority."

"*When* we share a bed?" she said, looking full at him. "I've never liked being taken for granted."

His eyes were a compelling midnight-blue, depthless and inscrutable. Charismatic eyes, which pulled her to him as though she had no mind of her own. She felt herself sway toward him, the ache of desire blossoming deep in her belly and making nonsense of all her defenses. Reaching up, she brushed his lips with hers as lightly as the touch of a butterfly's wing, then just as quickly stepped back.

Her heart was hammering in her breast. So much for keeping him at a distance, she thought, aghast. What was wrong with her?

For once Slade found himself bereft of speech. Going on impulse, he lifted her hand to his lips and kissed it with lingering pleasure, watching color flare in her cheeks. Then, calling on all his control, he looped one arm lightly around her shoulders and led her back to the lobby. The light from the crystal chandeliers seemed excessively bright. He said, "The Genoese. In three weeks. If you need anything in the meantime, call me."

"I won't call you," Clea said. Turning on her heel, she crossed the vast carpet to the elevators.

Nor did she.

CHAPTER FOUR

THE Genoese Bar on a cool damp evening in November should have been a welcome destination. Slade had walked from his hotel, with its magnificent view of the Port of Monaco and the choppy Mediterranean, past the obsessively groomed gardens of the casino to a curving side street near the water where a discreetly lit sign announced the Genoese. It was exactly seven-thirty.

The bar, he saw with a sinking heart, was underground, down a flight of narrow, winding stairs.

His nightmare, once again.

He was thirty-five years old now. Not eleven. He should be able to walk down a flight of stairs and spend six hours in a windowless room without hyperventilating.

Yeah, right.

Clea, he was almost sure, wouldn't arrive until Friday. If this was some sort of test, why would she meet him any sooner? Unless she thought he wouldn't bother turning up until Friday, and in consequence came tonight.

It was useless trying to second-guess her. Taking a deep breath of the salt-laden air, Slade walked slowly down the stairs and pushed open the heavy, black-painted door.

The noise hit him like a blow. Rap, played as loud as

the sound equipment could handle it. He'd never been a fan of rap.

He let the door shut behind him, his heart thudding in his chest. The room was vast, tables all around its circumference, a small dance floor in the center under flickering strobes that instantly disoriented him. A big room, he thought crazily. Not cupboard-size, like the one he'd never been able to forget.

Come on, buddy, you can do this.

Leaning against the wall, he let his gaze travel from face to face, wishing with all his heart that Clea's would be among them. It was a young crowd, in expensive leather and designer jeans, the women's silky hair gleaming like shampoo ads, the energy level frenetic.

Clea was nowhere to be seen.

Slade claimed an empty table near the door, where he could see anyone who entered or left. Shucking off his trench coat, he sat down and ordered a bottle of Merlot and a dish of nuts. Automatically he located the Exit signs, wishing the ceiling didn't feel so low, wishing they'd turn off the strobe lights. Wishing that he'd never met Clea Chardin.

His hormones were ruling his life, he thought savagely. How he resented the hold she had on him, with her slender body and exquisite face! But no matter how fiercely he'd fought the strength of that hold, he couldn't dislodge it. God knows he'd tried hard enough the last three weeks.

She, in all fairness, had no idea how arduous a test she'd devised for him by making him wait in an underground bar.

As the array of bottles at the mirrored bar splintered and flashed in the strobes, dancers writhed to the primitive, undoubtedly hostile music. The little underground room had been quiet. Dead quiet. Frighteningly, maddeningly quiet.

All these years later, Slade still did his best never to think about the kidnapping that had so altered his life. At age eleven, he'd been snatched from the sidewalk near his school, drugged and kept in darkness in a small room below the ground, for a total of fifteen days and fourteen nights.

The kidnappers, he'd learned later, had been demanding ransom. The FBI, working with admirable flair and efficiency, had tracked down the hiding place, taken the kidnappers into custody and rescued him. Apart from the drugs, aimed at keeping him quiet and administered from a syringe by a masked man who never spoke to him, he was unharmed.

He'd never forgotten his mother's silent tears when she'd been brought face-to-face with him at the police station, or the deeply carved lines in his father's face.

The lasting aftereffect had been a phobia for dark, underground spaces. Right now, to his mortification, his palms were damp, his throat tight and his heart bouncing around in his chest. Just like when he was eleven.

A woman in a black leather jerkin and miniskirt sidled up to his table. Pouting her red lips, she said over the thud of the bass, "Want to dance?"

So she'd picked him out as an American. "No, thanks," he said.

She leaned forward, presenting him with an impressive cleavage. "You didn't come here to be alone."

"I'm waiting for someone," he said in a clipped voice. "I'd prefer to do that alone. Sorry."

Smoothing the leather over her hips, she shrugged. "Change your mind, I'm over by the bar."

By 2:00 a.m., when the bouncer closed the bar, Slade had been propositioned six times, felt permanently deafened and was heartily tired of Merlot and peanuts. His claustrophobia had not noticeably abated.

He climbed the stairs and emerged onto the sidewalk. Thrusting his hands in his pockets, he strode east along the waterfront, where buildings crowded down the hillside to a pale curve of sand. Useless to think of sleeping until he'd walked off those agonizingly long hours.

He should leave Monaco. Forget this whole ridiculous venture. Was any woman worth two more evenings in the Genoese Bar? After all, what did he really know about Clea? Sure, she'd given her word. But was it worth anything? What if she didn't show up? What if she'd spent the evening in Milan with one of the many men she'd mentioned, laughing to herself at the thought of Slade sitting in a crowded bar on the Riviera in November?

She was making a fool of him. He hated that as much as he hated being confronted by the demons of his past.

And how could he lust after a woman whose sexual standards, to put it mildly, were by no means exacting? Promiscuous, he thought heavily, and knew it was a word he'd been repressing for the last three weeks.

She looked so angelic, yet she'd slept with men the length and breadth of Europe. The clippings and her own admission proved it.

He should fly back to New York in the morning and forget the redhead with the vivid eyes, dancing intelligence and lax morals. Hadn't she done her best from the beginning to discourage him? The Genoese Bar was the final touch. After three nights of his life wasted in a futile vigil, he wouldn't be in any hurry to search her out.

Which meant, of course, that she'd won.

At three-thirty Slade's head hit the pillow; at five-forty-two he was jerked awake from a nightmare of a syringe impaling him to a dirty mattress; and at eight that evening, he was again descending the stairs of the Genoese Bar. Clea didn't show up that night, either. Nor had she appeared by one-thirty the following night.

By Friday Slade's vigil in the bar had become as much a test of his courage and endurance as anything to do with Clea. He was intent on proving to himself that he could stick it out for one more night; that the low ceiling and dark corners weren't able to drive him up the stairs in defeat.

That night he was drinking Cabernet Sauvignon. He had a headache, he was sleep-deprived, he was in a foul mood. He sure didn't feel the slightest bit romantic.

At one-forty, Clea walked down the stairs into the bar.

Slade eased well back into the shadows as she stood on the stairs looking around, her red hair in its usual wild swirl. Her jade-green evening suit boasted a silk camisole that clung to her breasts. He fought down a jolt of lust that infuriated him.

Be damned if he was going to fall at her feet in abject gratitude because she'd finally shown up.

From his stance against the wall he watched her search the room from end to end, checking out the men at the bar, the dancers, the seated, noisy crowd. On her face settled a look compounded of satisfaction, as though she'd proved her point, along with a sharp, and very real, regret.

The regret interested him rather more than he cared for.

Clea took the last of the stairs into the bar and wormed her way across the dance floor, her eyes darting this way and that. She couldn't see Slade anywhere. So he'd failed The Test. Given up. If indeed, he'd ever been here at all.

I'll wait, he'd said. But he'd lied.

A cold lump had settled in her chest. Hadn't she believed him when he'd said he'd wait for her? So, once again, her low opinion of the male of the species had been confirmed, rather more painfully than usual. She straightened her shoulders and tried to relax the tension in her jaw; when she reached the bar she ordered a glass of white wine and gave the room one more sweep.

Two men and a woman were edging toward her, old friends from Cannes; she hugged each of them, tossed back her wine and, with a defiant lift of her chin, walked out onto the dance floor with the taller of the two men.

Slade, watching, saw how the man's arm encompassed her waist, how his fingers were splayed over her hip. His anger rose another notch. *Playing the field...*her specialty.

He put his glass down on the table and strode across the room. Tapping the man on the shoulder, he said loudly, over the pounding rhythms of drums and bass guitars, "She's mine. Get lost."

Clea gave a shocked gasp. "Slade!"

"Did you think I wouldn't be here?" he said with disdain. "Tell your friend to vamoose. If he values living."

"I'll talk to you later, Stefan," she said, her heartbeat competing with the drums. "It's okay, I know Slade."

"Oh, no, you don't," Slade said, standing so close to her he could see a tiny fleck of mascara on her lower eyelid. "If you knew me, we wouldn't have had to indulge in this stupid charade."

"You agreed to it."

"You know what I want to do right now? Throw you over my shoulder, haul you out of this god-awful bar and carry you to the nearest bed."

He looked entirely capable of doing so. She said faintly, "Bouncers don't like it when you do things like that."

"It'd make me feel a whole lot better."

"I suggest we have a drink, instead."

"Scared of me, Clea?"

"Of a six foot two, one hundred ninety pound, extremely angry male? Why would I be scared?"

"I like you," he said.

She blinked. "Five seconds ago you looked as though you wanted to throttle me."

"Five minutes ago you looked extremely disappointed when you thought I wasn't here."

"You exaggerate!"

"I don't think so. Let's dance, Clea."

"Dance? With you? No way."

"I've sat in this bar for three long nights," he grated. "I've been propositioned, I've drunk inferior wine and I've been bored out of my skull. The least you can do is dance with me."

He'd waited for her. He'd passed The Test. Now what was she supposed to do? "You asked for it," she said recklessly.

The floor was crowded and the music raucous. Her eyes blazing with an emotion Slade couldn't possibly have named, Clea raised her arms above her head and threw back her mane of hair as movement rippled down her body. Lust stabbed his loins, hot and imperative. Holding her gaze with his, he matched her, move for move, and deliberately refrained from laying as much as a finger on her.

He didn't need to. Pagan as an ancient goddess, hips swaying, nipples thrusting against the thin silk of her camisole, Clea danced. Danced for him alone. Danced as though they were alone. Danced until he thought he might die of unfulfilled desire.

The music ended abruptly. Into the ringing silence, the barkeeper said, "Closing time, ladies and gentlemen."

Clea bit her lip, her breasts heaving. "You did it again," she whispered. "Made me forget who I am."

Slade dropped his hands to her shoulders and kissed her full on the mouth. "Good," he said. Dancing with her had also, for the space of four or five minutes, blanked out the fact that he was underground in a dark room.

Quite a woman, this Clea Chardin.

"Let's get out of here," she said. "I need some fresh air."

So did he. Slade took her firmly by the hand and led the way up the narrow stairs.

Outside, under a star-spattered sky, Clea took a long, steadying breath, trying to forget how wantonly she'd swayed and writhed on the dance floor. "I'm hungry," she said in faint surprise. "I forgot to eat dinner."

He'd been gulping air obsessively, hoping his enormous relief at being in the open air wouldn't show. But Clea said, puzzled, "What's the matter? Are you all right?"

He spoke the literal truth. "I spent far too long cooped up in that bar—not sure I've got any eardrums left." Tucking her hand in the crook of his elbow, he added, "Food—that'll help."

He set off at a killing pace along the brick sidewalk, which was lit by lamps atop curving iron posts. Distantly he could hear the soft shush of waves against the breakwater. A breeze rustled the tall cypresses, while palm fronds rattled and chattered edgily. Clea said breathlessly, "I said I was hungry, not starving. You could slow down."

"Sorry," he said, and moderated his pace. "How do you know Stefan?"

"I met him in Nice last year. He designs yachts for the very, very rich."

"Have you slept with him?"

"No."

"Do you own a yacht?"

She grinned. "I get seasick on a sheltered lagoon."

"But if you didn't, you could afford one of Stefan's yachts."

"My grandfather left me the bulk of his fortune. Payton Steel, have you heard of it?"

"Very, very rich," Slade said, tucking the name away in his mind. So her parents must be dead: a loss contributing to what he was beginning to suspect was a deep, underlying loneliness. Or was he way out to lunch? "Do you have any brothers or sisters?"

"No."

"So what do you do with your life, Clea? Other than play the field?"

"I have no need to do anything else."

He said, from a deep well of conviction that took him by surprise, "Don't give me that—you're far too intelligent to spend your life flitting from party to party."

They'd reached the floodlit façade of the casino, with its turrets and crenellations, its huge windows. The formal gardens were lit by tall lanterns; a fountain splashed in the light, the water falling like elegant bracelets of gold. Clea said tightly, "Where are we going to eat?"

"My hotel's five minutes from here. One of the restaurants is open all night."

"I'm not going to bed with you, Slade!"

"Just don't pretend you don't want to."

"It's a little late for that," she said irritably.

"You're damn right. Anyway, I didn't say room service, I said restaurant. Then I'll walk you straight back to your hotel."

"I leave here first thing in the morning."

"Covering all the angles, aren't you?" he said.

"I'm protecting myself—why wouldn't I?"

"You sure don't act like someone who goes from man to man, footloose and fancy-free."

"You're not like the rest!"

He stopped under one of the graceful street lamps, in front of a pink stucco house with charming iron-railed balconies and tall white shutters. "How am I different?"

"Too intense, too forceful, too—" she hesitated "—disturbing."

"Well, that's a start."

A red Ferrari roared past, drowning any reply she might have made. Tugging at his arm, she headed up the hill as if all the demons who'd assaulted him in the bar were after her. She had her own demons, he was convinced of it. He could have found out what they were with very little effort; one good private detective could unearth whatever he needed to know within twenty-four hours. But he wanted Clea to tell him what haunted her, why she was so adamant against any kind of commitment.

Usually he had very little interest in the motives of the women he dated.

His hotel had an exquisite stucco courtyard filled with exotic trees and flowering shrubs, leading into a neoclassical lobby with a marble floor on which Clea's heels tapped decisively. The restaurant overlooked the cliffs with their fur of vegetation, and the dark silky water. Hadn't Clea once compared his eyes to that enigmatic midnight-blue?

As they sat down, Slade said easily, "I've never really liked Monaco—tiers of buildings all the way down the slopes to the water's edge. No room to breathe."

"Where do you go to breathe, Slade?"

Her eyes were flickering down the menu. He let his gaze wander her features, rediscovering them with secret hunger: winged brows, delectably kissable lips, determined chin.

Sensing his scrutiny, Clea looked up; the expression in his eyes brought a wash of color to her cheeks. "You just have to look at me," she said in a strangled voice.

"And...?"

"Never you mind. Bad for your ego."

He threw back his head and laughed. "You make me feel as though I own the entire principality of Monaco."

"Casino and all?"

"The gamble paid off, didn't it? Here we are, having a meal together."

She bit her lip. "I didn't expect to see you in the bar tonight."

"Are you sure that's true?"

"Most men wouldn't have stayed." She gave him an unhappy smile. "I call it The Test. I figured you'd fail it."

He grinned. "That's what I figured you'd figure."

Feeling hunted, she burst out, "Why did you stay? The noise, the crowds, hours and hours with nothing to do but wait…you must have hated it."

"You and I are meant to be together. In bed. That's why I stayed."

Clea's knuckles on the leather-bound menu tightened with strain. "You say that as though it's an immutable truth."

"It is."

The clippings had always been her first line of defense, The Test her second. She had only one more weapon: this one had to work. "I told you I date lots of different men, Slade. Take it or leave it—because I won't change for you or for anyone else."

"So the battle lines are drawn," he said softly.

"If sailors have a girl in every port, I have a man in every major city in Europe." She slammed the menu shut. "I'll have a Salade Niçoise with tapenade."

The waiter materialized beside their table. "Madame? M'sieur?"

After Clea gave her order, Slade requested a bottle of wine by the number on the list, and for himself *daube,* wild boar simmered in red wine with herbs and garlic. Red meat, that's what he needed.

As though they hadn't been interrupted, he said, ticking off his fingers, "First, I'm not dating anyone else and I have no plans to do so—you're the one I want. Second, I've shown you tonight that I'm capable of hanging in. Of passing your ridiculous test." He allowed a little of his anger to surface. "When and where will our next date be? And this time it'll be a specific time on a specific day."

The waiter appeared with the bottle of wine Slade had ordered, a Burgundy from a château in the north of Burgogne. Clea glanced casually at the label. The color drained from her face; her gasp of dismay was audible. Puzzled, Slade said, "I should have consulted you—you don't like Burgundy? It's an excellent wine, I've had it before."

"No," she muttered, "it's fine. I—someone I know owns the vineyard, that's all."

She looked as though she could very easily burst into tears. The man who'd hurt her, was he the vintner? Another mystery, Slade thought, and went through the ritual of sniffing the cork and tasting the wine.

As warm, crusty baguettes were put on their table, Slade lifted his glass. "To the places where we can breathe."

She picked up her glass as if she were about to drink poison. "To freedom," she said, and for a moment looked as though her heart could break. Then she tossed back half the glass. Promptly the waiter refilled it.

Slade said easily, "My parents for as long as I can remember have owned a house on the coast of Maine. A rambling old place with a wide veranda facing the sea, its own private beach and acres of woodland. I've always loved it—the wind blows all the way from Portugal, and the air's so pure you can fill your lungs with salt and fog."

"You're very lucky," Clea said stiffly and took another gulp of wine.

Slade was drinking almost nothing. He wanted all his wits about him; he had no idea what was going on. Every time he saw her, wasn't he being drawn deeper and deeper into the mystery that was Clea?

"I was exceptionally lucky to have done a lot of my growing up in Maine," he said, telling her some of his escapades as a boy along the rocky shoreline, hoping she'd relax. The level of wine in the bottle sank steadily.

Their meals arrived. Clea looked down at her salad and the toast spread with olives, capers and anchovies; her appetite had vanished. As she picked up her fork, Slade said, "I'm unavailable for the next two weeks. A tour of some factories in Russia and Siberia that's taken the better part of six months to organize. But we could meet after that."

She swallowed some more wine. "On my terms," she said.

"For now," Slade said softly.

Implacable, she thought. Immovable. Irresistible. She should run away as far and as fast as she could. She said rapidly, gazing at her leafy green salad, "I'll be in Denmark the week after that. We can meet at Tivoli in Copenhagen—their annual Christmas market will be open."

"What are you doing in Denmark?"

That was her secret, one she had no intention of sharing with him. "Freedom means not having to account to anyone for the way you spend you time."

"Or does it mean—as the song says—that you've nothing left to lose?"

"You can't lose what you've never had. Pour me some more wine, Slade."

As he complied, he said evenly, "You said your grandfather left you his money—when did your parents die?"

An anchovy dropped from her fork. "If you meet me in Tivoli, do you plan to take me to bed?"

"Yeah," he said, "that's the plan."

"What if I say no?"

"I'll just have to change your mind, won't I?"

She said with the dignity of someone who'd drunk a half

a bottle of full-bodied Burgundy in a very short time, "Lust is overrated. That's all that's between us…the oldest instinct in the book. Once you got sex out of the way, you'd forget all about me. So what's in this for me?"

"How about the best sex you've ever had in your life?"

With an inner quiver of laughter that edged on hysteria, Clea knew she'd have almost nothing to compare it with. Another secret she wasn't going to share. She said haughtily, "You're much too sure of yourself."

Slade wasn't as sure of himself as he might have sounded: his gut was in a turmoil and the wild boar could have been hamburger. She was like quicksilver, he thought. Impossible to pin down. As for analyzing her in any rational way, forget it.

The waiter appeared and topped up Clea's glass. "Would m'sieur like to order a second bottle?"

Clea said, "M'sieur would not. Madame has drunk more than enough."

Not sure if he wanted to laugh or hit her on the head with the nearly empty wine bottle, Slade said tightly, "After we have sex in Copenhagen—because we're not talking about making love here—we go our separate ways…is that how you see it?"

"Once you have sex," she parried, "you lose interest. Right?"

She was, unfortunately, rather too close to the truth. "Who's the man who owns the vineyard, Clea? And what did he do to you?"

She put her glass down so fast that wine slopped over the rim onto the back of her hand. Red as blood, Slade thought, and saw that she was very lightly trembling. She said, "You could easily find out—we both know that."

"I could. But I'm not going to. You have a right to your privacy. Plus I'd much rather you told me yourself."

"As if that's going to happen."

"Bitterness docsn't become you."

"Not everyone has led your charmed life, Slade."

He thought of that dark, cold room, quiet as death. "I guess I've been luckier than most," he said noncommittally.

Her head jerked up. "I hit a nerve, didn't I?" she said evenly. "I'm sorry."

Taking his napkin, he wiped the wine from her hand, then covered her fingers with his own. The words that came out of him were totally unplanned. "Why do I get the impression you're the loneliest woman I've ever met?"

"Stop," Clea whispered, her hand curling into his in a way that touched him to the heart. "Or you'll have me crying like a baby."

"I have two shoulders and they're available anytime you want to cry on them," he said, and knew this simple offer felt unlike anything he'd ever said before. He'd never wanted women crying on his shoulder. Or on any other part of his anatomy.

She mumbled, "You make it sound so easy."

"Clea, I wish you'd tell me what's wrong."

"I can't. I never do." She tugged her hand free, and dabbed at the tears that were hanging on her lashes.

At least she wasn't denying that something was wrong. But what had the man who owned the vineyard done to her? And why did he, Slade, care?

He said, "Tivoli. Three weeks. When and where?"

"The first Saturday in December at five in the afternoon. There's only one patron saint for the season. Find him and you'll find me."

"I'll do that," Slade said. But by then, he thought, all her defenses would be firmly in place in again.

"Maybe you'll meet someone else in the meantime."

"Maybe the casino will go broke."

"You're right," she snorted, "I'm never bored with you. I want a piece of chocolate torte."

"After anchovies? You'll have nightmares."

"I don't dream," she said lightly. "Do you? What's your worst nightmare?"

He wasn't going to tell her about the underground room. So how could he fault her silence on the subject of the vintner? "That my mother will lose her recipe for smoked salmon fishcakes with rhubarb chutney," he said promptly.

The conversation went from cooking to country inns, and from there to the winners of the Cannes Film Festival. Slade ordered a cab to take her to her hotel in Fontvieille. As they crossed the courtyard to wait for it, he noticed for the first time that there were two large birdcages against the far wall, each covered by a linen cloth. "They're probably songbirds," he said. "A barbarous practice to keep them in cages, I always think."

She couldn't agree more. "Why don't we set them free?"

"Great idea," Slade said with a grin.

Swiftly they walked over to the cages. But when Clea lifted the first cover, she saw that the bird in the cage was a parrot, its feathers a deep blue. The second cage held a lime-green parrot. Both were sleeping, heads tucked under their wings.

Slade said, "We can't set them free, Clea. It's November, they'd die."

"Yes," she whispered, "they'd die," and let the cloth drop to cover the cage. She felt unutterably sad.

His one desire to comfort her, Slade slid an arm around her shoulders. The contact, warm, unbearably intimate, brought Clea back to her senses; she pulled away, her face wiped clean of any emotion. "The cab'll be waiting," she said.

"Let it wait. What's up?"

"I'm tired, I drank too much wine and I want to be alone."

"I don't care how many men you date, you're alone too much. In a cage of your own devising."

"You have no idea what my life is like!"

"I've seen enough of you to make an educated guess."

White-faced with rage, desperate to get away from him, she seethed, "If you ever get tired of windmills, you can take up psychiatry." Then she whirled, hurrying alongside the ornamental pond with its filagreed fountain, and the bougainvillea tumbling down the stucco walls. At the gateway, as she came to a halt beside two imposing urns filled with pale canna lilies, Slade caught up with her. The taxi was waiting, its engine running.

He was in no mood for subtlety. Seizing her by the arm, he rasped, "You can't run away from me...you know that, and so do I."

"I can run as far and as fast as I choose."

"Just make sure you end up at Tivoli in three weeks."

In an incendiary mixture of rage and desire, Clea reached up, took his jaw in her two hands, her nails digging into his skin, and kissed him hard on the mouth. Then she pivoted, opened the back door of the cab and slipped into the seat.

Reckless laughter sparking his eyes, Slade grabbed the door handle, holding it open. "For me, the earth just moved. Did it for you, Clea?"

"Too much wine," she retorted, wishing it were the truth, and gave the name of her hotel to the taxi driver. "Goodbye, Slade."

"Self-deception's a dangerous game," he said. "See you in three weeks."

As he very gently shut the door, her features were a study in conflicting emotions. The taxi drove away, Slade watching until its lights disappeared around the corner.

The parrots, in the morning, would still be in their cages. But what of Clea? Where would she be?

CHAPTER FIVE

COPENHAGEN in early December was unexpectedly cold, with a couple of inches of fresh snow. Slade had just flown in from Latvia; so he was wearing a sheepskin coat and fur-lined boots as he walked under the brightly lit archway at the main entrance to the Tivoli Gardens, on Vesterbrogade. He felt as strung out as a seven-year-old on Christmas morning.

Clea had haunted his thoughts for the last three weeks.

Tivoli in winter was far from a mere ghost of its summer festivities. Directly in front of him was a huge restaurant, its Moorish façade outlined in gold, red and green. Everywhere he looked was extravagantly lit, music lilting through the chill air. The lake gleamed with a thin skim of ice; from fairy-tale cottages drifted the warm odors of pastries and hot coffee; the pagoda's elegant roofline dominated the roller coaster's long coils and the tall spire of Det Gyldne Tårn, the Golden Tower.

Now all he had to do was find jolly St. Nicholas. And Clea.

He was forty-five minutes early, so he had lots of time. Although he spoke virtually no Danish, the first person Slade asked for directions replied in impeccable English; so within ten minutes, he was standing to one side of an arcade that sheltered a herd of stuffed reindeer, sacks of toys and a red-clad St. Nicholas with a white beard and gold-rimmed glasses. He was attended by several pixies, little gold bells jingling on their red-and-green costumes. None of them was nearly tall enough to be Clea. A crowd of children surged around St. Nick's knees, their parents watching from the sidelines.

From behind a big red sleigh a woman emerged, her arms laden with packages. She handed them to a couple of the pixies, then bent to speak to a little girl near the back of the crowd. Another little girl grabbed her sleeve, and soon a cluster of children was laughing and chattering around her.

Slade stood very still in the dark shadow of the building. This was a side to Clea he hadn't yet seen, and wouldn't have suspected. She looked completely at ease. She looked, he thought, as though she loved children, this woman who couldn't abide the possibility of commitment.

One more layer to the enigma that was Clea.

Then she glanced at her watch and stood up. A small boy was seated on the saint's knee. She walked over and lifted him off, handing him back to his mother. St. Nick said something to her. She laughed, giving his beard a playful tug. Then she went back to her job of taking presents from the sleigh.

Under his red costume and ripple of white beard, St. Nick could be anyone. As, for instance, one of the players in her famous field.

Slade checked his own watch. It was five minutes to five, time he made an appearance. He walked into the arcade.

When Clea appeared from behind the sleigh, passing her pile of gifts to the pixies, he said clearly, "*Goddag,* Clea. And that's fifty percent of my entire stock of Danish."

Although Clea was expecting him, she gave a tiny start, as always disconcerted by his sheer presence, so laden with animal magnetism. Forcing a practised smile to her lips, she said, "*Hej,* Slade…so you came."

"Did you expect otherwise?"

"I didn't give it much thought," she said loftily.

"You're a very bad liar," he said, and looked her up and down, taking his time. She was wearing a long hunter-green cashmere coat, against which her hair flared like a torch. The hood was lined in velvet and edged with white faux fur; her mittens were fluffy white mohair, her boots polished black leather.

He stripped off his glove and rested his hand against her cheek; it was pink with cold. Clea said, sounding not quite as adamant as she should, "Don't even think of kissing me in front of all these children."

"Not the kind of kiss I have in mind."

Color mounted her cheeks. She could imagine that kiss all too vividly. With a rather overdone pout she said, "You have a one-track mind."

"How are you?" he said abruptly.

She widened her eyes innocently. "Getting my Christmas fix out of the way early...I'm fine."

So that was the way she planned to play it, he thought: on the surface, everything light and easy. But when had he ever backed down from a challenge?

"You look gorgeously, sexily and utterly beautiful," he said. "Am I the first man to tell you that today?"

"As a matter of fact, you are."

"St. Nick must be blind—have you known him long?"

Her lashes flickered. "Three years."

The question was out before he could censor it. "Have you slept with him?"

"Pixies and children have big ears," she snapped. "Let's walk for a while, I love looking at all the lights."

"Let's," he said agreeably. But once they were outside, Slade pulled her into the shadow of a giant evergreen, his kiss fueled by three weeks of sexual frustration and far too many erotic dreams.

Despite her best intentions, Clea grabbed the collar of his jacket and kissed him back, her tongue entwined with his, her teeth bruising his lip. And was lost.

Heat surged through Slade's body, heat and a depth of hunger that overwhelmed him with its demands. He wanted to haul her behind the tree and make love to her against the trunk. Make love until neither one of them could breathe, until they were saturated with the body's sensations…and all the while, he savored the dart and thrust of her tongue, the yielding sweetness of her mouth crushed to his.

His heart hammering in his chest, Slade wrenched his head back. "If we don't quit right now," he gasped, "we'll be flat on the ground underneath this tree."

Her rapid breathing made little puffs of white in the cold air. She said shakily, "That'd ruin my coat."

"We certainly deserve better than pine needles for a bed the first time we make love."

"We're not going to make love—ever!"

His heartbeat had settled to a steady throbbing. "You haven't answered my question yet."

"I forget what it was," she muttered.

"Jolly old St. Nicholas, was he a lover of yours?"

Patches of hectic color staining her cheeks, she said, "I don't keep asking you about your sexual history."

"You showed me the clippings, so I'm not expecting you to be a virgin—you're twenty-six years old, you come with a past. But I sure as hell don't want to be tripping over ex-lovers every step we take."

Wondering when she'd ever been so angry, Clea snapped, "I hear you, Slade. Put your voice one notch higher and all of Tivoli will hear you."

"Just so long as you do." Taking her by the hand, he led her away from the tree and deliberately changed the subject.

"I've just come from Latvia—I had to make a side trip there after Moscow. The weather was cold enough to encourage mass emigration to the Caribbean."

His profile, predatory as a hawk's, was etched against the lights. "What were you doing in Latvia?"

Being as entertaining as he knew how, Slade began describing some of the ups and downs of the last three weeks, and was rewarded by her delightful cascade of laughter. They wandered some of the boutiques of the market, where Clea suddenly stopped by a long table. She picked up a small pin, an enameled teddy bear with a charming grin. "I'm going to buy it for you," she said. "Not that you resemble a teddy bear."

"Not a chance," Slade said, pleased beyond measure by the simple gift.

She took out her credit card. "It'll remind you of Christmas in Tivoli."

"Do you seriously think I'll forget it?"

"*Ja,*" she said. "Men have short memories." Frowning in concentration, she pinned the teddy bear to the collar of his shirt. Her fingers brushed his throat; she was standing very close to him, her perfume wafting to his nostrils, complex and seductive.

*Men have short memories...*how he hated it when she lumped him in with half the human race. He said casually, "*Tak*—my only other Danish word. I have something for you, I found them on Fifth Avenue."

He took a small box out of his pocket and passed it to her. Clea blinked at the name of the jeweller, tore off the silver ribbon and opened the box. Inside were gold earrings in the shape of birds with wide-spread wings.

"They're free," she said blankly. "The birds, that is. I don't mean the earrings didn't cost—"

"I know what you mean. That's why I bought them."

For a horrible moment Clea wondered if she was going to

burst into tears. She struggled to subdue them, smoothing her features into the mask she'd perfected over the years, and tucked the box into her black leather shoulder purse. "They're lovely, thank you."

Her defenses were a mile high, just as Slade had suspected they'd be. What, other than kissing her, could breach them? Wasn't that what he was here to find out? "Let's walk some more," he said.

They followed the circumference of the lake. On the far shore, a small group of teenagers came into sight, shoddily dressed, not as clean as they might have been. Clea stiffened, horrified; she had to get out of here before they recognized her. "Let's go this way, Slade," she said hastily, indicating another path and tugging at his sleeve. "We can get a better view of the roller coaster."

Going on instinct, he said, "We'll come back to the roller coaster in a minute—I'd like to take a look at that building up ahead."

"But—"

The girl in front, who had studs in her ears, nose and lower lip, cried out Clea's name, ran toward her and launched into a rapid stream of Danish. The other kids crowded around Clea, all of them obviously delighted to see her.

Who were they, Slade wondered, and what was their connection to Clea? Who, noticeably, was making no attempt to introduce them to him.

She was carrying it off, he thought, although beneath the banter she was exchanging with the kids, she looked thoroughly discomfited. Fiercely he wished he spoke Danish.

After a loud chorus of goodbyes and several sidelong glances at him, the teenagers kept going. Slade said casually, "What was that all about?"

"You couldn't follow?" Clea asked, keeping her voice casual with a huge effort. "You really don't speak Danish?"

"*Goddag* and *tak*—that's the extent of it."

She said with partial truth, "They panhandle by the station. I gave them money once and started talking to them, that's all."

"I don't think so," he said in a steel voice.

"Are you calling me a liar?"

"What's the rest of the story, Clea?"

"I liked them," she said. "I made long-term arrangements for them to sleep in a hostel at my expense." Which was also a partial truth. "Now can we please talk about something else?"

"That was kind of you," he said.

"With the amount of money I have? Scarcely."

"You got personally involved—that's what's kind. Anyone can give money away."

Belle, he thought, making a lightning-swift connection. Belle gets involved, too. Was that the root of the connection between Clea and Belle?

Mystery piled upon mystery. He said, "Let's find somewhere to eat."

"There's a very classy restaurant at my hotel," Clea said stiffly.

Seduction looked like the last thing on her mind and he wasn't formally dressed. "I saw a place near the concert hall," he said, and within five minutes they were seated in a folksy cottage whose menu was in both English and Danish. Once they'd dealt with the waiter, Slade said evenly, "You still haven't answered my question. So I'll answer it. I'd be willing to bet you haven't slept with St. Nick."

Clea looked at him warily. He was, of course, right. "Why do you say that?"

"Remember the clippings? The more I see of you, the less I'm inclined to believe that they're evidence of—what should I call it?—promiscuity? A very active love life?" He paused, struck as always by the intelligence in her gaze and the vulnerable curve of her mouth. "There's something about you," he went on slowly. "An almost untouched quality…"

Skewered to her seat by his dark eyes, Clea said in a brittle voice, "You can believe what you want to believe."

"Smoke screens—they're your specialty."

"You know the saying," she retorted, "no smoke without a fire."

"You didn't know what a fire was until you met me."

"How can you say that?" she flashed.

"I scared you witless the first time we kissed—on Fisherman's Wharf, remember?—because I got you in touch with the passionate woman you're meant to be. Who's a far cry from the woman in those clippings."

"You should be writing novels," she said sarcastically. "Fiction's definitely your specialty."

He said with growing conviction, "Nothing you could show me will persuade me you're shallow and flighty, changing men as easily as you change your shoes. It doesn't go with the Clea I'm starting to know. The one who wants to free caged parrots, who befriends a bunch of down-at-heel teenagers, who talks to little children as though they're real people." He took a deep breath. "I think that's the real woman."

"You're making this far too complicated!"

Was he? "You're a mass of contradictions. You sleep around, or so you're implying. Yet you won't let me near you. I—"

Someone was speaking to him in Danish. It was the waiter, holding out two platters of steamed mussels in apple cider broth. Slade raked his fingers through his hair. "*Tak,*" he said.

He felt frustrated, stirred up and confused. The one thing he didn't feel was hungry.

As the waiter vanished, Clea impulsively reached over and rested her hand on Slade's "This is what I was afraid of—that

I'd cause you pain," she said jaggedly. "It's why I did my best to send you away the very first time we met."

Her fingers were slender and ringless, her nails tinted a soft pink. He could see the tracery of blue veins under her smooth, ivory skin. As though he couldn't help himself, he lifted her hand to his mouth and closed his eyes, inhaling her scent, feeling her warmth lance through his own skin, intimate and desired. His pulse began to hammer; his groin hardened.

Was he being a fool to ignore the evidence she'd presented him with? Or was he simply being true to his deepest instincts?

When he looked up, Clea's gaze went straight through him, for it was blurred with desire and helpless longing. Tears hung on her lashes; her turquoise eyes were as vulnerable as he'd ever seen them. If a simple caress laid her so devastatingly open, how would the act of love affect her?

There was only one way to find out.

He said with iron implacability, "I'm not like the rest of your men—I won't jump at your whim, or conveniently disappear when you want me to. I'm different, you said so yourself. So why don't you try something different? Radically different. Exclusivity. With me."

She tugged her hand free and swiped at her eyes, knowing his caress had touched her in a place she strove to keep untouched. Inviolate. "Whenever I'm anywhere near you, I want so desperately to make love with you—even though you scare me half to death. But I don't do commitment, Slade. Not for anyone."

His gut churning, Slade said forcibly, "Spend Christmas with me and my family. Get to know me. Change your mind."

She picked up her fork and extracted a plump mussel from its shell. "I spend every Christmas with friends in Trinidad," she said repressively. "No St. Nick, no turkey dinner, no children, no snow."

"No family?"

"Definitely no family."

He remembered her lifting the little boy, the way the child had laughed down at her. "Don't you want children of your own?"

She flinched. "Perhaps. Someday."

"Then you're going to have to make a commitment, aren't you?" he said, and saw that, for once, she had no glib reply, no clever retort.

He began to eat, noticing that tonight she was scarcely touching her wine. He was the one who felt like getting drunk, he thought wryly. Had he ever met a woman as stubborn as Clea Chardin? As determined to avoid anything that remotely smacked of exclusivity? Usually it was the other way around, women latching on to him with wedding bells ringing in their ears.

Poetic justice, that's what his father would call it.

"There's a lot of garlic in these mussels," he said easily. "Good thing we're both eating them."

"Don't assume you'll be kissing me again."

"It's not an assumption—it's a certainty."

Her eyes flitted down to her plate. "We'll see about that," she said, and determinedly led the conversation into the murky field of Russian politics.

It was a conversation Slade was quite capable of sustaining. After they'd finished eating, they took a cab to her hotel, Clea sitting as far from him on the seat as she could.

In an elegant enclave of eighteenth century rococo buildings, the cab drew up in front of a stone hotel named after Den Lille Havfrue, the Little Mermaid. "She was the daughter of the sea king, who lost herself when she fell in love with a human," Clea said, a slight edge to her voice. Then panic tightened all her nerves as she saw Slade reach for his wallet. "You don't need to get out," she added jerkily.

"I'll see you indoors," he said, and paid off the cabbie.

Clea didn't want Slade accompanying her into the hotel: not when her own body was so intent on betraying her. "The name of the hotel is one reason I stay here," she gabbled. "Plus it's wonderfully comfortable, and small enough to be friendly without being intrusive. I love strolling around Frederiksstaden, all the palaces and the cobbled square—the guards look so solemn in their blue trousers and fur hats."

Clea wasn't a woman to make small talk; she was nervous, Slade thought, and covering it with chatter. The doorman in his deep plum coat ushered them into the lobby, where gilded columns surrounded an antique table crowned with a huge bouquet of lilies.

Clea turned to face Slade, her voice higher-pitched than usual. "Good night."

He said curtly, "We haven't made any arrangements for our next date. And we're not going to do that in a public place. What floor's your room on?"

She could throw a tantrum, or she could scream for help: either of which would ruin her reputation here forever. She said helplessly, "My suite's on the top floor."

The elevator smoothly whisked them up five floors, depositing them on a thick floral carpet outside four tall, gilt-engraved doors. Clea chose the one on the left and inserted her card. The door opened with a click. She walked in, throwing back her hood and tossing her coat on a velvet-upholstered chaise longue. Swiftly Slade surveyed his surroundings. More rococo elegance; the bedroom door was wide-open. Through it, he could see the wide bed, canopied and draped in plum brocade.

His heartbeat quickened. He brought his gaze back to Clea. Her dress was black, severely cut, yet all the more provocative for the way it skimmed her hips, and gently outlined the swell of her breasts. Awkwardly she kicked off her boots, her high-arched feet and slender legs exquisite in black hose.

Beneath a thin veneer of composure, she now looked outright terrified.

A cold fist clenched around his heart. How could he seduce her when she looked like a wild creature at bay? "Clea, I don't force women," he said flatly, "it's not my style. You'll come willingly to my bed or not at all. So there's no need for you to look so frightened."

"It's myself I'm frightened of," she said wretchedly. "I thought you knew that."

With a tiny sound of compassion, Slade took her in his arms. She held herself rigidly; at the base of her throat the pulse fluttered under her skin. He smoothed her hair with one hand, tipped her chin and kissed her gently on the mouth.

Had he ever kissed a woman with this overwhelming need to comfort her?

Her body gradually relaxed, her lips soft and warm, opening to him. With all the control he could muster, Slade moved back, and knew he'd never done anything more difficult.

"Florence," he said. "In ten days. My house there is small, but it has central heating."

Aching for the touch of his mouth, Clea gaped at him. "Florence?" she croaked. "Our next date?"

"Yeah…do me a favor, will you? Don't date anyone else in the interim."

Almost, she weakened. She'd felt safe in his arms, she thought unhappily. Protected. Yet nothing in her experience encouraged her to trust either feeling. "You're putting me in a cage, Slade. Like the parrots."

"If that's what you truly believe, then you're in trouble."

She said, despair flattening her voice, "If we keep on

seeing each other, we'll get involved more and more deeply."

"That's right," Slade said inflexibly. "I'll give you my address in Florence and I'll meet you at the airport."

"You wear me down," she muttered, then heard her own words replay in her head. She sounded defeated. Beaten. Like the coward he'd accused her of being.

She could handle Slade Carruthers, she decided in a flare of defiance; certainly she could be every bit as stubborn as he. "I love Florence," she said steadily, "I always have."

"Along with New York, it's my favorite city in the world."

"I'm not responsible if you get hurt, Slade."

"We're all responsible for the consequences of our actions."

"There's a costume museum one street north of Ponte Vecchio," she said rapidly. "I'll meet you there. Three in the afternoon on the sixteenth."

"Do you promise there'll be no one else between now and then?"

"If you're talking sex, it's highly unlikely in the next ten days," she said, her cheeks flaming. "But I have two dinner dates I'm not going to cancel—I won't have restrictions put on what I do."

Forgetting all his good intentions, Slade stepped closer to her, pulled her the length of his body and kissed her parted lips with ferocious hunger; she responded instantly and with a fervor that set his pulses racing. His hand found the sweet rise of her breast, where her nipple was tight as a bud; she moaned deep in her throat as he drew her hips into the hardness of his erection.

If he didn't stop now, he'd be lost.

On his terms. Hold that thought, Slade. Pushing her away, he said with assumed calm, "Then I'll say good night."

Her whole body on fire with needs she'd never known she possessed, Clea faltered, "You—you're not staying?"

"That's right."

"Why did you kiss me, then?" she demanded, her eyes blazing. "Leading me on this way?"

"Would you rather we'd had this discussion in the lobby?"

She wrapped her arms around her chest. "I'd rather you'd stayed in the cab," she said bitterly.

"I hoped, when we actually got within the vicinity of a bed, that you'd tell me you wouldn't date anyone else for the space of ten days," he said with matching anger. "It doesn't seem too much to ask."

"It's not the ten days—it's the principle of the thing!"

"Or," he rapped, "from my point of view, the lack of principle."

"So Florence is off," she said in an unreadable voice.

"Florence is very much on."

"What's that saying? A sucker for punishment—that's you, Slade."

"Have you ever heard of New England cussedness? It's another way of saying obstinate as a stone wall. That's me, Clea."

"The unbendable force meets the immovable object," she said softly. "That's us, Slade."

He tweaked a strand of her hair. "You got it, babe. See you in ten days at the museum. Sleep well—and if you dream, make sure it's about me."

Her eyes were brimming with a turmoil of fury and frustration. Desperate to get away from her, because if he didn't he'd end up in her bed despite all his fine pronouncements, Slade marched across the carpet to the door and let himself out. It closed with the same decisive click with which it had opened. He ran down the stairs and out into the cold night. Alone.

He was, he was sure, the very first man who, with the prospect of a night in Clea Chardin's delectable arms, had walked away from her.

More fool he.

CHAPTER SIX

SLADE walked down Via De'Benci toward the Arno. The light was golden and the sky a cloudless blue. There were few places he'd rather be than Florence on a sunny afternoon in December; especially when he'd be seeing Clea in a few minutes.

He dove into the network of streets that led him ever closer to the river, toward the famous Ponte Vecchio and the much less famous costume museum. He must ask Clea why, of all the illustrious museums in the city, she'd chosen that one.

He was going to make love to her this evening; he was tired of waking in the night and reaching for her, his body one big knot of frustration. Enough was enough. Besides, if he took her to bed, he was sure to break down some of the barriers she hid behind, even change her mind on the subject of fidelity.

The museum boasted Romanesque arches with Corinthian capitals, its stone frontage flanked by two fountains. The enormous oak door creaked as Slade pushed it open. The lobby was cool and high-ceilinged, peopled with astonishingly lifelike mannequins wearing everything from polished armor to the diaphanous robes Botticelli had immortalized.

The receptionist had classic Tuscan features and a warm smile. Slade paid the fee on his VISA; as she noted the name on his card, her lashes flickered in a way he was later to remember. Keeping his eyes open for Clea, he meandered from room to room, hard-pressed to resist such a beguiling tour of Florence's history.

Visitors with guidebooks and art students with easels were wandering around, but there was no sign of the woman he was looking for. In the last room his gaze flicked over the mannequins, a cold lump settling in his belly. She wasn't here. Had she given in to her fears and stayed away? Or had she been delayed in one of Florence's ubiquitous traffic jams?

He'd go back to the lobby and wait for her there. She'd turn up.

As he turned to leave, his gaze brushed over the figure of a woman standing on a pedestal. Her eyes gleamed in a way that was almost lifelike, he thought idly, and turned away. His steps faltered imperceptibly. Almost? They *were* lifelike. The woman's face was Clea's.

She'd moved slightly; that's why he'd noticed her in the first place.

With a superhuman effort Slade kept going, until he was hidden from her by one of the foot-thick walls. He leaned against it, wanting to laugh his head off. He had his answer: he now knew why she'd chosen this museum. Once again, she was testing him. With, he thought, her sense of humor very much to the fore.

Why wait for him by the front door like any other tourist? Much too boring and predictable a course of action for Clea. Wasn't her sense of fun one of the several reasons he was pulled so strongly toward her?

Two could play that game.

Approaching one of the art students, he said in Italian, "Would you do me a favor, you and your friends? Would you spend a few minutes sketching one of the costumes in the next room? The woman in the long green dress…I'd make it worth your while."

The students, all of whom looked like they could do with a square meal, talked in rapid-fire Italian for a couple of minutes. Then the bearded young man, who appeared to be their leader, pocketed the sheaf of bills Slade had produced. *"Si, si…grazie."*

They picked up their gear and went into the next room. A few moments later Slade followed them. Clea was still stationed on the pedestal, her gaze demurely downcast. Her gown cupped her breasts, falling in long folds down her body; her starched white wimple completely covered her hair.

He said, a little too loudly, to the nearest of the students, "How fashions change. That woman wouldn't be called particularly beautiful today…yet in her time, she was probably considered a fine catch."

Clea's mouth twitched. He went on, "A pious and dutiful wife…her head full of heaven and the blandishments of her latest lover. And a mouth full of bad teeth."

"Unwashed, too," said the bearded young man, whose shirt was far from clean.

"Lice in her hair?" Slade suggested. "Not exactly a turn-on…I'll be back in a few minutes—I'm supposed to meet someone here, and she's late."

He walked away. But in ten minutes, judging that was long enough to have made Clea suffer, he was back. For a moment he stood in the doorway, looking at the scene with private pleasure. The setting sun was slanting through one of the high windows, dust motes floating gently downward on the silent collection of medieval knights and their ladies. The women's costumes glowed like jewels.

But Clea's face, he saw with sudden dismay, was ashen-pale. As he stepped out of the shadows into the light, she swayed on her feet, her eyes glassy.

He thrust through the group of students and leaped onto the platform on which her pedestal stood. As her head fell forward and her body slumped, he caught her in his arms.

Her forehead bumped his shoulder; she was as limp as a rag doll. Cursing himself for making her pose too long, Slade lowered her to the edge of the platform and pushed her head between her knees. Kneeling beside her, he said with a gentleness new to him, "Take your time—you fainted."

She made a tiny sound of distress. "Slade?" she whispered. "Is it you?"

"Yes, I'm here...I'm not going away."

"I...the room suddenly started to sway and I couldn't make it stop."

"It was my fault," he said harshly, "I shouldn't have left you standing so long."

She was pushing against him. "I need to lie down."

He put an arm under her knees and another around her back, lifting her in a single smooth movement. "I'll get a limo right away." He glanced over at the bearded student. "*Grazie.*"

"Slade, put me down!"

"No," he said. "I feel like a louse, and you must let me make amends."

He carried her through the series of rooms, ignoring the curious stares of the other visitors. In the lobby he asked the receptionist to call the limousine driver he always hired in Florence, whose station wasn't far from Ponte Vecchio. "Tell him to hurry," Slade said.

Quickly she did as he'd asked. Then she said, "The signora, is she all right?"

"She fainted...the rooms are very warm." He added, almost certain he was right, "You know her?"

"She's one of our best benefactors."

"Maddalena, be quiet," Clea gasped.

Maddalena went on, "This is, of course, why the signora is permitted to wear one of our gowns."

"We'll return it first thing tomorrow," Slade promised.

"That will be fine."

"I'll take good care of the gown, Maddalena," Clea said faintly. "Could you get my case?"

"Of course." The receptionist took a small black leather case from the cupboard behind her. "The signora's clothes," she said, handing it to Slade.

Five minutes later, Slade was easing Clea into the backseat of a sleek black limo. "*Buon giorno,* Lorenzo," he said. "Thanks for coming so quickly. Take me home, would you?"

Clea pushed herself upright against the seat, striving to gain some control over a situation that had the potential to thoroughly mortify her. "Slade, I want to go to my hotel."

"For once you're not getting your own way."

"Please—I just need to be alone for a while."

"Relax, we'll be at my place in ten minutes."

With something near despair she said, "I can't fight you— I don't have the energy."

"Then don't try," he said, smiling at her to take the sting out of his words. "Let someone else take charge of your life for a change."

If only it were that simple. If only her impulse to have a little fun in the museum hadn't backfired so badly. Clea leaned back, closing her eyes.

It was nearer twenty minutes before the limo drew up in front of an old stone house in the artisans' quarter. The cobbled street was narrow, the houses seeming to lean into one another, their walls illumined reddish gold as the sun sank further to the west. The limo driver got out and took the key Slade had passed him, unlocking an old oak door nestled in a masonry arch.

Slade smiled his thanks, lifted Clea as carefully as if she were breakable, and carried her inside; she was still pale, bluish shadows under her eyes. As the door closed behind them, he snagged the double latch and quickly disarmed the alarm system. The steps were wide, carpeted in rich burgundy; frescoes in earthy browns and reds adorned the plaster walls. He said easily, "I use the two bottom floors for business meetings, and keep my personal stuff on the top three floors."

His bedroom was on the very top floor, its little balcony with a view of the splendid gold-tipped spire on the Duomo and the faraway, misty outline of the Tuscan hills; it was a view he never tired of. His few treasures were set into alcoves in the wall: a small Donatello, an inlaid box that had belonged to one of the Medicis, a Verrocchio bronze of a young hunter. The bed was large, the wood with the patina of age, the spread the same faded red of the tile roofs of the city he so loved. Nothing matched in the room; yet it made a harmonious whole.

He put Clea down on the bed. She said, trying to push herself upright, "I wish you'd taken me back to my hotel."

Standing beside the bed, he said, "Let me look after you for once, Clea—independence is all very well, but it can be carried too far. And, to put it bluntly, you look awful."

"I never let anyone look after me," she said with a spurt of her normal spirit.

"We should all be open to new experiences," he said dryly. "Do you think I make a practice of looking after women?" Going over to the tall walnut wardrobe that took up the better part of one wall, he took out a shirt. "You can wear this. The first thing is to get that headdress off—it looks tight enough to make anyone faint."

"I can manage."

"I'm sure you can. But you're not going to."

He found the snaps at her nape, under the gauzy white

folds, and carefully removed the wimple, laying it on an old oak chest under the window. Then he reached for the buttons on the back of her gown.

In a strangled voice, knowing she couldn't postpone it any longer, Clea said, "I—I have to ask you to go to the *farmacia* for me—the drugstore."

"I've got a first-aid kit—what do you need? Something for a headache? A muscle relaxant?"

She wasn't wearing a bra; the long line of her spine filled Slade with a desperate longing to run his finger along the small bumps of her vertebrae. He eased the gown from her shoulders, picked up the shirt and slipped it around her.

She clutched the shirt to her breast as the gown fell to her waist. "You wouldn't have what I need," she muttered. "Or maybe you do and I'll hate you for it."

She was talking in riddles. "Stand up," he said, "and let's get rid of the gown. I'll get you something to warm your feet once you're in bed, then I'll find whatever it is you need."

"I'm early," she blurted, her eyes downcast, "that's why I'm not prepared. I'd never have done this silly skit with the gown if I'd realized...wrong time of the month, Slade. My period."

"Do you faint every month?" he said, appalled.

"No...but I don't stand on a pedestal trying to emulate a statue every month, either. I get cramps and I feel horrible for about twelve hours, that's all."

It sounded like more than enough to Slade. "Then I'm doubly glad you're here so I can look after you, and doubly sorry about the art students," he said. "Once you're settled, I'll go to the drugstore, there's one four streets over from here. Because no, I don't have what you need."

I'll hate you for it...did that mean she was jealous of any other women in his life?

She frowned at him. "This isn't what you'd planned for the evening."

As he helped her to her feet, the gown slithered to the floor. Clea automatically stepped out of it, kicking off delicate gold shoes at the same time. Slade said, "Roll with the punches. Always been one of my mottoes."

He pulled back the covers and eased her onto thin cotton sheets that smelled sweetly of lavender. "Lie down and stay down," he ordered. "Do you want something hot to drink? Herbal tea, perhaps?"

"I—no," she said clumsily. "But it was nice of you to ask." In a gesture that tore him to the heart, she snuggled into the pillow. "That feels better," she sighed. "Maybe you could bring me a muscle relaxant for the cramps."

Slade hung her gown in the wardrobe before running downstairs, where he found the vial of pills and poured some water into a crystal goblet. He'd bought a dozen pale yellow roses for the dining room table; picking them up, he carried them upstairs, too.

Clea was nearly asleep. "They're lovely," she mumbled. "My favorite color, how did you know?"

"I didn't. Happens to be my favorite, too."

"So we're meant for each other?" she said with a weak grin.

"Who knows?" Slade said soberly. He passed her the water along with the pill, propping her up as she took it. Warmth from her skin seeped through the shirt she was wearing. He said with a wry smile, "So here you are in my bed, Clea. Although not quite the way I'd imagined it."

She sank back on the pillows. "I must look about as seductive as a mud hen."

"You'd look seductive in a garbage bag. Are you warm enough?"

"Wonderfully warm," she said drowsily.

He wrote down his cell phone number. "The phone's here by the bed. Call me if you need anything more. I'll be back in fifteen minutes."

"Thanks," she murmured and closed her eyes.

He was still wearing his jacket over a Guernsey sweater. On the street he threaded through the people getting off work, his mind very much on Clea. If she'd had her way, she'd be back in her hotel right now, and he'd be a million miles away.

The thought of her in his bed filled him with an unsettling and poignant emotion he couldn't call by name. What was happening to him? She'd looked so fragile, so vulnerable, that his sole urge had been to look after her.

A whole new experience.

The drugstore was crowded. Slade stood in front of the dismayingly large array of neatly arranged boxes, knowing this was another new experience. Grabbing three different kinds, he marched toward the counter, paid for them and chastised himself for cowardice because he was relieved when the cashier put them in a brown paper bag.

Give him ten angry CEOs any day of the week.

Within twenty minutes he was climbing the stairs to his bedroom. When he walked in, Clea was asleep. She was lying on her back, her face turned sideways to the pillow. Her hair seemed to have drained her cheeks of all color; her eyes still had bruised shadows beneath them.

He left the package beside the bed and drew the curtains over the two narrow windows. Then he walked downstairs to the kitchen. They wouldn't be eating out tonight. So the meal was up to him.

Ribollita, he thought, with crostini spread with olive oil, wild mushrooms and chopped tomatoes. He had two helpings of outrageously expensive tiramisu from his favorite delicatessen, and if Clea liked to finish a meal with espresso, he always had that on hand.

After opening a bottle of red wine made from the Sangiovese grape of the Tuscan hills, he rolled up his sleeves and started making the rich vegetable soup, turning on one of the local radio stations to hear the news.

Sometime later, when the kitchen was redolent of herbs and garlic, Slade suddenly became aware he was being watched. He swiveled. Clea was leaning against the doorpost, his shirt falling to her thighs, her face delicately flushed. She said, "The apron becomes you."

He smiled. "I'm a messy cook. How are you feeling?"

"Better. Slade, I should go back to my hotel, you—"

"Supper's nearly ready. Would you like it in bed?"

"No! I—"

"Let me find you some sweatpants and a top, then we'll eat."

She looked around at the vegetable peelings on the butcher block, the crushed herbs and the bottle of thick tomato paste. "You cooked. For me," she said blankly.

"Yeah…" He put a little of the broth in a ladle and walked over to her. "Careful, it's hot. Enough salt, do you think?"

She sipped it gingerly. "It tastes heavenly."

"You don't have to sound so surprised."

She said stiffly, "I'm not used to a man who can make *ribollita* as though he was born here."

"I told you I was different," he remarked. "Let's eat in the kitchen."

The kitchen walls were sponged a soft blue, with terracotta accents. Herbs hung in bunches from the ceiling, while geraniums bloomed in bursts of red against the squared windowpanes. The table and chairs had come from an old Tuscan farmhouse; Slade had lovingly polished them until they shone.

"It's charming," Clea said, wondering if Slade would ever stop surprising her.

He pulled out one of the chairs. "Sit, Clea. I'll bring something for you to wear."

"This place," she said in a rush, "it's like a real home."

She looked strained and unhappy. Not bothering to disguise his compassion, he said, "Where's your real home?"

"I don't have one."

"We all need a place we can call home."

She should never have revealed her lack of a home to a man as acute as Slade. "I'm hungry, Slade. Feed me."

"Sure I will," he said. "But we're not done with this conversation."

He took the stairs two at a time, grabbed some clothes from the wardrobe and went back to the kitchen. She had to roll the waistband of his sweatpants several times to get them to stay up, even with the help of his Gucci belt; the cuffs of his sweater swallowed her fingertips. He said, "Armani wouldn't hire you for the catwalk."

She gave a snort of laughter, tightening the belt. "I wouldn't be seen dead on Via de'Tornabuoni right now."

He served her a bowl of soup, putting the crostini on the table, and pouring her a glass of wine. Then he lit the beeswax candles in a battered silver candelabra that had come from a fifteenth century Benedictine abbey. Sitting down across from her, he raised his glass. "May you find your true home, Clea."

She sent a hunted glance around the kitchen. "This is all so domesticated."

"Domesticated, from *domus*. Which means home."

"I'm not used to it, that's all I meant."

"I know what you meant."

She took a big bite of toast slathered with wild mushrooms. "Mmm…delicious. Do you cook like this all the time?"

"Mostly when I'm here. I get tired of fancy restaurants—don't you?"

She closed her eyes in bliss as she savored a mouthful of the broth. "I've never thought about it."

"Time you did."

She didn't want to. "Who does the dishes?" she asked.

"I do. With the help of the most modern of dishwashers that I keep hidden in the pantry so it won't wreck the decor."

"No servants?"

"Caretakers live in the flat behind the house. Cleaners come every week. But when I'm here I like the place to myself." He cut her a chunk of cheese. "I spend a lot of time with people, most of whom want something from me. Or whose minds I'm trying to pry away from instant profits to long-term considerations—like an environment that'll be fit for their grandchildren. So here I prefer my own company."

"And the company of women."

"Not here," he said.

Her spoon halted halfway to her mouth. "You must bring your women here   why wouldn't you?"

"I told you—this is my retreat." He leaned forward. "You're the first woman to be in that bed."

The spoon sloshed back into her soup. "I don't believe you!"

"You'd better. Because it's true."

Something in his face finally convinced her. She said uneasily, "Why did you bring me here then?"

"The alternative was to abandon you in a hotel," he said. "Be damned if I was going to do that. Eat your soup. You wouldn't want to insult the cook—he's bigger than you are."

Her eyes narrowed. "It's a measure of the excellence of the soup that I'm doing what I'm told."

"I'm flattered," Slade said, and asked her what other museums she frequented in Florence. From there, the conversation ranged easily over many subjects, until finally he was pouring espresso into tiny pottery mugs.

Then Clea said, feeling like a dog worrying a bone, "This house—it must have cost a fortune."

"Several, when you include furniture, taxes and upkeep."

"I don't understand how you've made it into a home…"

"It's because I love it. And everything in it."

Restlessly she wriggled her shoulders. "I'm a hotel person—here one day and gone the next. No attachments. Nothing to hold me down."

"Then, in my opinion, you're the loser. This place is real, Clea. Real and lasting and loved."

She was glaring at him as though he was an enemy. "I don't get it."

"Get what?"

Sweeping her arm to encompass the messy kitchen, she said choppily, "You put me to bed, you went to the *farmacia* for me, you cooked for me—what's in it for you, Slade?"

"I did it because I wanted to."

"There's no payoff—we both know that."

Anger uncoiled within him. "You mean sexual payoff?"

"Of course."

"What kind of men do you date?" he exploded.

"The kind who'd have put me in a taxi and sent me back to my hotel. Alone. Which is what I wanted you to do."

"How many times do I have to tell you I'm different from the rest?"

She said with icy precision, "What was the real reason you didn't you go to bed with me in Copenhagen?"

"I told you—I'm not going to tumble in and out of bed with you while you date men from every corner of Europe. Both of us deserve better than that. You'll commit yourself to me for the duration of our affair—or there won't be one."

She pounced. "And which one of us decides when the affair is over?"

He didn't have a clue. "We can argue about that later," he said, knowing it for a weak reply.

She pushed back her chair, wood scraping on the ceramic tile. "I really hate this conversation."

"Because I'm not jumping to your tune like the rest of your men?"

"Because sooner or later you'll dump me like you've dumped all your other women. So I'm dumping you first. Right now."

"Sure—run away. You're good at that."

"Yes," she said, "I am. It's called self-preservation."

She stood up. She should have looked ridiculous in her borrowed clothes; instead she looked beleaguered, defiant and very unhappy. Slade got to his feet, too. With raw honesty he said, "I'm offering you the best gifts of my body, Clea. I'll be as good to you as I know how, give you all the pleasure I'm capable of. But I'm not offering marriage, and I won't share you with anyone else."

The best gifts of my body...

A wave of flame swept over her; for a crazy moment she wondered if she was going to faint again. "I'm going upstairs to change," she said jaggedly, "then I'll get a cab to my hotel."

She walked past him, hitching at his Gucci belt, the shoulder seams of his sweater halfway to her elbows. Slade stood still, breathing hard. He'd give her five minutes. Then he was going after her.

After pouring the last of the soup into a plastic container, he loaded the dishwasher and left the kitchen, taking the stairs two at a time. Outside his bedroom door he paused for a minute to gather his wits; and with a jolt realized he could see Clea in the reflection from his mirror. She was standing by the bed in a chocolate-brown suit, the skirt several inches above the knee, the jacket smoothly skimming her body. She was holding his sweater to her face, her nose buried in it, her eyes closed.

Then, in a gesture of shocking suddenness, she flung the sweater on the bed and bent to put on her shoes.

Slade walked into the room.

CHAPTER SEVEN

"I'M NEARLY ready to call the cab," Clea said tightly. "And don't you dare blame this whole mess on hormones."

"I wasn't about to blame it on anything but sheer cussedness—you'd make a fine New Englander." Slade took her by the elbows and spoke from somewhere deep inside him. "You're as white as the sheets on the bed—stay here, Clea, sleep in the bed, and I'll sleep in the guest room."

"Stop treating me as though I'll break—this happens every month," she said irritably. "And the answer's no."

"Then you're still being a coward."

She broke free, marched over to the bureau and picked up a silver-framed photo, waving it wildly in the air. "These are your parents, aren't they?"

He'd taken the snapshot of David and Bethanne on the verandah of their house in Maine, the sea a sparkling backdrop; both his parents looked happy and relaxed. "That's right."

"If their marriage is so great, why are you still a bachelor? You're a decent man, don't think I can't see that—put decency together with a whole lot of money and that sexy cleft in your chin, and the women must mob you. Yet here you are, having one carefully orchestrated affair after another."

"I've never met a woman who tempted me to change that pattern."

"So you expect me to fall into it."

"You know what? I bet none of the rest of your men has ever made you lose control—made you so desperate for love-making that you can't sleep or eat. Tell me I'm wrong."

How could she, when it would be a blatant lie? "None of them frighten me, either," she retorted.

"You can't spend the rest of your life scared of your own shadow," Slade said forcefully.

He'd had more than enough of words. Taking her in his arms, he began kissing her, enveloped in a hunger that threatened to devour him. His hands ranged her back, buried themselves in her tangled curls, cupped the sweet curve of her breast and soft rise of her hip. And all the while his lips feasted on her, his tongue dancing with hers.

Knowing she couldn't help herself, Clea kissed him back, her fingers tugging at the buttons on his shirt, slipping beneath the fabric to trace the arc of bone and heat of muscle. Was this home? she thought in true confusion. The only home she'd ever known?

As she rubbed against him, inflaming him beyond any control, Slade muttered, "Stay with me, Clea. I don't care if we can't make love—let me at least hold you, have you in my bed where you belong."

"You make the bones melt in my body," she whispered. "I want you as I've never wanted a man before…you're right, that's what I can't deal with—how I'm so out of control."

He slid his mouth down the entrancing tautness of her throat, finding the little pulse at its base, feeling through every nerve the frantic racing of her blood. "We're not going to make love," he said huskily. "So you're safe to stay."

"And what about next time? What do we do then?"

"Let's take one day at a time."

Her eyes held all the turmoil of the ocean. "You'll still want to make love to me, and—"

"Sure I will. But only if you promise that we'll stop chasing each other all over Europe, and that you won't date anyone else. As for me, I swear I won't dump you between one night and the next, as if you're disposable. As if you have no feelings. Do you think I can't see how vulnerable you are?"

Trembling very lightly, on the verge of tears, she cried, "You terrify me, Slade. If we had an affair, you'd turn my life upside down, and then you'd leave me with nothing. I can't do that. We mustn't see each anymore, it's too painful, it tears me apart."

Pulling free, Clea picked up the phone by the bed, punched in some numbers and spoke in rapid Italian. Banging the receiver back into its cradle, she announced, "A cab'll be here in five minutes—I have a regular driver when I'm in Florence."

Then she grabbed her long gown, her wimple and gold slippers and her black case. Head high, she marched out of the bedroom.

Slade stood still. The sheets were crumpled from Clea's body. His parents smiled at him from the bureau. The thick curtains masked any view of the city he loved.

Raking his fingers through his hair, he started down the stairs, his steps muffled by the thick carpet. Clea was standing at the bottom by the big oak door, leaning against the wall, her eyes shut. She looked frighteningly fragile. He said harshly, "You leaving like this, it's all wrong."

"For me to stay would be wrong."

"Running away is what's wrong. I don't have a clue who hurt you so badly, although I'd sure like to punch the bastard into the middle of next week. But you can't hide from him all your life—because then he's running the show."

"You don't understand!"

"Then explain it to me so I can. Tell me about him—that way, there'll be no risk of a repeat."

She shook her head, her hair falling forward to hide her

face. Inside Slade, anger defeated compassion. He was living in the wrong century, he thought savagely. If he were a Medici, he wouldn't be standing here like a block of wood letting the woman he desired walk out the door. "No matter where you run, I can always track you down," he said in a voice that he scarcely recognized as his own.

"If you have any feelings for me at all, you won't do that," Clea said, her turquoise eyes full of pleading. "I—the taxi should be here by now."

As she tugged the door open, a white cab pulled up and blasted its horn. "Goodbye, Slade. Take care of yourself," she muttered. Then, clutching her clothes, she dived into the back-seat of the taxi, and it drove away.

Slade closed the door. The thick walls of his house deadened most of the street noise; had he ever felt so utterly alone?

Grabbing his jacket from the hook, he went outdoors, into the bustle and confusion of one of Florence's narrow alleys. The taxi had disappeared.

The shops of the artisans and restoration workers, the ice cream parlour near Santa Croce, the crenellated twelfth century tower of the Bargello where executions had run rampant, Slade strode past them all, hardly seeing them. Even the magnificent Piazza del Duomo for once failed to move him.

He headed back toward the Arno, into the western quarter of the city, marching along street after street until it was well past midnight. The smell of roasted chestnuts died away as the vendors went home. The traffic lessened. And still he walked.

He'd let her get away: the only woman who'd ever touched him in depths he hadn't known were his.

At seven-thirty the next morning, Slade was dreaming. Hands and ankles in chains, his elbows gripped by two armored guards, he was being led toward a scaffold in the arched courtyard of the Bargello. Somewhere high above his head a bell tolled, once, twice, heavy with doom.

Sweating, his heart pounding, he sat up in bed. A bell was ringing. The telephone.

He picked up the receiver and said hoarsely, "Carruthers."

"Slade?"

He cleared his throat. "Clea?" he said stupidly.

"Are you all right? You sound terrible."

"I was asleep. Where are you?"

"I'm at the airport and—"

All his anger surged to the surface. "Of course you're at the airport. That's what you do best, isn't it? Here one day and gone the next. Believe me, I—"

"Will you please shut up and listen! I want you to meet me in Paris. On Tuesday. For dinner at La Marguerite, do you know it?"

"Everyone knows it. Best restaurant in Paris. The answer's no."

"Look, I know I didn't handle last night very well and I'm sorry. I'm not playing games, really I'm not. There's someone I want you to meet," she said, her words tumbling over each other. "He usually eats at La Marguerite on Tuesdays. It'd help you to understand why I'm the way I am—that's why I'm suggesting it."

Slade rubbed his eyes, trying with all his willpower to fight off the dread and foreboding of his dream. "All right," he said curtly. "What time?"

"Eight-thirty. I'll look after the reservation...thank you, Slade." There was a small pause, during which he could hear a loudspeaker announcing the next flight. She said in a rush, "I've got to go, they're calling my flight. I'll see you on Tuesday."

The connection was cut. Slade put down the phone and got out of bed. Pulling back the curtains, he looked out over the ranked rooftops of Florence, and belatedly his brain began to work. Clea was—finally—taking the initiative. Reaching out to him.

In three days he was going to meet the man responsible for her terror of commitment. He couldn't very well pound him to a pulp in the august surroundings of La Marguerite. But he was fully prepared to hate his guts.

If he hadn't been stunned by lack of sleep and a nightmare so vivid he could still feel the weight of the chains, he'd have told Clea how brave she was. How much he appreciated the import of her phone call.

Wasn't it the first chink in her armor?

His thoughts marched on. She was willing to open her past to him, expose wounds that had gone frighteningly deep. He, Slade, couldn't add to that hurt. Couldn't dump her, to use her own words. It would be unconscionable. But—if they embarked on an affair—how could he avoid hurting her?

By marrying her? He couldn't do that if he didn't love her.

Start small, he thought. How about allowing her needs to supersede his for now? A whole new perspective for him: one that, at a level he scarcely understood, scared the wits out of him.

Sunlight gilded the Duomo. Through the glass he could hear the ceaseless roar of traffic. Quickly he rummaged for his palm pilot in his trouser pocket, and checked his appointments for the next few days. He had some rearranging to do if he was to be in Paris on Tuesday.

He'd do a lot more than cancel a meeting or two to understand why Clea was the way she was.

La Marguerite on Tuesday…it couldn't come quickly enough.

* * *

Paris was cold and wet, filled with bad-tempered Christmas shoppers and equally bad-tempered drivers. Rain slanted through the wide boulevards, pinging in the puddles, turning the roads into black mirrors and slowing the traffic to a crawl.

Gamely a tiered Christmas tree entirely made of lights glinted from the metal girders of the Eiffel Tower. The tree was topped with a brilliant star.

One moment Slade felt like that star, because Clea was opening her life to him. The next moment, though, he felt as cold as the sleety rain. She'd promised nothing other than an explanation. Explanations didn't necessarily entail change, or mean that she'd end the evening in his bed. And just who was the man she wanted him to meet?

Because Slade was impatient to see her, he was early at La Marguerite. Named for a flower, the restaurant surrounded an idyllic courtyard whose shrubs and trees sparkled with tiny white lights. Inside, cherrywood paneling and Fragonard-style murals were set off by gold chandeliers; thick carpeting muffled the sounds of conversation.

Slade was well acquainted with Gérard, the maître d', and was escorted to the table he was to share with Clea. Eight-thirty came and went; the restaurant started to fill up. Eight-thirty-five, eight-forty…had she changed her mind?

Then, with a tightening of his nerves, he saw her step into the entrance hall. The doorman took her long coat, and Gérard gave her a welcoming smile.

Not everyone who dared to be late at La Marguerite would be so generously welcomed.

As she was escorted to their table, Slade stood up. He was wearing his best Italian suit, a dark pinstripe, with the blue shirt and silk tie he'd worn at Belle's garden party.

But Clea wasn't looking at him; her gaze was skittering around the restaurant, checking out the occupants of every table, the look of strain on her face deepening. As Gérard pulled out her chair, Slade leaned forward and kissed her on both cheeks, making no attempt to hide how happy he was to see her.

Her dress was sea-green, long-sleeved, elaborately embroidered with silver thread; its neckline dipped low, a slender silver chain nestling between her breasts. Her hair was piled high on her head, stray tendrils caressing her cheeks.

He said huskily, "You take my breath away."

She blushed, taking her seat. "I look better than the last time you saw me."

She had yet to meet his eyes. He said matter-of-factly, "I gather the man we're to meet isn't here yet."

"No, not yet…I could have asked if he has a reservation for tonight, but Gérard's the epitome of discretion and probably wouldn't have told me…I'm sorry I'm so late, the plane was delayed and the traffic, as I'm sure you know, is horrendous."

She was speaking very fast, her fingers restlessly toying with the embossed menu. "It's called Christmas," Slade said dryly. "Why don't you decide what you want to eat, and then we'll talk?"

Quickly she chose truffle *feuilleté* followed by roast duck marinated in orange and coriander. Slade ordered a green salad served with chèvre, and *croustillant* of lamb; he picked a very dry red wine from the same château whose owner she had claimed to know. Clea was checking out the room again, noticing every arrival; her eyes were too bright, the color in her cheeks almost hectic.

Whoever the man was, he was foremost in Clea's thoughts. Slade sure wasn't.

Slade didn't care for this at all. He began describing a important contract he'd landed in Hamburg, her uneasiness transferring itself to him. What if tonight he found out something he really couldn't accept? What then?

Would he still take her to bed?

Their entrée plates were removed. Clea was drinking sparingly, and eating less. "If you don't eat your dinner," Slade said, "Gérard will be insulted."

She looked at him as though she wasn't sure who he was. He added brusquely, "Whoever this guy is, I sure hate the effect he has on you."

"Not half as much as I do," she muttered. "I'm sorry, Slade. I seem to be doing nothing but apologizing to you—how very tedious of me." She gave the waiter a bright, insincere smile as he put the roast duck in front of her. "That looks delicious," she said and stared down at it with something like loathing on her face.

The waiter put Slade's plate down with a flourish, topped up their wine glasses and disappeared. Clea picked up her fork, then suddenly dropped it with a clatter. A brown-haired man with a curvaceous blonde on his arm was approaching their table. Awkwardly Clea got to her feet, her serviette falling to the floor. In a voice Slade scarcely recognized, she faltered, "Papa?"

Papa, Slade thought, stunned. The mystery man was her father. His assumption that her parents were no longer living had been just that: an assumption. Clea had never actually told him they were dead.

He, too, stood up. But he might not have existed for all the attention Clea and her father were paying him. The man said in a voice as chilly as champagne, "Clea...well, what a surprise."

"I know you often eat here on Tuesdays," she said raggedly. "I thought I might see you."

"So this isn't a coincidence."

Trying to subdue a flood of rage that anyone, let alone her father, should speak to Clea with such brutal lack of feeling,

Slade said clearly, *"Bonsoir, M'sieur Chardin.* My name's Slade Carruthers."

"Raoul Chardin," the other man said with minimal politeness; he made no attempt to introduce the woman clinging to his arm, whose violet eyes were avariciously taking in every detail of Clea's appearance.

"Papa, can the four of us meet after dinner for a drink?" Clea asked. "It's been a long time since you and I have had the chance to talk."

"That wouldn't be convenient, no." He tugged at the blonde's fingers, which sparkled with an assortment of rings that could only be called garish. "Our table is ready, *chérie.* Come along.*"*

The blonde said chirpily, "I'm Sylvie Tournier. I hadn't realized Raoul had a daughter...you must be younger than you look, Clea."

Clea gave her a blank look. "I'm twenty-six," she said. Then she turned back to her father. "How about tomorrow, Papa—I'm not leaving Paris until midafternoon. Could we meet for a coffee in the morning?"

She was openly begging. Clea, in Slade's experience of her, wasn't a woman to beg.

"I'm going back to the château in the morning," Raoul said curtly. "The vineyard doesn't run itself, you of all people should know that. Certainly you benefited from it financially for far too long."

"I haven't taken a penny of your money for years."

"Unlike your mother."

Clea flinched. "I'll call you the next time I come to Paris," she said. "Or I could visit you at the château."

"Perhaps. Sylvie, we're keeping Gérard waiting."

Sylvie gave Slade a look that was unquestionably a come-on. "I've heard about you," she said prettily. "I'm delighted to have made your acquaintance."

"Mam'selle Tournier, M'sieur Chardin," Slade said with cool formality and walked around the table to help Clea into her seat. Briefly he rested his hands on her shoulders, his fingers warm on her skin. Then he sat down himself.

He said crisply, "How could a man with ice-water in his veins have fathered a woman as passionate and full of life as you?"

She stabbed a piece of duck with her fork; tears were shimmering in her eyes. "I'm not passionate and full of life! I'm—to quote you—scared of my own shadow."

"That man's got as much feeling in him as a dead codfish. Has he ever given you the love a daughter should expect from her father?"

"No."

"But you keep hoping."

"Oh, yes—more fool me. Even when I'm begging him for five minutes of his precious time, I'm despising myself for asking." She took a sip of wine, her mouth twisted. "That's why I didn't ask him to meet us here tonight—he'd have refused. I had to leave it up to chance."

"Is your mother alive?" Clea nodded. "What's she like?" Her lashes flickered. "You don't want to know."

"Yes, I do," Slade said mildly.

"Raoul's more than enough for one evening."

"He dyes his hair," Slade said.

She gave a choked laugh. "He has for years. That's one reason he doesn't want anything to do with me—Sylvie's younger than I am. The older he gets, the younger his mistresses."

"Sylvie will drop him in a flash when a bigger bank balance walks in the door."

Feeling minimally more cheerful, Clea said, "She'd drop him for you."

Slade shuddered. "I prefer redheads...did you live with your father until you were old enough to leave home?"

"No. He left first. When I was seven. The money he mentioned—that's how he discharged his parental duties. He stopped paying anything as soon as I turned sixteen."

"He doesn't love anyone but himself, Clea," Slade said gently.

Another tear gathered on her lashes. "I don't want to believe you. Which is really silly of me, I know."

"He withheld what you most needed from him...with the result that you're continually searching for it." Manfully Slade erased any anger from his voice. "Is he the reason you don't believe in commitment?"

Clea winced, the full import of her behavior washing over her. She'd meant this meeting with Raoul to be businesslike, cut and dried, with everything on the surface. Slade would meet her father, she'd describe some of Raoul's many mistresses and her own inability to commit would be tidily explained. Instead, her strategy had backfired: she'd humiliated herself in front of Slade by begging for her father's attention like a starving puppy. How could she have been so stupid?

"I can't tell you how many mistresses my father's had. I've lost count," she said in a brittle voice. "I have one of the wedding photos when he married my mother...they're gazing into each other's eyes in adoration. But by the time I was seven, they hated each other's guts. That's what marriage does, Slade. It changes people. Turns love to hatred."

"My mother and father still adore each other."

"Then they're the exception that proves the rule." She pushed an exquisitely glazed piece of meat around her plate. "I couldn't bear to have you speak to me the way my father does—that's why I'll never risk intimacy. Ever. And isn't that what commitment implies? Intimacy?"

It never had for him. Yet the scene Slade had just witnessed, which had roused in him a fury that went far beyond the casual, had unquestionably been intimate.

"Well," he said, leaning back in his chair, "at least I'm starting to understand where you're coming from."

"Five minutes in my father's company will do that."

"How about five seconds?" Slade smiled at her. An intimate smile, he realized, and wondered if he should be calling for help. "Try and eat something, Clea, you'll feel better if you do."

"When you look at me like that...I don't know how to handle it, Slade!"

"You don't have to handle anything. Eat up, we'll skip dessert and get the hell out of here—I don't even like being in the same room as your father."

"For once, we're in agreement," she said with a watery grin.

A few minutes later Slade signed the bill and slipped his credit card back in his wallet; he doubted that La Marguerite's admirable food had ever received so little attention. Getting to his feet, he pulled back Clea's chair. "Your father's hanging on to Sylvie's every word, not to mention her cleavage, and don't you dare look his way," he said in a conversational tone of voice. "In fact, why don't you gaze at me adoringly as though he's the last person on your mind? Sylvie will notice, even if he doesn't, and I'm sure she'll let him know."

Clea blinked. "That's deceitful."

He felt a bubble of laughter rise in his chest. "Try it—the adoring part—you might like it. You love me to distraction, darling Clea, and you can't wait to get me to your hotel room so you can strip the clothes from my back."

She was scowling at him. He added patiently, "Quit looking as though you want to strangle me. Rest your arm on my sleeve and kiss me—once will do. But be sure to keep upper-most in your mind a very wide bed with both of us in it. Stark naked."

"You're behaving extremely badly," Clea said, then reached up, her lips brushing his in a touch as delicate as gossamer.

Briefly he cupped her face in his palms and kissed her back. "Mmm," he said, "roast duck."

Her sputter of laughter was unforced. "The last of the ro-mantics, that's you."

"I want you, I desire you, I need you," Slade said, naked truth edging his voice. "We'd better get out of here before I make love to you on the carpet."

"Gérard would have a heart attack," Clea said faintly.

"I imagine he would." Slade put his arm firmly around her waist and steered her toward the door. There he buttoned up her elegant long coat with its fur-edged hood, taking his time, his eyes lingering on her flushed features. Then he put on his raincoat and took his big umbrella, and they stepped out into the night.

Had he really said he needed her?

CHAPTER EIGHT

STANDING under the canopied entrance, Clea said quietly, "Thank you, Slade. For getting me out of there without—one more time—begging for a sideways glance from my father. I couldn't have done it alone."

It was a huge admission. "My pleasure. Want to walk for a while?"

"I would, yes." She tucked her arm in his as he put up the umbrella and they set off into the rain; to leave the vicinity of La Marguerite filled her with relief. "I could have told you about Raoul in Florence, I suppose—but having you meet him was probably more effective."

"You should congratulate me for not putting my famous left hook into practice—believe me, I was tempted. Why did he leave your mother, Clea?"

She might as well expose the whole sordid picture. "At the time, I had no idea. Another woman, I expect...when my mother told me he was leaving, I waylaid him at the door, pleaded with him to stay. He looked at me like I was dirt under his feet and asked why he would stay with a whining brat who hadn't even had the decency to be a boy."

"I should have decked him tonight. Gérard or no Gérard."

"I always feel about five years old when I'm anywhere near

him," she burst out. "It's so humiliating—even now I'd give my entire inheritance to have him say he loves me."

Rain pattered on the roof of Slade's umbrella; cars swished by, throwing up small fountains of spray. Clea talked on, filling in the portrait of the self-absorbed man who was her father. She almost never mentioned her mother, Slade noticed, filing this fact away for future reference.

They were approaching one of the metro's art nouveau entrances, with its fan of green-lit glass and intricately scrolled ironwork. Clea said impulsively, "Let's take the metro to Champs-Elysées—the Christmas decorations are always so pretty there. They'll look lovely in the rain."

She tugged at his sleeve, pulling him forward, smiling up at him. Slade's heart sank. He'd have done almost anything to keep that smile on her face. But ahead of him loomed the steep stairs with their iron railings, the dark cavity leading deeper and deeper under the ground. "I can't," he said.

"What do you mean? I've got tickets—come along."

She looked as excited as the little girl she'd once been. He said flatly, "I never take the metro. Or the New York subway or the London tube. I get—claustrophobic."

Her smile faded. She drew him to one side, keeping her grip on his sleeve, her eyes trained on his face. "Claustrophobic? Why?"

After the courage she'd shown tonight, she deserved the truth. He only hoped she wouldn't laugh her head off because he, a grown man, was scared to go down a few steps into the black tunnels of the Paris metro. "When I was eleven, I was kidnapped and held for ransom," he said rapidly. "Plucked off the street near my school, drugged, and kept in the basement in a dark cupboard for two weeks. Ever since then, I can't abide enclosed underground spaces."

"How were you rescued?" she whispered.

"Police and the FBI. I was one of the lucky ones."

Her eyes widened. "The bar!" she exclaimed in horror. "The Genoese. It's underground. Oh, Slade, I'm so sorry."

"It was probably good for me," he said. "Isn't that what all the pop psychology books advise—confront your fears?"

"Don't joke about something that's not remotely funny," Clea said fiercely, her words tumbling over each other. "If I'd known, I would never have suggested the Genoese...I can't believe you stayed there for three whole nights. If only I'd showed up on the first one—but I was so determined to test you, to prove myself right."

His smile was crooked. "You tested me, all right."

She didn't smile back. "You hung in," she said, touched to the core. "You didn't know me, you must have wondered if I'd keep my promise to show up. And yet you stayed there for three nights."

"Don't make me into some kind of knight errant," Slade said uncomfortably.

"I'm not. But I'm starting to realize how strong a man you are. How determined. I feel—" she sought for the right word "—humbled. That you should go through all that just because you want me."

"There's no *just* about it."

Ignoring him, she said slowly, "Your courage...and your integrity. I haven't wanted to see you as you really are, because then I can't dismiss you as easily." Unconsciously her fingers tightened on his sleeve. "I don't understand why you want me so much—and no, I'm not fishing for compliments."

"I don't understand, either," he said roughly. "All I know is that you haunt me day and night, I can't sleep because you're not beside me, and I don't even want to look at another woman."

"Well," she said shakily, "that's plenty."

"But then there's the C word. Commitment."

"By now I thought you'd understand why that word drives me crazy! My father changes women as easily as he changes his tie. The men I go around with—their affairs are turned on and off like the kitchen tap, because there's always another beautiful woman around the corner."

Hit by a sudden insight, Slade said, "You don't trust me to abide by the terms I'm setting up. To be faithful to you."

"Why would I?" she flashed, knowing he'd unearthed one more layer to her resistance. "Nothing in my background or my present life leads me to believe men are trustworthy."

"If I can last three nights at the Genoese, I can handle commitment to you for as long as we're an item, Clea."

"An item," she said bitterly, "an affair—I even hate the language."

"An exploration," he heard himself say. "A voyage of discovery. Maybe we'll be lousy in bed together. Maybe you take all the covers."

"Or snore," she said with a sudden grin. "I bet you drop used towels all over the bathroom floor."

"And expect you to pick them up." His smile faded. "Clea, I desire you with every fiber of my being. As I believe you desire me. We'd be fools to pass that up because we're afraid of what might happen."

"You'll get what you want and then you'll leave," she said in a stony voice.

"I won't," he said, hearing the two little words echo in his head. "But I can't prove that until after we've made love."

"By which time it's too late."

Her shoulders were drooping, her face drained of its usual vivacity. Could he hope to defeat, even temporarily, the damage Raoul and his like had inflicted on her? "You're tired," Slade said.

She was; her father always had that effect on her. "I'd like to go back to my hotel."

"There's a taxi stand just down the street."

When they were seated, Clea quickly gave the name of her hotel. Then she leaned back, closing her eyes. Her profile flashed in and out against the streetlights, her hair seeming to weigh down her slender neck. Slade put his arm around her. Despite all the power and money at his command, and no matter how much he wanted to, he couldn't make Raoul Chardin give her what she craved.

Twenty minutes later they drew up outside an eighteenth century mansion south of the Seine, its tall black-painted doors flanked by boxwood in terra-cotta pots. "Clea," Slade said, squeezing her shoulder, "we're here."

She roused herself, rubbing her eyes. "Will you come in?" she asked.

He had no idea what she was thinking. "Sure," he said, and paid the driver.

She led him through a long tree-lined passageway into an open courtyard. "I love this hotel," she remarked, talking fast. "It's like the one in Copenhagen, small enough to be intimate. The gardens in summer are exquisite, and from here I can easily walk along the river, then across the bridge to Jardins des Tuileries."

Once again she was nervous, he thought, as they entered the charming lobby with its antique furnishings and air of quiet comfort. Without looking to see if he was following, Clea headed straight for the elevators, and within moments they were walking along the corridor to her suite. She ushered him inside, and made quite a business of hanging up their coats and spreading the umbrella wide so it would dry. She looked as brittle as a Dresden figurine, Slade thought in a rush of protectiveness. "I'm going to ask the obvious—why did you bring me up here?"

"I don't know," she said jerkily, striving to be as honest with him as she knew how. "Maybe I thought I could finally do it. Make the leap. Trust you enough to go to bed with you."

Heaven knew he wanted that. But just as strongly he was convinced tonight wasn't the night. "You're exhausted, your father upset you—"

"Do I look that bad?"

"You look like you'd shatter into a thousand pieces if I said *boo.*"

She kicked off her shoes, walked up to him with none of her usual grace and rested her forehead on his chest. "Hold on to me," she said in a muffled whisper.

He put his arms around her, drawing her close to his body, his cheek resting on her sweetly scented hair. Only gradually did he realize she was crying, slow tears soaking through his shirtfront. Knowing exactly what he was going to do, he picked her up and carried her through the sitting room with its rose-pink Aubusson carpet into the bedroom. The bed was a four-poster covered in ruffled white eyelet. Putting her down, he reached for the zipper on the back of her dress. "Where's your nightgown?" he said matter-of-factly.

"Under the pillow. Slade—"

"Hush," he said. "This is getting to be a habit, undressing you and then walking out the door. Talk about a test."

"You're not staying?"

Was he imagining that hint of relief in her voice? "No."

She reached for a tissue and blew her nose. "Yankee cussedness versus Parisian lust."

He passed her the silk gown, which was the color of café au lait, turning his back as she stood up to remove her dress and slip on the nightgown. "How about common sense coupled with admiration for your courage?" he said. "I like that version better."

"Courage? When I'm still afraid?"

"Yes. Courage."

"You mean you still want me?" she said in a low voice. "Now that you've met my father?"

He turned around; she was sitting on the bed. "Clea, I want you so badly I can taste it. Yeah, the Genoese was a test. But—trust me—for me to walk out of here tonight is almost more than I can bear."

Shivering, she muttered, "I wish you wouldn't say things like that."

"I say them because they're true." His smile was rueful. "They take me by surprise, too."

She blurted, "Once we go to bed, this crazy attraction between us will fizzle out."

"Do you honestly believe that?" Not waiting for a reply, Slade said forcefully, "When we make love, I'll enter every cell of your body. And you'll encompass every cell of mine. That's how it'll be—I know it, and, deep down, so do you."

Her eyes were downcast; her gown was clinging to her breasts, her skin pale ivory. And what a lot of skin, Slade thought, taking in the vulnerable slope of shoulder, the graceful curve of arm, her high-arched bare feet. To walk away from her was going to take more strength than he possessed.

He sat down beside her, took her face in his hands and kissed her mouth with slow sensuality, savoring her, letting all his pleasure show as he slid his fingers down her throat to her bare shoulders. Her surrender was instant, yet oddly gentle, like spring rain. His heart overflowing with an emotion new to him, one he wasn't sure he could name, Slade nibbled at her lips. "Fizzle out, did you say? Not a chance..."

Clea put her palms flat to his chest, pushing him away. "Every time you kiss me, I change," she cried. "I go up and down like the stock market. The way I behave, the things I say, the feelings I have when I'm with you—I never know what I'm going to do next."

"Life demands change of us," he said roughly. "And change is difficult."

"My father's never changed," she whispered.

"That's right. And likely never will. Is that what you want for *your* life?"

"You're so relentless," she said, the heat from his skin burning into her fingers. "Is that how you got to the top?"

He moved his shoulders restlessly, once again allowing the truth to spill out. "I'm not just fighting for me here—I'm fighting for you, too. If you turn your back on me, we both lose." He smoothed her forehead with his lips. "Do something for me—meet me at Kennedy Airport in New York City right after the New Year. I'll take you for the most fabulous lunch you've ever eaten, and that includes every Michelin-starred restaurant in France."

Her head reared back. "Your parents live in New York City."

"They do."

"Just because you've met my father doesn't mean I want to meet them."

"So far, you and I have gotten together in Monte Carlo, Copenhagen, Florence and Paris. Three of those cities were your choice. Now it's my turn."

"You make it sound so reasonable."

"That's me—reasonable."

She made a rude sound. "I'm out of my mind. Yes, I'll meet you in Manhattan."

Trying to mask a relief that scared him with its force, Slade said, "Once you've booked, let me know your flight time. I've got meetings after the fourth of January that I can't put off, but until then I'm free. And wear something warm—Trinidad to New York in winter is a shocker."

"A dress-up lunch?" she asked.

"Just as long as you turn up, I don't give a damn what you wear." He leaned forward and kissed her again. "Good night, Clea."

The question was out before she could censor it. "You're really going to leave?"

"Have you changed your mind about commitment?"

"Commitment's the very opposite of freedom."

Almost sure she sounded less convinced by that magical word *freedom,* Slade said tautly, "I stayed the course at the bar. I've rearranged my schedules and jetted all over Europe for you. I'm doing my level best right now not to use sex as a weapon. What the hell else do you want from me?"

"I don't know!"

"When you figure it out, we'll go to bed," he said in a hard voice. Getting up, he jammed his hands in his pockets. "Until then, I'm going to keep on walking away from you even though it half-kills me every time."

"Me, too."

The quiver in her voice went right through him. "God, Clea, the last thing I want to do is fight with you after the night you've had. Get into bed, pull the covers up to your chin so I can't see all that enticing flesh, and go to sleep."

In a flash of bare thighs she slipped under the puffy white duvet. "I'll see you in New York," she said.

"In the meantime, happy Christmas. Enjoy Trinidad."

Leaning over, he switched out the bedside lamp. The darkness giving her courage, Clea announced, "Until I met you, I was always the one calling the shots."

He laughed. "You know what? The same's true of me."

"We can't both call the shots."

"If we want the same thing, we can...good night, captivating Clea."

"*Bonsoir,* sexy Slade."

His eyes adjusting to the gloom, he strode toward the door of the suite. His whole body ached with frustration. He'd walk all the way to his hotel, which was across the Seine in the Opéra Quarter.

Perhaps it would take his mind off sex. Off the beautiful redhead alone in her hotel room, where he'd left her.

The woman who was changing his life.

It was the third day of the new year. The plane from Miami was half an hour late, and there were delays in customs. Gradually a slow trickle of travelers started coming through the frosted glass doors, their tans ranging from copper to scorched pink.

Then Clea walked into the arrivals area. She was wearing turquoise wool pants with a matching collarless long coat; an off-white turtleneck sweater hugged her throat. Slade waved his present at her to get her attention, and watched her smile, a dazzling smile that made his heart thud in his chest.

As she eased through the crowds toward him, he saw that she was wearing the earrings he'd given her, small gold birds with their wings outspread. Then she was standing in front of him. "Is that for me?" she asked.

He was carrying a six-foot-tall stuffed giraffe with a big red-and-green bow tied around its neck. "Merry late Christmas," he said, wrapped his arms around her and the giraffe, and kissed her with a pent-up passion that spoke volumes.

When she emerged, she looked thoroughly flustered. "You still want me," she said.

"That's one of the things I like about you—your grasp of the essentials." His smile felt as wide as the giraffe's neck was long. He held it out to her. "His name is George."

Her laugh was a joyful ripple. "What am I supposed to do with him?"

"Put him in your apartment," Slade said promptly, "and whenever you look at him, think of me."

"My apartment is furnished in minimalist style."

"I figured it was. He'll brighten the place up."

"One more step in your campaign?"

"Campaign? What campaign?"

She was gazing into the giraffe's face. "I wish I had eyelashes like his."

"Your eyelashes—along with the rest of you—are perfect, Clea," Slade said huskily, his eyes drinking in every detail of her features.

Clea gave a tiny shiver. How could she resist him, so ardent, so intense? Tucking the giraffe under her arm, she pulled Slade's head down and kissed him with an explicitness that spoke volumes. He said unsteadily, "I guess that means you still want me."

She compressed her lips. "I guess it does. A bit. Sometimes."

"Live dangerously—say yes."

"All right, yes. Yes, I do want you. In Trinidad I even found myself wishing you were with me. You'd have loved the beach, Slade, it was in a sheltered cove and every morning the frigate birds swam there, and once I saw a green turtle..."

While they waited for her luggage, she talked animatedly, Slade watching the play of expression on her face with its delicate tan. Would she ever capitulate and open her arms to him? And if so, would he ever have enough of her?

Outside, the ground was bare and the wind sharp. Clea hugged the giraffe to her, shivering for a different reason. "We should have met in the Bahamas."

His car was in the parking lot, a sleek Mercedes coupe.

Sinking into the leather seat, she said, "Mmm...nice. Where are we going for lunch?"

"Uptown," he said evasively. "Tell me about your friends in Trinidad."

The traffic was heavy, but by one o'clock he was driving along Madison Avenue. Turning onto a side street, he parked by the curb. "We're here," he said.

"I don't see any restaurants," Clea said, her brow furrowed with suspicion.

"We're having lunch with my parents. Smoked salmon fish cakes with rhubarb chutney."

"Dirty trick, Slade."

"All part of the campaign, Clea. I'm showing you the opposite side of the coin from your parents' marriage."

Her temper climbed another notch. "I wondered if you'd want me to meet your parents while I was here. But I never thought you'd take me there for lunch without checking with me first."

"I didn't check because I knew you'd say no."

"I can still say no."

"But you won't. Admit it, you're curious to meet them. To see if they're real, this saintly couple who are still in love after nearly forty years."

"See the sights of New York—the Empire State Building, the Faithful Couple," she said crazily.

"You'll like them—I swear you will."

"You take far too much for granted!"

"Not you, Clea," he said hoarsely. "Never you." And bit his tongue in exasperation. Why did he persist in mouthing feelings he hadn't previously known?

She let out her breath in a small sigh. "Can I take the giraffe in with me?"

"You want to embarrass me in front of my parents?"

"It would give me considerable satisfaction to do so."

They got out, Clea clutching the giraffe to her chest as Slade locked the car. The elevator carried them smoothly to the top floor. Slade said nothing the whole way up. When they arrived, Clea planted her feet in the wide hallway. "You're nervous," she said in sudden discovery.

"Yeah."

"I talk too much when I'm nervous, and you clam up."

"That's because I'm from New England."

"Let's hope your parents aren't nervous, too. Or it'll be a very quiet lunch." Frowning, she added, "Just what have you told them about me?"

"That I met you at Belle's. That they'll like you…that's about it."

Her frown deepened. "Why do I get the impression you're omitting something?"

"You're too clever by half."

"Come clean."

"You're the first woman I've ever brought here," he admitted. "For lunch, dinner or breakfast. I know that and so, of course, do they."

Dismayed, Clea said, "They probably think we're in love. Planning to get married."

"Then they'd be wrong on both counts, wouldn't they?"

"You're darn right." She tossed her head, hiding a sudden and unexpected shaft of pain that Slade, despite wanting her so badly, wasn't even remotely in love with her.

Not that she wanted him to be in love with her.

He said abruptly, "Why are you wearing the earrings I gave you?"

"So you won't forget I need my freedom."

Inwardly he winced; hadn't he hoped she'd been wearing them for sentimental reasons? "You tell it like it is, don't you?" he said, unable to erase the edge in his voice. "Shall I ring the bell?"

"Do," she said sweetly. "The housekeeper we had when I was six did her best to instill good manners into me—I promise I'll behave."

The housekeeper, he thought. Not her father or her mother. Reaching around her, Slade rang the doorbell.

CHAPTER NINE

SLADE'S father swung the door open. "Slade—and you must be Clea. Do come in."

David Carruthers was nearly as tall as his son, his build athletic, his hair a distinguished gray. His blue eyes were full of life. He introduced himself to Clea, giving her the full benefit of his smile.

Clea said the first thing that came to mind. "You look astonishingly like your son."

David laughed. "Twenty-five years older—a minor detail. Uh...that's a fine giraffe."

"His name is George," Clea said limpidly, setting the giraffe down in the corner. "My Christmas gift from Slade."

"Anyone can buy sweaters and jewelry," Slade said with a lazy grin. "Hello, Mum."

"Slade, darling," Bethanne said, kissing him on the cheek with unaffected love, her patrician features flushed with pleasure. Then she turned to Clea. "Welcome, Clea," she said, wiping her hands on her ruffled apron before shaking hands with Clea. "I'm so glad you could join us today."

Although her words were conventional, the warmth behind them was genuine, Clea sensed that immediately. David said easily, "Here, let me take your coat...Slade said you've just flown in from Trinidad."

The talk gathered momentum as they walked into the spacious living room, with its panoramic view of the bare-limbed trees of Central Park. Bethanne's eye for color was everywhere evident, from the glowing hues of the Persian rug to the rich red cushions on the navy-blue chesterfield. Impressionistic art adorned the walls; a small jungle of tropical plants was grouped near the windows.

David offered Clea a drink; Bethanne brought out broiled shrimp and a dip; and Slade sat down with his back to the light, where he could watch Clea. This room was as familiar to him as the office downtown where he spent so much of his time; to have Clea sitting in it was disconcerting.

Her fiery red hair clashed with the cushions.

"An incredible martini," she said to David. "And, Bethanne, the shrimp are luscious."

"David can also make plants flourish indoors and out; and steer a kayak down a raging torrent, emerging right way up at the other end," Bethanne teased. "Rivers with big waves on them make me run for cover—but I love to garden. You've seen Belle Hayward's garden, Clea…it's lovely, isn't it? She's an old friend of ours."

Clea smiled her assent, and segued to some of the famous gardens she'd visited in Europe. The conversation moved from topic to topic, Clea neatly fielding any questions that approached her private life.

As they got up to move into the dining room, Slade said curiously, "The painting in the corner—it's new, isn't it?"

"David gave it to me for our anniversary," Bethanne said, giving her husband an unselfconscious hug. "I adore it. Just look how the sun falls on the water…"

"Thirty-nine years," David said, smiling into his wife's blue eyes. "And each one better than the last."

Clea's mouth tightened, her eyes suddenly liquid with pain.

Her lashes dropped; absently, she brushed her fingertips over the glossy leaves of a fig tree. Then, as if she felt Slade's gaze on her, she looked right at him. The pain had vanished from her eyes as if it had never been. He said hastily, "Good choice, Dad. Did I tell you I'm bidding on a small Ghiberti bronze? Early fifteenth century."

"For the Florence house?" Bethanne asked. "Have you been there, Clea?"

Heat rose in Clea's cheeks. "Oh—er, yes, I have."

"Just once," Slade said.

"You must get him to cook for you there," Bethanne went on, starting to ladle out a thick leek soup. "His kitchen is a dream."

"He made soup for me," Clea said. And looked after me, she thought, the memory bittersweet.

"I taught Slade the difference between basil and oregano at a very early age," Bethanne remarked. "I was determined not to bring up a son who thinks the kitchen is solely for women."

"Not a hope, Mum," Slade said.

He passed freshly baked cheese sticks and talked at some length about his latest project near Hamburg; Bethanne brought in smoked salmon fish cakes with rhubarb chutney. Clea said, "You're famous for these, so Slade told me. In Trinidad we ate fish cakes made from shark..."

She began describing some of the meals they'd had in the beach house over Christmas. It was, Slade thought, a rather unsubtle message that she had many friends, and had chosen not to spend Christmas with David and Bethanne's son. He replenished everyone's wine, and changed the subject to the hurricanes that had lashed Florida last September.

When they were finished with the fish cakes, which had indeed been delicious, Bethanne and David got up to clear the table for dessert. As they carried plates into the kitchen, Clea also got up, taking the dish of chutney and the basket of cheese sticks from the table. Slade followed with the side plates. In the kitchen, Bethanne was rinsing the plates under the tap, David standing very close to her, his arm around her waist, his lips nuzzling her ear.

Clea stopped dead in her tracks. Slade cleared his throat. "Okay, you two, break it up."

Bethanne gave a little start. "Oh, I didn't mean for you to help," she said, flustered. "David, stop!"

Her husband patted her on the bottom. "Whatever you say, sweetheart. Should I whip the cream?"

"That would be a good idea," Bethanne said firmly, and took the plates from Slade. "The chutney goes back in that jar, Clea, and the cheese sticks in the bag on the counter."

Dessert was a compote of fruit laced with Grand Marnier and slathered with cream. David tucked in, winking at his son. "Back to skim milk tomorrow," he said.

Clea launched determinedly into a discussion of the latest fads in diets. Coffee was produced and drunk. Bethanne took Clea on a tour of the penthouse; David discussed plans for repairs to the Maine house. And then, finally, it was time to leave.

Clea thanked his parents with a pleasure Slade would have sworn was unfeigned. "I hope we see you again soon," Bethanne said, kissing Clea lightly on both cheeks.

"That would be delightful," David added. "Talk to you in a couple of days, Slade, when I've got the estimate for the roof."

"Great, Dad...thanks, Mum."

"Love you," Bethanne said, as she always did when they parted, whether for ten minutes or two months.

Clea picked up George the giraffe, and she and Slade went downstairs in the elevator. She tossed the giraffe in the back of the car before getting in the passenger seat. As Slade slammed his door, she said with icy politeness, "Shall we fight now or later?"

Her eyes were the blue of a glacier. "Now," Slade said, and went on the attack. "My parents are real people, Clea. They haven't always had it easy. Their families never got along...the kidnapping was a terrible time for them...they always wanted more children but Mum had a series of miscarriages instead. And, I'm sure, they've had the usual difficulties of any long-term marriage. But they love each other deeply, and that's carried them through—it's called commitment."

"The perfect antidote for my father."

"Okay, so bringing you here for lunch wasn't overly subtle of me. But I'm not going to hide my parents just because they happen to be in love."

"They can't keep their hands off each other," she cried. "They were necking—at their age—in the kitchen."

"They do it all the time. I look the other way...I don't want to know about my parents' sex life, thank you very much. But what's their age got to do with it? Don't you think you could be the same?"

"No, I don't!"

"I can only think of one way to prove you wrong," he said incautiously.

"And what's that?"

"For you and me to live together for thirty-nine years and then have this argument again."

His words hung in the air. What had possessed him to say them? He'd never wanted to live with anyone, for one year or thirty-nine. And now he was suggesting living with Clea? Obstinate and argumentative Clea?

Desirable, fiery, beautiful Clea...

She glared at him. "Stop treating me like a big joke!"

"That's not my intention. All I did today was introduce you to two people who've loved each other through thick and thin. To show you it can be done with grace and courage, and that the end result is happiness."

As had so often happened, Slade had sliced the ground from under her feet. "Okay, so I've never met anyone like them before. And I get your point—people can stay married and be happy. Or at least, your parents have been able to do so." And how it had hurt, she thought, to see such deep, unaffected and enduring love.

With fierce intensity she went on, "I don't know how to do what they've done. I never learned. I had no models. So marriage is the last thing I'd ever embark on." She took a short, sharp breath. "I hardly dare ask what's the next step in your campaign."

"Get you into bed," he said promptly. "Without that stupid giraffe watching our every move."

"Then we'll live together for thirty-nine years? Very funny," she said tightly. "The next step in the campaign is mine—do you have plans for tomorrow?"

"Nope. I leave for Oslo the day after."

She snapped open her purse, took out a small pad and pen and her cell phone, and punched in some numbers. Then she spoke in very rapid Italian, waited a couple of minutes for a reply and jotted down some numbers on the pad. *"Grazie... arrivederci."*

She passed the pad to Slade. "That was my travel agent. You and I are flying to Kentucky tomorrow morning. Lexington."

"To meet your mother," he said intuitively.

"Precisely. You might as well know the whole sorry story—and no, I'm not going to talk about her. You'll meet her soon enough."

"Let's go for a walk," Slade said abruptly. "Too much to eat and too much emotion in the last couple of hours."

"I have an appointment at a bank downtown."

"Then we'll meet after that."

She said, her heart racing in her breast, "I can't. I'm having dinner with a friend."

His gut clenched. "Male or female?"

"He looks after a portion of my portfolio. I've known him for years."

So angry he could scarcely talk, Slade grated, "Do I mean anything at all to you, Clea? Or am I as disposable as all your other men?"

"I don't know what you mean to me, that's the whole problem." It was absurd of her to feel guilty. So why did she? "This was a good opportunity to see Tom, that's all," she said. "I'll take a cab to my appointment."

"You do that. Have fun explaining the giraffe at the bank."

"Having lots of money means you don't have to explain," she retorted, her cheeks bright pink.

Moments later she was marching away from him toward Madison Avenue to hail a cab, the giraffe's long legs sticking out behind her, the smaller of her two suitcases in her other hand. Slade banged his fist on the steering wheel. Right now she was calling the shots, and how he hated it.

Tomorrow he was going to meet her mother.

The Darthley Stud Farm was nestled in Kentucky bluegrass country, near Lexington. Classic, Slade thought, as he and Clea drove along a winding paved road between white-painted rail fences, the branches of massive oak and beech trees black against a gray sky. Mares and foals were clustered around loose piles of hay near an immaculately maintained barn. Every one of the horses looked healthy and exceedingly well-bred.

He'd been disinclined to make small talk ever since he'd met Clea at the airport. He flat-out refused to inquire if she'd enjoyed her dinner; nor was he going to ask if the man who managed her portfolio was thirty-five or sixty-five.

Let her do the talking.

But Clea, the closer they got to the stud farm, became equally quiet. As they drew up outside a magnificent brick mansion wreathed in wisteria, she finally broke the silence. "I called my mother this morning. She's expecting us. The name she goes by is Lucie DesRoches, even though she was born Amy Payton in Pittsburgh, Pennsylvania. Byron Darthley, who owns all this, is her eighth husband."

Then she got out of the car. This morning she was wearing a severely cut pair of dark gray wool trousers with a moss-green cashmere blazer and a white silk blouse; small gold hoops hung at her lobes. Her hair was ruthlessly tugged into a knot on the back of her head, although Slade was heartened to see several stray strands curling on her nape.

Eighth husband, he thought. No thirty-ninth wedding anniversaries for Lucie DesRoches.

Clea pushed hard on the doorbell. It was opened by the butler, his face as sour as last month's milk; he led them into an overdecorated and completely soulless living room and left them there. She paced up and down, picking up an ornament, putting it down, checking her hair in the mirror, twitching at the hem of her blazer, and wishing she were anywhere else but here.

"Clea…what a nice surprise."

The first thing Slade noticed was that Lucie DesRoches was an outstandingly beautiful woman; the second, that it was taking considerable effort to maintain that beauty. Her russet hair was expensively dyed, her makeup a work of art and her clothes, rather too fussy for a morning in the country, reeked of money.

"Hello, Mother," Clea said, and took a step toward Lucie,

her hands tentatively outstretched. Casually Lucie retreated behind a spindly antique table; Clea dropped her hands to her sides, schooling her face to a protective mask.

So that's the story, Slade thought, unsurprised, and said calmly, "How do you do, Mrs. DesRoches...I'm Slade Carruthers, a friend of Clea's."

Lucie transferred her emerald-green eyes to Slade. Contacts, he thought unkindly, and smiled down at her.

"Why, Clea, honey," she drawled, "you got yourself a real prize here. How do you do, Mr. Carruthers—or may I call you Slade? And please call me Lucie, we don't stand much on ceremony in these parts."

She put her palm in his, squeezing his hand just a touch too meaningfully. "I'm pleased to meet you, Lucie," he said. "You have a lovely place here."

Discontent dragged at the corners of her mouth. "Nice of you to say so. I wanted Byron to refurbish the entire downstairs, but he insisted on buying another stallion instead. Four million dollars for one horse when the country club down the road has better drapes than I do."

"Where is Byron?" Clea asked.

"In the barn. Where else would you find him?"

"The horses are in great shape," Slade interjected.

"So's the new stablehand," Lucie said waspishly. "A girl. In her early twenties."

"Mother..."

"Don't you *Mother* me, Clea! Byron's always had wandering eyes, and now the rest of him's in on the act. What he doesn't understand is that I'm keeping tabs on him and passing it all on to my lawyer."

"Not another lawyer," Clea said, her heart sinking. "You were madly in love with Byron a couple of years ago."

Lucie's eyes filled with decorative tears. "It's a terrible

thing when a man turns his back on his vows, Slade—wouldn't you agree?"

"Yes," he said, "it is."

"Have you ever been married?" He shook his head. "You planning on marrying my Clea?" Her voice quavered. "I had her when I was almost a child."

He said evasively, "I see where she gets her beauty."

"Why, thank you," Lucie simpered. "Clea, why don't you get Byron? I told him we'd have sherry in the drawing room. But I guess he's got other things on his mind, like that little bitch in the stables—he doesn't pay much attention to me anymore."

"Certainly, Mother," Clea said and fled the room as though sixteen stallions were about to trample her.

Lucie poured a glass of sherry from a Baccarat decanter and passed it to Slade. Then she put her hand on his sleeve, directing the full force of her emerald eyes at him. Deliberately she moved closer, until her breast brushed his arm. He fought the impulse to run out of the room after Clea, and stepped back.

Lucie's fingers tightened until he could feel the bands of her rings digging into his flesh. "Clea's way too young for you, honey," she breathed. "You look like a man who'd appreciate a mature woman. Someone ripe and understanding…"

"It's Clea I want," Slade said loudly. "Unfortunately commitment is a dirty word to her."

Venom thinned Lucie's mouth. "The difference between Clea and me is that she doesn't have the decency to marry her men. She uses them and tosses them aside like they're no more than an outfit she's bought."

From the corner of his eye Slade saw a tiny movement near the door. Clea was standing there, and must have heard every word. He said curtly, "I don't believe that to be true of her."

"Then for all your handsome face, you're a fool," Lucie snapped. "Clea, sugar, is Byron coming?"

Clea stepped inside, wishing she could erase from her mind the sight of the buxom brunette locked in her stepfather's embrace against the paddock fence. "He says he can't spare the time."

"Did you meet darling little Kimberley?"

"Why don't we have a drink?" Clea said. "We don't need Byron."

"So you did meet her." Lucie snapped the stopper from the decanter again and sloshed amber sherry into two more of the long-stemmed glasses; for a moment, Slade was convinced that the emotion that had flickered across Lucie's perfect features was nothing short of terror. He passed Clea a glass, took a healthy gulp of an excellent Spanish dry sherry, and determinedly steered the conversation into safer channels. Half an hour later, he and Clea took their leave.

Quickly Clea brushed her lips to Lucie's cheek. "Take care of yourself, Mother."

"Don't talk to me as if I was in my dotage," Lucie snapped. Switching on a smile, she added, "A pleasure to have met you, Slade. You remember what I said."

"Goodbye, Lucie," he said, and hoped the note of finality in his voice was as obvious to her and Clea as it was to him.

The big door swung shut behind them. Clea marched to their car and Slade slid behind the wheel. As they drove past the first bend in the road, Clea said bitterly, "She put the move on you, didn't she? My own mother!"

"Yeah," he said. "But you must have heard what I said."

"I'm so ashamed of her," Clea muttered. "She cheapens everything."

"She didn't cheapen either me or you, Clea. No one can do that to us."

"She doesn't know the meaning of love. Or vow. Or fidelity. Would you like me to tell you what it was like growing up with my mother and her succession of men?"

"Go ahead," Slade said evenly.

"The man I call my father—because who knows if he really is?—was number two. I don't remember number one, she met him at a debutante ball and the marriage lasted exactly six months. I was an accident, by the way, so she told me as soon as I was old enough to understand. She never wanted me. After all, I'd ruined her figure."

Slade pulled over to the side of the road and turned off the ignition. "Who was number three and how long did he last?"

"A Spanish bullfighter. A year and a half, when it became as obvious to Lucie as to everyone else that he loved the Plaza de Toros a lot more than he loved my mother. Number four was an Austrian businessman, who tried to take the wildness out of me by a combination of discipline and terror tactics."

"For God's sake, Clea…"

"I hated him. But then she married Pete. He was a sailor, he owned a racing yacht that was the most beautiful boat I've ever seen. We lived in a cedar house by the ocean in British Columbia, and I had the run of the woods and the shore, and for two whole years I was happy…" Her face clouded. "Mum had already started divorce proceedings—living in the woods wasn't her scene—when he drowned in a freak accident."

Slade sat very still. "How old were you?"

"Thirteen. I was shipped off to boarding school in Switzerland and Mother took up with an Italian art collector. I graduated at seventeen, inherited enough of my grandfather's trust at eighteen to set up my own apartment in Milan, and the rest is history…oh, yes, there was a Swiss banker after the art collector and before Byron—have I missed anyone?"

"I can understand why you're bitter, Clea—it's a wonder to me you didn't plunge knee-deep into booze and drugs."

"I tried getting really drunk just once when I was young. But it made me so sick I decided it wasn't for me. And I've never done drugs. I like being in control too much, I guess."

"For once, I'm all for you being in control." He took her hands in his, gently rubbing her slender, ringless fingers. "Your mother's running scared, Clea—she knows she's getting older, that she can't keep up this kind of lifestyle. Yet she's got nothing to replace it with."

"Byron's a sleaze, I thought that the first time I met him. But he has tons of money."

Slade asked something that subconsciously had been bothering him for a while. "Why did your grandfather leave his money to you, and not to your mother?"

"He was a straitlaced old tyrant who didn't condone divorce. My mother inherited my grandmother's fortune instead—peanut butter and mustard pickles. One more reason Mother changed her name from Payton to DesRoches."

"One more reason she resents you?" Clea nodded. "You said your father vanished from the scene when you were seven."

"Mother sent me to stay with him the first summer after the divorce, so she'd have a clear field—or should I say arena?—for the bullfighter. Raoul was furious. He left me in the care of his horrendous old housekeeper, who threatened me with dungeons and rats. I ran away and refused to stay with him ever again."

Despite her best intentions, she was trembling. But when Slade put his arm around her shoulder, she pulled away. "Let's go back to the airport," she said in a dull voice. "I hate being within ten miles of my mother."

To remove her from the vicinity of the Darthley Stud Farm seemed an eminently sensible idea to Slade, and she'd given him plenty to think about. Besides, it would give her time to collect herself.

She'd had a lot of practice doing that, he thought, his heart aching for the little red-haired girl who'd been dragged from country to country and stepfather to stepfather; only once had she been given anything other than indifference and outright hostility.

No wonder she was wary of commitment; finally he understood the source and depth of her antipathy.

He drove on through the rolling countryside. They'd spend the night in his apartment in Manhattan, he decided. He'd rustle up something for supper, and do his level best to banish the stricken look from Clea's eyes.

However, just before they reached the airport, his cell phone rang. He flipped it open. "Carruthers," he said. Then his voice sharpened. "Backing out? *Why?*"

Clea glanced over at him. His jaw was a hard line, his fingers clenched around the phone. The ruthless businessman, she thought with an inward shiver; plainly she herself had vanished from his mind.

The conversation lasted a couple more minutes, then Slade said, "You've organized a jet for Lexington? I'll leave right away. Thanks, Bill."

He folded the cell phone and thrust it in his pocket. "That was my assistant. I'll have to fly straight to Oslo. There's been a major screwup and four months' work could go down the drain." He moved his shoulders restlessly. "I'm sorry, Clea— more sorry than I can say—to leave you now, so soon after seeing your mother."

The feeling uppermost in Clea's body was relief. She could be alone, she thought. She could regroup, figure out what she was going to do about the man sitting so close to her in the car. The man who knew more about her than anyone else in the world. She said evenly, "It's okay, I understand how important your work is to you."

His work was important to him. All-important. So why did he feel torn in two at the prospect of leaving her? "Where will you go?" he demanded.

"Oh, back to Europe, I expect," she said vaguely. "Skiing, maybe. The powder's great in the Alps at this time of year."

"Europe and the Alps cover a lot of territory," Slade rapped. "Can you be a bit more specific?"

"St. Moritz, or possibly Chamonix."

He pulled up in the rental area and turned off the ignition. "Let Bill know what you decide. He keeps track of the various phone numbers where I can be reached."

As she made a noncommittal noise, he added impatiently, "Do it, Clea. We're past the stage of playing cat and mouse, for God's sake."

"All right, I will," she said, over an immense lethargy. Her mother's coldness, Byron's infidelity...which was worse? David and Bethanne, with their happy marriage, seemed a million miles away. "Where do you go to find your jet?"

"It should be out on the tarmac. I'll have to go through customs."

Slade got out of the car. For the first time in his life, he found himself resenting the demands of his own corporation. He didn't want to fly to Oslo. He wanted to be with Clea. It was that simple, and that complicated. "Come in with me, while I find out what the score is," he said.

Ten minutes later, he was ready to go through customs. Standing by the door, Slade took Clea in his arms, rubbing her taut shoulders; her mask, the mask he hated, was very much in place. But he had to go to Oslo. He had to. He said, sounding brusque and efficient rather than concerned, "Look after yourself, won't you? I'll be in touch in a couple of days."

Her smile was stiff, barely reaching her eyes; stabbed by a deep unease, he said without finesse, "Years ago, when you were too young to know the difference, Raoul and Lucie put you in a cage. But now you know where the key is."

"You're the key," she said tonelessly, "that's what you mean, isn't it?"

He nodded. "Have any of your other men met your parents?"

"Of course not."

"I rest my case," Slade said. "And now, much as I don't want to, I've got to go." He bent his head, kissing her with all the confusion of emotion she aroused in him just by existing, feeling her resistance. Against her lips, her delectably soft lips, he said roughly, "That day in Belle's garden, it was as though something in me recognized you. Desire calling to desire…a force of nature."

His kiss and his words seared through Clea's flesh, all the way to her soul. Panic-stricken, she mumbled, "I hope you'll be able to straighten things out in Oslo."

The challenge wasn't Oslo, Slade thought. The challenge was Clea, so desirable and so elusive. He pulled her the length of his body, holding her with all his strength, then releasing her with a reluctance that shuddered through his frame. Turning on his heel, he strode into the customs area. The doors closed behind him.

Was he man enough to meet that challenge?

CHAPTER TEN

FOUR days after leaving Clea in the airport at Lexington, Slade was stepping out of the shower in his hotel suite in Oslo. It was a marble shower with multiple jets. The water had pummeled some of the exhaustion from his muscles; anticipation would do the rest.

He'd worked day and night, calling on all his formidable skills of negotiation and his iron will, and he'd won. One more chain of environmentally sound paper mills in the world.

He liked winning, he thought, scrubbing himself with the luxuriously thick towel. But now it was time to switch gears, to call on other skills which weren't nearly as well honed. It was time to meet Clea, and win her.

He'd find out where she was from Bill. Some alpine skiing would suit him just fine.

Clea in his bed would suit him better. Despite his single-minded focus the last four days, she'd never been far from his thoughts, and as always had tormented his sleep.

From Manhattan, Bill relayed the information that two days ago Clea hadn't been sure if she'd stay in St. Moritz or head for Chamonix; she hadn't been in touch since then.

His jaw set, the towel cinched around his waist, Slade made half a dozen quick phone calls, ascertaining that Clea had been staying in a chalet in Chamonix the last couple of nights.

She hadn't bothered letting him know where she was.

Anger bit through anticipation. He was through playing games. He was going to Chamonix and he was going to bed Clea. In bed, with her naked beside him, he'd bring her face-to-face with the woman she was meant to be—passionate and passionately generous—trusting the consequences to luck and his own skills of persuasion.

If he could enforce his will on a boardroom of obdurate businessmen, he could surely handle one red-haired woman.

Slade arrived in the French town of Chamonix well after midnight. Early the next morning, he stationed himself near the base of the cable car, enjoying what must be one of the most spectacular views in Europe as he waited for Clea to appear.

In front of him Mont Blanc pierced a sky that was a dazzling blue. Snow, rock, the dark green of fir trees, the serried peaks of Les Grands Montets: no claustrophobia here, he thought. Not even a whiff of it.

He was in ski gear, goggles looped around his neck. He could have walked to the small private chalet where Clea was staying; but from his contact in Chamonix he'd discovered that she'd skied early the last two mornings, either alone or with a guide, so he'd decided to wait for her outdoors.

He was going skiing with her, whether she wanted him to or not. It was all part of his campaign.

And then he saw her, walking toward him in a slim-fitting yellow suit, her hair pulled back, dark glasses perched on her nose. She was carrying skis and poles over one shoulder. She could have been wrapped in a tarp, he thought, and he'd still have known her; his heart was thumping in his chest as though he'd just run the moguls half a mile from here.

A man in blue racing gear came out of a building advertising instructors and guides. Hailing her, he kissed her on both cheeks with a familiarity that made Slade's hackles rise. After they'd talked for several minutes, the man went back inside, the sun slanting across his thatch of blond hair. Clea kept walking, the smile still on her face.

Slade stepped onto the road. "Good morning, Clea."

She stopped as if she'd been shot, as if the breath had been slammed from her body. Very slowly, she reached up and took off her dark glasses. "Slade," she said. "Your assistant didn't think you'd be leaving Oslo until tomorrow."

It was information that had been true enough at the time. "I wrapped everything up last night," Slade said.

She needed time to catch her breath. "Successfully, I hope?"

"Very. Were you planning to let me know where you were?"

"Later on today." As he raised one brow derisively, she snapped, "It's true. Not that I needed to bother—you found me anyway." Why was she behaving like a shrew, she thought despairingly, when the sight of him had filled her with a wild torrent of joy?

Why was he making no move to kiss her?

"Where are you skiing this morning?" he demanded.

"Off-piste," she said briefly. "To get away from the crowds."

"Suits me fine."

Her voice was sharp as the ridges on the mountain. "So you're skiing with me?"

"That's the plan."

"You don't look overjoyed at the prospect."

"Looks can be deceiving." He reached out, tracing the line of her cheekbone with one finger. "You haven't been sleeping well. Why not, Clea?"

"The latest downturn in the stock market?" she retorted,

yanking her head away from his touch. "So *are* you overjoyed to see me, Slade?"

His laugh was devoid of amusement. "I never know what I'm feeling when I'm anywhere near you. Although it sure isn't indifference."

"Is that supposed to be a compliment?"

"Whatever you feel for me, Clea, it isn't indifference either," he said softly. "Are we going skiing or are we going to stand here half the morning exchanging brilliant repartee?"

"It's not brilliant, it's stupid," she said irritably, "and I truly was going to let Bill know that I was in Chamonix."

Her eyes were flaring with emotions Slade couldn't have named to save his soul. "Okay, I believe you," he said, and cupped her face in his palms, feeling the early morning chill on her cheeks. His voice roughened. "Maybe all along I've been in as much of a cage as you have—all those carefully orchestrated affairs I had, and the distance I kept between myself and my emotions. But it's too easy to stay locked up, Clea, everything safe and under control. You and I mean something to each other, I swear we do. Whatever's between us, it matters."

Staring down at her shiny white-and-yellow ski boots, Clea said rapidly, "I think about you all the time, I'm awake half the night every night, and food is the last thing on my list. But it's not because I'm in love with you—it's because I'm afraid."

"It's yourself you're afraid of, not me," Slade said bluntly.

"Maybe. Maybe not." She moved her shoulders restlessly. "Who are you afraid of? You? Me? An avalanche?"

"You have the knack of asking unanswerable questions," he said. "How about all three? And now let's go skiing."

"Okay," she said, gave him a rueful smile and headed for the cable car.

Using their passes, they got on the car that would carry them up eight thousand meters to the top of Les Grands

Montets. Slade was blind to the scenery; he hadn't really got used to the simple fact of Clea's presence at his side. Was he in danger of falling in love with her?

Another unanswerable question.

They said almost nothing to each other on the ascent; the car was crowded and Slade wasn't in the mood for chitchat. After they'd disembarked and were clipping on their skis, Clea asked with impersonal briskness, "Do you know the territory?"

He shook his head. "Then you'd better hang close," she said. "This is no place to get lost—glaciers, crevasses, rock outcrops, and after a while they all look identical. Ready?"

She was adjusting her goggles. Slade did the same, feeling a rush of adrenaline at the prospect of steep slopes and deep, powdery snow. Coupled with a cloudless sky, it was an unbeatable combination.

Well, not really. He and Clea in bed together would be the ultimate unbeatable combination.

She pushed off, her skis carving graceful S's down the fall line as she gathered speed. They stayed on the trail for the first few hundred meters. But then she took a sharp turn to the left, kicking up a spray of fine, dry snow. Virgin snow, Slade noticed, with another rush of adrenaline. He was, quite literally, putting his life in her hands. He knew it, and so, he was sure, did she.

As the couloir opened up, he accelerated to join her, their skis leaving a series of wide, snakelike curves. Pushing in his heels at the turns, flexing his legs to keep his skis from sinking, Slade was filled with an exhilarating sensation of floating, weightless, over the snow, and was filled, too, with a deep certainty. He was going to win Clea if it was the last thing he did.

They skirted a deep bowl, then plunged down another corridor. Her arms relaxed, knees flexed, Clea jumped over a rock outcrop, landing so smoothly that Slade laughed out loud and took the same jump, the wind flattening his jacket to his chest, his knees absorbing the impact.

They were alone with the mountains and the sky.

Of course he was going to win her, he thought exultantly. What other ending could a day such as this have? Wasn't that why he'd wanted to go skiing in the first place?

On her next jump, Clea did a spread-eagle, then swirled to a halt. Not to be outdone, Slade did a variation on the mule-kick, watching her wave her pole in acknowledgment, her teeth gleaming white in a wide grin.

Like all good things, their solitude had to end. Ten minutes later they rejoined the piste, with its neat signposts and small clusters of skiers. Tucking her poles under her arms, Clea schussed down the slope, coming out of it in a spray of snow near the tree line. More decorously, she continued her descent to the bottom of the trail, where she came to a dramatic stop in another swirl of snow.

Slade pulled up beside her and shoved his goggles up on his forehead. "Fantastic!" he said, laughing for sheer pleasure from that wild descent.

She was laughing, too, her cheeks pink from the wind, her eyes as brilliant as sky and snow. "I can't really compliment you for being a mean skier, because I was nearly always ahead of you."

"I was an idiot to ever call you a coward," he said, put his arms around her, pulled her close and kissed her with all the reckless passion with which they'd skied. She strained her body to his, her lips parting, her tongue darting to find his. Slade said thickly, "My hotel's right across the street."

"Let's go," she said, leaning into him as he put one arm around her waist.

Outside the ultramodern hotel, they locked their skis and poles in the racks. In the lobby they headed for the stairs, walking side by side, Slade aware of Clea through every pore in his body. She was yanking off her toque, shaking her hair free in a glorious mass of curls. They took the stairs at a run, hampered by their boots, and within moments Slade was ushering her into his suite.

He locked the door and pulled her toward him, finding her mouth with his, drinking deep of her sweetness. "Your lips are cold," he muttered. "You're all I want, all I ever wanted—come to bed with me."

"Yes," she said, yanking the zipper down on her jacket. Her white sweater clung to her breasts; she was still breathing hard. Bending down, she started to unclasp her boots.

Slade kicked his own boots aside and stripped off his jacket. Clea, he noticed, his breath catching in his throat, was stepping out of her yellow trousers and pulling her tights down her legs. Quickly her turtleneck and synthetic T-shirt followed the tights. "Clea," he said hoarsely.

Now was the time to unlock the cage, she thought. Now, with Slade, the one man who was the key. She said with a daredevil tilt of her chin, "You're letting me get ahead of you again."

Her sports underwear couldn't really be called sexy. But had he ever seen anything more beautiful than the woman leaning against the wall as she pulled off her socks? He hauled his sweater over his head, the air cool on his bare flesh, and dropped his ski pants to the floor. Then he jammed her against the wall, kissing her until he thought he'd die from pleasure and unassuaged desire.

Her hands were frantically exploring his chest, his shoulders, the bone of rib cage and muscle of belly. His erection was instant and fierce; when she pushed herself hard against him, his heart felt as though it was trying to hammer its way out of his chest.

Her hips writhing of their own accord, Clea gasped, "I've dreamed about this—"

"Me, too." He kissed her more deeply, his tongue caught between her teeth. With one hand he found the swell of her breast, teasing the nipple beneath the soft fabric of her bra. She pulled back and in a swift movement drew the bra over her head, throwing it to the floor; her breasts, full and rose-tipped, gleamed softly in the morning light.

Slade lowered his head, tracing the rise of her flesh with his tongue, taking her nipple and suckling her as she moaned his name over and over again, her hair rippling to her shoulders in a dance of fire, her body arched. And all the while she was thrusting her hips against his.

He pulled her underwear down her thighs, and hastily she stepped out of them. "Your turn," she said thickly, reaching for his waistband. Moments later her body was pressed to his, naked, warm and infinitely desirable. He was losing control, Slade thought dimly, everything vanishing but the imperative need to enter her. "The bed," he muttered against her mouth.

She seized his hand and drew it down her belly to the juncture of her thighs, to the wet heat that told him how ready she was. "Touch me," she whispered, losing the last remnants of shyness. "Oh, Slade, I want you, I want you."

Stroking her, his own body drumming in response to hers, he drew back, watching the storm gather in her face. She gave a sharp cry, her slender frame shuddering and trembling, her breathing frantic as a trapped bird's. And still he stroked her, eliciting from her a passion that excited him beyond belief.

She was whimpering now, faster and faster, until she broke against him with one last cry of repletion. He pulled her close, feeling the pounding of her heart like his own. But as he went to lift her in his arms, Clea looped her thighs around his waist and drew his head down to kiss her once again, her features still dazzled with surrender.

He couldn't wait; it would be more than anyone could ask of him. Hard and sure, Slade drove into her, watching her face convulse with reawakened longing. Slick, hot, welcoming, she took him in. And he was lost.

From a long way away, he heard his voice cry out her name and hers answer him, urgent, imperative. Her body's inner throbbing seized him, inflaming his own rhythms until, in a convulsion of need he couldn't have withstood, he emptied himself deep within her. Burying his face in her bare shoulder, he held her tight, never wanting to let her go, wishing this moment could last forever.

Her hair smelled sweetly of flowers; her skin was damp with sweat. Drinking in every sensation, Slade for the first time in his life knew what it meant to become one flesh. Old-fashioned words, he thought. But hadn't making love with Clea banished any boundaries between her body and his? Linked her to him even more strongly?

"Slade, Slade," Clea muttered, feeling as though she'd just fallen over a precipice. "I've never...I mean, that was so—"

"Fast," he supplied, looking up with the faintest of smiles, his chest still heaving.

Her cheeks were suffused with pink. "Was it too fast? I should have—"

"Two of us are involved here, so let's leave *should* out of the equation. Anyway, we're going to do it differently next time. Properly. Taking our time."

Her flush deepened. "There's nothing remotely proper about making love against a wall. I can't believe I did that."

"I can. And being improper with you...what better way to spend the day?"

"So we're going to do it again?" she said saucily.

He ran his lips down the taut line of her throat, feeling her tremble to his touch. "I think we should," he said.

She chuckled deep in her throat. "That kind of *should* I can deal with." Then her smile faded. "I've only just started taking the pill," she blurted. "The doctor thought it might help with the cramps I have every month—I told him how I'd fainted. But I don't know if the pills have kicked in yet."

So she hadn't been on the pill prior to meeting him; wasn't that one more clue that she wasn't nearly as promiscuous as she'd indicated? Slade said flatly, "I always use protection anyway. But it never entered my mind."

"Or mine."

Shifting her in his arms, Slade carried her through into his bedroom, which overlooked a range of startlingly white peaks etched against a blue sky. He put her down on the bed and rested his body on top of hers, his weight pressing her into the mattress. "This time we'll remember," he said. "Because this time we won't rush—we have all the time in the world."

In the turquoise depths of her eyes he saw the stirrings of panic coupled with desire. Leaning down, he kissed her forehead, her cheekbones, the spun silk of her hair; panic was his enemy, he knew that. "You're so beautiful, so soft and warm, so unbelievably sexy...your skin smells of lilacs."

"Soap," she said, her eyes drifting shut as he continued his exploration, nibbling at her lips, parting them with his tongue, kissing her with all tenderness welling within him.

Tenderness. Another new emotion.

"Your eyes remind me of the sea," he said, "your hair's like embers."

"You could write a Shakespearean sonnet," Clea murmured, her heart melting within her. "You say such lovely things to me."

"It's not difficult. In fact, it's superlatively easy. Although maybe we could leave the sonnet for another time."

She smiled, taking his face in her hands and kissing him almost shyly; oddly, she felt as though this was the first time they'd really been together. He took his cue from her, easing down to lie beside her so he could slowly move the length of her body. Exploring as he went, playing on all her sensitivities, he exulted in the eagerness with which she met him, and in the little starbursts of surprise that overtook her, but most of all in the wonderment that suffused her flushed features.

Wonderment, he thought. As if making love with him was giving her far more than she'd anticipated or imagined.

He pushed the thought aside to feast on every inch of her, feeling tension gather in muscle and sinew, hearing her tiny moans of pleasure, her whispered requests, each punctuated by small, frantic kisses. "Oh, yes, Slade…oh, again. Again."

And all the while, her hands were smoothing his shoulders, wandering over his torso and hip bones. She tangled her fingers in the dark hair on his chest, tugging gently, and with her lips traced collarbone, breastbone and ribs; her cheek was resting over his heart, with its imperious tattoo.

It was like a dream, Slade thought, and yet simultaneously more real than anything he'd ever done before. The woman he'd desired for months was in his arms. In his bed. What more could he ask?

With a gentleness that disarmed him, her hands drifted lower, delicately encircling him. "So silky, so hard," she marveled, her eyes trained to his face, her blood thrumming in her veins. "You like me doing that."

"God, yes," he groaned. Then, as she lifted herself to straddle him, he quickly dealt with the protection he'd earlier put on the bedside table, and slid inside her. With the same exquisite, agonizing delicacy, she rode him, up and down, side to side, overwhelming him with the sweet ache of longing and the fierce impulsions of his own blood.

Rolling sideways, carrying her with him, he buried his face in the soft valley between her breasts. "Stop," he muttered, "or I won't be able to—"

"Do you have any idea how that makes me feel?" she said. "Where did I get so much power?"

He could have joked. He could have called her a sexy chick and made her giggle again. He could simply have kept quiet, kissing her into another of those tranced silences. Instead Slade said, his breath wafting over her skin, "I'm so happy to be here with you, Clea. Happier than I thought possible."

A tiny shudder rippled through her body; and he knew it for a resurgence of fear, not delight. Dammit, he thought, you're not going to be afraid of me or of my feelings. I'm not going to give you the chance.

Taking her nipple in his mouth, he tugged at it, feeling it tighten like a pebble on the beach. As her heart began to race beneath his fingertips, he stroked her other breast with hypnotic slowness until her tiny cries of delight danced in the air. Only then did he wrap his thighs around hers and touch the wet petals of her flesh, hearing her gasp, feeling her body buck and arch. Her climax ripped through her, her single sharp cry echoing in his ears.

Clea collapsed into him, boneless in surrender, hearing her own breathing ragged against his shoulder. "You did it again," she gasped.

"We're not done yet," he said, smiling into her eyes as he lifted himself on his elbows, his big body hovering over her. Very slowly he again eased inside her.

Her eyes widened. "I still want you," she whispered, awestruck. "How can I?"

"Because I'm irresistible," he teased. His voice deepened. "Because you're passionate, more passionate than I could have imagined. And believe me, Clea, where you and bed are concerned, my imagination's been working overtime."

"You talk too much," she said spiritedly, and suddenly thrust against him, again and again, her irises darkening, her hair spread like a silken fan on the pillow.

The fire caught him in its heat and willingly he entered it. Crushing her breasts against his chest, he moved with her, two rhythms as one, falling into the flames, falling as one, falling and falling...and distantly heard his own hoarse cry of satiation.

Beyond words, almost beyond feelings, Slade rolled over to lie beside her, enfolding her in his embrace. "You've done me in," he muttered.

Gently as the brush of a bird's wing, Clea kissed him on the mouth. "It's mutual," she whispered, and felt her lashes drifting down, her body languorous with the need to sleep.

The image was imprinted on Slade's brain: Clea, her hair tumbling over his bare shoulder, her lips swollen from his kisses, falling asleep. Then he, too, closed his eyes and slept.

Although the sun had fallen behind the mountains, it was still daylight. What was he doing in bed?

Slade reared up on one elbow. He was alone in the bed. "Clea!" he called. "Where are you?"

But somehow he knew, even before he opened his mouth, that he was the only one in his suite. As he put his feet to the floor, the first thing he saw was a folded piece of hotel stationery lying on the bedside table. His name was scrawled on the outside.

His heart cold as a glacier, he picked up the paper and flattened it on his knee. "Slade," he read, "I lose myself when I'm with you, I don't know who I am anymore. I have to be alone so I can think this through. I'll be in touch, I promise. But please don't follow me."

The writing was agitated. There was no signature.

He didn't need a signature.

She'd gone. But when? His gaze fell on the digital clock, also on the bedside table. Five-thirty, he thought in dismay. How could he have slept so long?

Easily. Because he'd been sleep-deprived for days, and he'd just made impassioned love with the woman he'd wanted more than any other woman in the world.

Buck-naked, Slade strode into the next room. All Clea's clothes were gone. The scent of lilacs lingered in the air.

With a muttered curse Slade headed for the bathroom. Moving fast, he showered, dressed and packed up his gear. Then, doing up his jacket as he went, he hurried downstairs.

Her chalet wasn't far from his hotel. But when he stopped outside a charming wooden building enclosed in evergreens, its balcony facing the mountains, he knew intuitively that it was empty. He banged on the door, unsurprised when he got no response.

Again going on intuition, he walked to the guide office and stepped inside. Giving the receptionist his best smile, he said in French, "I'm looking for a blond-haired man in a blue ski suit…a friend of Clea Chardin's."

"Lothar Hesse. He's our best guide and instructor."

"Is he around?"

"No. He and Clea left together, actually, a couple of hours ago. They were driving to the airport at Geneva."

"I'm sorry to have missed them," Slade said through a red haze of fury and jealousy. "Do you know where they were going?"

"Lothar had plans to fly to Hamburg. Ardlaufen, his home town, is only ten miles outside the city." She lowered her voice conspiratorially. "Clea and Lothar were a very hot item a couple of years ago, so I wouldn't be surprised if they've gone to Ardlaufen together. Lothar has the next two days off, and there's a lot more privacy there than in Chamonix."

His jaw clenched, Slade said, "He'll be back in a couple of days, then?"

"Oh, yes, he's very reliable." The receptionist pouted. "I wouldn't mind being in Ardlaufen with him, he's such a hunk and a sweetheart into the bargain. But what chance have I got against someone like Clea Chardin? Beautiful and rich. Some people have all the luck."

Managing another smile, Slade said, "Thanks for your help," and walked outside again.

Fifteen minutes later he was on the road to Geneva. With him traveled demons of doubt, demons Clea herself had planted over the weeks since they'd met. Was she incapable of fidelity, as she'd suggested? Had she gone right from his bed to Lothar's?

She couldn't have. Not Clea. No, their lovemaking had indeed turned her world upside down, forcing her to confront her own passionate nature. Guarded and defensive as she was—and who knew that better than he?—she'd run away from her new knowledge, and from him. Opportunely Lothar, an old friend, had offered her a drive.

Being in bed with Clea had turned his own world upside down, opening a floodgate of emotions new to him. Clea, more vulnerable, must have found it devastating to her carefully constructed image of herself. Of course she'd fled for cover.

Please don't follow me...

He had to. What other choice was there?

CHAPTER ELEVEN

TAKING out his cell phone, Slade got the number of a private investigator from his contact in Chamonix, phoned him and gave him some terse instructions. Within fifteen minutes he had his answer. Clea and Lothar were on their way to Hamburg. Clea had booked her passage at the airport. Lothar, on the other hand, had purchased his ticket two weeks ago.

Choosing to be encouraged by this, for it meant their traveling together hadn't been premeditated, Slade drove on. The investigator had stationed someone at the arrivals terminal in Hamburg. So once he, Slade, arrived in Hamburg, he would know where Lothar and Clea had gone.

Please don't follow me.

You're not running away from me, he thought. I saw your face in the moment of climax, I watched your every reaction. And I'd swear that in bed with me you found a woman new to you. A woman whose existence you'd scarcely guessed... that's who you're running from.

If he was wrong, then what?

He wasn't wrong. Clea's shyness, the wonderment rising in her face like the morning sun, her unbridled passion, all of them cried out to him that he was right.

Hold that hope, he thought grimly. And he was still holding

it at dusk, when he finally arrived in Hamburg. There he found out that Lothar and Clea had driven to Ardlaufen in Lothar's blue Volkswagen. They'd gone to a restaurant for dinner, and were on their way to a nightclub on Günter Strasse.

Slade picked up yet another rental car, checked a local map and left the airport. Ardlaufen was a pretty little town on the Elbe, its streets lined with tall gabled houses and neatly trimmed evergreens. The nightclub was, Slade discovered, on the ground floor of an old warehouse; among the cars parked along the curb was a blue Volkswagen.

He got out of his own car, stretching his shoulders. The day felt as though it had gone on forever, from early this morning when he'd stationed himself by a ski lift in Chamonix to now, when he was standing outside a nightclub in a small town in northern Germany.

Taking a deep breath, Slade walked into the club.

Swiftly his eyes adjusted to the gloom. Too swiftly, because he saw Clea right away. She and Lothar were dancing to a slow and lazily sensual blues rhythm, his arms around her waist, hers around his neck, her face pressed to his shoulder. His head was downbent, his lips against her hair.

They were totally absorbed in each other.

The knife that stabbed Slade to the heart went far beyond jealousy to an agony he'd never experienced before. He blundered out of the club, dimly aware that the bouncer was watching him in surprise, and found himself outside on the brick walk. His lungs heaving, he drew in great gulps of air, desperate to loosen the terrible constriction in his chest.

Once, in university, as a novice boxer, he'd been hit by a pro. He had the same sensation now of gut-wrenching violence and total disorientation. The primly decorated houses swayed on their foundations. The stars dipped and shimmered, and the clipped branches of the trees whirled in front of his eyes.

Slowly, painfully, through a storm of emotion, a single fact confronted him. All along, Clea had been telling him the truth. She *was* incapable of fidelity. She did go from man to man, from bed to bed.

From him to Lothar in less than twelve hours. The evidence had been seared into his brain only moments ago. Unarguable. Ineradicable.

It took Slade three tries to unlock his car door. Carefully he eased into the seat and pulled the door shut. Then he sat very still, concentrating on his breathing.

Gradually the world righted itself. The trees were simply trees, their boughs without movement on this windless night. The stars stayed in their appointed orbits, glimmering coldly, speaking of distances beyond imagining, and of incredible loneliness.

Clea was like her mother: the cure for any difficulty was to change men. The only difference being, as Lucie had said, that Clea didn't bother marrying them.

She'd fooled him from beginning to end. Or had he, all too willingly, allowed himself to be fooled? Because, of course, he'd learned something else the last ten minutes. Something just as devastating. He was in love with Clea.

He loved her wholly, desperately and irrevocably. Had for weeks, probably, disguising it behind words like *sex* and *desire*.

How stupid could he be, he thought with brutal truth. For a man known for acuity, he'd been unbelievably obtuse. He not only hadn't realized he was falling in love; he'd done so with a woman who'd left his bed for another man's within a matter of hours.

At least she didn't know he loved her.

His secret.

Pain slammed through him, and momentarily he dropped his forehead to the wheel. His secret and his burden.

How the gods must be laughing. He'd fallen in love, finally, with a woman incapable of loving him back. Beguiled by her beauty and her intelligence, he'd made the worst mistake in his life.

He had no idea how to undo that mistake.

How did you fall out of love?

Slade was no nearer a solution to that dilemma a few days later when he pulled up outside Belle Hayward's Victorian mansion in San Francisco. He was on his way home from trade shows in Vietnam, South Korea and China. Had he been in the best of spirits it would have been an exhausting trip. As it was, he felt far beyond exhaustion. Numbness was what he was seeking, and that was what he'd achieved.

He'd dropped Clea from his life as if she'd never been part of it, making no move to find out where she was or who she was with. The first thing he'd done after leaving Ardlaufen was to leave a message with his assistant, Bill: if Clea contacted him, she was to be told that Slade was permanently unavailable.

Please don't follow me. How ironic a request, given the circumstances.

He still hadn't come to terms with how awry his judgment of Clea had been from beginning to end. Sometimes a lightning bolt of denial would shoot through him: Clea was innocent of wrongdoing, had been honest with him all along. At times like this, he'd reach for the phone, desperate to locate her. But then, inevitably, the image that had burned into his brain in the nightclub in Ardlaufen would confront him once again, and hope would drown in a bitter sea of regret.

He loathed this seesawing of his emotions, with its plunges into denial, hope and despair. He also hated his own self-doubt; he'd always prided himself on knowing his own mind and the minds of others.

Not anymore.

Was he going to sit here all afternoon staring at Belle's front door? Or was he going in to say hello? His flight east didn't leave until tomorrow, because he'd learned from hard experience to take a day's break when the jet lag was so extreme. So he certainly had time for a visit.

What was he, a man or a mouse? So what if Belle knew Clea? So what if he himself had gate-crashed Belle's dinner with Clea last October, and had ended up driving Clea from this very house back to her hotel? He wasn't going to cut Belle out of his life on Clea's account. Belle had been a friend for too long to do that.

He got out of the car, marched up the steps and pressed the bell. Within moments the door was opened by the butler. "Hello, Carter," Slade said. "Is Mrs. Hayward in?"

"Come this way, sir."

Slade was ushered into the formal parlor, where the stag's head sneered at him from over the mantel. His gaze winced away from the dark little oil painting of the man in shackles being led into the cave. Self-portrait, he thought, and passionately wished he'd gotten on the first flight east.

"Slade," Belle cried, walking in the room and giving him a quick hug. She was wearing purple pants with a bright yellow top, her gray hair fluffy as a seed head.

"Hello, Belle," Slade said with genuine affection, kissing her cheek. "How are you?"

"Have you come to see Clea?"

The muscles in his face froze. "Clea?" he repeated stupidly.

"She's at the site right now, but she's staying here. You should join us for tea—she'll be home by three-thirty."

"Site? What site?"

Belle said sharply, "Didn't you know she's here? Have I put my foot in it again? It does seem to be a talent of mine. One of the few that's expanding with age—like my waistline," she finished gloomily.

Slade said flatly, "No, I didn't know Clea was here. I came to see you."

"Oh," said Belle. "Then I've put both feet in it."

"What's she doing here?" he snarled.

Belle put her head to one side, assessing him. "The two of you look like half-starved insomniacs," she announced. "Clea clams up if I as much as mention your name, and you obviously had no idea of her whereabouts. Yet it's as plain as the diamonds on my fingers that you're in love with each other. I just wish you'd get on with it."

"She's not the slightest bit in love with—"

"Do you know where Rosa Street is?"

"No. She's not—"

"I'll get the map. You stay right here." And Belle bustled out of the room.

He was thirty-five years old. Was he going to allow Mrs. Henry Hayward III to boss him around as if he were six? Slade strode out into the hall just as Belle reappeared holding a San Francisco street map. He said brusquely, "If Clea's staying with you, I'm out of here."

"This is how you get to Rosa Street. You'll find her at a building site on the corner of Rosa and Ventley. The rest is up to you."

Slade stared at the map. "What kind of building site?"

"You'll see." Unexpectedly Belle put her hand on his sleeve. "I try very hard not to ask anything of the younger generation. But I'm going to break my own rule. Go and see her, Slade. Please."

Belle disliked displays of emotion. He said, "Clea and I

went to bed together in Chamonix. Then she ran away with another man. I'm sure you've heard of her reputation—believe me, it's earned."

"Are you telling me she's promiscuous?"

"I'm telling you she wasn't faithful to me for the space of a single day."

"I don't believe it."

"Belle, I saw her," he said harshly. "She ran away with a ski instructor she had an affair with a couple of years ago."

"It can't be true." Belle's bosom swelled indignantly. "There's got to be an explanation." Then she frowned at him, her eyes narrowing. "Anyway, what do you care? She's just another woman. Dump her."

"I've fallen in love with her."

"In love? *You?*"

"Yeah." His smile was wintry. "Serves me right—is that what you're thinking?"

"Give me a little more credit than that. Go to the building site, Slade. Ask her about the ski instructor. Because if she's promiscuous, I'm—I'm—"

She was flapping her arms, at a loss for words. "A lousy judge of character," Slade supplied dryly.

"She's a good woman. I'd stake my fortune on it."

Belle had always had the knack for seeing through any pretensions to the real person. Deep within him he felt, once again, the agonizing stirrings of hope. "All right," he heard himself say, "I'll drive to Rosa Street."

"Off you go, then."

Nearly forty minutes later Slade pulled up near the junction of Rosa and Ventley. A two-story building was going up on the north corner, an institution of some kind, judging by the window placement and the wide entranceway. A small crane pivoted serenely over the roof, scaffolding scaled the walls and a cement truck was parked on the street. Workers were visible on both floors, wearing jackets against the cool air.

A man holding a sheaf of blueprints came out of the front door. Clea was walking at his side. She was wearing overalls, her vivid red hair tucked under a yellow hard hat. She and the contractor stood on the sidewalk having an animated discussion, Clea gesturing at the second floor, the contractor nodding every now and then.

A couple of the workers joined them on the pavement. Clea said something to them, and they laughed.

What the hell was going on?

She and the contractor shook hands. Then Clea headed across the sidewalk toward a small green car. Slade got out of his own vehicle and crossed the street. She was tossing her hard hat in the backseat when he came up behind her. "Hello, Clea," he said.

She jumped as if he'd dropped a brick through her windshield. Whirling, she gasped, "*Slade!* What are you doing here?"

"I could ask the same of you."

Shock was instantly routed by rage. So angry she could hardly talk, she spat, "It didn't take you long to disappear after Chamonix. I phoned your office to tell you where I was and was given—oh, ever so politely—the brush-off. *I'm sorry to tell you Mr. Carruthers is no longer available.*" Her voice rose. "Thanks, Slade. Thanks a lot."

"Quit playing games, Clea! There was a damn good reason I cut you out of my life."

"Yes, there was," she seethed. "You got what you wanted. Me in bed. Game over."

"That's not true and you know it," he blazed. "Tell me— how's Lothar?"

"Lothar?" She blinked. "As far as I know, he's fine...but what's he got to do with it?"

Slade took her by the arm, his fingers digging into her flesh. "You went straight from my bed to his. How could you do that, Clea? How *could* you?"

Her jaw dropped. "You're saying I went to bed with *Lothar?*"

"Don't play the innocent—we're way past that."

"We sure are! Let go—you're hurting my arm."

"I'm not letting go until I've gotten a few answers. Truthful ones, for once—if you're capable of them."

"You told me I could trust you," she fumed. "That you wouldn't dump me, you'd—"

"Trouble here, Clea?"

Slade turned his head, still gripping Clea by the arm. The contractor and two of the workers had gathered on the sidewalk, all three of them assessing him warily. "No," Slade snapped.

"Yes," said Clea.

"The only trouble she's in is that the past has caught up with her," Slade grated. "I want answers and I'm going to get them. So you guys can butt out."

The contractor said easily, "You want us to leave, Clea?"

She shot Slade a hostile glance. "Maybe not. Although—"

"Let's start right here," Slade rasped, glaring at the contractor. "What the devil's this building and what's her connection with it?"

"It's a school for disadvantaged kids," he said. "Street kids. Reformed druggies. Clea's paying for it, along with Mrs. Hayward."

Slade looked straight at Clea. "Is that true?"

"Yes."

His brain made a lightning-swift connection. "You do this in Europe, too, don't you? Those kids we met at Tivoli—were they in one of your schools?" Again she nodded. "Why didn't you tell me?" he lashed.

"I don't talk about it. To the press. To my friends. Certainly not to my parents."

"Or to me." It was odd, he thought distantly, that she still had the power to hurt him.

"I didn't know you well enough."

"You knew me well enough to get in bed with me."

"The worst mistake I ever made!"

"It didn't take you long to get over it. With Lothar." He turned to the contractor. "I've fallen in love with this woman. Which is the dumbest move I—"

"You're not in love with me!" Clea gasped, her brain whirling.

"Yes, I am." Again he addressed the contractor. "Clea might have more money than she knows what to do with, but she comes from a lousy background. Instead of looking after her own needs, though, she builds schools like this for troubled kids. Very admirable of her. But until she comes to terms with her own family, it doesn't do her—or me—a pick of good."

"Be quiet, Slade—I hate the way you're talking about me as if I don't exist."

"I followed you to Ardlaufen," he grated. "I saw you and Lothar on the dance floor of that nightclub, wrapped around each other like a couple of mating seals. You and I made love, Clea—that very day. Or at least, I made love. There are other words for what you did."

She said carefully, "You saw me and Lothar in the nightclub?"

"Congratulations—you're finally getting the message."

"I've never gone to bed with Lothar," she said with fierce emphasis. "He's a friend, a good friend, and that's all."

"That's not what it looked like to me."

She shot a glance over her shoulder at the three men on the sidewalk. "Slade, do we really have to discuss all these intimate details in front of an audience?"

"Yep," said the contractor. "He's a big guy, Clea, and plenty mad. We'll just hang around till we see how it shakes."

"Okay, Slade Carruthers," Clea announced, "you asked for it. I ran away from you in Chamonix. I'm not going to apologize for that—you turned my world upside down and scared me half to death. Lothar was going home for the weekend, so I went with him. What you saw in the nightclub was him comforting me after I'd spent the better part of two hours weeping on his shoulder…because I was so unhappy. Because I didn't see how I could stay with you, and yet I couldn't bear leaving you."

He stared at her in silence. The breeze was whipping her hair around her head. Her eyes blazed with honesty. He said, "You had your arms around his neck."

"I was exhausted," she snapped. "I'd have fallen down if he hadn't been holding me up. I knew if I stayed in that hotel in Chamonix with you, I'd be in danger of falling in love with you. And what then? Marry you? Like my mother marries all the men she falls in love with? Not likely."

"Are you in love with me, Clea?" Slade said urgently.

She ran her fingers through her hair in unconscious drama. "No! Maybe. I don't know. I've never been in love in my life. And once I'd spoken to your assistant, I was so angry I did my best to stop thinking about you altogether."

"Did you succeed?"

She glowered at him; the truth was, she'd failed miserably. "Never you mind."

"Tell me anyway."

She said shrewishly, "I was going to ask Belle tonight if you'd moved on to another woman."

"Oh sure," Slade said, "I've dated nine different women in the last nine days. For Pete's sake, Clea, I'm in love with you—don't you get it?"

By now she'd totally forgotten their audience. "I'd had exactly one lover up until Chamonix," she announced. "At age nineteen I went to bed with an acquaintance of mine because I wanted to find out what sex was all about. I didn't like it very much, the earth very definitely did not move—the bedsprings scarcely moved—and I was never tempted to repeat the experience."

"All those newspaper articles?" Slade flashed.

"You know the media. If I look sideways at a man, I'm sleeping with him. It sells papers."

He'd had exactly the same experience with regard to women. "Lothar's an old friend," he repeated slowly, "and you were crying on his shoulder."

"His girlfriend was arriving from Trieste the next day."

Slade rubbed at the back of his neck where the muscles were as taut as steel. Prior to Chamonix, Clea had had one lover, an inadequate one at that. He remembered their own lovemaking, with her little starts of surprise, her wonderment, her air of awakening in a new place almost as if she were a virgin, and knew she was telling the truth. She'd never been promiscuous. Far from it. She'd been virtually chaste.

"I totally misjudged you," he said painfully. "There's no possible way I can apologize for that."

"I suppose it must have looked pretty convincing," she said grudgingly.

"Yeah…"

She asked the crucial question. "Do you believe me, Slade? Because if you don't, it really is game over."

"Yes," he said quietly, "I believe you."

He glanced over at the three men. The younger of the two workers said raptly, "It's like a soap opera, right here on the sidewalk."

The contractor said with genuine interest, "Is your mother the reason you don't want to get married, Clea?"

Slade said, "Her mother's been married eight times and her father goes through mistresses quicker than you can pour cement. So Clea's decided marriage is the ultimate dirty word."

"You're doing it again," Clea complained. "Speaking for me."

"I've had plenty of time to think about it in the last week," he said grimly.

The worker to their right, a man in his forties, shoved his hard hat back on his head. "I'm happily married to my high school sweetheart. It gets better and better as time goes along. Sure, we have our ups and downs—we've both got minds of our own, and while the kids are great they bring their own problems. But Liz and me? Solid as the foundation of this school."

The contractor grinned. "True Confessions. I've been in love with the same woman for fifteen years. Wouldn't want it any other way." He turned to the younger man at his side. "What about you, Mikey?"

"Divorced," Mikey said.

"Oh well," the contractor said, "two out of three ain't bad."

"Let's make it three out of four, Clea," Slade said, resting his hands on her taut shoulders, and knowing he was taking a monumental step. "The only way you're going to find out I'm in this for the duration is to marry me. Live with me. Have kids and bring them up, give them the love you missed out on. Then maybe, twenty years down the road, you'll realize how happiness and love—the lasting kind of love—go together."

"You guys are ganging up on me," Clea blurted. "Four to one's not fair."

Slade leaned over and kissed the tip of her nose. "Hey, you can handle odds like that."

The contractor said, "You could take on the whole crew, Clea...okay, guys, we'd better get back to work. Or else the boss'll fire us." And he grinned at Clea.

"I'll see you tomorrow," she said. "Eight o'clock."

Mikey rolled his eyes. "Better make it nine."

As Clea scowled at Mikey, Slade said lightly, "Belle's invited us back for tea. You know Belle, she's a stickler for punctuality."

Slade. Bill. Lothar. Mikey. And now tea with Belle. It was all too much. Clea sketched a goodbye salute to the three men and dove into her car. "I'll see you there, Slade," she said, and drove off in a screech of rubber.

Slade got in his own car and followed her back to Belle's. He didn't want to sit in the parlor and decorously drink tea. He wanted to be in bed with Clea. Only then would he believe she was back in his life again.

When she'd tried to contact him after Chamonix, she must have felt utterly betrayed to be told he was no longer available. How the hell was he ever going to make amends?

By the time he was climbing Belle's steps for the second time that day, Clea had vanished inside. Belle herself let him in. "We're in the sunroom," she said.

At least he was spared the parlor. Slade marched into the solarium, with its pleasant bamboo furnishings and drifts of orchids, hibiscus and orange blossoms. Clea, in her overalls, her back to him, was busily deadheading the Christmas cactus.

Belle said, "Ah, here's the tea. Thank you, Marlene. Sit down, Slade, you look about as relaxed as a caged cougar." She picked up the sterling silver teapot. "Clea, you sit down, too."

Clea, to Slade's surprise, did as she was told. Belle went on, "Help yourself to sandwiches. Milk, Slade?"

Slade nodded and swallowed an asparagus sandwich in one gulp. He was hungry, he realized in faint surprise, and took another. When had he last eaten? In mid-Pacific?

Belle said calmly, "By the look of both of you, nothing's been settled. Clea, I first saw Slade as a babe in arms. I know him through and through and I admire him greatly. He's—"

"Belle," Slade said, "be quiet."

"You be quiet," she snorted. "If Slade says he's in love with you, Clea, he is. No ifs, ands or buts—he doesn't do things in half-measures. So quit thinking that the moment you get a runny nose or decide to take a Ph.D. in Aztec mythology, he's going to vanish like your father and all your mother's husbands. He's not."

"That's what he says," Clea admitted reluctantly.

"Then listen to him." Belle waved her sandwich in the air. "Live with him if you're afraid of marriage."

"Either way is a commitment," Clea snapped.

Belle leaned forward. "Your schools are a wonderful gift to the world. But now it's time for you to go back to school. Unlearn the lessons Raoul and Lucie taught you, and learn what Slade can teach you. Build something new that's just for the pair of you."

Clea was frowning at Belle. "How did you get to know me so well?"

"I liked you from the moment you walked in the door last October proposing you build a school on my land on Rosa Street. Otherwise, do you think I'd have allowed you at the garden party without a hat?"

"In trousers, too," Clea said with a small smile.

"Forgive your inner child," Belle said grandly. "Nourish your heart chakra, run with the wolves—this is California, after all. Or just plain rely on your backbone. Of which you have plenty."

Clea was still frowning. "I have to learn to trust it first."

"Exactly," Belle said. "I suggest you go upstairs, pack your bag and go with Slade wherever he's going. At least for tonight—doesn't every journey begin with a single step?" She leaned back in her chair. "I'm spouting clichés and I've said more than enough."

"My turn," Slade said. "I wish you'd told me about the schools, Clea."

"They hit too close to home," she said clumsily, knowing she owed him an explanation. "If I talked about them, I might have to admit that I've always felt like an abandoned child—me, with all my money. Much easier to keep quiet."

It made perfect sense; it also touched him deeply. He took out his cell phone, called his favorite hotel in the city and booked his usual suite for two nights. Then he looked over at Clea. "Come and stay with me," he said.

The moment of choice. Stay or run. She said faintly, "All right, I'll come."

Into the silence, a grandfather clock in the next room chimed the hour.

CHAPTER TWELVE

CLEA scrambled to her feet. "I'll go and pack," she said and hurried from the room.

Belle said determinedly, "What did you find out in Beijing?" and Slade did his best to talk intelligently about something other than Clea. Then she herself was standing in the doorway, wearing her turquoise wool coat and trousers, carrying a small black suitcase.

"I'm ready," she said, her voice sounding almost normal. "We'll take both cars, Belle. That way I can go to the site when I need to."

So it wasn't until the door of the hotel suite closed behind them that Slade was alone with Clea. He said, wanting only to put her at her ease, "Those were very small sandwiches—would you like to go downstairs for something to eat?"

She put down her suitcase and rested her palms on his chest. "I can't promise I'll fall in love with you," she blurted. "Or marry you. But I do promise I won't run away again. And I won't date anyone else."

His vision blurring, Slade said huskily, "Those are huge promises."

Briefly she brushed his lashes with her fingers. "I need you to promise you won't turn me away again. Being given the brush-off by your assistant—I can't tell you how terrible that made me feel." In spite of herself, her voice shook. "Negated. As if I'd never even existed for you."

"Of course I promise. Clea, I'm more sorry than I can say. I should have marched up to you and Lothar in the nightclub and had it out with you. But I was, quite literally, stunned...all I could do was get out as fast as I knew how and cut you out of my life. And whenever I'd find myself hoping—trusting—that you were innocent, the image of the two of you on the dance floor would tell me otherwise."

"That, and the clippings, and all my protestations about going from man to man." She bit her lip. "I did a good job, didn't I? Too good."

"One of the worst things was feeling I couldn't trust my own judgment anymore."

Her brow wrinkled. "But you do love me—you mean that?"

"Today, tomorrow and forever," he said huskily.

"What have I ever done to deserve that kind of love?"

"I'm not sure we have to earn love," he said. "I suspect it's a gift."

As a single tear slid down her cheek, he wiped it away. "Let's go to bed, Clea."

Trust, she thought. "I've missed you terribly, Slade. I've been so confused, it's been awful. At some point you might want to thank Lothar—he's listened to far too much moaning and complaining."

"Next time, I'll hang around and you can introduce me."

Her smile felt almost natural. "It's a deal."

"Shower," Slade said decisively, "then bed." He swept her up in his arms, carrying her into the bathroom. "You've lost weight," he grunted. "I'll feed you strawberries and cream after we make love, would you like that?"

"Providing the lovemaking's very soon," she said. "Wow, what a lot of mirrors."

"The better to see you with, my dear," he smiled and started stripping off his clothes, tossing his shirt and tie on the chair.

Giving way to impulse, Clea flung her arms around him, almost knocking him off balance, and holding him so tightly he could scarcely breathe. "I can't believe I'm here with you...I'm so sorry I ran away, but I didn't know what else to do."

Burying his face in the fragrant mass of her hair, Slade said, "I love you, Clea. I love you."

Wishing she could say those three small words back to him, she begged, "Hold on to me."

One hand in the small of her back, the other at her hips, Slade drew her to the length of his body. "I'm holding the whole world in my arms," he said. "You can trust me, sweetheart. Trust that I'll always be there for you, no matter what."

Trust. That word again. Pulling back a little, Clea lifted her sweater over her head and quoted Belle. "Every journey begins with a single step," she said.

Her lacy bra, cupping the ivory swell of her breasts, made his head swim. "Take off the rest of your clothes...let me see you. All of you."

She stepped back, her eyes trained on his face, and let her trousers slip to her ankles. Her hose were held up by slender garters, also embroidered with lace. Taking her time, she slid her stockings down her legs one by one. Then she unclasped her bra, freeing the soft weight of her breasts, and eased her lace-edged bikini pants from her hips.

She said breathlessly, "When you look at me like that—I dissolve, Slade."

He tossed his socks on the chair, unbuckled his leather belt and threw trousers and briefs after the socks. He was, he knew, only too ready to ravish her. As she reached out and stroked all his hardness, his face convulsed. "I was on a plane most of the night," he muttered. "A shower's a necessity."

She gave a rich chuckle. "In that case, it's going to be the quickest shower on record."

As the hot water pounded his back, Clea ran the soap up and down his chest, her fingers playing with his wet, sleek body hair. Slade dropped his head and took her breast in his mouth, gently tugging at her nipple until she threw back her head with a sharp cry of pleasure. "I want you now," she gasped. "Now…"

"No hurry," he said, and smoothed her hips with leisurely sensuality. "Delayed gratification is good for the character."

In deliberate provocation she covered his face with tiny kisses, then sought his lips, her tongue darting to meet his. "I bet I could change your mind."

Raw hunger engulfed him. He muttered, "I bet you could," and kissed her back.

She was trembling very lightly, her body aching with desire. "I want to be in bed with you," she whispered.

He reached behind and turned off the shower. Then he grabbed two of the big, soft towels from the heated rack, swathing her in one of them, fastening the other around his hips. "There are little drops caught in your hair," he said. "Like mist. Sea mist."

"Could you live by the sea?" Clea asked with sudden intensity.

"Yes," he said, and forbore to add that he could live anywhere with her.

"When my mother and I lived with Pete in British Columbia, I loved waking to the sound of waves on the shore."

An idea blossomed in Slade's mind, along with a hope so powerful that it frightened him. He pushed both aside. "Bed," he said. "Your character is fine as it is."

So they were laughing as they tumbled into the wide bed. Slade opened his arms and Clea slid into their circle so naturally that it took his breath away. "You look as though you've been doing that for years."

"I've had lots of practice—you wouldn't believe the fantasies I've had about you," she said. "X-rated, I might add."

"How about some X-rated reality?" he murmured, and stroked the soft rise of her breast to its tip.

She shivered, her eyes darkening. Gracefully she lifted herself to hover over him, deliberately offering him the freedom of her body. With exquisite care Slade set about giving her all the pleasure he was capable of giving. His hands and mouth teased and roamed from head to toe, and all the while the tension tightened, notch by notch, caress by caress, until she was writhing beneath him, her frantic cries like those of distant shorebirds.

Only then did Slade slide within her. She arched to gather him, bucked and plunged, and the last vestiges of control left him. Riding her fierce rhythms, caught by them, he joined with her, and losing his own freedom, found a greater freedom.

His climax, long and shuddering, left his chest heaving and his body drained. He fell to the mattress, clasping her in his embrace. If his heart beat any harder, he thought dimly, it would burst from his rib cage.

Very gently Clea smoothed his sweat-slick hair from his forehead, her fingers unsteady. Capturing them in his, he brought them to his lips. "Beautiful Clea…"

She spoke the only truth she knew. "You give me more than I dreamed possible."

"Body and soul—that's what I give you. But don't you see what's happening? Everything I give, you're receiving. You're beginning to open your heart as well as your body."

With all her courage, she met his gaze and stated the obvious. "You're changing me."

"You're changing yourself." And then, because the last thing he wanted was to revive all her old fears, he added, "Strawberries and cream? That was the deal, wasn't it?"

"With champagne."

He reached for the phone. "I'll have to put some clothes on."

"But then you'll take them off and come back to bed." She gave him a wicked grin. "Why haven't any of my fantasies included licking champagne from your body?"

"How about me licking whipped cream from your breasts?"

She pulled up the sheets to hide her scarlet cheeks. "I want a couple of French pastries, too. Strictly for eating."

He picked up the phone and punched the numbers for room service. And, later, in the big bed, fantasy and reality blended in a way highly satisfactory to both of them.

Clea was late arriving at the site the next morning.

While Clea was at the construction site, Slade checked out several Web sites, phoned his father and asked some pointed questions about seafront properties, then contacted a number of real estate agents.

When Clea came back, he kissed her as if she'd been gone for three months rather than three hours. This led to a swift and impassioned lovemaking on the carpet. Afterward, lying still, her head on Slade's shoulder, Clea gasped, "I'm glad Mikey can't see us now."

"I'm glad any number of people can't see us."

She burrowed her face deeper into his chest. "You know what? I have fun with you, Slade."

"I aim to please," he said. "If you can get away, we'll fly east tomorrow. There's something I want to show you."

She lifted her head, her hair silky on his bare chest. "Sure, I can go, the school's shaping up beautifully. But what are you going to show me?"

"A surprise." He cupped one ivory-smooth breast in his hand. "No questions allowed."

Distracted, she said, "If we're going to make love again—because I know that gleam in your eye—it's going to be in bed. I've got carpet burn."

"What are we waiting for?" Slade replied, and wondered if this was what a honeymoon was like, this unsettling mixture of laughter, eroticism and overwhelming tenderness.

A honeymoon implied a wedding.

Two days later, Slade and Clea were driving the rocky shoreline of Maine. When they came to a secluded headland, Slade stopped the car near a pair of black iron gates, and unlocked them with the keys he'd picked up at the airport.

The driveway curved through a forest of pine and spruce, the boughs weighted with soft billows of fresh snow; then it opened into a vista of low granite cliffs and boundless sea. The house faced the ocean; built of stone, cedar and glass, it looked steadfast, as though it could withstand any number of storms. As Slade switched off the engine, Clea whispered, "The only thing I can hear is the waves on the shore…what a beautiful place."

"We could buy it," he said, his throat tight. "Use it as our home base."

She was chewing on her lip, her heart racketing around in her chest. "Are you proposing to me?"

"No," he said. "Shared accommodation and our own bed. That's enough for now."

"That's a lot."

"We'd just be taking Belle's advice," he said mildly, watching her like a hawk. "Live together, isn't that what she suggested? Do you want to go inside? I've got the keys."

"I'd love to," Clea said, knowing that once again Slade had thrown her off balance. Live with him…could she?

The real estate agent had kept her promise to turn the heat up. The furnishings had been moved out, the rooms echoing with emptiness and possibility. Clea wandered from one to the next, gazing out the windows at the stunning views of the bay and the offshore islands. She said dreamily, "We'd need a big oak dining room table and lots of carpets in rich colors—oh, Slade, look at the staircase!"

A gracious curve of highly polished walnut wound its way to the second floor. Like a woman enraptured, Clea climbed the stairs, her fingers caressing the railing. Slade followed, his attention more on Clea than on the details of the house. She liked it, he thought, his heart hammering in his chest. More than liked it.

The master bedroom faced the ocean. A stone fireplace was nestled between built-in bookshelves; the floor was pale birch. Clea went to stand by the window where she could gaze out at the gleaming blue water. How thoughtful of Slade, how loving of him, to find a house that reminded her of the one time in her childhood when she'd been truly happy.

He came up behind her. "It's a long way from civilization."

"If we kept our apartments in Manhattan and Milan, and your house in Florence," she said, "isolation would be nothing to worry about."

Our apartments, he thought giddily. "If there was a blizzard, we might be holed up for days."

"As long as we have a bed, that's fine with me."

"So buying a bed takes precedence over a fridge and stove?"

She turned to face him. Her sweater was tawny orange, her coat and slim wool slacks dark olive-green; once again, she was wearing the gold earrings he'd given her. Looping her arms around his neck, her eyes smiling into his, she said, "Are you suggesting I've got my priorities wrong?"

"I think you've got them exactly right," he said thickly, and kissed her at some length.

"I wish we did have a bed," she said, her voice muffled by his Aran-knit sweater.

He wanted, suddenly and desperately, to make love to her in this sun-drenched bedroom. "We could spread our coats on the floor, and there are a couple of blankets in the trunk of the car. For emergencies."

"This is an emergency. Why don't you go and get them?" she said, a gleam of pure mischief in her eye.

Slade took the stairs two at a time. He wanted to sing the Hallelujah Chorus. He wanted to waltz the length of the living room with Clea in his arms. He wanted to marry her.

One thing at a time, Slade. Blankets first. Marriage later.

When he went back upstairs, he stopped dead in the bedroom doorway. Clea was lying on the floor on top of her olive-green coat, wearing nothing but a smile and a pair of gold earrings. The light angled across her flank onto the smooth, pale birch.

Leaning against the door frame, the blankets draped over his arm, Slade started to laugh. "You have this unique capacity for taking me by surprise," he said. "But I bet you'd like a bit more padding between you and the floor."

"We're not using the missionary position—you're the one who's going to be underneath."

"Who says it's easy being a man?"

"Take off your clothes, Slade."

"Bossy, aren't you?" he replied, pulling his sweater over his head and starting to unbutton his shirt. "Imagine what we'll learn about each other should we live together." His fingers stilled. "Will you live with me, Clea?"

Sitting up in an entrancing flurry of bare limbs, she said, "I—I think so. I really am thinking hard about it." Then she frowned at her choice of words. "Not just thinking, that sounds too cold-blooded. I'm trying to feel what it would be like."

He asked the obvious. "How does it feel?"

"Terrifying—like I might fall off a cliff into the sea. Exciting—sharing a bed with you, joining our lives, traveling together." She tilted her head to one side. "We'd take turns putting out the garbage, right?"

"Absolutely."

"Oh God, Slade, I don't know. What if it didn't work out?"

"What if a comet collides with the earth?"

"Hmm...how long before you have to decide about the house?"

"I've got first refusal. It's not in my own best interests to rush you, Clea—I could buy the house anyway, and we'll wait and see." Every nerve in his body cried out against such a course; he wanted a decision from her now.

"I'm getting cold," she said. "Come and warm me, Slade."

Slade tossed her his shirt, warm from his body, and kicked the blankets over her way. "Don't forget how much I love you."

"I'm starting to trust that, too," she said in a low voice.

They made love slowly, almost in silence, as if it were a dream they were sharing: an intimacy all the more profound for its dependence on touch, on skin against skin rather than words. Afterward, rather than lingering on a floor that was rock-hard even with her coat and the two blankets underneath them, they got dressed and trailed downstairs through the empty rooms to the back door. Clea said softly, "I hate to leave."

"No one else will buy the house, I'll make sure of that."

She was holding his hand so tightly her knuckles were white. "We're going our separate ways tomorrow. You to Mexico City, me to Marseilles to see if a school there needs an addition."

"I'm back in two days and you're only gone for five."

She suddenly shivered, her features taut with distress. "I'm being silly. Let's go."

He ached to protect her, even to tell her to skip Marseilles and he'd deputize Mexico City. But that way, he knew, would lead to disaster: they both needed their independence. "I'm not going to disappear, Clea," he said forcefully. "I'm not going to let you down. Nor will I vanish when the going gets tough—which it's bound to, sooner or later."

"You sound so serious."

"Not all the vows are found in the marriage service."

She gave herself a little shake, doing her best to banish her unease. "Let's go back to the inn and try their fish chowder. New England in a bowl, isn't that what you called it?"

They got in the car and drove away from the house without a backward look.

Slade returned from Mexico three days before Clea was due back from Marseilles. Too restless to simply wait for her, he flew north to Maine the next day. After spending a couple of hours with a crusty old man who was researching wind power, Slade drove to the house. He was going to buy it right away, rather than wait for Clea's decision.

She loved the house. That was the clincher.

He went through the rooms one by one, taking note of needed repairs; in the bedroom, he stood in the doorway smiling foolishly at the smooth birch floor. Then he checked the spacious garage and the other outbuildings. Finally, tucking his trousers into his high boots, he started tramping through the woods behind the garage.

The real estate agent had mentioned that the original house, built by the first owners of the land well over a hundred years ago, was still standing. "You'd want to demolish it," the woman had said. "Hazardous in the extreme—I'm surprised the present owners didn't have it taken down."

The sun was sinking toward some low clouds, the temperature dropping. He'd give himself another ten minutes, then he'd head back to the car and civilization.

He'd be seeing Clea very soon. Had a man ever fallen in love so thoroughly, so inescapably, as he had outside the nightclub in Ardlaufen?

Through the gloomy trees, Slade saw the dark bulk of walls and a roof. Stepping carefully between the jagged-limbed spruce, he approached the old house. The roofline sagged. The windows were black holes, the front door hanging on its hinges.

A frisson traveled his spine. A family had lived here once, raised children, gone out in boats upon the sea. What was left to show of their lives but a tumbledown house, its dreams abandoned to the encroaching forest?

He almost turned back, wanting lights and warmth. Wanting to talk to Clea, and reassure himself that she was real.

Chiding himself for being overly imaginative, Slade pushed the door open. The hinges squealed like an animal in a trap. But the floorboards, he noticed, were foot-wide softwood, a few of them still with vestiges of polish. Others, though, were clearly rotten, where the roof had leaked.

He stepped inside, treading gingerly, keeping to the edges of the floor. In the parlor he found some old photos on the wall; as he reached for one of them to see if anything was written on the back, a signal shrilled from his jacket pocket, making him jump.

His cell phone. Symbol of the twenty-first century.

He took it out of his pocket and flipped it open. "Carruthers," he said.

"Slade? It's Clea. Slade, are you there?"

"Yeah, I'm here." He gripped the phone, the distress in her voice going right through him. "What's wrong? Where are you?"

"I'm at Lexington airport. I got a call from Byron—my mother's husband. Mother's had a heart attack. Byron says it's not serious, but I don't trust him—so I flew back from Marseilles early." She hesitated, then took the plunge. "Slade, could you come right away? I thought I could handle this on my own. But I can't. I—I need you. I need you to be with me."

"Sure I'll come," he said instantly. Clea, admitting that she needed him? He'd move heaven and earth to get to her side.

"You will?"

"Of course—isn't that what this is all about? I'll be there as soon as I can—I'm in Maine, at the house. Why don't I call you when I get to Newark? That way you'll know when to expect me."

"Thank you," she said, overwhelmed with relief. "How inadequate that sounds—but I really mean it."

"I'll be there sometime tonight, I promise. Hang in, sweetheart. Byron may well be telling the truth."

"You're right, he could be. I'm sorry, I'm so upset I can't think straight. I'd better go—I'm taking a cab to the hospital and I'll probably stay there all night. But I'll see you later on."

"I love you," Slade said forcefully. "Don't ever forget that. I hope your mother will be all right, and I'll see you as soon as possible—I can stay at the hospital with you. Bye for now." Still clutching his cell phone, his mind totally focused on Clea, alone in an airport in Kentucky, Slade rushed out of the parlor and across the kitchen floor.

With the soft, doughy sound of rotten wood, a whole section of the floorboards gave way. Thrown sideways, he made a frantic grab for the edge of the boards. His cell phone inscribed a graceful arc in the air, landing with a small thunk near the bottom of the stairs.

The boards crumbled in his fingers.

His arms flung wide in a desperate attempt to find purchase, Slade plunged through the hole into the darkness of the old cellar. His head cracked against a rock, one arm doubled under him. For a split second his whole body was enveloped in a burst of jagged light and in pain beyond belief.

Then, mercifully, darkness encompassed him.

CHAPTER THIRTEEN

HE WAS eleven years old. Alone, in the dark. Not knowing where he was, or why. Knowing nothing but an atavistic terror of the night.

His eyes were closed, Slade realized in a surge of relief. That was why it was dark. Slowly he opened them. Blackness pressed down on him, surrounding him with a dead, suffocating and impenetrable silence.

But he wasn't lying on the floorboards of the underground cupboard, whose pattern of cracks he'd memorized because there was nothing else to do. He was lying on rock. Hard. Cold. Damp, even through his clothes. Where was he?

His head hurt.

As he tried to shift position, a hoarse cry of agony burst from his lips. His arm was on fire, the bone lanced with a pain that made the darkness swoop and whirl. He lay very still.

As though ice water had been thrown in his face, Slade remembered where he was: in the cellar of the old house on the property in Maine. He'd fallen through the floor.

Clea. He'd been on his way to see Clea. Because she needed him.

With his good arm, he fumbled in his pocket for his cell phone, and then recalled with a wave of horror how it had flown from his hand to land at the foot of the stairs.

It might as well have landed on the moon.

Think, Slade. Think.

He had a pounding headache. When he lifted his fingers to his forehead, they came away sticky. He'd hit his head on the rock, that's what had happened. It had been dusk when he'd been exploring the old house. So he'd been unconscious; now it was night.

He wasn't a young boy locked in an airless cupboard. He was a grown man who couldn't afford to panic.

Then his memory supplied the last, devastating piece of the puzzle. Clea was spending the night in Kentucky with her mother. She must be wondering where he was, for she would have expected him to have arrived by now.

He'd promised to phone her from Newark.

From her perspective, he'd failed her, running away when the chips were down. Just like her father. Just like her mother whenever there was the slightest problem with any of her husbands.

He had to get out of here. Phone Clea and explain why he was in Maine and not in Kentucky.

In a single swift movement Slade rolled over. Pain engulfed him; his groan sounded like that of a wounded animal.

He bit his lip so hard he could taste blood, and looked at his watch face. Glowing in the dark, the numbers said 06:50. Ten to seven in the morning, he thought sickly. He'd been unconscious for over twelve hours.

Clea had spent the night at her mother's bedside alone.

He pushed himself upright on his good arm, the other one hanging limp at his side. Then, gritting his teeth, he got to his feet and staggered across the uneven floor, one hand held out in front of him so he wouldn't walk face-first into the wall. When his fingers brushed cold stone, he followed the wall along its length to the corner.

What felt like an age later, Slade arrived back where he'd begun. There was no door leading to the outside. But while he'd been searching for it, he'd stumbled over several loose rocks, some of them flat. He'd pile them up and climb out of the cellar that way.

Say it fast. Nothing to it.

His knees weak as a kitten's, Slade sank down onto the nearest rock and fashioned his belt into a sling for his broken arm. Afterward, he sat very still for a while, struggling to recover his strength.

Then his heart leaped in his chest. Was that light seeping through the floorboards? So that he could, for the first time, actually see the hole in the floor?

The very faintest of gray light—but it was still light. Hugely encouraged, his claustrophobia dissolving, Slade pushed himself upright again, and headed for the wall where he'd stubbed his toe against the largest of the loose rocks.

The rock was far too large to lift one-handed. Using his feet and one arm, he moved it, inch by slow inch, underneath the hole. And this rock, he thought grimly, was the easy one. The next one would have to be lifted on top of it.

The hole looked an enormous distance above his head.

Clea. Remember Clea.

Three hours later, grunting with effort, Slade got a fourth rock on the pile. Two more and he'd be home free.

Despite the cold, Slade was sweating copiously. He'd give his eyeteeth for a bottle of cold spring water. And a doughnut, he thought. Covered in maple cream and laden with trans fat.

Whipping cream, champagne and Clea…how he loved her. And how terrified he was that she'd fly straight from her mother's bedside to Europe, where she'd go into hiding, convinced that he'd betrayed her newfound trust.

How could he blame her for coming to that conclusion?

With renewed energy he got the fifth rock on the pile. Although the last rock was the hardest, eventually he got it in place, then spent half an hour jamming smaller stones into the gaps to stabilize the pile.

Afterward, Slade never wanted to remember how he got out of the cellar. He did know it took every last ounce of his strength and determination. He simply couldn't afford to be defeated. Too much was at stake.

The hardest part was finding an edge of the floor to cling to that wasn't rotten, meanwhile teetering on the pile of rocks. With a final shove, using all the power of his leg muscles, he thrust himself onto the floorboards and rolled onto his side, panting, his eyes closed. He'd never again dismiss a broken arm as a trivial injury.

His cell phone was at the foot of the stairs.

Craning his neck, he looked at his watch. One o'clock, he thought through the red mist in his head. Clea could be in mid-Atlantic by now. Winging her way east.

He pushed himself to his knees and, inch by inch, distributing his weight as evenly as he could, crawled toward the stairs and his cell phone.

"Slade! Are you inside? Slade, where are you?"

He was hallucinating. He had to be, if he was hearing Clea's voice when she was hundreds of miles away. Digging his nails into the old plaster of the wall, Slade hauled himself to his feet.

A shadow fell across his body. He looked over his shoulder.

Clea was standing in the open doorway. As she stepped over the threshold, he gasped, "Stop! The floor's rotten."

Her dazed eyes went from the gaping hole in the floorboards back to him. "Your head," she said in a voice he scarcely recognized. "It's bleeding. And your arm—"

"I fell into the cellar," he said, suddenly acutely uncomfortable. "It's taken me all this time to get out."

"Slade, you could have been killed…"

"No more than I deserved—it was a damn fool thing to do."

She made a tiny gesture with her hands, unable to bear feeling so useless. "I'm coming to help you—you look like you're going to fall flat on your face."

"Stay put, Clea. That's an order."

He edged toward her, keeping as close as he could to the walls with their peeling wallpaper. Finally he reached the doorway, standing only inches from her. She was wearing a blue parka and jeans, her eyes huge, her face pale. "I've been out of my mind with worry," she faltered, and burrowed her face into his shoulder, needing to know he was real. Safe in her arms.

Keeping his broken arm out of the way, he pulled her toward him, resting his cheek on her hair. "I'm so sorry, Clea," he muttered. "I figured you'd head straight back to Europe and I'd never see you again."

"I thought of it, believe me."

"Why didn't you?"

"I'm here, that's what counts," she said. "My car's parked by the house—luckily you left the gates unlocked. I'm taking you to the nearest hospital and we'll talk after that."

"I don't suppose you have any coffee with you? Or even water?"

"Hot coffee and blueberry muffins, in the car."

"You're nominated for sainthood."

"Some of my thoughts the last twenty-four hours have been far from saintly. Put your good arm over my shoulder."

"I can manage on my—"

"Do as you're told," Clea flared, wondering how she could be angry when he'd just scared her out of ten years' growth.

"Okay. Only because I'm not sure my legs can hold me up. Do you promise to turn the heater on full blast?"

"I do. Let's go."

"Like I said, bossy." But as he looped his arm over her shoulder, he added huskily, "Thanks, Clea. For hanging in."

Her vision wavered. "You're welcome."

The ground was uneven, and the trees too close for comfort. But eventually they reached Clea's rented car. "We'll leave your car here and send someone for it," she said. "Give me the keys and I'll lock the gates on our way out."

"My overnight bag's in my car, could you get it?" He passed over the keys and sank down into the passenger seat. His heart was thudding and his hairline wet with sweat. Clea shut his door, walked around the hood and got in beside him.

She reached down by his feet, picking up a thermos and pouring him a mug of steaming coffee, glad to have something concrete to do. The alternative was to break down and weep like a baby, which wouldn't be the slightest bit helpful.

"This coffee's divine," Slade mumbled. "You did say muffin, didn't you?"

As he devoured the muffin, Clea circled the driveway, stopping beyond the gates. After she'd locked them behind her, she took a blanket from the backseat and bundled it to support his sling. "Is your arm broken, do you think?"

"Gotta be—hurts like hell."

"We'll be at the hospital in half an hour," she said, turning onto the highway.

He had to get it over with. "I was rushing across the kitchen right after getting your phone call, not watching what I was doing, and the boards gave way. Cracked myself on the head on the rock in the cellar and was out like a light for over twelve hours."

"In an underground place in the dark…no wonder you look so awful. You shouldn't be talking, Slade—just rest."

"I need to talk…I couldn't bear to think about you waiting for me to arrive, waiting and waiting, then gradually realizing I wasn't going to come just when you needed me. That I'd failed you. Betrayed you in the cruelest way possible."

She said steadily, "I did feel all those things. It was a very long night, and I hope I never again feel as low as I did at four a.m. The only bright spot was that my mother was much better than I'd anticipated, so at least I didn't have to worry about her. Although I did make the mistake of telling her you were flying down to be with me."

Slade's very pungent swearword brought a smile to Clea's lips. "You said it. Early this morning when it was all too clear you hadn't turned up or sent a message, and that you weren't even answering your cell phone, Mother started to rub it in. Men, she said, bastards all of them, their promises as useless as—er, certain other parts of their anatomy. None of them can be trusted, and the rich ones are the worst…you get the picture. At first I went along with it because it really had been a dreadful night—every time I heard footsteps in the corridor, I thought it was you."

"And it never was," Slade supplied grimly.

"But around the time the sun came up, I told Mother to keep her opinions to herself, and I started to think. About you. How you said you'd never let me down because you were different from my father and all my mother's husbands. That's when I decided something must have gone wrong. Then Bill—with whom I'm on speaking terms again—told me you hadn't come back from Maine. I got on a flight north by the skin of my teeth, and drove straight to the house."

"You trusted me," Slade said dazedly.

"Once I stopped paying attention to Mother, I did." Clea hesitated, her eyes on the winding road. "I still do. And I was right to, wasn't I?"

"I can't tell you how I regret putting you through all that."

"Nothing like listening to my mother on the subject of men for bringing me to my senses." She glanced sideways at him. "There's something I really regret, too—I ought to have called the police before I flew up here. You'd have been rescued so much sooner."

"I'm glad you didn't," Slade said emphatically. "Sirens. Ambulances. Reports to file. Omigod."

"We both did okay, then," she said contentedly.

"You did superlatively, Clea. Splendiferously."

Her smile felt as wide as her face. "To have finally realized that I can trust you—what an amazing feeling."

"Worth falling into several cellars."

"Will you be able to make love with your arm in a cast?" she said pertly.

"Trust me," he said.

"I will," she chuckled. "After all, I've got to keep in practice…we should be nearly there."

Within five minutes Clea was parking near the emergency entrance of the local hospital. As they walked toward the glass doors, Slade caught sight of his own reflection: unshaven, dried blood encrusted in his hair and down his face, his skin and clothes filthy. "Is that me?" he gasped.

"They wouldn't hire you for the cover of *Gentleman's Quarterly*."

"An ad for detergent, more like."

"The heavy-duty kind," she said, holding the door open. The inevitable forms had to be filled in, they waited for the appropriate doctor, then for X-rays, and finally the cast was applied. By the time they left the hospital, Slade was too tired even to be hungry.

Clea said easily, "I booked a room in a country inn down the road. They'll have dinner ready for us. The nurse said you can have a shower as long as you keep the cast dry."

The medication he'd been given for his headache was making him drowsy; it seemed a very long time since he'd last slept. The inn, decorated in a romantic extravaganza of roses, was a blur to him. He showered and dressed with difficulty, ate what was put in front of him and climbed the stairs again with Clea at his side.

The wide bed, canopied and with a rose-strewn duvet, looked as near to heaven as he could imagine. Clea helped him undress. Wearing only his briefs, he lay down. "Come here," he muttered, "I want to hold on to you." And fell asleep.

When Slade woke, the first thing he saw was a pretty flowered lamp shade, its bulb a soft glow in the darkness, sitting on a table with a long flowered skirt.

Clea was curled into his chest, her breathing the deep, even rhythm of sleep. Her hair was a tangled, fiery mass of curls on the pillow. The pillow slip was embroidered with roses.

Such an uprush of love filled his body that he could scarcely contain it. She hadn't run off to Europe without him. She'd come looking for him instead.

How did he ever get to be so lucky?

She must have left the lamp on so he wouldn't, even for a moment, think he was still trapped in a dark cellar.

With his good hand, he stroked the hair back from her face, then kissed her cheek, letting his mouth slide down the slender column of her throat. Her eyes flickered open. "Slade?" she murmured.

"Hello, my darling."

As she stretched lazily against him, her eyes widened. "Well," she said, "you're recovering just fine."

"Do you think we should find out if I can make love with a broken arm?"

"Nothing like the present," she said, wriggling to face him and running her fingers up his bare chest.

He said huskily, "Everything I've ever wanted is here in my arms," and bent his head to kiss her.

They made love with a quiet intensity, broken only by little bursts of laughter as the cast inevitably got in the way. When he slid within her, knowing he'd come home, he could feel her trembling and throbbing with need in every nerve he possessed. As climax shuddered through her, he rose to meet her, emptying himself even as he was suffused with a love so strong, so overwhelming, that he could scarcely breathe. Their hearts, he thought dimly, were hammering as one, even as their bodies were one.

In the lamplight Clea smiled at him. How could there be a better time than this, she thought, and said, "I have something to tell you."

"You're flying back to Marseilles first thing in the morning."

"And leaving you here? No way."

"You're going to wear a red leather miniskirt to Belle's next garden party."

Chuckling, Clea pressed her fingers to his lips. "Be quiet and listen. Slade, do you know what's happened? It's so wonderful—I've fallen in love with you."

He lay very still. He was dreaming. He must be. "Say that again."

Shyly she looked up at him, her lips swollen from his kisses, her cheeks a warm pink. "You heard me—I love you."

"I've wondered if I'd ever hear you say that. Oh, sweetheart, I love you, too."

He held her close, filled with a happiness as deep as the ocean, as sure as the tides. She said, easing herself into the circle of his arm, "Now that I look back, I guess I fell in love with you in Chamonix. But I was into denial in a big way. Me, in love? Absolutely not."

"I noticed," Slade said dryly.

"It wasn't until I was waiting for you, hour after hour, at my mother's bedside, that I realized the truth." She gave a reminiscent shudder at the memory of that excruciating vigil. "Terrible timing. I'd finally fallen in love, but with a man who'd abandoned me just when I needed him. I told you it was a long night. And then when I figured something must have happened to you—that was even worse."

"Marry me, Clea."

"Yes," she said.

"Just like that? You're sure?"

"I love you, I'll marry you and live by your side, we'll have children, we'll invite your parents for lunch on Sundays and I'll learn how to make smoked salmon fish cakes."

"Nothing half-hearted about you, my darling."

"I can't tell you how happy I feel! I love you, Slade. And I love telling you that I love you."

As he laughed deep in his chest, his arms hard around her, she added, "Maybe, once in a while, we'll even invite my mother for lunch. Because you're right, Slade, underneath it all she's scared silly."

He smiled at her, his heart in his eyes. "We can invite Lothar, if you like. And Bill—you and he are practically old friends."

She gave a contented sigh. "No more meeting in bars."

"No more costume museums."

"No more strobe lights. Are we going to turn into a deadly boring couple sitting by the fireside night after night?"

"I can't imagine life with you being the slightest bit boring," Slade said. "In bed or out."

"Let's phone your parents and invite them to the wedding."

"Later," he said firmly. "For now, just in case you're worried about boredom creeping up on us, I think we should stay exactly where we are."

Clea ran her fingers suggestively down his body. "The dining room doesn't open for another two hours."

"Good," said Slade.